ONE BOSSY OFFER

AN ENEMIES TO LOVERS ROMANCE

NICOLE SNOW

ABOUT THE BOOK

Grandma left me the life of my dreams with one ginormous catch.

Miles flipping Cromwell.

Workaholic king of grumps. Control freak. Older billionaire next door.

We didn't exactly hit it off when he showed up with an offer to buy my land and my hyperactive dogs yanked my robe open right in front of him.

I wish running him off my porch totally mortified was the worst part.

But re-opening Washington's cutest inn gets crazy expensive.

When Seattle's hottest crankyface bachelor comes knocking again, he has me cornered.

This time with a high-paid job offer I can't refuse.

I thought I was strong.

I thought I could force a smile, work, and laugh off his rude demands.

I thought I could ignore his obscenely good looks, his innuendo, his incendiary glares.

Never once did I think he'd ambush me on a date with another man and take my soul with one jealous kiss.

He's a walking contradiction.

Hating him is easy.

But falling recklessly in love with Miles and his heart-wrenching secrets?

Oh, God.

Will his final offer claim my heart or demolish me?

I: NO BIG DEAL (JENN)

"enn, you don't have to do this. Taking on this place —this burden—it won't bring her back. You know that, right?"

I sigh and stare out at the sea for the third time today, pressing my phone closer to my ear until it burns.

The sunlight turns the water into dancing silver.

I've always loved the ocean, and the Bee Harbor Inn has a view second to none.

Just lovely enough to endure this agonizing conversation.

Sure, the place needs some work, but at least I'm not packed into that tiny Seattle shoebox masquerading as an apartment anymore.

"Dad—"

"I can set you up with a realtor anytime," he cuts in. "Angie's the greatest. She flipped your mom's spec house in Bellingham for over a million solid a few years back. I know the inn is far from turnkey and stuck in the middle of nowhere, but that woman works miracles."

"Pinnacle Pointe isn't nowhere." My fingers tighten. "I don't know why you despise this place so much. Does Mom know you hate her childhood home?"

He snorts loudly.

Who are we kidding? Of course she does.

He's never made an effort to hide it. Mom herself even frowns on Pinnacle Pointe these days.

But it's beautiful here.

Less noisy. Less rushed. Less stressful.

I don't care if they don't like it. Gram loved her sanctuary, and so do I.

"You have no experience in real estate. You're twenty-six and single—"

"Whatever shall become of me?" I do a mock gasp, covering my open mouth with my hand, which is pointless since he can't see it, but it still makes me smile. "Also, you're forgetting I have years under my belt with an international hotel chain. I know a thing or two about hospitality."

"That's not what I meant." His voice is stern. "You're in no position to keep that relic running. It'll cost you a fortune just to make the necessary repairs."

"Good thing Gram left me her business account, Dad. I'm honoring her wishes."

"Jennifer, that account doesn't begin to cover the work it needs, and it's not a DIY job. Goddamn, what was she thinking?" he whispers. I can just see him shoving his spectacles up on his forehead like he always does when he's frustrated. "Lottie shouldn't have dumped a dilapidated money pit on you. You could barely handle your own bills before your last big raise. I still don't understand why she did this."

Ice churns in my veins.

It's a struggle to remind myself he's just trying to be sweet, overprotective Dad—not a prick who looks at me like I have a brain the size of a walnut.

"She didn't *do* anything to me. It's a blessing, just wait and see. And it's not *that* bad. You talk like it's falling down." No way. Though I wonder if I should be standing on the third-floor balcony when it feels kind of flimsy. I'm pretty sure that last

2

breeze *swayed* it. "You got what you wanted out of the will. Let me enjoy my inheritance, too."

"I want you to enjoy your life," he mutters. "I'd rather see you cash out the equity and invest in a better future, honey."

"If you think it's such a craphole, it'll sell for way less than it's worth."

"The market's on fire right now," he rushes out. I'm sure he has dollar signs flashing in his eyes. "Some developers would buy that place for the land alone. Think about the new construction you could put there."

And raze my family homestead?

Not happening.

I shake my head. "You have to admit this view is worth a million bucks and it's right on the beach, too. It's beautiful and peaceful and I owe it to myself to try to make this work."

There's a long pause.

I can tell he's holding back from saying, *are you sure you owe it to yourself or a dead woman?*

"I still can't believe you quit your nine-to-five at the rate they were paying you to dabble with this place. You know Brock Winthrope's wife personally. It's not too late. I'm sure he'd hire you back in a heartbeat if you just talk to them and—"

"Stop." I cringe at the thought. "I've made up my mind. I'm not spending my life trapped behind a desk for ten hours a day. Gram left me the inn because I'm the only one in this family who gets it like she did."

I hold a breath, my mind stewing with frustration.

You got what you wanted, Dad.

Money. Now why can't you leave me the hell alone?

After another long silence, he says, "I'm only making you second-guess because I love you, Jenn. I can't stand to see you making mistakes that are easily preventable."

"But they're mine to make, aren't they?"

"Yes, and you're still my only daughter. I worry about you, believe it or not."

Damn him, I smile. "Believe it or not, not everyone needs money piled up in some stocks to be happy."

"No, but it certainly makes emergencies easier to handle and buys you all the fancy coffee and pastries you could ever want." He laughs.

He just had to go and mention food, didn't he?

My stomach rumbles, thinking about those mammoth cinnamon rolls from Sweeter Grind, my favorite shop back in Seattle. I miss it.

"Maybe you're right, though," he says quietly. "I shouldn't worry about this."

I cock my head and stare at the phone. "What's that supposed to mean?"

"You love that place because it's sentimental. You'd spend a few weeks there every summer and again at Christmas growing up. It was a change of scenery. Your special escape with Grandma where she'd spoil the living daylights out of you. Jenn, I *lived* there with your mom under their roof for a few years. In a couple months, you'll see what I mean. Then you'll get bored and come home."

I dig my teeth into my lip, more determined than ever to prove him wrong.

"You should be happy I'm taking care of it. Somebody has to."

"Well, Lottie should've sold and moved to town years ago. God knows we tried to convince her. Especially when she was getting older and less mobile. We were always so worried about her out there, living alone..."

"Miles away from civilization? *The horror*," I tease.

He clears his throat.

"Gram loved this place for a reason. Honestly, I think it kept her alive to a ripe old age."

He goes quiet again.

Yeah, this conversation is a waste of time. My parents have never appreciated the beauty of the ocean without a twinkling city skyline and a thousand conveniences.

They never stopped to admire the vibrant colors of Gram's roses, the nights talking in her kitchen while savory homemade pasta sauces simmered behind us, or the fresh honey at breakfast from the bees she kept.

And now that she's gone, they aren't going to start.

They aren't going to figure it out any more than they'll start understanding me.

I'm about to get off the phone when a loud *woof!* from below grabs my attention. I look down.

Cream stands at attention next to the fence with her huge white head thrown back, barking for all she's worth.

A black nose pokes out of the dirt on the other side of the fence behind her, and then the jet-black head its attached to.

Inwardly, I groan, even before I see it.

There's a new trench dug under the fencing—almost in the same spot I filled in a few days ago.

Another reason I can't let this place go.

Gram's two beasts are almost two hundred pounds of Doberman Pinscher trouble.

"Coffee! Again? You're such a pain." I push away from the railing—and is that another board swaying under my feet?

"What now?" Dad asks sharply.

"Coffee tunneled under the fence again. I'd better go before he takes off on the neighbor's property." I hang up while I have a chance.

Coffee and Cream are another good reason to stay and fight.

What Seattle rental would ever let me move in with two hulking Dobermans?

I'll never land a place with a yard, and I can't handle the thought of giving these dogs away. I don't care what Dad thinks.

I run inside the house, toss my phone on the king-sized bed, and start down three flights of stairs to corral Coffee before he's rocketing around someone else's acreage like a wild man. Hopefully before Cream follows him out, too.

The dogs are guardians, brats, and huge babies all in one.

Trying to shepherd both of them is almost impossible sometimes.

By the time I get to the beach where Coffee is galloping around in the sand with his tongue hanging out, Cream pops out of the hole. She sees me and starts backing away from the fence.

Good.

While Coffee tires himself out with a few more flying laps, I grab his collar and start gently walking him back toward the house. I'll let them chill in the sunroom—their favorite spot—until I can get that hole filled.

But I barely make it five steps before more loud barking starts.

Coffee bolts out of my grasp.

I whirl around, just in time to see Cream prancing around in circles, happily kicking sand up with her long white legs.

He jumps up to join his sister, and I topple over. Thankfully, the sand cushions my butt as I hit the ground.

And now they're both free again, and more hyper than ever.

Lovely.

With the battle lost, I relax and stare up at the clouds rolling in, searching for some divine intervention.

What if Dad's right?

What if I'm in over my head?

I get my answer from above.

The sky rips open out of nowhere and rain starts pouring down.

Not exactly the inspiration I was looking for, but the dogs also hate getting drenched. The sudden shower makes them more cooperative.

Ignoring the entire universe stacked against me, I stand up and grab Coffee's attention again. Then we close in on Cream together.

This time, they obediently follow me back to the house—or maybe they're walking me.

All I know is, I'm moving faster than I want to.

Upstairs, I towel them off and lock the dogs in their sunroom while the rain turns into a proper Pacific storm.

"Relax. You guys can nap until your next bathroom break." I lock the glass doors behind me and head upstairs to wash the dirt and dog hair off.

After the world's longest shower, I'm in a better mood, but now I'm freaking starving and light-headed.

On my way to the kitchen, I stop by the sunroom and see a black nose smashed against the glass. Coffee sits in front of me, giving me the saddest deer eyes ever.

Oh, he knows he's in trouble, but he also knows I'm a terrible softie.

Cream ambles over when she notices me, wagging her tail. Unlike most Dobermans, Gram never cropped their ears or had their tails docked, so they both sport long curly question marks for tails.

"Fine, but you two better behave." I try to sound stern as I open the door, but I must fail totally.

A second later, I'm being licked to death by two giant tongues.

I throw the dogs some treats from my pocket and pilfer through the casseroles in the fridge. Every person in a thirty-mile radius must've dropped one off since Gram died, and I'm still thawing out the backlog.

Nothing shows respect like food, and she was a fixture in Pinnacle Pointe. I go for classic cheesy chicken and rice.

As nice as it is not having to cook—*not that I can cook*—all of this sympathy food is a constant sad reminder of what I've lost.

Honestly, just being here is a reminder.

I wish I'd quit Winthrope sooner and moved in with Gram while she was still alive. Maybe if I'd been here to take care of her, she'd still be around.

But she was eighty-seven years old. You couldn't have saved her from old age.

Still, someone should have been here for her until the end.

Trying to shake off the regret, I warm up the casserole and take it to the living room. I don't want to eat at this huge table by myself.

Lounging on the couch with my leftovers, I stare at a bone-white envelope with my name scrolled neatly across it.

I sigh, fighting not to lose my appetite.

It's been here since the day I arrived, untouched and neglected.

I'll have to read it sooner or later, won't I? Why wait?

After stuffing a few more bites in my mouth, I put my plate on the table, tear the envelope open, and brace for a heart-sting.

The first two words alone are a gut punch.

It's insane how a silly nickname can mean so much.

MY QUEEN,

Dry your eyes.

Rejoice.

I'm with my William again, and it's been a long, long fifteen years.

You're the only person I can trust my home to because you're the only one who learned to love it the way I did.

Did you know it was untamed land when I bought it?

We were so young. My father didn't like Will very much.

He'd forbidden me from seeing him, so Will snuck me out of my second-story window one night, drove off, and we were married the next day.

Your grandpa got a job as the maintenance manager at a Seattle hotel. Women didn't work much back then, but I was so bored at home.

One day, I brought Will lunch when I knew the hotel manager would be there and convinced the man he couldn't afford not to hire me.

It only lasted about ten months until your Uncle Henry came. But with my money saved up, I bought that piece of land in an adorable little town far away from the city hubbub.

It wasn't easy. Women didn't buy land for themselves in those days.

The bonehead who owned it told me he felt bad for offloading it on a "schoolgirl." He wanted to make sure my husband knew what I was getting myself into. Your grandpa thought it was hilarious he'd try to lecture me and offered to go "take care of it" before I drowned the poor man face-first in a banana cream pie.

Please.

I let him know real quick that I didn't need my daddy to tell me who to marry and I damn sure didn't need a man telling me what to spend my money on.

The property sat and sat and sat some more.

It was just virgin land and it would take a Herculean effort to make it shine. So I waited a few weeks and started writing the knuckle-head landowner as L. Risa, a busy investor too busy to come to town for a proper look and signing.

He fell for it and I had my land.

You already know the rest.

I turned it into the best bed and breakfast in a hundred miles and raised a family in Pinnacle Pointe in between.

Oh, I loved watching my babies grow up in that house, and then watching you play there every summer in your little red bathing suit with the strawberries. Remember that?

Bee Harbor gave us a life, but it gave us so many more sweet memories. How could I ever leave it to someone who doesn't cherish them?

You, my Queen, are so much like me—

I look away with burning tears.

Then I laugh harshly because I'm nowhere near as gutsy as my grandmother.

I couldn't have kept up this castle of rooms alone in my twilight years. And in high school, I never would've had the guts to sneak out of my window and elope.

I wish we were more alike.

But I shake my head and keep reading.

You can find your dream in Pinnacle Pointe the same way I did. Just keep an open heart.

An open heart? Did she mean an open mind?

I frown, reading it over again.

Gram was slipping toward the end, especially with words and phrases. Someone should have been here with her.

"I'm sorry," I whisper out loud. She's not around to hear my excuses, but I know we let her down. I finish the letter, wiping another tear off my cheek.

Take care of my home and my babies. Most of all, take care of yourself.
Love,
Gram

HOW CAN Dad want me to walk away?

After reading that, I'd rather walk on knives.

Gram bought this place when she was twenty and invested so much more than money. She put her entire life into her dream.

I don't care what my parents think.

The letter leaves me feeling heavy all afternoon. I'm not hungry anymore, but I could use a glass of wine.

Coffee looks up from the antler chew he's gnawing and trots over. His head swings back and forth between me and the remaining bits of food on the coffee table.

"Don't even think about it. Too much cheese and garlic for you." I scrape the remnants into the trash before one of the dogs gets an early dinner and pour myself a large glass of wine from the bottle of red blend I opened yesterday.

At least the house came with a nicely stocked wine cellar.

I start up the stairs with the dogs close behind me. Coffee's big black bulk squeezes between me and the railing. He must push against the spindles too hard because one pops out, lands on the living room floor, and spins like an empty bottle.

Awesome.

One more thing to fix.

One more problem.

But as a hand flutters to my chest, I realize no repair on the massive maintenance list compares to the yawning chasm in my heart.

I miss her too much for words.

All I have left is to make Gram proud.

* * *

Bang!

Woof!

So many woofs.

Then more banging.

I blink my bleary eyes open as a black mass launches at me. My heart jumps up my throat.

What now?

Coffee cannonballs down next to me on the bed and puts his paws on my chest.

What was that banging, though? The weather or just a dream?

Maybe just thunder. Cream's alert yip turns into a proper howl at her brother's side.

"Okay, okay. Get off and let's go investigate. Um, I can't take you out if I can't get up," I say, pushing at Coffee's weight.

Bang! Bang!

There it is again.

I wonder what time it is. I'm missing my phone somewhere under the heap of Doberman.

"Coffee, you want a treat?"

He leaps off the bed with a grunt and sits like a total gentleman.

I smile and crawl out of bed. Even if it hasn't completely robbed them of their wily ways, Gram made some headway with training over the years.

They actually listen. *Sometimes.*

But another round of loud knocking pulls me from my thoughts.

I grab my robe and throw it over my Taylor Swift tank top. The dull light streaming in through the window hints that it's early morning.

Who brings a casserole around this early? It must be another mourner, dragging in late to pay their respects. They've been my only visitors over the three weeks I've been here.

Not that I can blame any would-be patrons from out of town, either. I'm not remotely ready to deal with hosting random strangers here, but the Temporarily Closed sign out front is an easy miss.

"I've got to put up a better sign," I mutter as the dogs trail after me down the stairs.

That banging blares through the house again, this time more insistent.

This is ridiculous.

Did anyone stop to think that I'm mourning, too? And it's a little past eight in the flipping morning.

When I get to the door and tear it open, I'm ready to confront the early bird on the other side with my coldest glare.

But it's not another smiling old lady or solemn-faced couple from church clutching food trays.

Instead, a tall, broad man stuffed into a three-piece suit and black sunglasses stands on my step.

Holy dark knight.

Before I can breathe a word, he dips his shades, revealing the most startling grey-blue eyes I've ever seen.

He's older, maybe in his mid thirties.

A single glance cuts through me. I actually rock back a step, straining to find my footing again. Even the dogs seem tense behind me, frozen in place with their ears perked.

"Miss Landers? Good morning." He reaches inside his jacket.

My blood glazes over.

Is he going for a weapon? What if he's some kind of mafia gun coming to wipe me out?

Except he only pulls out a sleek white envelope.

I'm already looking for a bank logo before he pushes it toward me.

Yep, here we go. Gram had some loan or lien I didn't know about, and I'm being foreclosed.

She kept impeccable records, though. I've sifted through the office several times.

The mortgage on this place was paid off thirty years ago, and she had just enough in the business account to keep the day-to-day going.

"Are you well?" the stranger asks, raking me with those wintry eyes. "Miss Landers, you're pale. If this is a bad time—"

The second I start shaking my head and open my mouth to reply, Coffee lunges past my legs, straight at my visitor.

Oh, no.

He rears up with a loud, curious bark. Then a massive paw catches the barely fastened belt of my robe as he crashes down on his long legs, pulling it open.

A cool breeze rushes through the thin cotton of my tank top and panties, winding down my bare legs.

But all I feel is *fire* as I reach down, desperately trying to make myself decent again.

When I look up, there's a smirk stabbing across the banker man's face.

A gentleman would've turned around or at least glanced away.

This man stares, his eyes roaming my bare flesh, making me feel naked and vulnerable in front of him.

Fury throbs under my cheeks as I yank my robe shut with both hands.

Coffee's big, wet nose presses against the hand gripping the envelope.

"Coffee, sit!"

Of course, he chooses now not to listen. He just stands there with his curly tail flicking.

The man doesn't move, turning his amused gaze to the dog.

My stomach knots.

I don't have a clue who he is or what he wants, but all I need is for this guy to scare my very large dog into bowling him over.

"He doesn't bite. Can I help you?" I need to end this and get the dogs inside.

Not to be left out, Cream bounces past me too, sniffing the stranger's hand. It's big and calloused, more like a workman's hand than the cool professional it's attached to.

He looks at Cream, not me, and says, "Not today, lady."

Wait. He knows the dogs?

I clear my throat loudly until he holds his hand out.

"Miles Cromwell. Your neighbor—of sorts."

I blink, taking his hand loosely.

"I know who you are," I lie.

Actually, I've heard the name before. It totally doesn't match this angled face, all sharp edges and moody dark windswept hair with a dusting of stubble around a mouth that looks like it's made to give commands.

This is not the recluse I pictured who owns the neighboring lot.

He's owned it for years, but I've never seen him before. Not that it's easy when there's a pretty huge acreage separating the houses.

Aren't rich hermits usually over sixty years old?

Grizzled, ancient, eccentric men who keep the shades drawn and hoard strange things like pop-up turkey timers.

"Oh, right. You're here about the intrusion on the beach, huh? If the dogs dug a hole on your side—"

The cool eyebrow he lifts stops me mid-sentence.

"I'll never complain about Coffee and Cream." He glances at the dogs before his eyes flick over, trailing my body again.

Annoying.

14

I'm not used to being ogled, especially by strange men with sky-spanning shoulders and dusky eyes from a vampire romance book.

My cheeks burn hotter, unsure how to feel. And even though I'm completely covered by my fluffy robe, there's a tingle in places no stranger should ever touch.

"They do seem to be more than you can handle," he points out bluntly.

I raise a brow this time. Is that a joke?

Ha. Ha. Ha. So funny, McDick next door.

"Can I help you, or what? Did you come to borrow a cup of sugar?" I ask again. "If you're just here to gab, this isn't the best—"

"I came to offer my sincerest condolences. Lottie was an amazing woman. I'm sure you know everyone here respected her. We're all worse off without her, but you know that," he says.

I bat my eyes numbly.

He knew Gram too? What's going on?

He extends the hand grasping the envelope again, shoving it toward me. "Also, a special delivery. Given the circumstances, I thought it was best to make you an offer in person."

"Offer?"

What on earth is he talking about?

"I trust you'll find it compelling. Please take it in the spirit Lottie would have intended."

I shake my head loosely, taking a step back into the house. "What offer are we talking about?"

He doesn't answer until I take the envelope.

Sighing, I rip the thing open, pull out the contents, and—it's a check?

"Hold up. Bee Harbor isn't for sale," I say, steeling my voice as I look up. "Sorry, but this is really sudden. Do you think I'll just take your money and agree to it on a whim?"

Thick, dark brows pull down, casting a standoffish look.

"You're offended—that wasn't my intention."

"Well, the next time you want to try to buy a dead woman's property when she's barely cold, have the decency to use a realtor. Maybe try the phone first. Then I can just say no, thanks and hang up without tumbling out here in my—"

I don't finish that thought.

His lips curl up in that insufferable smirk again.

"I promise you, I didn't see much," he says. But his tone makes it sound like that's a tragedy.

God, give me strength.

Because even when my last boss was a billionaire ogre, I never rolled out of bed before nine a.m. with an instant urge to choke a man before.

"You should go," I bite off.

"Miss Landers, surely you must know who I am."

"I don't. Frankly, I don't care. My grandmother never mentioned you."

The harsh head shake I throw back only sharpens those silver daggers for eyes.

"Don't misunderstand my intentions. I wanted to do this in person, so you'll know the property is in the best hands. I fully intend to preserve its natural beauty, without any sales to developers. Also, I thought you'd be thankful to have the burden lifted off your shoulders promptly." He pauses. It must be the lashing flames in my eyes. "What are you so mad about? The maintenance cost on this old place alone exceeds any projected revenue. You can't possibly intend to stay."

"Oh, I intend. *Possibly,*" I throw back, each word so sharp it tastes metallic.

He studies me slowly, his eyes frosting over me with amusement.

"*You?* Alone? Without any capital backing?" He scoffs loudly.

That does it.

My mouth drops open and I take a halting step forward.

"What do you know about maintenance on *my* property?

Have you been snooping around? And why do you care so much if I'm staying? I just got here!"

Deep breath.

Try not to scream.

I almost want him to do something dramatic and angry and full of assholery so I can run him off my porch. Maybe even get him a visit from the sheriff.

But he's too smug to be reckless. Too calm and levelheaded.

"Naturally, I do my research before any new real estate deal. This one is personal and close to home. Literally. It's even more warranted when a man tries not to shit where he eats."

I groan.

"Does that research usually make you crap yourself? Because I'm not interested. Bye."

Before I can slam the door in his face, he throws an arm out. A happy-looking Cream darts between us and stops in the doorway, wagging her tail.

Perfect timing.

"Wait. I'll round up my offer to an even two million, but I can't warrant going higher. That's well above market value and I'm nobody's sucker," he growls.

"Two million?" I can't feel my toes.

I realize I never glanced at the numbers on the check he basically shoved in my face.

I stare at him as he nods.

"What kind of psycho offer did you make?" I mutter. I hate that I was too rattled to look until now.

"A painfully generous one. Nothing less."

I pull out the check, grinding my teeth together so my jaw doesn't drop.

Yep, those are zeroes.

Many, *many* zeros.

So many life-changing zeroes, I don't think there's any way this can possibly be real. The whole inn and its acreage might be worth a hair over a million dollars at best.

He's offering almost double.

I'm at a loss for what to say, what to think—until he smiles like he thinks he's won me over.

That same sinful, almost smarmy smile that spoils a face molded by the gods.

"Don't think on this too hard, Miss Landers. You'd be surprised how far instinct has always gotten me in business. What does your gut say?" His voice is so gentle, but the intention is all brute force.

Hell no.

While I still have my wits, I hold it up and tear the cursed thing into a dozen pieces. A sharp wind blows the confetti in his face, now set like unblinking stone.

"Well, it's safe to assume you didn't make your fortune in real estate, I guess," I say dully.

The paper scraps flutter onto his expensive black shoes.

He watches them with disinterest. I hate that he doesn't flinch.

"Bad move. You won't get another offer like that. Hell, you'll probably wind up selling at the bottom to some second-rate developer with a taste for gold watches. He'll turn Bee Harbor into another row of cookie-cutter houses in no time. Congratulations, Miss Landers."

I shrug and look away. That's not happening while I'm alive and solvent.

"Amazingly, that sounds like a better option than dealing with you."

For the briefest second, his eyes heat to blue mercury.

"Shit," he mutters, turning away. "When Lottie said this wouldn't be easy, I didn't know I'd be dealing with a goddamned wolverine."

I don't even want to know what that means.

But I reach into my robe pocket and retrieve the stress ball I fought away from Coffee earlier today.

"Coffee, go fetch." I throw the ball over my shoulder to make sure the dogs stay inside where they belong.

Once they're off on a mad chase, I smile at the would-be shark I just had the courage to harpoon. "Have a blessed day. And stay the hell away from my dogs."

Boom.

I slam the door in his face and run.

It's the only thing that keeps me from dwelling on the proud, stupid thing I've done.

II: NO FREE LUNCH (MILES)

I grind my shoulders against the leather cushion of the car seat.

I can't get comfortable even though I've been in the back of this car a thousand times.

"Of all the shitty, stubborn, pigheaded things she could do—"

"A little advice, boss?" Benson chuckles from the front seat as we pull onto the road.

I glare back at his eyes in the rearview mirror.

"Perhaps it was a tactical error to think she wanted to sell so soon. Her grandmother's passing was recent and rather sudden. She's still grieving. Now might not be the best time while her emotions are swirling."

"Like hell. A million dollars over fair market value would mend my broken heart."

His eyes hold mine silently until he says, "We can't all be you, Mr. Cromwell. You were born cold-blooded."

Finally, a compliment.

I sigh.

"I got the letter from Lottie's lawyer, Waldo, three days after she died. It was practically begging me to make a good faith offer. She said the old inn would be a handful for her granddaughter to take on. I thought it was a done fucking deal. Never imagined I'd have to reach for the moon to convince this cactus-woman to sell."

I'm not used to this insanity.

People don't tell me no.

Some negotiations are tougher than others, but until today, I've never had a check unceremoniously torn up and tossed in my face before.

When the dog flung her robe open, I thought I knew what I was dealing with.

A distraught splash of auburn-haired beauty with long lashes and legs made for sin.

Not a complete ballbuster who seemed to enjoy the dumb look on my face when she set my olive branch on fire.

Not someone I ever imagined going to war with.

Benson laughs again. "Lottie always was one to inject some fun into life, wasn't she?"

"This is not my idea of *fun*." However, the late Lottie Risa was the only local I ever trusted with the code for my gate. I'll miss the apple pastries and fresh honey she foisted on me every time she dropped by. "You should've seen her, Benson. Tossing that hair of hers, cheeks all cherry-red, ranting and raving like I was some goddamned intruder who came there to chop her up instead of pay double for that old place."

My hand forms a fist, balanced on my knee.

"Since the negotiations didn't go so well, now you'll have to see a pretty lady *twice*. Tragic."

Again, my gaze daggers him.

Again, he isn't fazed.

"How do you mistake stubborn mule for beautiful?" I demand.

In fairness, Miss Landers is easy on the eyes. Disarming when she shouldn't be.

I figured as much going in, but the photos I've seen over the years with Lottie didn't do her justice. I did a basic scan of her before putting together the offer. In the portrait on her new business page, she looked professional, all prim and proper in her turquoise cat-eye glasses and tight updo.

I thought professionalism would come naturally to her.

Not a hopeless desire to cling to old houses that are nowhere near the trendy Seattle coffee shops and yoga places she probably frequents.

Fuck, I thought this was a done deal.

Benson smirks, forming lines under his weathered eyes, making me ask why I keep him around. "You forget I was around when other deals fell through. You usually climb in the car roaring about some bloodsucking leech scheming to drain you dry. Frankly, sir, I don't recall another business meeting where you left mentioning your adversary's hair or her flushed cheeks."

I jerk my face to the window, fumbling to form a response.

"She's striking, I'll give you that," I say slowly. "But a starving goddamned tiger has a better personality. I can think of a billion things I'd rather do than deal with her," I snarl.

"Enlighten me." He throws back a skeptical look full of innuendo.

"Why do I keep paying you again?"

"Because no one else wants to haul you around while they put up with a litany of insults, I imagine."

I nod briskly.

He's right about one thing.

Doug Benson has also been around long enough to warrant his shit-talking. That's because I demand the best.

Normally, I get my way.

Which is why I can't fathom how a crumbling bed and breakfast that's seen its better days *still isn't mine.*

"What the hell do I have to offer to grab that lot?" I mutter absently.

"You may not want to use that word with Miss Risa's granddaughter, for one."

"What word?"

"Grab. If she thinks you see her grandmother's property as a spot on a Monopoly board, you won't make this any easier."

I roll my eyes. "Why must people be so damn sentimental? It's no game at all. It's the last piece I need to ensure total privacy from the townies and tourists forever. You know that."

"I do," he agrees quietly. "Just like I know you'll never face much competition for happiest loner on the planet."

* * *

I HOLD the canvas in place, feathering the extra-fine detail brush against it with my other hand.

This is my oasis.

Sweet tranquility, creating entire worlds with each stroke, untainted by wretched surprises or gorgeous, obstinate women destined to drive me insane.

For once, I'm not even thinking about my father as I stroke long fluid lines across the width of the canvas.

Then my phone vibrates on my desk, tearing me from serenity.

My eyes flick over. My executive assistant's name flashes across the screen.

Shit, didn't I just talk to her a few days ago?

Sighing, I drop the brush into a cup of water, grab a paper towel, and wipe the cobalt-blue smudges off my hand, so I can take the call.

"Louise."

"Hi, I'm just calling with your regular update, Mr. Cromwell. We've had an uptick in advertiser revenue driven by special interest groups invested in the Seattle city council race. We should expect to see an upward trend there until the election. As you know, the last debate came to blows. It's hard to imagine lobbyists backing off with things more heated than a *House of Cards* episode—"

I should care about this.

I really should when a single change in the council's makeup could mean regulatory heaven or hell for my company.

Except, I just don't give a damn.

"Go on," I say flatly.

"Um, the series of short videos we did on the Bainbridge Seal Sanctuary to attract the younger crowd went viral on TikTok. You asked if we were making progress there…"

"I worry about this new generation." I sigh.

She laughs. "Boss, take the win! It was pure candy clickbait, just like you wanted. Everyone loves cute animals. And I'd say it did the job because Pacific-Resolute launched a copycat effort with some sea otters a few days later—"

"Don't use their name—or *hers*." My gut clenches. "And why do you think I care?"

"Well, the copycat failed miserably for one…"

Ordinarily, I'd bask in being a trendsetter, even if it's a bit annoying to watch someone else build their media business off my strategies, but it's Pacific-Resolute.

It's enough to know it failed and I don't have to hear about it.

"Louise, this is my time off. Unless something disastrous happens and needs my immediate expertise, let's make these calls bi-weekly. Okay?"

"Bi-weekly?" She pauses. "Does that mean like twice a week, or two times a—"

"Less often. Definitely."

"You're only checking every two weeks?" There's a note of fear in her voice.

Last time I checked, I was the boss at Cromwell-Narada Media, and I make the rules. If that means I want to step back from being a workaholic android for what's left of summer, my people should wrap their heads around it, and fast.

"If the clients want my head on a pike or Mount Rainier blows up, call me. Otherwise, you should see this as an exercise in trust. You run a tight ship like all my senior people. Nothing will go wrong," I promise, hoping like hell that's true.

"Can creative at least stop by?"

"Creative?"

"You remember you had them scheduled, right? They're coming out there to film content about Pinnacle Pointe for—"

"Right," I throw back.

Right.

The deal I made with the town council here to help drum up tourism. I need a positive local image if I want to be left the hell alone.

I want to be the aloof rich guy who's viewed like Santa Claus and enjoys North Pole level privacy, too. Apparently, that's going to cost me a meeting or two with the creative wonks during my summer off.

"Send them over when they arrive. By the way, I need you to comb through anything public you can find about a small Seattle consulting firm owned by a Jennifer Landers in marketing."

She pauses.

"Are you trying to buy out some small-time marketer? Um, I know our in-house marketing hasn't been impressive lately, but I didn't know it was that bad."

Hardly.

The fact that I'm even wasting time on this ornery spitfire thumbing her nose at my generosity feels like a thorn in my side I can't extract.

"It's a personal matter. I want her land, but I need help figuring out what motivates her if I'm going to convince her to sell."

"Ohhh, I like it. Everybody needs a little turf war drama. I'll see what I can come up with."

"Understood," I say, ignoring her 'turf war' comment.

I throw the phone down and stare out my floor-to-ceiling window.

NICOLE SNOW

Outside, it's a picturesque summer day, illuminating the source of my misery.

Green grass stretches out like an ornate carpet, exploding into wildflowers and the faint outline of an old stone inn with red shutters.

The house next to it is tall, worn, but somehow still as bright as the landscape around it. I think the stone was locally sourced a long time ago, probably cheap to come by when the inn was built.

It's a cross between a whimsical cottage and the best small-town charm the 1950s had to offer, all odd angles, fearlessly perched on the side of a bluff overlooking the Pacific.

I look at my cobalt-blue canvas.

Now I know why I picked that shade of blue. I also know what's wrong with the painting.

Moving back to my easel, I mix black and white on the palate until the color turns into the kind of moody grey you'd expect to find belching from a chimney. I layer smoke over cobalt blue until the background is no longer blue, but not completely grey either.

It's dark, but a certain brightness peeks through.

When Louise calls back roughly an hour later, I'm putting the finishing touches on a faded Gothic castle perched over a cliff with thorny vines clawing up the sides.

"Louise. Didn't we say bi-weekly?"

"I've got the info you asked for. I thought you'd want to know."

"Right." She could've just emailed it, but that's Louise. Whenever she hears tension in my voice, she prefers the phone.

Damn. Am I letting that insufferable woman get to me? All over this unbelievable rejection?

I need to knock that shit off right now.

"Give me details," I say.

"It's a pretty new company. There's a list of services offered and a few testimonials on their site. She also has a Facebook group with less than a hundred people in it. It seems like a barely open kind of startup thing. I did some poking around on LinkedIn and see she's gone full-time with the business just recently, but she used to have a senior marketing position for Winthrope International."

"Winthrope? Send me all the links you can find for her." Clearly, my initial scan wasn't enough.

I'd like to know just how senior that position was. It could mean she's sitting on more money than I thought, and that might explain her laughing off my offer.

"Will do, bossman. Anything else?" Louise asks cheerfully.

"No. Just send what you have on this marketing startup, and I'll figure out the rest."

The email comes through shortly after I end the call. I find the attachments with all of Miss Landers' social media profiles along with the startup's website.

A quick glance at her Instagram shows it's filled with pink quotes about the joys of marketing and bringing dreams to life.

Spare me the fluff.

I rake a hand through my hair, wondering why every person and their dog is a freelance marketer now. The biggest *joy* of marketing seems like making money without doing any real work.

After scrolling through a few short videos with mundane 'inspirational' quotes, another video pops up. She's standing on the beach in a bikini.

Holy fuck.

I'm instantly ripped back to a giant Doberman pulling her robe open, revealing a sight I couldn't tear myself away from.

I didn't mean to stare.

Hell, eyeballing a woman in an accidental state of sudden undress isn't me at all.

But when she rocked curves that called my hands and mouth to roam, well, I'm not fucking dead.

I still have a pulse—and that pulse bangs like a war drum as I stare at a half-naked Jennifer Landers.

Even the way she sweeps her hand through wet cinnamon-red hair while she giggles makes my cock jolt.

The video begins to auto-play with her talking.

"This is the best part of my workday. Yes, *work* day! I get so many ideas from being out and enjoying the fresh air. If your clients are raving about you but you're stuck in a feast or famine cycle, it's not because you need another certification. You need marketing. You need to be getting your fine work out there for the world to see. If you don't know how, I can help. And if you think you can't afford marketing, you can't afford not to."

A water droplet slides down the curve of her breast, accenting everything.

Goddamn.

There should be a law of reality against a demoness being stunning enough to strike me down.

I check out her website next. The left side is an image of a devil who looks like an angel wearing a turquoise dress and those matching glasses I suspect she only wears in front of a camera.

They bring out the natural green of her eyes too well.

Here, she looks professional and proper, but innocent. If you didn't know her, you'd expect a total sweetheart.

And aside from spitting fire over unexpected land offers, maybe she is.

There's another video on her sales page, too.

She's wearing the same turquoise dress and sitting at a desk.

"I know. I know you've tried everything. Instagram, Twitter, Facebook, TikTok, and Reddit. Endless hours pumping out videos. And for what? If you're like a lot of my clients when they come to me, it's not getting you results. What if I told you the problem isn't that you need to work harder? What if you're working *too hard?*"

"What if you make fucking a cactus look delightful?" I mutter to her smiling face on the screen.

"I have a three-step process for finding you an easy flow of new leads." She holds up three fingers. "First, simplify. You don't need to be on nine different platforms. Pick one to master, and preferably one you don't hate. I'll help with the SEO. If you want to find new clients, you have to be easy to find. And you don't have time to learn a whole new skill. I'll do it, so you can just keep being awesome at what you do best. Finally, make connections. Engage with the content you like. Take the time to respond to DMs. A conversation keeps you first in a customer's mind, and more importantly, builds a referral system. I know, it's a lot to take in. That's why I'm willing to take the time to walk you through it. Just call Odd Little Bee and ask for Landers!"

Odd Little Bee? That's seriously her company name?

The stinger fits, I suppose.

Although her advice isn't bad, this still smells like a textbook startup. A starving one damned near begging for business.

After scrolling through her other social media, I'm convinced.

This must be a passion project for her, even if she appears to know what she's talking about, and that's an opportunity.

Maybe offering her flailing business a lifeline will help sweeten the deal to make that land mine. I click over to her website again, clench my teeth, and call the number on the contact page.

Voicemail. Of course.

I wonder if she's busy torturing other hapless men with her skimpy swimsuits.

My jaw tightens as I wait for the beep to leave a message.

Fuck.

If this doesn't close the deal, I'm going to be pissed.

"Jennifer, this is Miles Cromwell. My executive assistant found your marketing company, and I have a project I'm hoping you can help us with. Please give me a call back so we can discuss the details. I'd love to forget what happened earlier and start over with a clean slate."

Surely, I'll hear from her soon.

From the looks of things, it's not like clients are beating down her door.

I check my phone before I shower and start to wind down for the night. Nothing new.

Damn.

I gave her the right number, didn't I?

But she doesn't call the next day either. Maybe she really didn't get the message?

Either that, or she'd rather rip my throat out than shut up and take my money.

A thousand other possibilities roll through my head until I can't stand it.

Grudgingly, I try again.

Another voicemail greeting.

Another message.

Another gaping hole of radio silence.

Miss Landers can't be as passionate about marketing as she seems, or else she'd rather set her bee-loving heart on playing volleyball with a live wasp's nest than deal with me.

This is where I question my sanity.

It's time to rethink my strategy for acquiring Bee Harbor, even if I loathe working through proxies. Except now I'm extra pissed that she's ignoring my calls for marketing help.

What kind of miracle does it take to *pay* this woman?

And how can some copywriter who was earning typical Seattle corporate money afford to turn down easy cash from a billionaire?

Money isn't always the shortcut people think it is, but everyone appreciates a payday they don't have to sweat for.

Don't they?

Scowling, I pick up the phone and call her again, drumming my fingers on my desk as I wait for voicemail.

"Jennifer, Miles Cromwell again. I'll be blunt. If you want my business, this is your last chance. Call me back by the end of the day, or I'll find someone else. Thanks."

That last word tastes like ash.

Of course, I'm second-guessing every damn word, and I never second-guess.

Great job, Miles. That's really going to help you get the land from a lady who already thinks you're bear vomit.

I'm sure I've sealed my fate—until my phone lights up and starts blaring a minute later.

I can't help the wry smile. My little threat must've gotten her attention.

I pick it up before I even check the number.

"Great to see you come to your senses, Miss Landers."

"Um—it's not time for our bi-weekly call. Sorry. I was afraid you'd be upset if I called without a true emergency." Louise.

Dammit.

"I thought you were—never mind. Why are you calling? What's wrong?"

"Nice to talk to you too, Mr. Cromwell," she says with a fluttery laugh. "Anyway, one of our tech clients wants to tweak their advertising strategy and—"

"That sounds like a job for Clarence in marketing. He's the head of the department and deals with our jumbo accounts."

"Well, yes, but the marketing lead said the guy insisted on talking to you. You know how persistent they get when they're desperate—and between the stock crashing and that dumb virtual reality thing they're blowing billions on, they're hair-on-fire freaked. They want your direct approval for the new campaign setup."

I cringe, knowing exactly what company she means.

"Send it over," I clip.

I should be more annoyed with this. Yet it's only a faint spark against the flaring wildfire coursing through me every time I think of Jennifer Landers laughing at my messages and instantly deleting them.

"Already done. And I hate to dump more on your plate, but they requested you get back to them by end of week."

Beautiful.

"I'll take care of it, Louise. It's not your problem anymore, okay?" I tell her.

"Okey dokey, Eeyore."

"Eeyore?"

"The donkey. It's probably none of my business—"

"It isn't," I throw back, thoroughly annoyed.

"—you sound a little more tired than usual." Louise sucks in a deep breath. "Is everything okay, Mr. Cromwell?"

"Never better," I lie. "I'm away from Seattle and enjoying the quiet when my damn phone isn't drilling through my eardrums."

"Oh, good. *Right*," she adds quickly as it clicks in her head.

"While you're on the line, you didn't find out anything else about Jennifer Landers or her Odd Little Bee, did you?"

"I sent you everything," she says, her voice going up an octave. "Wow, Mr. Cromwell. You must *really* want this property."

I can tell by the lilt of her voice that it's not the property she means, but its owner.

"It would mean a lot more privacy, and that's invaluable."

She's quiet for too long.

"Is there something else, Louise?"

"...with all due respect, sir, you're holed up in that middle of nowhere town on its own island. How much more privacy do you need?"

"Never enough. Since I haven't burned my fortune investing in lunar rockets, this will have to do for an eccentric billionaire quest," I growl back.

She laughs like it's the funniest thing she's heard all day.

At least someone appreciates my humor, even when it's more than half serious.

"Well, good luck with the tech people."

"Remind me, does my office phone have voicemail or does it route to you?" Maybe the marketing genius called my office instead of my cell phone.

"I check your main voicemail at six a.m. and six p.m. I forwarded you everything pertinent this morning. Do you need me to check it again?"

"No, it's fine."

"Are you looking for something specific?"

"No. I appreciate your attention to detail, as always."

By the end of the day, Jennifer Landers hasn't returned my call.

There's no way I can call again without looking like a desperate goblin.

When my doorbell chimes and I tap my phone to see who's at the door, I'm almost praying to the gods she decided to drop by in person. Any negotiation would be a thousand times more interesting face-to-face.

"I picked up your dry cleaning," Benson says. "Should I leave it in the mudroom for you?"

"I'll let you in. Hang on."

A couple minutes later, I open the door, and he hands me a garment bag.

"You want a scotch while you're here?" It's not like I have anything better to do tonight except brood. I'm not closing any remarkable land deals anytime soon.

"Would I ever turn down a free drink from your stash?" His smile is timeless.

Aside from his hair going full silver, he's the same portly, pleasant man I've known since I was just a fresh-faced kid.

We walk to my bar and I pour out a few fingers from the top-shelf stuff I never bother saving for a better occasion. I haven't celebrated anything with expensive booze since the days when Dad had my job.

Those days were very different. Every triumph was warm, full of big speeches in crowded rooms, and dammit, *meaningful.*

"Where are you tonight, boss? Any reason you're glued to your phone?" He tosses back the last of his drink with a satisfied sigh.

I shake my head. "I'm trying to close on the place next door, as you know, and I'm having trouble reaching her."

He smiles, holding up his glass wistfully. "Ah, yes. Lottie's little tigress. Be careful when she's already shown you her claws."

I snort, reaching for the bottle to refill our glasses.

"Haven't I learned that the hard way? I'm going to get that land, Benson."

"She does live next door. I know it's a bit of a walk and we're too drunk to drive, but you could just pay her a visit."

I could, I think, drowning a growl in my scotch.

I just wonder if I'm up for being tackled and possibly mauled like an overstuffed lion facing down a Bengal tiger—especially when another shit-fight with teeth is not how I'd love to devour every inch of Jennifer Landers.

III: NO LOFTY PROMISES (JENN)

*L*ast night, I walked out onto the balcony deck attached to my bedroom, and a stiletto heel went clean through a decrepit knot in the wood.

Ugh.

I never dreamed it was actually this bad.

I also never thought I'd be contemplating paying out almost a hundred thousand dollars to update all the massive decking with modern composite materials—if only the old house didn't have several other pressing issues.

It's still on my mind when I move my morning yoga practice to the downstairs patio. I'm not going down with that deck if I bounce around and shake the wrong rusty screw loose.

No soaring ocean view here, but it's still gorgeous.

Everything is so lush, so green, so alive. A few tiny hummingbirds flit around the flowering bushes like little jewels in the morning light.

I'm panting away in downward dog position—desperate to get back to the shape I was in before Gram's funeral—when my phone rings.

I nearly tumble over trying to grab it off the chair next to me.

A new client? I could use a lot of those.

Nope!

The number flashing across the screen is the same one that's called at least four times over the past three days.

I should have known it was Dracula, once again demanding I invite him into my dumpster fire of a life.

The latest message? "My original offer stands."

Like he hasn't made that as clear as a shot to the face.

Like he's doing this for poor widdle me.

Right.

It's amazing how Gram never mentioned living next to the prince of all jackasses. I wonder if he only knows the dogs because he went after them for trespassing on his precious kingdom.

I'm sad to say I'm not above doing my own digging.

Know thy enemy, or whatever.

The results that came back from my best Google-fu were all too predictable.

Miles Cromwell.

Media titan.

All around anti-people jerkoff.

Single—*no surprise.*

Silver-blue eyes sharp enough to cut steel and shoulders wrapped in imported suits big enough to haul around his ego.

And just like the bloodsucker he is, his looks are too good at concealing his shriveled up heart.

Look, I know billionaires are used to getting their way, but he needs to take the L here.

He's not getting Bee Harbor.

Not for any amount.

I don't care if he rides in on the world's cutest pony holding a check for infinity dollars.

His crap reminded me I still have principles, and Gram would spin right out of her grave if she knew I signed the inn over to the devil next door.

Still, I can't live with these pesky messages forever.

So I reject the call and pull up a text message instead, biting my cheek as I try to type out something more polite than he deserves.

Mr. Cromwell, thanks for your interest, but like I've said, I am not interested in selling to you or anyone else at this—

Knock! Knock!

That distant banging is followed by Coffee and Cream barking up a storm.

I guess I didn't answer the phone fast enough, so Dracula decided to show up on my doorstep.

Cool.

At least I'll get to see the look on his face when I shoot him down.

Sliding my flip-flops on, I storm inside through the sliding glass door, march straight to the front door with the dogs trotting behind me, and throw it open.

"Let's cut to the chase, I'm not—"

Oh, crap.

I've already started tearing into the guy before I realize it's not the grump next door. Is it one of his minions coming to do his dirty work instead?

Hmm.

The stranger isn't quite as tall as Dracula, but probably broader.

He's my age, not ten years older like Dracula. Muscular. Smiling like it won't break him.

And he's wearing a flannel shirt with a toolbelt hanging around his waist.

My asshat neighbor wouldn't be caught dead in flannel.

"This a bad time?" The man loops a thumb through his belt.

"Uh—no." I shake my head. "Sorry. I thought you were someone else." I offer him my hand before I remember I'm still sweaty from yoga, so I wipe it on my leggings with my face burning. "Uh—yoga. Sorry again!"

He laughs loudly and shakes my hand anyway.

"No problem. I'm Ace. I was Lottie's repair guy. Just wanted to finish a few fixes we were working on before she—well, before—"

I nod warmly. He doesn't have to say it.

Ace, huh?

It's even a sexy name.

This day suddenly feels brighter.

"What repairs?" I don't even know where to begin, and I worry any renovations will eat into my nonexistent fortune. "Listen, I'm happy to go over anything you'd like, but I'm not sure I have the budget right now for anything too major."

He holds up a hand. "Don't worry, miss, it's on the house. I just want to finish a few things we were already working on. Lottie fronted me the money six months ago. Wouldn't feel right leaving them undone when I already got paid. I wasn't sure if you'd be keeping me around, but I want to make sure I've done what I can."

When he smiles, he looks like the lead in one of those Christmassy romance specials, and he's just as charming as any small-town hunk of handy love too.

Okay.

So I get a little googly-eyed and suddenly start thinking this could be my very own rom-com—the kind where Mr. Fixer Upper sails in and helps save my flailing bed and breakfast from total ruin.

"That's kind of you." I smile back.

"We were in the cottage last, trying to get it spruced up and functional so she could rent out the spare rooms again. But I could walk you over to the main building, point out the repairs, and explain the larger items that are gonna need some bigger renovations, if you'd like."

I nod, biting my lower lip as charmingly as I can.

"Yes, thank you. I'd appreciate that."

"Do you want to start with the cottage since that's where we left off? We can start out back."

"Sure." I follow him around to the back door, wishing it were winter.

It's easy to let my brain rabbit away, imagining us walking through the snow, making a snowman over hot cocoa, him in a fisherman sweater and me in fluffy pink mittens. Later, we'd get more cocoa, and he'd wipe a bit of foam off my lips before kissing me, and then—

I shake my head, clearing my throat as he looks around.

"This was a storage building a long time ago. My grandpa converted it when business picked up like fifty years ago. With everything the inn needs, I'm a little surprised she started with the cottage."

"Oh, yeah. I tried to get her to start with some little things inside that I thought were safety concerns—not just for her guests, but for her own well-being. She stayed on the third floor since she loved that ocean view so much. Honestly, I didn't think it was safe for a woman that age to be walking those stairs every day. But you know Lottie. If she didn't like being told, she wouldn't listen."

I laugh, despite my heart pulling down.

"That was Gram, all right."

Ace smiles. "She said the cottage still brought in the most rent with the summer crowd and she wanted it up and running by now. Plus, she was still pushing her morning crew aside and doing most of the cooking and serving herself. Right till the end."

I'm in a losing battle against stinging tears.

It's too soon for this.

But I dislodge the knot in my throat and keep walking with him.

By the time we've roamed through the cottage and the first floor of the main house, me listening to his long list of recommended fixes, I've stopped thinking that this is the start of my happily ever after.

More like a horror movie.

We're over fifty thousand dollars of renovation in and that doesn't even touch the crumbling deck and balcony. A lot of that's just basic repairs to make the three guest bathrooms fully functional.

Good God.

I'm already overwhelmed, and there are still *two floors* to go.

That business account Gram left me is going to run dry in no time at this rate, and so will my own savings from my old job at Winthrope.

Our next stop is the second floor bathroom. Ace turns the faucet on the porcelain sink.

I gasp at the rusty red liquid oozing out.

So much for a cozy Christmas romance. I'm pretty sure this happened in *The Haunting* or one of those paranormal movies.

Ace throws me a gentle smile. "It's just rust. The pipes are old and temperamental. The whole place needs new piping, I'm afraid. I told her, but—"

"She always had her own order to things," I finish for him.

"Yep. That sink looked like this for a while, and I guess folks never complained in the warmer months when there were other bathrooms and that neat little outdoor shower. I tried to get her to replace the pipes then, but she didn't want to. I put a temporary fix in, but I'm not sure how long it will hold."

More great news.

I don't say anything. Still, my face must show what I'm thinking because he says, "It's an old building. I know it's a lot to take on. I do this for a living and the amount of work this place needs is a lot to think about, even for me. You considered selling?"

I tense.

"Dracula didn't put you up to this, did he?" I ask. Probably a longshot, but who knows how much of the town he's bribed with his bottomless pockets.

"Dracula?"

I wave a hand. "Never mind. But no, I'm not selling this

place. I'm going to take a stab at making this work. I don't know what to do about all the work just yet, but I'm glad you're available."

He shrugs. "We can take it one piece at a time. Start with whatever makes it safer, and we can go from there."

"Umm—is it bad that the master bedroom balcony is rotting off?"

He gives me a pained look. "Yeah, that's probably not safe. Could be termites or dry rot. No cure for old boards like that short of replacement."

I let the wall hold me up, leaning into it. A blow to the face would've been less painful, even if I knew it was coming.

"What if I just don't go out there?"

"I guess if you don't use it, it's okay to wait another year or two. But you'll have to block it off and make sure nobody else walks out there either."

"That's easy enough. I'm the only one here." But it's my favorite place in the house and it kills me. It would suck to never be able to use it again. "Maybe we should start there, though. It's a good place to work while the weather's warm, right?"

He nods.

"Before we go any further, are there any other bloody nightmare faucets I should brace myself for?"

"If you haven't noticed that red color anywhere else, we're good. Back in the winter, I did quick fixes on the kitchen, main floor bathroom, and third floor bathroom. A few more of the guest sinks look like this. We could try letting 'em run for a few minutes and see if the water clears up. If so, it's probably okay. If not, I wouldn't use them."

I take a deep breath. "How much does it cost to replace the pipes?"

"For a place this size? You might be able to get it done for thirty thousand if it's mainly the bathrooms, but I'm not sure. Major piping isn't something I can do. You'll need a real plumber for that. I just cleaned up as much as I could and then tightened it, hoping to get rid of the rust."

I hate to admit it, but maybe it wasn't pure ego and threats when the vampire next door warned me about keeping this place up.

Thirty thousand dollars? Just for pipes?

On top of everything else?

Oh my God.

This place is going to send me home to my parents with my tail forever tucked between my legs.

It also hurts knowing Gram spent her last days like this.

She shouldn't have.

My stomach sinks.

I wish I'd been out here more often, at least enough to know what was going on. If it hadn't been for that mess with my bestie and the boss and that creeper trying to sabotage the entire company, I would've stayed longer on my last trip.

But woulda, coulda, shoulda were curse words to Gram.

If she were standing here, she'd drag me into a bear hug and tell me not to bother looking back.

"So, how close to the top of the list should piping be?"

Ace scratches the back of his neck. "If the water stays clear, you can wait a little while. If it rusts up again like a murder scene, I'd call a plumber ASAP. I can try to clean it out for you again and do any drywall torn out by the plumbing fix, but I can't promise how long it'll last."

His smile is very good at softening the blow.

For the briefest second, I'm able to push Miles Cromwell and his diabolically handsome crankyface out of mind.

"Thank you for taking care of my grandmother and putting up with her quirks," I say. "She could be crazy stubborn."

"It was only right. Miss Lottie took care of the whole town. I still dream about her apple squares. They were missed almost as much as her at the fair last month."

I smile at him. In those silly movies, this is where the leading man graciously offers to help with the repairs, for free, just because he has a sweet spot for the hapless granddaughter.

In real life, big nope.

When Mr. Fix-It leaves, I pour myself a tall glass of wine and start hatching a plan.

There's no way around this financial crunch.

I need income, and that means I need more clients now if I want to avoid more debt, or I need to start renting the place out.

That's risky, though.

I shudder to think how many state regulations I'd violate with this place in the shape it's in for long-term tenants. Plus, it would make it that much harder to keep it as a bed and breakfast.

As much as I love striking out for myself, I miss that steady paycheck from my corporate gig.

But if keeping Bee Harbor for Gram was never easy, why should it be for me?

And why should I flippantly shut down a business offer without at least hearing it out?

Yes, even from a man who's allergic to crosses and garlic.

There's the tiniest chance he could be genuinely interested in my services and not just strong-arming me out of this house.

* * *

I'M FLOPPED down on the couch with a glass of wine, texting Pippa, when a painting over the fireplace catches my attention.

I've noticed it before, but in my grief fog I haven't stopped to admire it until now.

It's the spitting image of the rose garden in its prime in front of the cottage, all vibrant reds and greens and purples before it blurs into wildflowers cheerfully crowding a familiar old stone wall.

"Wow," I whisper.

She must've had it commissioned. But Gram was always so

pragmatic with her money, I wonder why she bothered when the house needs so much work.

Another text from Pippa comes through. *So when are you coming back to civilization? I miss you.*

Jenn: The goal was never, but at this rate, it might be soon-ish.

Pippa: What's wrong?

I finish my wine and set the glass on the coffee table so I can type a reply.

The house needs major work. When everything is said and done, the renovations will probably run into six figures. You know, more than I have.

I wince. These are the times when I wish I had a hot billionaire husband like her.

Pippa: Just sell and come home! You can work with me again.

She sends a grinning emoji.

Jenn: You only love it because your boy toy is there.

Pippa: Still. Your apartment didn't stress you like this.

Jenn: No, but it didn't come with a letter from Gram giving me her most precious thing in the world.

I frown.

This whole conversation reminds me why I need to consider Dracula's offer. I hate giving in, but I'm in no position to return this place to its original glory without a leg up.

I open his contact, where I'd started typing a reply before Ace showed up. Maybe that was a sign from the universe that I shouldn't burn any bridges.

My phone buzzes again.

Pippa: You know, if you're hard up and hell-bent on staying, we'd be happy to front you a small loan. Zero interest. Brock wouldn't even bat an eye.

Jenn: Thanks, but no.

I swallow thickly.

If I were a better person, I might just take her up on that offer, knowing $100K is pocket change for the Winthropes.

But maybe Gram was right and we're more alike than I

thought. We're both too damn proud to take anyone else's money.

Let's find you a rich boy then. It would brighten your mood. Pippa's latest text flashes across the top of my screen.

I immediately reply.

Nah, no time for drama. I really don't want to sell this place, Pippa. It's bad enough I'm dealing with the vampire man next door. He's rude, pushy, and spoiled rotten.

It should be against the law for a jerk like that to be so flipping hot, I add, huffing with annoyance as I swipe away another annoying notification from some app.

I regret that last sentence.

Now, I'll never live it down.

It's a few minutes before she responds, which is fine because I'm staring at the empty text window, wondering if I can find the words to be polite to Cromwell.

Pippa: Vampire man? Are you five?

I laugh.

I expected her to ask why I hate him so much, but I guess she's right.

I should come up with a better nickname for a raging jackass.

Then my phone pings again. I brace for another round of teasing from my bestie.

Nice to know I'm 'flipping hot.' Is that why you've been giving me the silent treatment? You're cute too, and I typically prefer blondes.

Huh? Why would Pippa say—

Oh.

Oh, crap on a flapjack.

I just butt-texted Miles Cromwell. And my fingers were a hundred times clumsier than my butt.

The phone rings then, and his name flashes across my screen.

My heart leaps into my throat and for reasons unknown to me, I swipe to answer.

"That wasn't meant for you," I rush out.

"Hello to you too, Miss Landers," he growls back. "Relax. As much as I'd enjoy seeing you hot and flustered with your lying little tongue tied, I'd rather talk business."

Prick.

I don't know what else to say to that.

"It's not like you deserve an apology. I was just stating the obvious, everyone knows you're hot—and absolutely terrible."

"Am I?"

Oh, nonono.

I'm glad this is a phone call. He can't see my face throbbing red with anger or shame or something I don't want to acknowledge.

"You know exactly what you are, Cromwell. I'm sure you also know you're as graceful as a Neanderthal."

"I pride myself on it," he says smoothly.

"See? Nothing to apologize for then."

"Of course not. It's a compliment when a beautiful woman is so enamored with me that she has to text a friend about me on a Friday night. That's not why I called, though," he adds.

"I know. Goodbye," I say.

"Miss Landers, wait! Your little slip made it seem like you're interested in selling."

"Not to you, Dracula. Never."

"Stop with the flattery. Dracula was polished and devastating. I ate up every bit of Stoker's book when I was ten years old," he explains.

That figures. I roll my eyes. *So besides being so radioactive he glows, he's also well read.*

"Did you hear the part where I said 'never?'" I flare.

"Dracula was also a force of nature when it came to getting what he wanted," he says firmly. "An admirable quality, and awfully relevant here."

"Yeah, no, this conversation is over." My finger hovers over the red icon to disconnect.

"Fine. If you're still not selling, have you considered my other offer?"

I bite my lip.

"I don't date undead guys without reflections." I know that's not what he wants to hear, but it shuts him up for a second and gives me some control over this conversation again.

He laughs like it's the most ridiculous thing in the world. "You know I wasn't asking you on a date. I need you to work with me."

The grit in his voice tells me he's actually serious.

Exactly what I'm afraid of.

"I'm gainfully self-employed. But thanks for the offer," I lie.

"That's why I said *with*, not *for*."

"Do you even know what I do?"

"I'm well aware you're a free agent. I wouldn't be asking to purchase some of your Odd Little Bee magic otherwise," he says matter-of-factly.

"...what the hell do you want with a one-woman show? You own a whole media empire that has its own marketing department, right? I looked you up. You must have entire creative teams. There's no way you put out the amount of content you do without one. Don't play me."

There's an icy pause like he's amused with me calling him out.

"Always so feisty. For some unholy reason, I like it." His voice is a low purr, almost obscene. A chill sweeps up my back. "I have a strong creative backbone, Miss Landers. They're good at what they do, but like any company my size, they adapt to new developments at the pace of a giant sloth. Marketing has changed by leaps and bounds the past couple years, as you're aware. We can't ignore it forever. You specialize in Instagram and TikTok, don't you?"

"I'm pretty well versed in all major platforms, yeah. But I expect my clients to pick one and stick with it. Not that it matters. You aren't a client."

"I've been pushing my people for a bigger TikTok footprint for a while. They're still just reuploading the same content and flailing for influencers, and it isn't working out. The seal sanctuary series was the first thing that didn't bomb there—"

"Because they can't be good at everything," I cut in. "You're overwhelming them. That's why I recommend a platform focus."

"Regrettably, I don't have a single team who handles video shorts well. Past consultants have overpromised and underdelivered. That's why I'm trying to hire *you*, but you're making that so difficult."

"I'm making it impossible, you mean. And why does this feel like some weird tit for tat game? Does taking your money mean I'm on the hook to sell my place to you?"

He's too quiet.

"If I were really that devious, wouldn't your grandmother have warned you?"

"Leave Gram out of this!" I hiss.

But I've been wondering the same thing.

"Think about it. Surely, she would have mentioned living next door to a scheming bloodsucker, right?"

"She was a sweet old lady. She tried to see the best in everyone. Maybe she just didn't realize who you were."

"She knew me better than anyone else in town," he says cryptically. "Frankly, you're nothing like the late Lottie Risa."

Ouch.

Low blow.

I'm not even sure why it hurts.

"You did not just say that to me," I throw back.

"Miss Landers, I didn't call to bicker, and perhaps that was too harsh. Your grandmother brought my driver honey from her bees twice a week. She was practically the only person in town I opened the gates for. You have my apologies."

"No need to pretend you have a heart. You don't."

We're locked in cold silence again until he clears his throat.

"Regardless, will you consider my offer? I pay generously and

I'll make you a proper contractor, so you can work on your terms. If you want benefits, they're yours."

"I should go," I say, shaking my head sharply.

"So you can call your friend and tell her how the big bad vampire tried to give you a job when I suspect a cash infusion would do you a world of good?"

My hand clenches.

I hate this man with the force of a thousand suns.

"My life is none of your business. Neither are my problems."

"No, but there's one thing you should know."

"*What?*"

"I'm not walking away until you agree to at least consider the offer. Give me a goddamned 'maybe,' Miss Landers, and mull it over."

"...I think I'll just hang up instead."

"I'll call back," he throws back.

"And I'll block your number."

"You remember I live next door, right?" he snarls.

"And I can get a restraining order."

Sweet silence. He makes a strangled sound before he says, "You wouldn't dare. Nothing I've done resembles harassment."

"You think so, huh? You don't know me."

"I do know I'm 'flipping hot' and I can buy you some precious time. For fuck's sake, I'm offering to help you *keep* that place against my own best interests."

It's my turn to be choked. I don't know what to say to that.

"Goodbye, Dracula," I manage, pulling the phone away from my face.

"Listen, kitten—"

"That's not my name."

"Will you consider it?" he says, his voice so small as I peel the phone away from my ear.

"Bye."

I end the call and hang my head, totally boneless.

"Fine, you dick. I'll think about it," I mutter to myself.

Next to me, Cream gives me a puzzled look, her big white head creased with worry. I scratch her neck until the look eases.

Then my phone chimes with a new text.

Dracula: Call me every filthy name in the book. Write erotica about me with your friend. I don't care.

Just think about my offer, Miss Landers.

Good God.

He's going to drive me stark-raving looney.

My finger hovers over Pippa's number—who I now have four missed texts from, because she was texting me the whole time I was arguing with Dracula—but if I do that, he's right.

The terrible realization sets in that he's predicted my next move.

The only thing left to do is give him the shock of his life.

IV: NO SLOW BURN (MILES)

*I*t's been a couple of days, and I haven't heard from the auburn beauty next door who only speaks in words that drip venom.

I should storm over there and confront her, dammit, but my home has been invaded by the highest paid "creatives" in Seattle.

Smokey Dave walks up to me—a man who smells like he's thirty percent cannabis, but never fails to impress with his videography—and grins like I've just offered him a ten-pound pan of magic brownies.

"You wanna lead the grand tour, Mr. C? It'd be hella cool if we can get a local to show us around. The younger kids you're after love authenticity, y'know."

I've never heard any professional label people in the 25-40 age bracket 'kids.'

Also, since when do I look like the town's social butterfly?

The whole point of departing Seattle for the summer was to avoid people. CEOs don't babysit camera crews.

"You have a visitor, sir," Benson cuts in before I can lay down the law.

Clenching my jaw, I scan the crowded room and meet his eyes. "We're in a meeting."

"I believe you'll want to see this visitor, sir. You've been waiting for a response for days. If you're too busy, though, I can simply inform her to get on your books."

Her.

My chest swells as I draw in a ragged breath.

"Everyone, I have to step out," I say, not bothering to look behind me for their reaction as I blow past my valet.

She looks so small and out of place in my foyer. Her hands are clasped in front of her like she's afraid the walls of my house are about to chew her up.

Her bright-yellow sundress swallows her instead, and a sharp smile I can't decipher ignites her face when she sees me.

"What's this? You came to torment me in person? I'm honored," I say, extending a hand.

She doesn't take it, just steps toward me.

"I came for a job—don't make me regret this."

I nod coolly. "And upset a sun angel? No."

I'm annoyed that I sound so serious. I don't do reflexive flattery, but it's sincere here.

She's a glowing accent against the stark hypermodern black and white of my home, almost blinding in her dress.

"No need to kiss butt. I'm here, aren't I?" she whispers.

I step closer, inhaling a whiff of her perfume. My nostrils tingle, taking in cutting citrus and something softer and flowery, a smell that matches her radiance.

I glance away casually, trying like hell not to linger.

If my eyes wander her too long, they'll be diving up her sleek legs and down her cleavage in no time, destroying whatever progress we stand to make.

"Your timing is impeccable, Miss Landers," I say, taking her hand gently. "We were just about to get started on the project I need you for. You're welcome to join us in the—"

"Yo, Mr. C, you still busy? Just had a banger idea!" Dave calls behind me, leaning out the door and popping something into his mouth.

Probably another edible disguised as a mint.

Goddamn this talking THC factory. Can't he stay put for five minutes?

"I hope I'm not making a monster mistake," Jenn whispers, mostly to herself.

"What mistake?" Smokey Dave echoes.

"Go talk to your team. I'll be back in a minute." I put a hand on Jennifer's arm.

Something electric sears the air.

Her skin feels so soft, delicate and warm against my fingers.

If there's any mistake, it's right here. I rip my hand back, ignoring her heavy look.

"Come with me," I tell her.

"Who was that guy?"

"The video lead for Pinnacle Pointe's latest tourism push. He's annoying as hell, but surprisingly lethal with a camera. He'll help with the feel-good stories we need. We just need a tour guide first." I lead her into my library, where the others are gathered around in a messy circle.

She must sense the way I'm looking at her because she falls back a step.

"Wait, what? I'm a marketer, not a tour guide."

"And I'm a CEO who only goes into town for supplies. It can't be me."

Her jaw drops. "That's what you're hiring me for? To be a glorified babysitter?"

"That certainly isn't everything, but it's a start," I say carefully.

"I'm not available. Showcasing Pinnacle Pointe falls outside the scope of Odd Little Bee's services."

"It's a package deal," I say, seizing the opportunity. "Consider it a meet and greet with people you'll be working with. You'll be out with the creative team making sure they get started on authentic content. You can steer content production, and veto anything you don't like. Where's the problem, Miss Landers?"

"Cromwell, I am *not* some 'feel-good' reporter. And I don't know the first thing about shooting good video."

"That's why I keep Smokey Dave around—grudgingly. And what do you think content marketing is? You know where those cameras should be pointed."

She starts to turn around, huffing a breath.

"See, I knew this was a mistake."

I shut the door behind her before she can walk out.

"No mistake. An opportunity. Here are the terms of my offer. You give me three months on this project, helping my team satisfy the tourism booster promise I made the mayor. You'll walk away with a hundred thousand dollars and all the time in the world to fix up Bee Harbor. Plus, you'll have a corporate card to cover any incidental expenses while you're out with the team. By the end of this, if you happen to see me as a human being and not some soul-sucking demon aiming to buy off the world, I'd like the first option to buy your property—if and when you decide to sell."

She stalls and stares at me, barely breathing.

Her brilliant green eyes gleam with uncertainty.

"Jeez, you really are a vampire. The property is never going up for sale. Even if you're secretly immortal, you'll be in for a long wait."

"Forget the property then. I still need your expertise," I growl.

What I actually need is to stroke her ego enough to close the real deal. I'm willing to bide my time.

"I don't know. If giving you an exclusive option on the inn is one of your terms..."

I hold her gaze, drawing a breath, and give her an honest answer. "Miss Landers, I think eventually you're going to wonder whether or not a bed and breakfast is a bigger project than you're ready for right now. And even if you don't, you might ask yourself if you really want to spend your best years in Pinnacle Pointe. Should you change your mind and sell, I hope

I'm the buyer. I don't want to see that gorgeous landscape turned into a parking lot or a suburban exclave packed with cookie-cutter houses. An option is all I ask. First dibs."

"I'm not so convinced you'll give up that easy if I don't sell. My grandma isn't even cold yet, and you've already tried to buy me out multiple times."

My jaw sets.

"I didn't mean it to come across callously. I assumed you had a life in Seattle you'd want to get back to and taking the property off your hands would help. Since that's not the case, I'm willing to wait like a good boy for your scraps."

Her eyes narrow as she places a hand on her hip. "You just don't want my grandma's house turned into a development, right?"

I nod.

"Awesome. Then if I promise you it never will be, you can give up, right? Completely remove that condition from your offer, and maybe we'll have a deal."

"Listen, the thought of Bee Harbor becoming another marina or tacky chain hotel makes me sick. And it's not like I've asked you for price protection. I'm merely asking that if you think I'm not a vampire by the end of this experiment and you choose to pursue other plans, you *consider* selling the land at any asking price you decide."

"One hundred and fifty," she clips.

"What?"

"I want a hundred and fifty thousand dollars. Not for the inn, but for this 'experiment,' as you put it. Give me that and I'll agree to the other insane conditions."

My blood heats.

"Are you mad, kitten?"

She crosses her arms in front of her chest, trying to stare me down. "Crazy enough to stand here considering this while you call me that, I guess."

"A hundred thousand dollars is more than fair compensation

for roughly three months of consulting work on a project of this scope. Hell, it's practically charity. I'm running this venture at a financial loss."

"We'll call it a Cromwell premium. Fifty thousand dollars a month seems just barely tolerable for dealing with *you*. As for the property, *if* I decide to sell, I'll think about it. No promises."

The screaming sundress wrapped around her siren curves suddenly seems too fitting.

She's clearly intent on draining every drop of life from my bones.

My eyes narrow. "I know what you're doing. An extra fifty thousand dollars gives you more than enough to bring the inn up to speed. You won't need to sell then."

She smiles and nods.

"Yep. And who was it who said they're okay with helping me work against his own best interests?"

Damn her and those green eyes that could turn Medusa into stone.

This isn't working out the way I thought it would.

Though maybe by the end of summer with colder weather moving in and the stress of trying to score guests, she'll finally see reason.

"I'll go up twenty-five thousand. That's it," I say.

I wouldn't be Miles Cromwell if I didn't negotiate hard.

She rolls her eyes and turns for the door.

"I knew this was a waste of time."

Fuck.

She's got ovaries like cannonballs. I'll give her that.

"Fifty thousand dollars a month, even," I bark at her back. "But you turn around and start today."

Her mouth drops as she faces me again.

"Babysitting weed dude?" She shrugs. "Good to know not all guys in your company are hot bloodsuckers, I guess."

"You sound disappointed," I point out.

Her round face reddens. "You *are* a leech. Becoming my boss doesn't change that."

"As long as I'm a hot one," I remind her, bringing my face dangerously close to hers.

A small gasp slips out of her.

Then she glares at me with spinning green razors for eyes.

I chuckle and move past her, ushering her forward with a sweep of my hand. "Come on. I'll introduce you to the team."

I take her into the library where the whole creative team waits.

"Everyone, meet our new addition, Miss Jennifer Landers. She comes to us with considerable experience in cutting-edge marketing from Winthrope International. Since she has a background in hospitality and tourism as well as digital marketing, she'll be your best resource to ensure this gets done right. Nothing less than the usual Cromwell-Narada excellence. Now, it looks like the tour bus is here, so we should move."

Smokey Dave stops to introduce himself on the way out, shaking her arm like a tree branch.

"My friends call me Jenn," I hear her say.

Sarah is right behind him, and the other team members come strolling in one by one to greet her as they file out.

Jenn starts for the door.

"One more word, Jenn?" I call.

She stops and looks at me. "It's Jennifer."

"But you said—"

"My *friends* call me Jenn. Try listening."

I force back a smile.

"Okay, Miss Landers, since I have a personal interest in keeping the mayor of the town I live in happy, you'll be reporting directly to me on our progress. I hope that isn't a problem. After all, we're both well aware you have my number."

She glares, smooths her face, and shrugs. "It's you. Everything is a game with its own set of rules. I expected nothing less."

It's amazing how much she loathes me after a few brief conversations.

Usually, it takes a month without a single weekend off before people start adding my name to their list of curse words.

"I was hoping our new understanding meant turning a fresh page," I say, exaggerating my frown.

Not that I care what she thinks about me.

I promise you, I don't.

"You know how it goes with first impressions. They're hard to forget. You're not that hard to read. One brief meeting was all it took. You think you can buy people and places and the world is supposed to bend to your will. I just want to live and do right by Gram."

"A noble cause," I say, paying her a rare compliment.

"That's what makes this so personal, you know." She glances away for a second. "Selling you my grandmother's land she bought with her first paycheck and home she built from the ground up with my grandpa would be like selling you my grandmother. But you don't care. You only care if you get what you want."

"For the record, I'd never try buying a human being," I say, watching as she rolls her eyes right out of her head. "Although I respect your dedication, it's going to feel different when you're updating seventy-year-old plumbing and insulating room after room with an asbestos removal specialist. Also, I've always been transparent. I won't wake up to a goddamned subdivision on my doorstep."

"Why not? At least the developers had the decency to wait until she was buried to start circling like vultures."

Developers? Shit.

Has she heard from them?

"Has anyone contacted you?" I ask coldly.

"No. You're the only bonehead who's tried to come after my house."

I stop and stare.

This is the first time she's referred to it as *her* house. This may be harder than I thought.

"But you're not special; anyone else will get the same answer. Don't lose sleep over it," she tells me, batting her eyes.

"Miss Landers, I sleep like a baby. You'd do well to try it sometime. Now, let's get going."

She blinks in horror. "You're coming too?"

"Of course."

"What? Then why do they need a tour guide? You're at least as much of a local as I am. I'd argue more so since I just came back here weeks ago."

"I promise you in two weeks you've seen all the latest changes in this town. Shirley's Chowder Shop added a Fourth of July special and Max's Garage works on electric vehicles now." I give her a cutting look. "You do realize we have to interact since I'm signing your checks?"

"Unfortunately." She sighs. "This has to violate some kind of rule."

I snort. "You charged me an extra fifty thousand dollars for dealing with my temperament. I have to make sure you *are* dealing with me, or you aren't earning your keep."

"God, you must be miserable to work for."

I shrug. "Yet no one ever leaves for greener pastures. Luckily, you work *with* me, remember?"

"Oh, yeah. I'm working for fifteen hundred Benjamin Franklins. You just happen to be an unfortunate part of the arrangement."

Inwardly, I'm smiling my ass off at the claws this kitten has.

I just wonder if they'll wind up scratching my back in all the right places or ripping my throat out.

AN HOUR OR SO LATER, we're standing on the main pier in the marina, staring at a heavenly summer landscape.

NICOLE SNOW

Jenn and a couple others alternate between laughing among themselves and taking test shots of the gorgeous seascape.

No matter how hard I try to ground myself, the town cemetery across the street keeps grabbing my attention.

How many fucking years has it been?

I stopped counting a long time ago.

The tall, polished mausoleum—the only one that's regularly well kept—still looks out of place here, no matter how much time passes.

If I hadn't always had a soft spot for this town, I wouldn't be a Cromwell.

Still, I don't understand why anyone would pick this place to spend eternity. With everyone occupied in planning, I slip away and walk up the street to the florist a few blocks over.

The wreaths here aren't like the ones Lottie used to make by hand.

She'd clip her own flowers and do the arrangements herself, bright halos of appreciation that reminded the dead they were loved when the living couldn't.

Thanks to her, every grave had one a few times every year.

This town lost a guardian angel the day she died.

But I can't come this close to my mother's grave and not leave something, so I find a simple blue wreath and buy it for later before I walk toward the pier.

Even from here, I can see Miss Landers and the team still taking selfies, videos, and playing around. Smokey Dave becomes as serious as a sniper the second he's behind his camera, and I remember why I put up with his antics.

They haven't noticed I'm gone.

Good.

Another reason it's increasingly hard to care about what happens in Seattle. I'm not needed when the machine runs this smoothly, and if I'm not needed, I shouldn't be stuck there.

I text Benson to pick me up when I'm sure they're on a roll. Jenn seems to be doing a good job of handling the creatives, judging by the animated looks and gestures when they all huddle, listening to her advice.

A short drive later, I'm at the grave.

"I'm sorry it's not up to snuff. It isn't bright and pretty like Lottie's."

It hits me that I should have picked up a wreath for Lottie's grave too.

Fuck, I didn't think about it.

There's always next week, though.

"Still, you know me. I couldn't come here without bringing anything. Dad asked about you last month, too," I say, my voice burning. "It was a good day for him. He thought it was the nineties again, that time we stayed in Wyoming and you roped him into some bull riding thing for charity. He never made it a second, but he remembered how hard you laughed later, when he hugged you and he was still full of mud."

Pain is a funny thing. Every word stabs me through the ribs, but somehow, by the end of it, I'm smiling.

Wherever she is, I know she'll appreciate this.

Just like I appreciate the fleeting bittersweet moments when Dad still remembers her.

As I lay the wreath down, a small, shriveled bouquet catches my eye.

It can't be too old, a week or two at best.

Some of the flowers aren't completely dried out and wilted. A card almost as large as the bouquet itself is tucked between the flowers.

My pulse stops.

If this is what I think it is, I'm going to lose my shit.

I rip the small card out and scan it.

Goddammit.

God fucking damn *the nerve of that woman.*

With my throat vibrating, I tear the message into a million pieces and hurl them to the ground as I storm to the car.

Benson stands there, holding the door open when he sees

me. "Everything all right? I didn't know Miles Cromwell was a fan of throwing parties in graveyards."

"The bitch was here," I rasp, every word cutting my throat.

His face sinks.

I don't have to say anything else.

He knows exactly who I mean, and he just nods in bitter sympathy.

Benson knows me well enough to do his job quietly.

Today, though, I can tell he's worried as he climbs in the driver's seat and shuts the door. "Is it possible she's just paying her respects?"

"Fuck no. She wants to make sure I know she's not done with me yet."

"The woman is unhinged," he says glumly.

He's not wrong.

Psycho batshit bitch from Satan's waiting room is too mild a description.

"She does it to get a rise out of you, I'm sure. Don't give her the pleasure, sir," Benson says gently, looking back in the mirror.

I don't dignify that with an answer.

If he's right, I'm giving Simone Niehaus exactly what she wants, and I hate it.

Still, she crossed a line, and she fucking knew it.

She's not even here to know if I took the bait.

She damn sure knows leaving notes at my mom's grave is a bridge too far.

I lean into the back seat as a brief rain blows in, the kind that comes without warning and leaves with a blanket of vibrant green underneath.

My phone pings.

Jenn: Are you coming back? We were having content problems and I had to redirect your group. You weren't joking. Your "creative" strategy needs some work.

Welcoming the distraction, I text back, **You're a pain in the ass. I'm not sure I ever said my team sucked.**

Jenn: You didn't. You manager types are all the same. Mini-royalty. Can't call a spade a spade.

Miles: And you have no filter.

Jenn: Yeah, but you knew that already. Which is why I'm about to tell you the whole team is pissed at you, and I don't blame them.

What?

Do I have a mutiny on my hands?

Why? I hit send, clasping my phone like it's solid ice.

Jenn: You went AWOL. You didn't tell anyone where you went. We just looked up and you were gone.

Miles: Sorry.

Jenn: Tell them that. I felt like the sun came out when I realized you weren't leering over us. She sends a row of laughing emojis with the tears.

Miles: It's raining, Miss Landers. Tell me why my team sucks.

Jenn: It's not the people, but their ideas... Corporate, bland, and boring. Everything comes off like an ambulance chaser commercial. We're trying to sell a town, not a class action lawsuit.

Miles: The oldest guy on that team is thirty-six.

*Jenn: *Shrugs**

Miles: Where are you now? I know the weather turned.

Jenn: We're at my place, filming what's left of the gardens. I think I've half convinced them it's okay to have fun. We were going to make s'mores by the fire pits if the rain lets up, but I'm not sure it will.

I try like hell not to picture this slip of a girl with the glowing light from a campfire splashed across her skin.

I've seen her in a bikini, in skimpy sleepwear, too damn little that's still too much.

You have firewood? I send, hating that I can't pry her image out of my head.

When we had a week of storms last summer, I dropped by with Benson to leave some wood for Lottie.

Three laughing emojis come back. *I was going to send your most annoying employee to find some.*

Miles: Dave? Tell him there's an entire stack under the tarp by the dock.

Jenn: You know the place has firewood?

I don't answer.

A few minutes go by before she responds, *Okay, I mentioned it. So what did you have to do today that was so important, anyway?*

Miles: You were right to show them Bee Harbor. If the rustic look isn't authentic, then I'm Mr. Rogers. Nice to know you're more than just a pretty face.

And a nice piece of—land.

A nice piece of land.

Jenn: If I weren't just your consultant, I'd report that to HR.

I snort at my screen. My lip curls.

Miles: You're not easy to compliment, are you?

Jenn: I hate it when you're nice. It's weird.

Miles: I won't make it a habit. Relax.

Jenn: What should I do with your people now?

I send two question marks.

Jenn: Trust me, they can't be trusted developing this content on their own. Starting over is less work than trying to fix what they came up with. I planned to keep them here, snapping selfies and having fun, but my s'more making idea is gone with the rain. And I don't want half a dozen random strangers in my barely standing house, so what do I do with them?

"Who are you texting so seriously back there?" Benson asks.

I look up, surprised to find I'm almost home.

"No one important, Benson. Business," I say.

Miles: I'm almost home. When I get there, send the party next door.

Jenn: Will do.

Twenty minutes later, her impromptu party for my creative team moves to my large solarium. We're there for hours under the pattering evening rain, and once I've sent the team back to their hotel, I look at Jenn.

"I'll walk you home," I say. It's not a question.

"Um, I don't really need an escort. But sure."

We walk out the back. With the rain gone, everything smells fresh and alive, and I let her admire the grounds around my place.

"We have some of the same plants," she says, pointing to a square box of blooming flowers.

"Your grandmother was kind enough to give my gardener a few pointers. The heirloom seeds, too, I believe," I say.

She looks at me, startled, before settling into a disarming smile.

"I know why you abandoned us at the pier," she says.

"Yeah?"

I side-eye her nervously.

How could she know? Has she been doing her own research? Snooping into my life?

"Is she hot?"

"What?" I glance at her, taken aback.

"I saw you come out of the store with blue flowers." Curiosity flares in her eyes.

You didn't see too well, Miss Landers, or you would have noticed it was a funeral wreath, I think.

"Hot, sure. If you're into vampires," I say numbly.

"Oh, I knew that. It takes one to know one, right?" She grins at me.

"Opposites attract. Sometimes. But if it takes one to know one, what does that make you? You're a little monster yourself, Miss Landers," I say, loving the way her cheeks heat.

But that grin she's wearing just widens as she stops and leans in.

"That's where you're wrong. I've always been more of a stake driver."

V: NO GETTING OUT OF HAND
(JENN)

*T*wo days.

Two days of running this gauntlet I've agreed to take on to save my inheritance.

It turns out, coaching Dracula's team to make good shorts is harder than just taking the footage and making them myself.

I've thought about commandeering the whole project several times. I could have this town blowing up on every platform in under a week, but the people are friendly and eager, and they're all so invested in this project.

So later today, we're staging a little event we're calling 'Pints at the Pinnacle' for a photo shoot.

Pinnacle Pointe is still the kind of place where a few beers brings out the best in everyone. And there's nothing cozier than the only rustic tavern in town, Murphy's, with an Irish tricolor and the faded black-and-white photos plastered on the wall. They show off everybody's great-grandparents building this little town one fishing haul and giggling toddler at a time.

There's so much history here.

Unlike Seattle with its busy streets and glass high-rises and ever shifting cityscape, this history is loud and clear. It's in your face, real enough to reach out and touch in the bright smiles of every neighbor.

But first, the mail.

The mailbox is at the end of the street and the postman pulls away just as I'm driving by. I last checked the mail a few days ago, so I pull over and see what he's left me.

I fill my purse with junk mail that needs to be recycled and— a handwritten letter?

Hmm.

I don't recognize the return address, but it's probably another late bereavement card. Gram had obscure friends everywhere.

I slide my finger under the seal and pop it open to see who's sending their sympathies now.

But it's not another card.

It's a letter with an offer on my property.

Less than Dracula's eye popping offering, but it looks like he was right about developers being hot on my heels.

There's no real estate brokerage listed, just a number to call back.

Odd.

Don't realtors usually plaster their names and pictures all over everything?

Of course, I'm not ready to sell out to anyone, but if I have to, I should keep my options open. Never mind the ridiculous agreement I made with my boss...

So I tuck the letter in the front pocket of my purse for safe-keeping, away from the junk mail.

Staging Pints at the Pinnacle takes most of the day once I arrive.

By the time we've got it done, the tavern opens for the evening crowd.

"Jenn, how's this?" Sarah asks, a cheerful but shy blonde with a good eye for detail.

I lean over her laptop to see what she's showing me. It's a picture of the bar with the caption *'Drink to tomorrow!'*

"There isn't anything wrong with it, per se, but it looks more like the cover of Good Housekeeping than an Insta image. And photo slideshows don't perform as well on TikTok."

Her face falls. "I can do it better. No problem."

Ouch.

I hate that she takes it personally.

"It's not that I don't like it. It just needs a few tweaks before—"

"What makes a solid Instagram image?" she cuts in.

I have to think for a minute. "Well, you're thinking like a magazine, right? The cover has story teasers, page numbers, and photo credits all over it."

She nods.

"With these platforms, the image *is* the story. You want to bring your viewer right into the scene and let them imagine what it'd be like to be here. But Dracula—" Whoops. I didn't mean to call him that to her face. "Cromwell, I mean—"

"You call him Dracula?" Her face scrunches up with a smile. "Right on."

"If the glove fits... Anyway, I think Cromwell wants us to focus on TikTok and Reels first. How's the video coming?"

"I'll check with Dave before I dive back in and let you know." She holds up her phone sheepishly. "I got a few good shots of some drinks."

I grab it for a closer look and nod.

Her casual photo set shows off glistening amber and moody dark beers mingling with classy cocktails. It's not half-bad.

"Pretty decent. We can definitely use these on the website and foodie posts for the 'gram." I smile and pass her phone back, loving how her face glows red. "Realistically, we probably won't get great pics until more customers start coming in and ordering to make the tavern look busy. I want to go for a travel slash food mashup."

"Mashup?"

"They're all over TikTok. Can I show you?"

She nods and slides her laptop closer.

I pull up my account and show her my favorite travel shorts. They're under thirty seconds, brief scenes with simple transitions showing heavenly scenery and drool-worthy food set to punchy background music.

"See? The destinations are breathtaking, but the grub steals the show. Together, they make you want to hop on a plane and bring your appetite. That's the vibe we need."

"Good thinking!" Sarah looks up with bright eyes like it all clicks in her head.

I'm suddenly excited to turn her loose with a camera later.

Then I feel eyes on my back.

I'm almost certain I know who's ruining the mood even before I turn.

Holding in a sigh, I glance over my shoulder.

Sure enough, Dracula sits at a table tucked in the back corner, scowly as ever with a gaze razoring through me.

He takes a slow pull off a dark beer and sets it down, his eyes unwavering.

God.

Did he have to practice the whole intimidation look or was he born with it?

Before I can turn my head and pretend to ignore him, he's up and stalking toward me.

He stops beside me without saying a word.

It takes every ounce of willpower to flash him a cheery smile.

"Right on time to micromanage me?"

"I just came for a beer, Miss Landers. Sampling the food for myself seems like the best way to make sure this marketing lives up to its hype. Managing *you* is Dave's job."

"Really?" My eyes flick to the other side of the bar where Smokey Dave leans against the counter, pounding back a craft beer between loud laughs with a waitress. I smile up at

Cromwell. "You might want to rethink that. His videos are awesome, but I'm not sure he's manager material."

Dracula follows my gaze, his brow pulling down in grudging agreement.

"Also, if the goods don't live up to their hype, that's not on me. I don't make the beer or the corned beef-cheddar ale tots."

"No argument here. You can retract your claws," he growls.

He's still on that kitten thing?

Sigh.

And when did it get so hard to peel my gaze off him? There's just something about him looking down at me like Zeus with lightning in his eyes.

For the faintest second, I have a terrible image of being on my knees.

"What argument? That's against the rules at Murphy's," a happy male voice says behind me.

My eyes finally snap past the vampire.

Oh, no.

Ace steps forward and not so subtly tries to crowd out Cromwell. I turn toward him with my face on fire.

"Oh, hi! I was just telling him I don't make the beer. I just have to make it look pretty for the tourists..."

Oh God. Oh God.

Oh God.

Of all the things I thought I was ready for today, facing down two handsome, built men who make me *feel* things was not in the plans.

"I'm obviously missing something, but if you want to make beer, I can teach you. They've got two of the craft beers I brew with my brother on the regular menu here," Ace says proudly, the corner of his mouth quirking up in an irresistible smile.

He's so warm.

Nothing like the tall, domineering prince of pure ice and arctic frowns next to him, staring with an impudent look that's asking Ace why he's daring to run his mouth.

"You brew beer?" I ask, ignoring the bossman.

Ace nods. "In a town this size, everyone and their cat brews. Anyway, just wanted to let you know your roofing fix should be on for tomorrow like we talked about."

"Oh, thanks! I'm down with anything that stops a leak before it starts."

Cromwell clears his throat loudly, shoving Ace over a step with his shoulder.

"Can't you see you're interrupting a media shoot? She's on the clock," he growls.

Why the fuck are you encouraging him? his eyes ask.

I laugh. "Oh, leave him alone. We're going for candid shots with the locals, remember? Ace lives here."

"Nothing about social media is candid, Miss Landers. Eighty percent of it is staged. We want carefully planned shots that *look* natural. You know that much." There's an edge in his tone that makes me bristle.

Who the hell does he think he is?

"I must know plenty, Mr. Cromwell, or else your current social media strategy wouldn't need so much work." I stare back, my eyes all warning. "Let the people mingle and just be natural. Any unnecessary tension will only wreck the shots."

His jaw is clenched so tight as his eyes sweep to Ace.

Umm—what?

This feels like more than just being peeved over a business disruption.

Is Miles Cromwell jealous or is it just a very overactive imagination?

But the longer I see that volcanic look in his eyes, I wonder.

...this could be fun.

I stand and step closer to Ace, placing a hand on his bicep. "You've been so helpful, Ace. I don't know how I would have managed the inn without you."

Ace grins at me like there isn't a furious bystander staring him down. "I'm happy as hell to help out. It's what Lottie would've wanted."

"It was a beast to inherit, no question. I'd be a lot worse off if Gram didn't have great help."

He's drinking me in now, a new glint in his eye that says he's excited about more than the repairs. I definitely don't mind.

But Dracula might.

His glare is so molten it burns my skin, even as I pretend not to notice.

"It pays to have a strong, smart man around who knows what he's doing when he swings a hammer. And my, what big hands!" I can't resist grabbing one of his rough paws and holding it up. "I can see why she kept you around for so many years."

"Aw, now you're making me blush," Ace says with a rough laugh. "Miss Lottie only kept me around because I started working for her when I was sixteen and I barely raised my prices since."

I giggle like he's just said the funniest thing in the world.

"Oh, Ace!" I slap his chest playfully. "Are you always Mr. Modesty?"

My eyes flick back to Cromwell and—

Eep.

I may have overdone it.

He gives me a hardened look like I'm insane now, and he wants to have me committed.

It only lasts for two seconds before the flaring silver-blue rage in his eyes abruptly flicks back with something like—is that disgust?

But Ace chuckles and nods toward the back of the room. "Hey, Jennifer, my buddies are here, but I'll catch you later, all right?"

I nod. "Definitely. And if you don't, you know where I live. Feel free to drop by anytime."

I watch him as he walks away, keenly aware Cromwell's eyes are still tearing at me like hunting hawks.

I've been enjoying Dracula's reaction so much I didn't notice how full the room is now.

There's a steady murmur of evening laughter and friends clinking glasses, vibrant greetings and people rowdily narrating their summer adventures.

"You were laying it on thick enough to suffocate the man," Cromwell snaps when he finally speaks.

"...I don't know what you mean," I lie.

"His hands? Are you kidding me, kitten? The man is a bear. He looks like he should be pawing at the ground for grubs or raiding beehives for honeycomb," he rasps, shaking his head. "That's fine for swinging a hammer, but hands like that have no control. No poise. No grace."

Then he sweeps his own hand up and stares like he's comparing himself.

Oh my God.

"I've watched him put them to work. He's pretty deft. You'd be surprised."

Crankyface shoots me another glare and opens his mouth, but before he can clap back, Sarah sets a drink down in front of me.

"I brought you a cocktail since you were busy. This is their Northwest Mai Tai. On the house. I think I've got some good clips to show you from the kitchen, too."

"Later," Dracula clips.

"Um, sure. No problem." She nods and walks away.

I take a big gulp of the cocktail. There's a slight mintiness or pine taste that's surprisingly delightful.

Cromwell takes an angry slurp off his beer before he says, "You know, if I spent hours alone with a woman using my hands, I damn sure wouldn't settle for her saying all she did was *watch*."

Holy hell.

He can't be serious.

But the irritation lining his face does it.

73

I laugh so hard I spew cocktail, barely catching it with a napkin.

Cromwell manages to keep a straight face for a few seconds before he smirks. "The handyman, huh? Boring choice for a small-town crush if you ask me."

"Nobody did," I fling back. "Ace isn't a bad guy. He's gorgeous and hardworking. Just ask any woman here."

I gesture over to his group of friends. They're all tall, young, good-looking guys, and there are twice as many women in their circle, descending like hungry piranhas.

Dracula nods.

"He's a nice kid. I'm sure he'll settle down with some lady born and raised here and make her very happy." His voice is gruff. Demanding.

I have to bite my bottom lip to keep from giggling in horror or barraging him with insults.

"Must be weird, though, crushing on someone who basically works for you," he says, draining the last of his glass.

"He doesn't work for me, boss. He works *with* me. Like you said, big difference. Besides, I can think of worse things."

"Yeah?" He waits.

"Like crushing on your boss. Especially if your boss is some rich jerkoff who was born missing the smile muscles in his face. I've seen those situations before and they're always just...miserable. Pathetic, really."

His eyebrows dart up. "You talk like it's from experience, Miss Landers. Should I tell you now I'm not interested?"

My heart stops.

This man is determined to watch me die by embarrassment.

"No! Don't be ridiculous," I rush out, feeling my face ignite. "I'm talking about my friend. It's a miracle her office fling had a happy ending. That kind of craziness rarely does."

"Piper Winthrope?" he asks, using her real name instead of the nickname everyone calls her.

My eyebrows go up.

"You know Pippa? We've been besties since forever."

He shrugs. "I know you used to work for Winthrope. That scandal with her and Brock was front-page news for a while during the whole big hotel sabotage debacle. Then the wedding —" His face screws up with disgust. "I thought they went overboard to bury the scandal. Exactly why I'll always keep a low profile with the press."

"It wasn't a scandal—"

"The gossip blogs thought so. It was in my Twitter feed every time I opened the damn app."

"Yeah, and you saw what happened to Winthrope shares after the dust settled, right? I'm pretty sure Brock and Pippa have a few billion more than you."

His smirk disappears into granite disapproval. "So defensive. I'm sorry I brought it up, kitten."

Kitten again!

"Call me that one more time, and I *will* claw your face." I hold up my fingers and bend them so he can see my pastel-green nails. One of the few times I regret wearing them so short. "So what if I'm defensive? You're being rude and she's my oldest friend."

"My bad, kitten," he says with a shrug.

If I stare hard enough, can I light him on fire? Can loathing a man hard enough give you the kind of powers you only find in Stephen King books?

Yeah, but it'll be my mug in the news next for murdering this man.

Not fair.

"Brock Winthrope never had to bribe local authorities to protect his brand," I snap off.

"Bribe? That's a nasty accusation, Miss Landers."

I motion around the room I spent hours decorating with the creative team. "That's what this is all about, right? Bribing the mayor and town council. Letting them know Lord Cromwell pulls the strings."

"Hardly." He snorts. "I've never made it a secret that I'm spreading goodwill with the powers that be. I'm also doing this for Pinnacle Pointe because I respect this town—the same way I respected your dearly departed grandmother. Is that really such a sin?"

I hate that it isn't.

Gram loved this place with her whole heart. She'd be behind anything that helps put Pinnacle Pointe on the map.

She gave this little town a piece of her heart until the end.

She never dreamed of leaving. I even told her I'd find a bigger dog friendly apartment outside Seattle and she could stay with me, but she wouldn't abandon Bee Harbor for anything.

"Benson was damn near addicted to her honey," Cromwell says with a distant look.

"Benson?"

"My valet," he says with a snort.

I giggle at that.

"What?"

"You're like the guy in those regency books my grandma used to read. 'My valet.'"

"His duties are perfectly modern." His jaw locks. "I'm only telling you this to prove it's not all about money or power. I don't need bribes any more than Brock Winthrope does."

Wow. He *is* jealous.

The room swells with music, jaunty rock tunes spilling out of the speakers from the digital jukebox and its speakers wired around the bar.

Cromwell stares at his empty glass like he's contemplating another round. "You want another drink? It's on me."

"Thanks, but no. I should help Sarah with the food clips," I say, slipping away.

Actually, I'm way past the limit of what I can spend all night processing, and I don't need him adding more to my brain.

When I find Sarah, she's panicked. "Ugh, this lighting looks rough. What do you think?"

She holds her phone up and swipes through a few videos.

"These are good for TikTok. A quick filter change or a little third-party editing should do the trick. Here, let me try."

I pull up an editing app and find the right look and effects to make them pop. Ten minutes later, we have a dozen clips showing off savory appetizers alongside fish and chips plates that will make mouths water.

Someone taps my shoulder, and I look up to find Ace again.

"Dance with me." He asks like it's not even a question.

Whoops.

Maybe I did lay it on too thick earlier.

He must sense my hesitation, though.

"It's just a dance," he says gently. "But if you're not up for that—"

"Sure! Nothing beats having a little fun at work, right?" It's also not like the dating pool out here runs deep anyway. I might as well have fun with a guy who's easy on the eyes and dangerous in flannel.

He leads me onto the dance floor just as the song changes over. The next one is slower and rhythmic with barely any tempo.

But he places his hands on my hips and pulls me to him after a few beats.

O-kay.

I didn't really plan on dancing quite this close, but fine. Whatever.

He's far from repulsive and it's nice to know it when a man is into you, even if you're not after anything serious.

I don't know what to do with my hands, so I lock them behind his neck.

He's not the greatest dancer or else he's had too much beer, so we mostly just sway to the music in this cute awkward side-step that makes me laugh every few minutes.

I'm still mindful of the camerawork going on around us.

Honestly, I hope *this* won't wind up anywhere online.

Of course, Miles Cromwell catches my gaze from the side of the room when I look over. He's staring at us with a fresh beer and a fist coiled like a hammer at his side.

My stomach catches and I almost gasp.

Ace's grip tightens, his eyes asking if I'm okay.

I nod.

I'm not sure why it bothers me.

Until he appears behind Ace and taps him on the shoulder. Ace looks at him without answering, his eyes glassy with irritation.

"My turn," Cromwell grinds out, his voice pure smolder.

Oh, boy.

A beat of silence passes as the music thrums on and our swaying slows.

"Uh, okay—if it's all right with the lady." Ace gives me a sharp look.

"Who do you think I was talking to?" Cromwell says coldly.

My heart jumps as I look between them.

They're about three seconds away from throwing hands and sending someone home with a broken nose. I can't let a stupid man-trum bar fight ruin our work tonight.

"Ace, it's fine. He's just my boss. I'll catch you later!" It flies out of my mouth too fast.

Ace raises an eyebrow and slowly nods.

I drop my arms from his neck and take a step back.

Cromwell catches one of my hands before Ace even has time to move and jerks me to his chest. Before I can catch my breath, I'm watching Ace shrug and retreat to the corner with his people.

"Was that necessary?" My brows knit together.

"You agreed," he says like that's the end of it.

Holy crap.

And here I was annoyed that the Dracula nickname might be too kind when most vampires are mild mannered and charming when they aren't draining arteries.

Miles Cromwell is just the world's hottest horse's ass.

Thankfully, the song stops. I have good reason to take a step back.

But he doesn't release my hand. "Wait for the next track. This is my dance."

"You sound so sure, Mr. Cromwell," I say flatly.

His wrist snaps, pulling me closer to his chest again.

When I finish blinking in shock, I'm wedged against his slab of a chest with eyes like midnight raking me.

"I am sure," he whispers.

I shudder as he laces his long, firm fingers through one hand and drops the other hand to my hip. "Fair warning, Miss Landers, I actually dance. I wouldn't be caught dead with his drunken shuffle."

I hate him.

I hate him so much.

Still, my whole body tingles from his touch, begging to lean into him, to inhale more of his scent that's like a dark summer pine forest and some animal seduction.

But I don't give in.

I don't dare.

Jesus, I *work* for this maniac.

"You'd better not throw me around. The only dance I really know is cheer dance."

He snorts. "Why am I not surprised?"

His steps are wide and graceful and hard to keep up with without focusing. But after a few seconds, I stop fighting and match his movements. It's easy when I let him lead.

"What's that supposed to mean?"

"You still have the figure. If I had to write your biography, I would have guessed," he says, his eyes flitting over me, dipping over my neckline.

I definitely don't. I'm twenty to thirty pounds heavier than I ever was in high school, but the unexpected flattery makes this more tolerable.

"Yeah? And what does a cheerleader look like?"

"You." He smiles then.

A real human smile that makes me think he'll light up and sparkle like the good vampires you read about.

He doesn't, of course, but he makes me smile back like I'm a little broken.

"You're going in circles," I say.

"Really more of a square."

The dancing, he means.

I laugh.

He takes another one of those wide, too graceful steps that I've learned to keep up with. Only, this time I misstep and land on his toes.

I only notice because I almost fall as my foot slides off his shoe. "Oops. Sorry."

"No need to apologize. Just get ready to spin," he says, listening intently to the music's crescendo.

"What? I don't know if I can—"

"Trust me." He laces my fingers tighter to his.

Then with shocking dexterity, he uses the hand on my hip to guide me away from him.

I'm like a toy in his hands as he wheels me out, snapping me back toward him a second later.

It's amazingly fluid—flawless, even, if only I didn't mash his toes *again.*

"Was that so hard, Miss Landers? I think you'll find dancing with a man easier than a drunken boy."

"But I landed on your feet again," I groan.

And I step on his toes again as I'm saying it.

"Easy fix." He lifts me and places my feet over his, holding me so close I feel every breath, every pulse, every sweet degree of body heat.

I start to relax into him too easily.

"This can't be comfortable for long," I whisper.

I wish I believed it.

"You'd be surprised. Are you and the handyman really a thing yet or what?"

Oh, crap. So much for relaxing.

Are we?

"No. I don't think so."

"You had to think about it," he points out.

I wrinkle my nose. "Why do you care? It's like you're worried I'll sell *him* the inn instead."

He doesn't answer and the music thrums on.

"Well?"

He's quiet for a minute, those eyes wide with mystery before he finally says, "If you and the handyman hook up, you may have a real reason for staying here."

"And not sell you my property," I finish for him.

It clicks in my brain.

I should have known.

This lame dance was calculated from the very beginning. I wouldn't be surprised if he even feigned the jealousy act with Ace.

It's all about the land.

His stupid need to expand his little kingdom and wall himself off from the world, and honestly, maybe that wouldn't be so bad for everybody else.

It might save other clueless girls from thinking this devil of a man would ever be genuinely attracted to them.

"I get it now," I mutter coldly.

Cromwell doesn't answer.

"Okay, I think I'm out," I say, pushing back until he lets go. "I hurt my ankle. I should go sit."

"Your ankle? That's not possible. You're not moving like you're hurt."

The worst part is, his face gentles, and he looks at me with real concern.

"It just hit me now. I think it happened earlier on my way in, actually. I just didn't notice."

He walks closer, eclipsing me again.

"I'll help you find a seat."

I shake my head firmly. "No, thanks. I'm good."

With a messy spin, I flee across the room, not bothering to fake a hobble.

I sit down next to Sarah and some local man with a fishing cap. She's laughing at some dumb joke he tells her.

Cromwell stands in the middle of the dance floor, almost dumbstruck, staring like I'm the first woman who's ever had the gall to leave him stranded alone on a dance floor.

I find that so very hard to believe.

A minute later, he stalks past me without saying anything and retreats to his corner table. I chat with Sarah about the town and her past projects before I get up and go around the busy bar, taking pictures of antique fishing gear and photos from Ireland.

A server brings a divine-looking appetizer piled with mozzarella sticks and wings to a couple sitting at a table across from Cromwell. It's too perfect to ignore.

"Hi, do you mind if I get a quick shot of your food before you dig in? It's for my tourism video," I say.

"Go for it!" the woman says with a grin.

I'm well aware I have eyes on me the whole time.

Don't look at him.

Don't do it.

Focus.

I take a few shots and several five-second video clips and then start back toward my table at the front of the room.

But before I get there, Cromwell steps in front of me.

"Your ankle looks mended," he says sharply.

I'm too gobsmacked to answer.

Not before he storms past me like a tornado and exits the tavern.

What the hell was that?

I'm left wondering for the next half hour as I pretend to make small talk with Sarah and a couple others from the crew. Smokey Dave joins us halfway through, offering a handful of edibles so potent they make my nostrils flare.

No thanks.

I barely notice when Ace walks up to me. "Thought I'd see if you got a second wind. Less people on the dance floor now. It's all ours, if you want."

"Oh, um—that's sweet of you, but I was just going home. Rain check?"

He waves at me. "For sure. Need a walk home?"

"I've got it, Ace."

I start to rummage around in my purse to pay my tab, but Ace grabs the small receipt in front of me. "I've got it. Go on and get out of here."

Holy hell.

My heart could not be more confused tonight.

Despite the instinct to turn him down, I already know how pointless that is in Pinnacle Pointe. Kindhearted favors are almost a second language here and rejecting them is like a slap to the face.

"I owe you next time. You're such a good guy. Thanks!" I say, almost floating as I drag myself away from the bar.

Outside, I suck in the night air, loving how the stars twinkle overhead. There's so many more than I'd ever see in Seattle, and familiar constellations are colorful and sharper. All the classic legends in the sky aren't just ideas here, but living stories.

I'm fifteen seconds into enjoying the quiet night when I see him.

Cromwell. His arms are on the tall patio railing like he's been out for a while, waiting.

Waiting for me?

I start to move, praying he won't notice me, but his voice stabs my back like a dagger.

"Miss Landers, wait. Tell me what you're so pissed about."

My feet are lead as I turn.

"Nothing."

"Then why lie to me?"

"Uh—about what? Are you—"

"Your ankle." His eyes snap down my leg.

Oh.

Oh, jeez.

He's like a flipping dog with a bone. Too observant, too resilient, never letting go.

"You really want to know? Fine." I roll my eyes. "It was more polite than saying I'm allergic to egofreaks. A big bad CEO really should know how to handle rejection better, but that's not my problem."

His jaw sets like he's chewing glass.

"If you want to let me go for talking back, I get it," I say. "I can see nobody ever told you that before."

"What game do you think I was playing?" Every word is a bullet from his mouth.

My God.

Is he really that oblivious or is he just playing dumb?

But his voice is so sincere a more gullible person would think he really didn't know.

"The inn, dude. What else? What do you even really want with it?"

"I told you. Peace and quiet. The best chance to preserve its beauty. I won't let it turn into another overactive eyesore," he says tightly.

"And I told you that you don't have to worry about that. I'm not selling."

"I haven't tried to buy it from you since, have I?"

"No. You just wrote your option into my consulting contract. And I guess you're so worried about my crush on the handyman you had to go and—" I pause, my voice rusting shut with sadness. "—and make me think you actually wanted to dance with me instead of pump me for information."

His eyes widen, the stars adding their silver to his bewildered look.

"What the hell? I would never—"

I throw a hand up and turn again.

"You know what, save it. I'm exhausted. It's been a long day, and whatever did or didn't happen shouldn't affect our work. Don't mention the property again, and I'll shut my yap and give you a stellar heap of content, okay?"

I never stick around long enough to hear his answer before I bolt into the night.

The back of my hand hides the most ridiculous tears.

VI: NO BAD MEMORIES (MILES)

he next day, I'm with my father, my hand wrapped gently around his as he holds the brush.

"There, Dad. Keep going. Not so hard to bring the color out, is it?" I do a terrible Bob Ross, but I try, keeping my voice as warm and encouraging as I can.

"Show me," he answers feebly.

If I take my hand off his, he'll be trembling too hard to form anything resembling a straight line.

It's fucking hard to be here, but harder *not to be*.

Ignoring my urge to slash angry strokes across the canvas, I grip the end of his brush and lead him, gently but firmly.

A minute later, I think I see a ghost of a smile pulling at his thin lips.

He still enjoys this by muscle memory, I think, even if he doesn't remember how to paint without help.

Even if he can't remember his own son, and I have to explain who the hell I am every time.

The image comes out entirely formless, but it doesn't matter.

"A tree?" he whispers, looking up at me with pale-blue eyes.

"If you'd like a forest scene," I say, offering a real smile.

"India," he says suddenly. "I was there once."

My parents actually visited the entire subcontinent dozens of times, but I don't correct him.

I'm searching for my own muse, buried somewhere in the buffalo-brained fog of a night at Murphy's where I made a beautiful, obstinate young woman run off in tears.

An entirely reckless, preventable episode.

The only reason I care, I tell myself.

Except a man can only lie to himself so much before it gnaws at his bones.

Fuck, this is miserable.

On the surface, there's nothing special about that redheaded spitfire, and I'd better remember it. Auburn sirens with looks and brains damn near grow on trees.

But not all women with hair borrowed from the sun and emeralds for eyes are so good at turning me into an absolute gibbering imbecile.

And that's what I am now as I try to form a scene with my father, slowly bringing out a lush jungle landscape in six shades of green.

Dad smiles again, tapping his brush lightly over a fern. "I saw this once with her."

Hello, agony.

It's a good day. Hell, an excellent one. He hasn't mentioned Mom in months. I was starting to worry she was gone from his mind for good, just another distant shadow of the past he can't quite remember.

A few more strokes while he hums to himself, some old fifties tune I can't place. Blue Velvet, maybe?

Dad's halting, strange melody jumps around, possibly blurring lines between entire songs.

I hate that it makes me think of a woman who glows green and red, not blue.

What would have happened if I'd let her know that dance wasn't just about the goddamned property?

How would she have reacted if she knew I had another

reason for running off that oaf with the grizzly paws?

How could we keep working together if she thought I enjoyed every second of her skin fused to mine too fucking much?

And how the hell could I live with myself after demolishing Lottie's granddaughter?

I wish I could just blame it on the handyman clown and the way he blundered after her.

What kind of grown-ass man walks around named after a playing card, anyway? It sounds like some junior high football nickname he never outgrew.

And she was over there, lapping it up, eating out of his fat fucking hand.

I know, I know. I shouldn't care.

Shouldn't give a damn that around me, she's a tiger, tooth and claw and blood on her breath.

With Ace, she's like a little kitten, all smiles and play.

And here I am.

My brushstrokes get angrier before I catch myself, smearing my paint into a whirling storm. I'm not sure if Dad notices when I mix up a brilliant orange-yellow hue. He just watches me with his mouth slightly open.

"Dad? You game for more or do you want to watch TV?"

He shakes his head slowly. He looks like a bird that's seen too much shit, his feathers rustled and missing, the white tufts of hair he has left standing from the sides of his head.

"Is she here today? My Colleen?" His gaze locks onto me with a mindfulness I haven't seen in ages.

Fucking hell.

I'm so ready to hurl this canvas across the room, damages be damned.

Of course, I can't.

"She's still on vacation, Dad," I offer, the only answer that doesn't rip my heart out and leave it a grizzled mess on the floor. "I'm sure you're on her mind. You always were."

I throw myself back in my seat next to him, pondering the scene before I attack it again with new colors and a subconscious plan.

I've been stewing about this girl for too long.

Our next few minutes of quiet, peaceful brushwork helps, shaping an orange mass that's too low to be the sun through the trees. I have something else in mind.

"A tiger?" Dad asks, pausing to suck some water from the bottle I hold up.

"Sure enough."

Without fully realizing it, I've painted a regal tiger prowling through dark reeds.

Well, technically it's just a huge orange mess with a white muzzle and dark specks for eyes, but the outline is there.

Jennifer Landers shouldn't still be on my mind, dammit.

There are far more important things than what some junior marketer thinks of me.

This isn't me. I've spent thirty-five years on this warped planet and I'm not in the business of losing my head.

When my hands return to work, they aren't steady, messing up the stripes I try to detail.

I hide my frustration, chuckling at my errors.

Dad laughs along with me, at least. He's still got his humor, even if he has so little else.

Just incredible.

She's even ruining the very thing she inspired.

I turn the brush over, grumbling to myself as I try to use the end to cut through the excess paint. All I succeed in doing is smearing black paint on my hand, severing the neater lines.

Now I have two connected stripes, and they're both off.

A quick swipe and the animal has the beginnings of a hunter's scowl, though.

At least its mood matches my own.

Dad sighs. I look over to see his head slumping and his eyes fluttering.

"Mind if I finish? I can bring it back next week to show you," I whisper.

He's already out.

With a smile too heavy for my face, I pack the canvas up and step into the hall, waving down a nurse to get him into bed for his nap.

Once he's settled beneath the baby-blue covers, snoring next to an old wedding photo on his nightstand, I lean over and kiss his head.

"Rest up, Dad. I'll be back as soon as I can."

* * *

LATER, I'm still dabbing at that tiger scene in my office, less annoyed than I was earlier now that the details are flowing.

The sudden tapping at my door almost makes me jump.

Almost.

"Come!" I yell out, checking the time.

I'm expecting Benson, but Miss Congeniality waltzes in ahead of him, wearing a deep-blue short jumper that looks like a cross between shorts and a dress.

So much for ignoring the world's angriest hard-on.

She catches my eye, and I stare back grimly.

"All dressed up today." I can't help calling it out.

Does she have a date with the fucking playing card later?

She raises an eyebrow. "Is that a good thing?"

"An observation. Nothing more." I hold her gaze.

"An odd one. Does that mean I've been dressed down every other time you've seen me?"

Yeah, it's time to shut up now. I put the paintbrush on the pallet and stand, straightening my shirt.

"Right. I forgot you have no filter—"

"Excuse me?"

She shrugs. "See? I can make observations too."

"It seems like you two can manage." Benson clears his throat loudly. "I'll just let myself out."

He exits the room.

I'm glued to those cool jade eyes again. "You never answered my question."

"There's a reason for that. The last time I gave you an honest answer, I thought you wouldn't speak to me for a week."

"Yet you summoned me here." She steps closer. "You paint?"

"I dabble," I bite off.

She studies the canvas for a moment. "Not bad. Who knew you expressed yourself in images? Makes sense, considering your verbal skills."

I get that about my paintings a lot, and usually with a lot more subtlety than this terrible woman offers.

But somehow, it's different coming from her.

"My verbal skills are fine, and I suspect my art isn't what you came to discuss."

She looks at me and shrugs.

"I'll cut to the chase then. Pinnacle Pointe was founded on fishing, and the industry is thriving to this day. Focusing on the beauty of the sea should be a good way to bring in tourists. Boaters and fishermen are big spenders, and if there's one thing the town is after, it's more revenue."

She cocks her head. "I hope you don't think I'm going out on some rickety boat to shoot videos. It won't happen."

"No. You'll borrow my yacht and let Smokey Dave do the only thing he does best."

Her face relaxes.

"So charitable. I don't know how my grandma stood you as a neighbor all these years."

My jaw tightens.

I catch myself before I tell her that her grandmother and I were actually family friends.

The only person who treated me as a person, and not just the rich, reclusive shut-in who only shows up in town a few times a year for a drink or art supplies.

No point in correcting the record, though.

It wouldn't make a difference.

Jennifer Landers can't see me as anything except a jackass billionaire, and that's all I'll ever be to her.

"You should go home and dress for an evening on the ship," I say.

She stares. "You're telling me how to dress now?"

Goddamn, she's going to drive me to drink.

Without a word, I come around my desk and grab her hands.

"I'm advising you to dress for cooler weather so you don't freeze your fingers off—let alone anything more delicate." Her breath catches and my cock jerks. "You're a big girl, though. Prance around the yacht in that little short set if you want to turn blue."

I drop her hands.

She stares at me, her mouth hanging open.

"All this touching, after the bar—it feels unprofessional." She swallows harshly.

"You're right, but when have we ever been professional?"

Her chin juts out and she tilts her head back like she wants to argue.

"I don't have many other employees who answer the door wearing nothing but a t-shirt—"

"God, you *had* to go there. I was wearing a robe and for reasons I'll never understand, the dogs seem to like you. I didn't know you'd be my boss."

I step closer, the image of her sleek legs and ample tits engraved in my head. Even if she's far more covered today in that jumper, my brain goes back to the day we met, her standing there in that robe and damned near nothing else.

Surprisingly, she doesn't back away.

"And I didn't know I'd let you stand on my feet for three minutes of some stupid boy band song from twenty years ago."

She stares, scorn filling her eyes, unwavering.

I can't believe I'm about to do this, but I have to try.

"One more thing, Miss Landers. As long as you work with me, we need to clear the air. A little mutual respect can work wonders both ways. No more games or mixed signals. What do you say?"

"Coming from you? That's rich." She laughs.

"What do you mean coming from me?"

"All you do is scheme."

"You don't know me," I insist.

"Whatever. You hired me as a contractor over the stupid land and that's why I wound up on your feet. You suffered through twenty minutes of pretending to like me—"

"Suffered? It wasn't *that* bad," I snarl through my teeth. "I hoped you'd see me as a person instead of a pest."

She throws up a hand, pulling at a lock of strawberry hair before sweeping it over her ear.

"Yet you had to huff and puff and run off Ace, didn't you? Because if I like him enough to stick around in Pinnacle Pointe, you won't get your precious land. And this whole respect thing feels like a cheap psychology trick. You can train me into 'seeing you as a person—'" She makes her voice deep and puffs her chest out on those last three words. "Since you think that'll help you get the inn."

Fuck.

I can practically feel steam darting through my veins.

I'm not about to tell her that chasing away the Ace of Clowns had nothing to do with her dilapidated inn that isn't worth half the amount I offered for it.

Why does she always think the worst of me?

Am I really poison?

Did Simone make me such a cancer?

"Go home and come back ready to work," I tell her.

"It's not that cold. It's July." She glances away from me, seemingly annoyed that I won't turn this into a drag-out fight.

"The water will be."

"It's not like we're swimming," she counters.

"Have you ever been on a boat before?"

"Sure. Most yachts are heated, aren't they?" she says.

"Only in the cabin this time of year. You won't get good footage from there and my people prefer hands on."

She steps closer and points at me. "Let's get one thing straight."

My gaze hardens.

The only thing I want to get straight right now is tossing her against the wall and savaging her lips, destroying whatever point I've tried to make about professionalism.

I let myself imagine it, though.

What would it be like to taste her lips, tangle my fingers through her hair, chase her tongue until she whimpers with respect?

Her next words rip me from the fantasy.

"You're my boss, fine. But I'm still a free agent since I'm not on your payroll. You haven't paid me yet and I'm free to walk away anytime. It was in the contract, remember?"

"Your first check is coming soon. I suggest you try not to freeze your nipples off before it's in your account."

Her lips purse.

Her fingers twitch.

I wonder if she's about to slap me across the face.

Goddamn, would I welcome it?

Just to feel something with her again.

Just to prove I'm that fucked in the head so I don't have to wonder.

For a second, I wish like hell I wasn't dealing with her at all.

This entire working relationship is an exercise in patience and self-discipline.

She clicks her tongue. "What time should I meet you at the marina?"

"I'll text you. I still have your phone number from the night you texted me about how I'm so hot it should be illegal." I must be suicidal.

I just can't stop mashing her buttons.

"You mean because you were blowing up my phone for days and it was time to tell you to eff off?" Her face screws up with disgust, but her cheeks are rose-pink.

"Still. You think I'm hot."

Scoffing, she stalks past me to the door and looks back at me over her shoulder.

"I'll see you tonight. I'm never late to a client meeting—or an Anne Rice novel."

She disappears through the door.

I watch her walk away before I burst out laughing.

This is how it has to be, I guess.

Laugh at her incredible contempt for me because I can't change her mind.

It's either laugh, or break my hand punching the wall.

When I can set my face again, I put the tiger painting aside and pull out a new canvas.

I've painted it blue in no time, layering the top two-thirds of the scene with dark purple and the bottom third with a foamy green.

It does nothing to dampen the restlessness roaming my blood or my appetite for punishment.

How early can I tell her to show up and still call it an evening event?

* * *

I STAND on the top deck, looking down at the creative team below.

It's a blustery evening and they're fighting the wind more than I expected.

I smile every time Miss Landers catches my eye.

Thankfully, she heeded my advice.

95

Her curves are clad in black pants, a modest desert-brown pullover sweater, and a silver windbreaker over it. She switches off between huddling with the team for discussions and playing director, pointing people this way and that, while Dave pivots for shots that will either wind up spectacular or miserably faded in this weather.

She's simply infuriating.

There's no denying she's good at what she does.

I wasn't expecting this passion when I hired her, or this competence.

Honestly, I just hoped I could convince her I'm not Satan so she'd sell Bee Harbor. Now, it's a struggle to imagine anyone who'd be a better fit for this project.

A little while later, they must have gotten their initial round in.

Sarah and another woman walk away from a laughing Jennifer, and Dave digs around in his coat as he walks toward the back of the ship.

Another goddamned smoke break, probably.

We're slowly approaching the cliff Pinnacle Pointe was named for.

It's a natural gem for tourism shots, and it never fails to capture my attention no matter how many times I've seen it.

As soon as I look up at the majestic peak, a memory hits me in the face.

The first time I ever remember being here.

I'm knee-high and laughing, hunkered on Dad's lofty shoulders. My mother comes over and leans against his bicep, both of them laughing at some joke I'm too young to understand.

The late summer sunset streams through the cottony clouds on the horizon.

My old man draws in a breath heavy with life.

I feel it roll through him when he exhales.

"Take a good long look, little man," he tells me, shifting me higher for the best view while Mom rests her head on his shoulder. "This is

what's worth it, Miles. Right here. The times you'll remember for as long as you live and the people you'll share it with."

My jaw tightens like a vise.

There was so much sickening irony in his words, even if he couldn't have known it.

How many times have I told Dad that story, desperately trying to share that memory, only to get back a blank, glassy look in return?

Even memories aren't guaranteed. That's what I wish he'd told me.

And the people you hope will always share them, well, there's no guarantee they'll be here tomorrow.

The cliff hasn't changed in the slightest since I was a boy.

Yet, the landscape is the only thing that remains of that day with a happy family that stopped existing years ago.

It's a worn memory that's only mine now, and eventually it might just fade to black one fine day when I wake up and don't know who the hell I am.

Is that my destiny?

Sharing my father's fate?

Does he ever remember that day when Mom was still around to comb his hair, leaning sweetly into his ear and whispering—

"Hey, guys, you have to get this! Where's Dave?" Jenn's voice pierces my melancholy, dragging my eyes down to her again.

She's holding her phone in front of her face, filming the cliff as the ship reaches its closest approach and slows.

Everyone scurries closer, getting in their own shots.

They line up like an army of little photographers, capturing the cliffs from different angles.

I chuckle to myself.

This woman is the whirlwind my people need.

Half an hour later, when everything seems filmed to her satisfaction, the team disperses, but Jenn stays behind. She's still down there, pulling her windbreaker tight around her body and leaning up against deck railing, watching the landscape drift by.

This is probably a good time to talk to her.

If there's any such a thing as a 'good time.'

I'm not sure when I'll catch her alone again, though.

So I head down to the lower deck, wondering if we can trade twenty words before she's ready to flay me open.

A sudden gust blows just before I reach her. Her silver windbreaker flutters open, displaying an ample chest I've tried like hell to forget.

Goddamn, there's another memory I don't need.

Her, standing in front of me, dumbstruck and red-faced with her robe tossed open, baring everything and still not enough.

Even then, I wanted to devour her.

A craving that only intensifies. Because the first time I saw her, I didn't know she had the gumption to turn down an embarrassingly large offer for the inn. I didn't know she had zero problem telling people with twice as much experience what they're doing wrong and how to fix it.

My eyes wander and I beg the cold weather to fight down my hard-on. The peaks of those large tits dot her thin shirt, and it's harder to ignore them the closer I get.

"Miss Landers," I say, approaching over her shoulder. "That was damn good work."

She turns and smiles at me. "Have you come to gloat while I turn into an ice cube?"

"I'm here to admire the view." And though I nod at the cliff looming over us, my eyes never leave her.

Thankfully, she doesn't notice, returning her gaze to the ocean and the scenery beyond.

"I wish this town had a lighthouse," she muses. "It's the only thing missing from an evening like this."

Damn, this girl.

It's obscene how she turns me inside out without trying every time she smiles.

"I can't help you with that. However, we should have plenty of content over the next two weeks when everything gets compiled and edited. When the team returns to Seattle, they'll get to work on it and let you know when you're needed in the office."

That gets her attention.

She whips her head around now and meets my gaze.

"Office? You mean I can't just work remotely?"

I smile. "Only for a little while. Probably no more than a week or two. I wouldn't dream of keeping you away from paradise any longer than necessary. Hell, I don't want to wind up stuck in Seattle for more than a few days myself."

A stricken look lines her face.

"I don't know what I'll do with Coffee and Cream. My parents will flip if I drag them back home. Maybe I can get Ace to stop by and feed them. I'm pretty sure my grandma gave him a key."

Ace again? They're on pet sitting terms?

Venom courses through me.

"No," I say too quickly. "That's an easy fix. You can keep them at my place where there's constant security and space. Or I'll have my housekeeper go over and feed them and let them out regularly. You don't want the damn handyman alone with those monster dogs. Even if he could manage, it's too much liability."

Also, the idea of her turning to the Playing Card for help sours my stomach.

"They're good dogs! They don't bite. You know that."

I shrug. "Maybe so, but why take the risk? Besides, they're creatures of habit."

"That's what worries me. They've already had their routines upset so much when—" Her voice breaks and she sighs. "When Gram hasn't been gone *that* long. But I don't think the dogs can come with me to Seattle." She looks at me and smiles. "Anyway, if your housekeeper stops by to feed them, doesn't that mean *you're* taking on the liability? They're not even your dogs. I should just get Ace to do it when he'll be coming by for projects anyway. It's no big deal, and he doesn't seem like the type to sue me."

"I'll hire you a damned pet sitter. Company expense," I grind out.

Her eyes dance with amusement like the lethal little kitten she is.

Of course, she's enjoying this.

"Nonsense. They're my dogs and we've already negotiated compensation."

"Miss Landers, in case it wasn't obvious, I adore Coffee and Cream," I admit, hating how her eyes light up. "They've...grown on me since the day Coffee dug under my fence and destroyed a rosebush."

Her jaw drops. "He destroyed your bush?"

"They like to stomp around with those moose legs, don't they? Thankfully, he missed the thorns and didn't chew too much."

Laughing softly, she turns back to the seascape for a moment and then leans her head back and looks at the sky.

"You picked a beautiful evening for this. If I'm being honest, it's not just dog logistics that have me worried. I don't want to go back to the big city hustle when I'm settling in here."

I do a double take, wondering what the hell is going on.

Are we having a moment?

A real conversation without the constant sniping and tension and insults?

"You're from there, aren't you?"

"Born and raised, but this place was always my hideout. I spent most of my summers and quite a few holidays with Gram."

"Have you ever lived outside Washington?"

She shakes her head. "I even went to college in Seattle, and then it was off to Winthrope International as soon as I landed the internship. That's where I learned to appreciate beautiful places like this. I mean, I always loved Pinnacle Pointe, but I didn't appreciate the aesthetics the way I do now. Not until I started copywriting my butt off trying to sell resort stays in exotic places. This has all the makings of a cute resort town. I'm not sure what stopped it from being one."

"More development would be necessary. You'd need a few more bars and a couple high-end spas to attract the money crowd. Frankly, I like it the way it is. There aren't enough people here to bother me."

She stares at me for a second and bursts out laughing.

"What?"

What now?

"You surprise me. That's all. You just seem like the kind of dude who'd never leave the city unless you're bound for a five-star hotel with a restaurant that has crudo and a wine list a mile long."

"You don't know me," I flare, swallowing my annoyance before I ask, "Do you even want to?"

Her face blanks.

"Well... I mean, if it wasn't for the work arrangement and you lusting after my land—you wouldn't be half-bad. The painting thing knocks you down a bit on the ogre scale. It's interesting."

"Ogre, huh?" I puff out my chest and swing my arms, doing my best Shrek. It must not be totally awful since she doubles over with laughter.

"Oh my God, you... you have to stop." Her green eyes dance when she looks at me again.

I wait until she comes up for air. "One question for you. Is interesting better or worse than hot?"

Every last bit of her stiffens. More redness bleeds into her cheeks and it has nothing to do with the hysterical fit a second ago.

"You're never going to let me live that down, are you?"

"Why would I, Miss Landers, when you still can't handle the fact that you think I'm—" A strong wind abruptly hits me in the face before I can finish the sentence.

I look out over the railing and see whitecaps.

Shit.

"Be careful!" I yell.

Too late.

A strong evening tide rolls the boat up like the entire sea just turned into a thrashing carpet. Even a ship this size rocks violently when it's descending a hill of water.

The wave knocks Jenn off-balance and tumbles her toward me.

I sweep forward to catch her, and just manage to keep her from hitting the wooden deck.

Like every predictable romance movie, the next time I glance at her, she's cradled against my chest.

We stare at each other in stunned silence, too dumbstruck to move.

This compromising position feels too right.

She's so soft. So warm. So vibrant.

All lemony tart sweetness and a curl of hair against my cheek, her lips only inches from mine.

Every drop of blood I own goes molten as she slurs out a small whimper.

Fuck.

Our heads are so close, I could take her lips now, if I wanted.

And I do.

Goddammit, I do.

Neither of us make any effort to move as the boat rocks again. We're hoisted up and dropped down again by another dense wall of water.

My knees bang the deck as we fall, absorbing the blow as we tilt and I wind up on my back, still clutching her.

I wrap my arms tighter, securing her as she tries to scramble up.

For a second, she looks down at me.

Her eyes flutter shut, and she tilts her chin, giving me this tortured look I know all too well.

My lips hover in front of hers, so close I can smell the peach Bellini on her breath.

I want to lick it right off her tongue.

I want to drink every last drop of Jennifer Landers so fucking bad my spine throbs.

Only, she's caught up in her own slow-burn romance with an overgrown playing card.

Who the hell am I to ruin it, to blow up her life, even if I'd love to knock him out cold?

Also, she's technically an underling, consultant or not, and bound by all the company rules against fraternization.

My father made those rules God years before I ever took the CEO's chair. Cromwell-Narada was one of the first Seattle mega-corps to protect women from predatory bosses.

Plus, she still thinks I lured her into that dance to charm the land away.

Yeah. There are too many ways for this to derail catastrophically.

Too many invitations to ruin ourselves with a thousand cuts, or maybe just a few hacking slices cut by lips that shouldn't wander.

With a heaving sigh, I drop the arm around her waist and help lift us both so we're standing again.

She stares at me for a solid minute and clears her throat.

"But I—I thought—" She sighs and turns away from me, muttering something under her breath that can only be a curse.

So, she wanted it too.

Welcome to my personal hell.

I stand there speechless as we wait a few more seconds to make sure the big waves have passed before she heads toward the cabin door.

"You're welcome," I call to her back.

She spins around on one foot with flaming eyes. "For what?"

"Breaking your fall, Miss Landers. What the hell else?"

Her small hands curl into fists. "Right. *Thanks.*"

She's pissed, and she has a right to be.

Every bone in my body regrets not kissing her when I had the perfect chance.

We're all living a cosmic joke when doing the right thing wins this much scorn.

She doesn't say anything else, but she hasn't turned away from me.

If she's going to gawk at me like I'm in the running for world's biggest rhino dick, I'd might as well limp across the finish line.

"You never answered me, kitten. Is 'interesting' a promotion from 'hot?'" I flash her a shit-eating grin.

"Demotion. Definitely," she snaps.

Then I watch her trudge away, shaking her head, those silky strands of auburn that were almost mine fluttering in the breeze until she disappears.

VII: NO SECRETS AMONG FRIENDS
(JENN)

"*W*hoa, boy! Calm down!" Pippa jerks on Cream's leash as the dog rears up in excitement, releasing a muffled woof at a group of white birds pecking at the ground.

I laugh. "Careful. Cream isn't a boy, and you've got the calmer one."

"I can't believe you manage to walk both of these beasts by yourself every day."

"Shhh! They'll hear you," I say. "But seriously, they're usually pretty good about leash pulling. *Usually.*"

I just wish I had Gram's magic.

With her, the dogs were perfect angels. I'm still winning them over, and there are times when I have to repeat commands, but it hasn't been long.

Pippa laughs and screws her face up. "Sorry, Cream and Coffee. I didn't mean you were actual beasts. Just big, heavy, and independent-minded." She pauses and turns to me. "So, how are you *really* liking it here?"

A complicated question.

"Well, since my bestie stole her boyfriend's helicopter and flew in from the city to help me go dog walking, it's peachy. Before that—" I hold up a hand and rock it back and forth.

She rolls her eyes, her blonde hair more radiant than ever. I'd say it's the summer sun, but it's been somewhat cloudy this afternoon. I think that ring on her finger has a lot to do with her constant glow.

"I didn't steal the helicopter, Jenn. Brock had his pilot drop me off. They'll be back for me Sunday night."

"Oh, Mr. Winthrope himself is flying in? Stop the presses."

She grins. "He's too sweet. The man keeps texting about how much he misses me. He wasn't going to come on Sunday, but he says he can't stand another night alone in our bed."

"That is sickeningly sweet. *Woof.*" Coffee throws me a look with his ears perked.

It's also the gross lovey-dovey thing I've always secretly wanted but probably won't find in this lifetime.

"But how's it been settling in? You've been too busy to take my calls for a week, so there must be more to life than walking the dogs."

"You'd be surprised," I say. "It's been a lot to take in, Pippa. Setting up work with the inn, the new side gig, plus trying to get off the grief train... If Gram's ghost ever checks in, I'm sure she wishes she left me a year of her cheesecakes. God, I miss those."

"Me too! They were awesome every time you brought one home." She smiles. "But that's it? I thought small towns like these were packed with drama."

"I've always been boring," I say with a shrug. "Are you surprised?"

"Lady, if you're holding out on me..."

"Fine. I have a brand-new pain-in-the-ass client. Totally demanding and eats up too much of my time, but I did agree to the job."

"I hope they're paying you for any crap. You know you can come back to Winthrope whenever you want with a promotion, right?"

"I appreciate the offer, but I turned into a cog there. Gram leaving me her place was the wake-up call I needed."

Two little hummingbirds flit past. Coffee lets out a muffled woof. I stop for a break and motion for him to heel.

"I'm not sure what you mean?" Pippa says, shaking her head.

"It wasn't a bad gig. But you remember how taking that job was the last thing you wanted? It never fit your real plans—never mind the hijinks that snagged you a hubby. For me, it was a comfy check. Don't get me wrong, the benefits were incredible, but no career path there led to here."

"And this is what you've always wanted? Wow. I had no idea." She scans the greenery around us, taking it in. Then she turns back to me with a look like she's beginning to understand why I'm falling for Pinnacle Pointe. "Well, if you ever change your mind, I bet Brock could figure out some remote work for you."

"Pippa, I appreciate it, but the sooner I try to get the inn up and running again, the better. And even though the client sucks monkey balls, he pays decent enough. Like so well I don't need to worry about taking on new clients."

If only he didn't burn through my days with almost-kisses and invade my dreams at night.

If only Miles Cromwell was a little less... Miles.

She nods.

I wish she truly had a clue.

"As long as your new jerkwad pays you enough to be a royal pain in the ass."

"Yeah. It'll be over in three months, anyway. I'll have enough to tide me over to take an honest stab at the inn."

"From writing about fancy hotels to running your own. You're moving up!" she gushes, slapping my shoulder. "What are they paying you?"

I hesitate. It feels a little weird telling her when it's a generous amount, but she also shares accounts with a billionaire now, so any normal sum seems paltry to her.

"A hundred and fifty." I purse my lips.

"A hundred and fifty bucks an hour? Nice! I would've sat you down for a 'come to Jesus' if you sold yourself short again."

"...a hundred and fifty thousand, Pippa." I sigh, watching her eyes bug out.

"For three freaking months?"

"Yeah."

"Holy shit. Who are you working for? The mafia? No normal person pays a hundred and fifty smackers for three months of copywriting. That's almost an entry level C-suite salary at Winthrope."

"That's the sad part. I wound up with a bigger, broodier scrooge than your beau."

"Who?" She stares in disbelief.

"Miles Cromwell."

It *hurts* to say his name.

My eardrums vibrate when she claps her hands.

"O-M-G! Him! Brock always complains that guy charges him a fortune for ad space on his websites and broadcasts. He's got the whole radio market in the Pacific Northwest wrapped around his finger."

"Figures. He's pretty shrewd with real estate too. He tried to buy the inn out from under me before I was barely unpacked."

Her jaw drops again. "Are you serious?"

I fill her in on the rest of our anti-meet cute, thoroughly annoyed that I even consider it that.

Ugh.

"Whoa. Just weird. I never realized how many self-propelled dicks there are in big money until I became part of it." She sighs. "I got crazy lucky with Brock. Most of the moneybags he rubs shoulders with aren't remotely like him. They're full of bad habits and half of them cheat on their wives in the open. Every time some married rich guy walks into an event with his sugar baby, I gag. There are a few exceptions, though. That Cole Lancaster guy isn't half-bad."

"The coffee mogul? Right. He's an actual hero for the way he rescued his wife from that creeper," I say, remembering the headlines. "I wish my boss had a fraction of Lancaster in him, or even your Brock."

"Don't let him get away with anything, Jenn. He's totally buttering you up and trying to convince you to sell," she tells me.

I grin painfully.

"I know. That's why I negotiated just enough to fix up the inn with money to spare. The jerk knows he's basically helping me keep the place."

But while she laughs, I frown.

Is he really so awful when he's shooting himself in the foot to help me?

Maybe not.

But I can't say the same for the way he held me so close, his eyes all quicksilver and heated glances, and then dropped me like an ice cube after dancing.

I'm *not* mentioning either bout of that insanity to my best friend. She'll never let me live it down.

Luckily, Coffee whines and we start walking. I have to speed walk to keep from racing ahead, giving his leash a firm tug to slow him down.

"The boy's getting restless. I will say it's been an interesting few weeks. It might not be so bad if I hadn't drunk texted him—"

"Wait, what? You *drunk texted* Miles Cromwell?"

"Not literally. I was texting you and I got confused," I admit glumly.

"Classic Landers!" She snorts. "Remember when you sent that Tinder idiot *my* picture from your camera roll?"

I throw her a sour look. "Remember when we agreed to never discuss that again?"

Seriously.

The meathead fell in insta-lust with Pippa and bombed my phone with dick pics from four different numbers I had to block. Reason number 999,999 I want nothing to do with the hellscape of Seattle dating—or swipe dating in general.

"What'd you say to him?" she insists.

Heat pumps under my face. "I was telling you what a hot jerk he was and how it should be illegal for him to be so hot."

"You sent that? You're killing me."

"Yeah, and he's never going to drop it as long as he has a pulse."

"And this was before you signed on to work for him?"

"Dude. I couldn't turn down that kind of cash." I smile sheepishly. "You've seen the repairs Bee Harbor needs."

"I can't tell if you already have a crush on this guy, or a hate-crush."

"There's a difference?" I look at her and blink.

Even the dogs stare at me like I'm about to burst into flames.

"We just work together, Pippa. Hand to God."

Her mouth twists into a pout. "You're my best friend. If I had a crush, I'd tell you. You knew about Brock and all the crap he put me through from the second he came barreling out of the shower."

"Whatever. Maybe I do have a crush."

"See how easy that was?" she says smugly. "Now, since I know a thing or two about grumpy rich men and happily ever afters—"

"Not on Cromwell! On Ace," I spit.

"What's an Ace?" Her face falls.

Yikes.

I'm starting to think this guy's biggest flaw is his name.

"Not what. Who."

"Okay, *who* is Ace?"

I tell her all about how I inherited the hottest handyman ever. *Thanks again, Gram.*

"The handyman, though?" Jenn clucks her tongue. "Jeebus. You're the one who always made fun of those cheesy Christmas movies."

"Well, living one of those cheese flicks changes your mind."

Piper rolls her eyes and scratches Cream's ruff when the dog gives her a worried look.

We reel the Dobermans in closer as we head into town, slowly approaching the first corner with the general store.

We're about five feet from the door when Dracula himself walks out, his big arms loaded with—*what else?*—flipping paint supplies.

Too bad Coffee's excitement overwhelms his doggy brain.

The brat bolts, galloping to a genuine run.

Oh, no.

I try tightening the leash. I also don't want to hurt his neck and I didn't think to put them on harnesses.

Not fast enough.

He flies forward as my hand slips, the leash flapping behind him. I'm lucky I don't topple over onto Pippa.

"*Coffeeeee!* No!" she screams too late.

I scramble up, unpeeling myself from the concrete just as Miles shuffles the stuff in his arms and pulls out something wrapped.

Coffee spins circles and then settles into an excited sit as he rips off the papery covering.

Miles pats his nose and passes him a piece of beef jerky.

Heart, meet knees.

"...you're bribing my dog now?"

Make that *dogs,* plural. Cream isn't far behind, shoving her white muzzle greedily at his hand for her bribe.

"It's a treat, Miss Landers. He's better behaved than you. Aren't you glad I stopped at the butcher across the street? And for your information, I've given Coffee treats longer than I've known you."

Oof.

I hate that he has that flex, thinking back to the first day he came to the inn.

I expected Miles to freak out before my robe was unceremoniously yanked open, but he just said, *"Not today."*

Something doesn't add up.

How well did he know Gram and the dogs? Somehow, it feels

like more than random canine intrusions on his property and honey deliveries for his valet guy.

The longer I stare at him, I wonder.

He holds my gaze like he's pondering something.

"It's the weekend," I remind him before he has time to bark orders. "My day off. I wasn't planning to run into you."

He doesn't deserve a real apology and I think I deserve one day—*one day*—off from Miles Cromwell and his shit.

"It's my weekend, too. Just because I run a multibillion-dollar company doesn't mean I don't decompress," he grumbles.

My eyes dart to the blank canvas in his hands and back to his face. For once, I believe him.

"Looks as fun as watching paint dry. Literally."

A bad joke, but I can't resist.

He jabs his middle finger out, not so subtly flipping me off while he rearranges the load in his arms.

Then Benson comes out of the store behind him with more art stuff. They cross the street to load up a black SUV I haven't seen before.

Benson just stands beside the trunk patiently, flashing us a friendly smile. Miles takes things from him and does all the bending and twisting, which surprises me. I would've thought he needed his valet to spoon-feed him, much less drag heavy paints around.

I'm even more dumbfounded when Miles climbs in the driver's seat this time. *He's driving his driver?*

"Nice wheels. I think it's a newer electric model that doesn't suck. Brock has had his eye on that model for months. He just hasn't had the time for a test drive yet," Pippa says with a whistle. "Hey, at least you know he's a man of taste."

I glower as the engine whirs to life and the vehicle pulls away from the curb.

"I don't know about that," I say.

"You know what, Jenn? You suck at hiding things and you're an even worse liar," she says playfully.

"Did he notice me staring?"

"Duh. He *wanted* you to look, showing off his rig. That was fun."

That is way too close to becoming my new obsession.

Where's a hole opening under my feet when I need one?

I think I may need this Seattle visit to come sooner than later, just to clear my head. Preferably without King Dick Cromwell along for the ride.

A trip to my old stomping grounds might help. This town and this glorious idiot are doing strange things to me.

With the dogs back under control and licking their chops, we walk them in companionable silence.

"So, he paints?" Pippa asks.

"He dabbles. His word. I think he likes landscapes and animals and such."

Piper tries and fails to stifle another laugh.

"What's so funny?"

"Your answer. You know his style and you sound impressed." She holds up her finger and thumb with the tiniest space pinched between them. "Just *a little.*"

My face feels like it's about to melt right off.

"C'mon. We just passed a guy carrying an armload of canvas and paints. How dumb would I be if I didn't know something? And I don't know his style, exactly. I just... I've seen him while he's hacking away at the canvas. He was doing a tiger last time."

"Oh, man. You know we're going to spend the rest of the evening unpacking that symbolism, right? Kudos to Grammy for leaving you all that wine! Let's open a fresh bottle—the blueberry stuff, maybe. I love that." She thinks she's such a riot. "So, you've been to his house?"

"He lives next door and the creative team meets there," I say miserably.

"Dang. The boy next door on top of it? How many hot hero tropes are we up to, Jenn?"

Hopefully enough to get away with smacking her in the head.

There are times when I wonder why we're still besties after all these years.

"Brock and I started off at each other's throats, too."

"He's. Not. Brock," I stress each word, thinking I'm ready for that wine after all. "And you and Brock didn't get along because he was naked in your room. That didn't happen here."

I almost blurt out that he's the one who saw me naked—or near enough—but I bite my tongue before that slips out. It'd be the height of stupidity to hand her more ammo to give me a stroke from embarrassment.

"Look, can we just forget this?" I ask. "We'll go home and get pizza and drink wine, and you'll help me scare up a way to seduce Mr. Handyman. Cromwell will go on doing whatever giant grumpy asshats do, investing new ways to make everyone miserable, and that's that. The only thing he's getting from me is the best social media strategy a big check buys."

I clap my hands together like it's a done deal.

The dogs look up. They must know it's one of the few quirky mannerisms that rubbed off from Gram.

Oh, that hurts.

"Okay, okay. I'm your guest," Pippa concedes. "But just promise me you'll keep an open mind? Would it kill you to wind up with a hot billionaire if he's got a heart made of solid gold underneath? Trust me, it's kinda cool having a man cut his weekend short just so he can fly in desperate to see you again—and hot makeup sex never hurts."

My face scrunches up.

TMI, and yeah, I'm a little jealous of her sex life with a man who could be an affluent underwear model.

"You're living the dream and I'm legit happy for you, lady. But I'm not you."

Her eyes shine sadly as she asks, "What does that mean?"

"It's not something Miles Cromwell would be caught dead doing. And if he does, it won't be for me. I'm not you, and I'm okay with that. The idiot even told me once he prefers blondes. It's a billionaire thing, right?"

"No way!" she hisses. "I'm not standing here while you sell yourself short. You're beautiful, and I don't care if this wins me some crap, but that dude was *into you.*"

"He wants my land, not me," I fire back.

If she only knew the way he spun me around the dance floor in hopes of buying a bed and breakfast.

"He was staring, Jenn. Big desperate wolfy eyes screaming 'notice me.'"

"He's pissed I'm not working on the weekend, probably. For the rate he's paying, I might expect ninety days straight of constant work too."

"Live and learn." Piper shakes her head violently. "That wasn't an 'I have work for you' look."

"What was it then?"

"An 'I want to work you over' look. Huge difference."

Oh, boy.

There we go.

What's left of my face goes up in flames.

"Shut up." I slap Piper's arm with my free hand. Cream stops and groans, while Coffee lets out a whining yawn. Even the dogs are tired of this back and forth.

But my traitor friend just smiles ever so sweetly.

"Easy. I just pointed out the obvious. You're the one who's redder than a fire hydrant."

* * *

By the time we get back to Bee Harbor, we're both hot, sweaty, and our hands are covered in dog licks.

"Use the guest bathroom I showed you earlier. It's safe from the horror movie water now," I tell her after the dogs are down for their nap.

"Do I want to know?"

"Just take my word for it. Ace did a nice fix so it doesn't come out looking like a nightmare."

Later, we sit on the couch with our wine and a huge margherita pizza from the tavern in town.

"You have to admit he's hot. So you weren't out of line when you were texting," Piper says without looking up from her phone.

"Who?" But I grit my teeth because I already know.

"Your grumpy client man."

"Say it again and I'm telling Brock." I wag a finger in warning.

"Oh, don't get him started. He knows he has nothing to worry about but he's a caveman anyway. Also, your boy's a paid artist."

"I don't have a boy—and I'm not sure how you know that."

"Mr. Google told me."

I reach for her phone. "You're *Google* stalking him, now?"

Mostly, I'm annoyed she's stumbled on something I didn't. I never found out anything about Cromwell and his paintings.

She snatches her phone away. "Everyone Googles everyone else these days. Relax. I'm checking up on Mr. Handyman too. If these are the only two men you know in town—alone—a little background check can't hurt."

"You're so overprotective! Pippa, I can manage. You're not my big sis."

"You're basically my twin."

"And I don't know how you're going to Google Ace anyhow. I don't even know his last name, but he did work for Gram. All legitimate stuff. I checked the records in her office."

"What? You tried to convince me you were so smitten you couldn't possibly have a crush on your boss, and you don't even know his last name? Come on! The next time you want to lie, back it up. We'll give Ace a few points for your grandma hiring him, though. That woman didn't tolerate any BS."

She did not.

I sip my third glass of wine too quickly.

Then Pippa holds up her phone. "Look at this!"

The screen shows a painting. Fabulously bright wildflowers rioting over the side of an ancient stone wall, like something out of a Medieval fantasy scene or—

Hold up.

My eyes flick over, stopping just above the fireplace.

My breath catches.

Right there.

That very painting hangs over my mantle, and if it isn't the one, then it's an exact replica.

Holy Toledo.

...did Miles paint custom stuff for Gram? Did she buy it from him?

But it's hard to imagine.

Gram supported every cause ever in Pinnacle Pointe, but she wouldn't have ponied up the thousands I'm sure Mr. Billionaire would charge for his precious work. And why would he sell them off anyway?

I'm so lost.

"Piper?"

"What? Pretty cool, right?"

I raise my eyebrows, veering my head toward the painting until her gaze follows.

She sits up and looks in the direction I'm staring.

"Holyyy. Wow. O-kay then. So, bossypants knew your grandmother pretty well."

"You think so? Maybe she just bought it at some charity thing..." It's the only theory I can come up with.

"Uh, it's in your house. Safe to say they knew each other well enough to do art transactions." She flashes me a satisfied smile.

That's kind of what I thought.

So, why did she never mention Miles Cromwell being anything but a rich, mysterious hermit? If she ever used his name, it was only once or twice.

I glance around the room and stop on another painting on the opposite wall.

It's the beach off the downtown strip. I point to it, adjusting my glasses.

"That's the same artist, right?"

She sits up and follows my finger with her eyes. "I'm no art major, but it sure looks the same. Even the colors are close to identical."

The mystery deepens.

We grab our wine and start walking, scanning each room. Three other paintings in this house turn up by the only living artist I can't stand.

"Multiple paintings. She was either a huge fan, or she and your favorite bossman were kinda close. He can't be too much of a jackass."

I blink at her. "Why do you say that?"

"Your grammy knew she was leaving you the house next door to his. If she thought he was a jerk, she wouldn't have done it, or else she would have warned you first."

I laugh. "You only met my grandma a couple times."

"Yeah, but she wasn't the quiet type, and you were her favorite. She wouldn't have left you a house next door to a royal jerkoff without warning you."

I take another long sip of wine.

My vision sways, but it's not the alcohol.

"...I didn't know they knew each other like this. I'm freaking out. She barely ever mentioned him, but his paintings are all over her house!"

I'm light-headed now.

"Sounds like a reason to go have a talk with your favorite painter." She bats her eyes, wearing the most perfect grin.

"I do *not* have a crush. Even if I might have to ask about this."

"Keep telling yourself that," she mutters.

The rest of the night, we rehash old times and she talks up

her latest adventures with Brock and their weenie dog, Andouille.

But my brain is stuck on Miles, Miles, and also, *Miles.*

I don't dare text him while Pippa's awake.

She already thinks I'm wasting away without this idiot, but as soon as she falls asleep, I snap pictures of his paintings on my walls and open a new text.

Recognize these? I attach the pics.

My eyes burn as I stare at the screen, waiting for a response.

It never comes.

After an hour goes by, I try again. ***Cromwell, did you get my message?***

Nothing.

Jenn: Nice. So if I accidentally text that you're hot, you respond in thirty seconds. But you can't answer a legit question at all?

I barely sleep that night, repeatedly checking my phone for...anything.

I don't get it.

Morning comes with a dull headache and no answer.

Prick.

The only thing worse than developing a horrible crush on your vampire boss is when he turns into a bat and ghosts you.

VIII: NO TURNING BACK (MILES)

*I*t's been a solid week since the creative crew returned to Seattle, and with fourth quarter campaigns looming, my calls with Louise have picked up.

"The video work came out like a dream, Mr. Cromwell. Dave really outdid himself! Oh, and those shots on the boat, they'll grab a lot of eyes for sure. We just need Jennifer here to make sure everything fits her vision. Everyone said she's a delight to work with."

Of course they did.

Everyone who encounters Miss Landers experiences an angel—except for yours truly.

My fingers drum my desk.

"Go on, Louise."

"I was just about to mention that we're ahead of schedule. We can take our time with this, especially since it's a nonprofit side project."

"Agreed."

"The final review might be a good time for you to check in, too," she tells me cautiously. "If it won't disrupt any busy summer plans, of course."

"I'll be there. I won't miss the pre-launch phase. Too many

moving pieces and too many opportunities for something to go wrong." I turn to the window, staring out at Bee Harbor on the horizon.

It's incredible how something so idyllic can shelter a woman causing me so much grief.

I'm only half listening as Louise updates me on highlights from informal reports.

This company runs so smoothly it barely requires my presence anymore. It's a well-oiled machine that just needs my ideas, my discipline, my vision.

That should be liberating.

In reality, it's just annoying.

"By the way, HR needs to update the policy on hiring temps. Accounting has three women going out on maternity leave, and one of them wants to keep working from home so she doesn't burn her vacation time. The current process is to bring in a temp, which wouldn't allow her that—"

"Change the policy to three months paid maternity leave for everyone," I cut in.

"Are you sure? That's very generous, boss." She sounds so surprised.

"I'm not hemorrhaging talent over family matters. Plus, our Canadian office already gets more paid leave anyhow. It won't break the bank to give personnel here at home the same courtesy."

"Yes, sir."

I'm expecting her to sign off there, but she lingers.

"Is there anything else?" I ask.

"One more thing." Why does she sound so unsure? "A competitor reached out, offering to help host the big charity event we're sponsoring. Considering the celebrities flying into Seattle for the show, I didn't think it would be a disaster to at least hear them out. Rufus with our foundation loved the idea; he thought it could mean more money raised."

"That means sharing publicity," I point out.

"It will," she says. "But partnering also means twice the logistics and half the cost, doesn't it?"

"Yes." *So, what's the catch?* "What competitor?"

She freezes up and sighs slowly.

Fuck.

I already know what she's about to say, but I still hope I'm wrong.

"What competitor, Louise?" My voice turns glacial.

"Pacific-Resolute." It's barely a whisper. "Miss Niehaus herself sent the request personally."

Even after all these years, rage knifes through me instantly.

"Then you know where you can tell her to go. Don't waste my time on shit you know the answer to." Normally I'd feel bad chewing out my otherwise lovely assistant, but not with this.

"I know, Mr. Cromwell. You two have a complicated history. But it's still an offer. And it's for charity, not business. It's not like you'd be giving away any money or propriety secrets," she says quietly.

My chest swells and my nostrils flare.

I pace across the room, cutting a few brief circles, my only reprieve from fucking erupting.

"Louise, we've been through this. I don't do business with people I can't trust, and I'm not about to start. Do I have to explain this again?"

The last time was years ago and she never had the full story. Nobody deserves that.

If she thought time would heal my wounds, she never understood their severity.

"Right. My bad. Rufus, well, he didn't know the history and he lit up when he heard the idea. He was so excited. I guess I just ran with it, and I shouldn't have. My apologies." She sounds so defeated. So afraid.

"Is there anything else that needs my immediate attention?" I bite off, so goddamned ready to end this call.

The clatter of heels whips me around, and my eyes land on the very last thing I need right now.

Jennifer Landers, flouncing into my office in a vibrant green dress and heels that match her eyes. I think hell itself must be the same shade of green.

Apparently, my torture only began with hearing the name Pacific-Resolute.

"Louise?" I clip, demanding an answer.

"No, sir. That's all," she says.

I end the call without a goodbye and drop the phone on my desk before raising an eyebrow at the hellion in front of me.

"I see you no longer require an escort to traipse through my house."

She waves a hand. "Benson knows me, so he just sent me right back. Do I need to ask permission?"

Fuck, she's already won over my valet.

Or else he's having too much fun yanking my tail when he knows everything about Miss Landers is complicated.

"The project is with the team in Seattle for the next week, so what do you need now?"

She stops and tilts her heads, staring at me like I'm a disgruntled lion in its cage. "What are you so mad about? What did I *do* this time?"

Like you don't know.

"Nothing. I just don't know why you're here when it isn't necessary," I tell her.

With a shrug, she plops down in the chair across from my desk. "I came to find out why you're ignoring me. It's been a few days and I know you've seen my texts."

Her bare shoulders and low neckline draw my eyes to feast on her flesh.

"You're a difficult woman to ignore. The fact that you're in my office tells me ordering you out won't accomplish a damn thing," I say, trying and failing to pull my gaze off her.

"Yeah, so tell me. Why are you ignoring me again?"

"How can I ignore you if I'm talking to you right now?" I snort derisively.

"Stop trying to be cute—"

"I don't have to try, Miss Landers. I'm already illegally hot, in your opinion," I remind her.

Her breath catches and those strawberry lips part. With the sunlight splashing the room, she's a portrait of seduction.

A living, breathing cocktease so bright and alive and goddamned sexy I think this whole world must be purgatory.

Nobody ever said the devil and his minions were ugly.

She rolls her eyes. "Why didn't you answer me?"

I look down, ignoring her question. "I'm a busy man, and your questions weren't work related. Do you really expect me to just drop everything and—"

"Boss dude, all I asked about were the freaking paintings. Not your condom size. So chill." Her face heats as soon as she says it. I flash her a look that pins her in place. "Um, never mind. My point is, it could be related to the job. The art on the walls is a part of Bee Harbor and we filmed there plenty. Would it be so awful to mention there's a local artist in town? And I think I'll regret saying this, but a pretty *decent* one."

She's complimenting me?

Shit.

An insult from her, I know what to do with. This leaves me at a loss, especially when it's drifting dangerously close to forbidden waters.

"The paintings have nothing to do with the content for Pinnacle Pointe. There are ten thousand better things to show off in this town than my humble scribbles."

She stifles a laugh. "What, now you're Captain Modesty? You're talented, whatever your other faults. You do realize that could be a valuable part of your brand, right?"

"It isn't. Deliberately so. My painting isn't related to my profession. It's purely personal," I say, annoyed that I'm growling.

I don't know if it's hotter that she called me talented or the way the neckline of her dress melts into the crevice between her palm-sized tits with every breath.

I don't need to look down to know I'm hard again.

I also can't look away from her searching green eyes.

"Just to be clear, I counted. Five of your paintings are hanging in my grandmother's house and the inn next door. There's even a big one in the lobby, the marina scene." She clasps her hands and leans forward in her seat.

"And?" I force out.

"And?" she echoes.

"Lottie and I shared a mutual fascination with beautiful landscapes. Nothing more."

"So did Thomas Kinkade, but his paintings aren't in her living room." She throws her hands up and slaps her thighs—one more sound I don't need. "What's your deal? Why the big secret?"

"I auction off my work sometimes. Usually anonymously. She bought them at charity events. End of story." I'm lying my ass off, and it's so pathetic she sees right through me.

"Gram loved art, but she wasn't a collector. She also didn't have a crazy budget to compete with the type of people I'd guess are bidding on your stuff. She would've been your biggest fan to wind up with five paintings. I'm not a moron."

I scoff. "And you find that so unlikely?"

She blinks at me slowly. "You're really going to play it like this?"

"I'm *not* playing anything," I snarl. "You said the paintings were 'decent' yourself. Why is it so impossible to believe anyone would wind up with five?"

"It's possible, but it wouldn't be Gram. Not by any normal means."

What the hell does that mean?

Lottie always admired my work.

I look at her, taking a step closer, wishing I could glare this conversation to its end.

"Your paintings get high bids at these auctions. I did some sleuthing around the web and I caught a few mentions. One of your works sold for over eighty thousand dollars—"

"A commission for an associate." I sigh. "Again, for charity, but when he wanted a gold-plated dragon peeking out of the Hudson for his new penthouse in New York, it sounded like an interesting project for a good cause. So I obliged."

She smiles. "You didn't let me finish. Gram had some money, but not Cromwell art money. It's not believable she would have went stalking big money auctions in Seattle looking to pay an arm and a leg for your landscapes. The only charity events she went to were always here in Pinnacle Pointe, and usually for reading clubs, gardening, and bird conservation. Somehow, I don't think she bought your paintings at all."

Goddamn, am I *that* obvious?

"Maybe someone at the PTA had a painting or two on hand—"

"Or five."

"Or *five* they wanted to part with. Mystery solved. Would you like a Scooby snack to go for Coffee and Cream?" I counter.

She folds her arms, accentuating her chest.

"You're such an ass. I just wish I knew why." An exasperated noise rattles her throat.

"And you're surprisingly relentless over nothing."

"God, you—will you at least tell me if you painted them for her?" She exhales sharply and slumps in her chair.

"I painted them and they're hers, aren't they?"

I know I've officially leveled up in the giant dick department, being this evasive. If I knew this was coming, I would've come up with a better story.

"Specifically for her?"

"I wouldn't say that."

"Some of those scenes *are* Bee Harbor. Don't even try to deny it."

I can and I will.

If only I could tell you why, then this death by stupid fucking questions would end.

"The side that borders my land. Is it a crime to admit I admired your grandmother's gardens along with everybody else in town? Enough to paint them?"

We lock eyes.

"Why do you care so much, Miss Landers? You act like this painting mystery has the meaning of life."

"Like any normal human being, I'm curious. The way you're holding back just makes it worse."

"Curiosity killed the cat, kitten."

That wins me a hateful look like she's about to lunge for my jugular. I try not to laugh.

"One more time. Why are your paintings in my house?"

Goddamn. *Relentless.*

"If you must know, it was a simple trade between neighbors. Nothing deeper. Now drop it."

"It's *my* grandma and my house. I'm not letting you off easy." She pops out of her chair, takes one step toward me, and stops. "What trade? She got five paintings and you got what?"

A few rough seconds of silence burn by before I answer.

"*Honey.*"

"Honey?" She shakes her head like it's a foreign word.

"Honey. For Benson's tea."

"From her bees?" she says with disbelief.

"The only honey Lottie ever saw fit to put in jars. Good stuff. Now, if you're done with this bullshit—"

The anger in her eyes dissipates, and she turns with a heavy sigh. "Whatever, mister. Point made. I'll just stand by twiddling my thumbs until you need to yell at me for work again."

"Wait." I follow her when she starts moving.

"I'd rather die of cyanide poisoning," she says without glancing back.

Damn.

I shouldn't have snapped at her, but she just kept pushing. What other option did I have?

The only alternative was to tell her *why* I knew her grandmother so well, and that would be worse. Anything that provokes a thousand more questions from this hellcat is definitely worse.

Thankfully, she has an emotional skin like an elephant.

She'll get over being snapped at and come back to hound me before I know it.

I just wish I didn't have to leave it like this, so I follow her out of my office.

Just smooth it over, you fuck.

Don't let her leave like this.

But the longer I trail her, the harder it is to find the words. There's no subject to change, not when anything else involves work that's done or an inn she'd rather sell to a corpse over me.

When I drag after her to the front foyer, Miss Landers is already out the door, and Benson is staring out the window, watching her start down my long, winding drive.

He turns to face me. "What did you do to her today?"

"What? *Nothing.*"

"She blew out of here like a rocket, boss. She wouldn't even stop to talk to me like she usually does."

"She's being dramatic," I snap. "We had a disagreement—a goddamned stupid one. Nothing serious."

If only I believed my own words.

Benson stares at me like I'm the only stupid thing in the room.

I wonder if he's right.

"We just argued about the paintings I gave Lottie years ago. Is that so dire?"

"It's your business," he answers glumly.

Fucking ridiculous.

And I don't just mean today, where we went at each other like snapping turtles over nothing.

It's the fact that I almost kissed her, and we never talked about it. I ignored her for days over a few simple texts, only to lose my shit like a moody sixteen-year-old.

What's my malfunction?

What does Jennifer Landers do to me?

Obviously, this would be a bigger flaming wreck than it already is if I'd followed through on that kiss. Much less other desires that burn me down every time I look at her.

And today, my choices were either lie to her or admit the hellish truth, and it's no contest I took the gentle, simpler option.

I'm not reliving the worst parts of my life with this strange siren who wasn't supposed to blow into my world like a force of nature.

I don't do secrets and vulnerability anymore.

The last time I did, it cost me everything.

* * *

I WAKE up the next morning drowning in guilt.

Have I mentioned I fucking hate that I'm not the ironclad soulless ghoul the rest of the world sees?

She's grieving, and I didn't even try to be nice.

I just barked shit at her until she left me alone.

I could've had more tact.

I could've shown I had the tiniest heart without spilling everything.

Still, this will blow over. I just need to act casual.

I'll let you know when we're heading to Seattle. As soon as I hear from Louise, I send midday, fishing for a reply to judge how pissed she is.

The total nonresponse by evening says *very.*

Snarling a few curses, I pick up my phone and try again.

I received some interesting ideas to finalize the video montage. Meet me for drinks at Murphy's so we can discuss?

The fact that I add a question mark—rather than making it an order—tells me how fucked this is.

And I know I'm teetering on the brink of disaster when the cold shoulder continues.

Goddamn.

Before, she always responded to work.

At this stage, I hope she doesn't abruptly quit. She's given my creatives the swift kick in the ass they needed to help put this town on the map and build the credibility I need with folks who make the laws here.

I'm going over Dad's latest bills, contemplating a third round of humiliation by text, when my phone finally pings.

Jenn: I'm off the clock until you need me in Seattle.

Miles: Didn't you march over here insisting my paintings should be in the promos? Yesterday, you were happy to keep working.

She doesn't respond to that.

Beautiful.

I don't hear from her for another whole day, and I can't bury my ego enough to go chasing her again.

Playing it cool isn't working. There's one option left.

Apologize.

I suppose I owe her one, and even if she takes her property to her grave, she's crucial to finishing this project strong.

Boiling with nerves I can't believe I have, I jump in my SUV and blow through the gate, on the way to her place.

It's only a couple minutes of agonizing on the road, convincing myself I can sort this out without leaving her in tears or kissing her into oblivion.

Only, when I pull up, there's a shiny red pickup truck parked in front of Bee Harbor.

God. Fucking. Damn.

The Playing Card.

I should tear back down the dusty road and go home, if only I didn't see him so clearly in the house with her. Alone.

Fuck this. Why should this dolt in flannel run me off?

I came to apologize, so I will.

If Ace-hole has a problem with that, he can take it up with me.

I kill my engine and stomp to the front door, banging on it several times.

Coffee's deep bark comes first. Cream is right behind him with shriller yips.

My heart hovers in my throat and my head is full of all the awful shit I might be interrupting when Jenn pulls the door open. Her eyes instantly pop with surprise.

"Oh. Do you need something, Mr. Cromwell?"

Ace strolls in behind her with that overly friendly golden retriever look on his face. I'd love to punch that blankness right off his ugly mug.

What the hell, man? She needs backup answering the door?

"Coffee," I say as politely as possible, ignoring them both.

My old buddy bounds toward me and rears up to lick my face, chasing every bit of attention as I scratch behind his ear.

"Down!" Jennifer grabs his collar and tugs him back. "Do you have to get him so worked up?"

"I'm just saying hello." I push the door open and walk inside.

She gives me just enough space to enter and anchors herself to the ground, folding her arms.

"Listen, I came to apologize for our misunderstanding over the paintings."

"Paintings? What happened?" Ace butts in.

I shoot him a look straight from hell before my eyes flick back to her.

"I was rude to you. I shouldn't have gotten so defensive and blown everything out of proportion," I say roughly.

131

She staggers back with surprise and my eyes fall on the coffee table behind them.

There's a fresh case of beer sitting there and—four hand-picked roses beside it.

My heart fucking detonates.

This jackal.

This talking beef slab wrapped in flannel thinks he's going to sink his dick in my kitten?

The whole world turns red, and I have to count breaths to keep myself from launching past her and grabbing his throat.

No, I'm not stupid enough to assault a man for no good reason. I've made it damn clear I have no claim to her.

But if I'm not careful, I might be dumb enough to turn this miserable apology into a screaming match.

I think those flowers also bother me because they're so familiar. I've seen them before.

Then the chucklefuck leans in and whispers, "Jenn, if you don't want to talk to this guy—"

She raises a hand.

"It's cool. He's just making more of everything than it deserves."

Her comment pulls my attention away from him—away from the coffee table that tells me everything I need to know—and before those cool jade pools for eyes waver, I see a red toolbox beside the fireplace. My eyes naturally tick up to where the picture hangs.

Fuck.

Now I know where I've seen those flowers before.

What kind of shitbrained punk picks flowers out of a girl's own garden to give her?

Scratch that. I don't care. I shouldn't.

I should shut my yap and finish what I came here for, and nothing more.

"I hope this isn't a bad time." It takes major effort to keep my voice light.

"No. Ace just dropped by to help me fix a light fixture." She combs a hand through her auburn hair and glances at him.

I look at the oaf, who stands there like a stack of bricks in his always red shirt.

"I'll help you. No charge. I need to make amends for what happened—"

"Cromwell, chill. There was no misunderstanding. I understood you perfectly. You don't need to—"

"We were just finishing up." Ace flashes a disarming smile and sends her a hungry look I want to peel right off his face. "You two need some privacy, I get it. I'll be upstairs so you guys can talk."

The way she smiles up at him guts me. "Thanks, Ace."

It's so different from the way she looks at me.

Even her tone is all butter.

I lift one corner of my mouth in a snarl, fighting the nausea swirling in my gut, counting every hellish second until he's upstairs.

"So, I appreciate the gesture, but there's no need for this," she starts.

"Bullshit. I shouldn't have lashed out earlier. The truth is I painted those flowers for your grandmother specifically because I admired her gardens. Nobody put in the effort like Lottie Risa." A surface-level truth, but for now, it'll have to do. I nod at the coffee table. "For the record, I'd never pick a girl's own flowers for her."

"Here we go. I thought you were being nice for once." She rolls her eyes. "Lay off Ace. He's a good guy."

She's defending him now?

Damn.

Have they already—

No. Don't let your stupid jealous monkey brain go there.

I shift my weight, searching for words.

Technically, she isn't wrong.

If he didn't have his nose trapped up her butt, he'd be a

perfectly competent worker. Decent enough for Lottie to keep him around for years, even if I still want to bash his head in.

Nothing is the right thing to say.

She crosses her arms.

"So, what else? I get the impression you aren't done," she ventures.

I clear my throat, all simmering tension and uncertainty.

"You might remember how your grandmother used to leave flowers for every grave at the cemetery in town?" I start slowly.

She nods. "Yeah. She did that a few times a year. One time school let me out early and I went with her on Memorial Day to put little flags on all the veterans' graves."

"Do you remember the day you saw me coming out of the general store with the flowers and asked me if 'she was hot?'"

She smiles reluctantly, trying to hide it.

"How could I forget? That's the day you ghosted the whole crew."

"My mother's buried in the Pinnacle Pointe cemetery. I was visiting her grave, a family ritual of sorts I do a couple times a year."

A ritual that's my responsibility alone because my father can't anymore.

Her mouth drops. "Oh. I'm so sorry..."

I hold up a hand, cutting her off.

There's only room for one apology at a time, and right now I'm on deck.

"It's okay. Not long after I moved here, I noticed someone kept bringing fresh flowers to her grave and I knew it wasn't the grounds people. They don't have the resources for that."

"Gram did *all* the graves. Even the ones from the 1800s who don't have any people around who'd remember them," she says softly.

"She was too kind for this world. One day, I ran into Lottie while she was laying a bouquet at each grave and saying a quick prayer. I had to thank her. We had our first real conversation." I pause, pulled back to that day when my family falling apart was so recent, so raw, so real. "I knew she owned the place next door. I saw her in passing, but I had no idea she was the flower lady. Before I knew it, she started bringing flowers and honey over. She made me feel at home in a town where I hardly knew anyone. She also had the best damned blueberry-honey cheesecake in the known universe—*in Benson's opinion*," I add quickly.

I've already said too much.

Jennifer Landers does not need to know I have a terrible sweet tooth.

She laughs, but a single tear slides down her face she's slow to wipe away.

"Oh, a lot of folks would agree. But I have to say, you're scaring me, Cromwell."

I cock my head, searching her eyes.

"You're making me think you might have a heart bigger than a raisin."

I raise a brow. "Why would you say that? We were doing so well."

"Because you're still a liar. *You* obviously loved Gram's cheesecake. Why can't you just admit it?"

"Benson," I bite off, turning away as my face heats behind my shadow of a beard.

"I'm grateful for the heart-to-heart. Really. But all of this could have waited until tomorrow. You didn't have to drag your-self over here so late," she says.

"The hell I didn't." The conviction in my voice surprises me. "I'm just glad I got here before Ace started working on *your* wiring."

I know I'm risking her throwing me out.

I don't care.

When her eyes soften, I'm surprised. She scrapes her teeth against her bottom lip and moves closer. "And what if he does?"

Her chin tilts up.

Her face is already red as it comes as close to mine as it was on my boat that night I should have taken her lip with my teeth.

I missed my chance once.

Never again.

Before I can ground myself, I grab her and throw her against the wall.

My lips chase hers like a hunter.

My tongue flicks against her soft lips ravenously, forcing her mouth open.

I don't have to try hard.

She melts like her grandmother's honey, all willing sweetness.

Fuck, I've never tasted anything so sweet.

And if I could ignore the hurt in my cock, the braising sting to take more, to take everything, I might never come up for air.

I'm sure she's caught in the same delicious pain.

Her arms curl around my neck, pleading for more.

I kiss her until I can't, tearing myself away with a scorched breath.

"Tell Ace to fuck off, kitten. No one—no one but me—ever touches you."

Every word makes me more delirious.

I don't recognize who or what the fuck I am saying this, spouting jealous demands I've never made to any other woman.

But her eyes burn back into mine, green witchfire enchanting my soul.

She nods, her nails dragging through my hair, urging my mouth back to hers.

This time, it's incandescent, a slow burn with a building hunger.

Her tongue explores mine, and I meet her urgency, groaning into her mouth, filling her with the voice of my need because I can't fill her with anything else.

Not fucking yet.

Soon.

Her leg skims farther up my calf and her fingers roam my hair, scratching sweetly at my scalp.

"It's all—" Ace's voice falls flat. "Finished."

I look up from Jennifer without pulling away.

I hold on tighter.

Here he comes, ambling down the stairs. The expression on his face says everything.

He's seen us. He's shocked as hell.

I made him watch my tongue claiming her.

Jenn's still flushed as she goes stock-still, frozen and unsure what to do next.

I'm about to take over and tell him to scram when she says, "Thank you."

"No problem." He grabs his toolbox. "Hey, it's late. I should get going."

She sprints away from me, straightening her clothes, throwing a confused look back at me.

"Ace, wait. If you want to talk about the next steps for the inn—"

"Tomorrow, maybe. Sorry. I have an early job in the morning." He damn near rips the door off as he runs out.

My heart bangs triumphantly until it hits me.

When did a gushing apology become an outright conquest?

What the fuck have I done?

I just pushed a woman *who works for me* against the wall and kissed her like tomorrow's the apocalypse. Hell, the only reason it didn't go further was because the flannel fuckboy barged in.

I did this with someone else in her house.

Even if she wasn't an employee, it would have been insanely disrespectful.

This...this isn't me.

This is my dick highjacking my senses and driving me off a cliff.

I'm sure it's just a matter of time until she realizes how bad this is, possibly mere seconds.

"I should probably go too," I tell her, the instant she looks back at me.

Her brows dart up. "What? Really?"

"Yeah. I'm glad we had this—talk, Miss Landers. I'll update you soon about Seattle."

Shit, shit, shit.

Shit!

"Miles—"

I bolt out the door without glancing back until I've thrown myself in my vehicle face-first.

When I look up again, she's gone, just a wilted silhouette behind the blinds with two big dogs next to her.

IX: NO MORE SUGAR (JENN)

*O*h my God.

Oh my God, what was that?

I haven't heard from the prince of jackasses since he kissed me and ran, and that was three days ago.

Three of the most bewildering, soul-crushing days of my life, right up there with Gram's funeral and that time I had to save Pippa from her own case of heartbreak with a freezer full of ice cream therapy.

I'm not so lucky. I can't even work up the courage to crawl to the grocery store for a couple pints of banana-chocolate ambrosia.

I'm tired.

So drained with his games.

But I should've known the second I opened my door.

That's the thing about vampires. They'll only wreck carnage if you invite them in.

But the jerkwad was so sincere with that apology and his sob story about Gram. I sure didn't mind when he ravished my lips until they were sore the next morning.

I hate that I can still taste him.

I definitely regret that it wasn't Ace.

Don't get me wrong. Ace isn't Dracula meets Henry Cavill hot.

He doesn't have the whole chaotic broken bad boy vibe. He's less mysterious and less intriguing. He's not rich and all powerful.

But he's attractive.

He's muscular and good-hearted and *fine.*

If Gram were here, I'm sure she'd be ecstatic if he were the man I shacked up with.

Sweet baby Jesus, I wanted to be attracted to him—*I wanted him to drive a stake through the vampire's heart*—and I probably could have been if he was a halfway good kisser.

It didn't even need to be toe-curling, hair-bending, panty-soaking hot like that shameless attack Miles Cromwell made on my body.

But I'll never know now, will I?

Ace was a perfect gentleman. He made his move with flowers and it ended there.

All because Cromwell blindsided me just long enough to blow up my hilariously thin dating life.

Coffee comes bounding over, carrying his tug rope. I give in and play, almost toppling over, fighting him for it until my arms burn.

He loves it, of course, and so does Cream when she comes diving in to join us.

But I think I have some rage I need to work out, preferably without pulling the dogs' teeth or breaking my tailbone if I hit the floor.

There must be healthier ways to deal with rich dickheads.

Plus, the pups are always game to go outside.

Seeing a break in the rain, I might as well kill two birds with one stone. I get up and grab their leashes.

My phone pings before I can leash up Cream.

I pat her nose.

"Stay, girl. We'll leave in just a minute."

Awesome. It's a new email from Satan.

Miss Landers,

I roll my eyes. I'm still Miss Landers.

I've never seen a man who stays this formal after sucking my tongue.

Gotta love billionaire weirdos and their emotional damage.

Dave will email you the initial edits soon. Your feedback will be appreciated and help guide further edits.

Cool. Let Dave email me then when he puts down his pipe.

Jerkoff.

I actually make a stroking motion with my hand, which confuses the eavesdropping Dobermans.

Sighing, I shove the phone in my pocket and scratch Cream's head. I give her a couple salmon treats from a bag by the door before we head out.

"Good job." I get Coffee on his leash, treat him, and take off with the only creatures here who don't drive me insane every waking second.

We've barely made it through the gardens when my phone pings again. Another message from hell.

MISS LANDERS,

If the silent treatment is the punishment you've chosen, so be it.

I know you'll still read this.

See the attached link to a cloud folder with preliminary edits of several videos for the Pinnacle Pointe tourism project. Tell me what you think whenever you stop hating me.

Yours,

M. Cromwell

Chief Executive Officer, Cromwell-Narada

ALL ASS.

All the time.

I use my whole body weight to pull the leashes tight enough to bring the dogs to a halt and hit play on the first video. I need an immediate distraction from Miles and his infinite crap.

The video starts with the company logo that looks like it's aimed at YouTube or other streaming sites.

It's a basic montage with the lighting adjusted.

Beautiful places and beautiful people.

Lots of smiles.

Quarter second glimpses of majestic cliffs and decadent Irish pub food.

In other words, it's fifteen seconds of rapid-fire commercial fluff that flies by too fast to really see anything.

I regret my life.

How? How did they do this?

They got good video. Sarah practically memorized the whole ten pages of editing pointers I wrote up for video. I made sure of it.

So why is this hacked up into some kind of 1990s ad that looks like it'd play between daytime soaps?

My freaking parents would barely bat their eyes.

The name of the town only flashes for three seconds.

"Ugh!" I sputter, cringing as I flip to the next video.

Yep, yep, more of the same.

The same stiff, overpolished corporate commercialism that's going to bomb on all the big digital platforms and cause brutal costs on the ones where it could work. Barely.

But it does make my response very easy.

I open my email, hit reply, and type a simple answer.

FRANKLY, the videos suck and so do you.
Never yours,
Jenn

. . .

WHY DOES it feel so good to type my name?

Cream whines since we're not moving, nosing at the little pouch of treats I clipped to my belt. She just wants a fish nugget, I know, but it feels like she's trying to tell me not to be stupid.

I groan and throw them both treats.

As much as I want to, I can't send that last part.

I have to stay professional.

I have to muddle through this.

I have to make sure I'm not setting myself up for another apology and another kiss that occupies my brain.

So I delete the last four words and hit Send.

We're walking again, taking the winding paths between town and the shore.

A few bright butterflies dart past and the Dobermans stomp their paws.

At least they're happy as the breeze blows in their faces.

I regret everything.

A hundred and fifty thousand dollars is a lot of money, but I shouldn't have taken it.

He was trouble the second he showed up on my doorstep.

I'm still in shock it isn't just a dream turned nightmare.

Leaving and ignoring me after what he said that night—*no one but me ever touches you*—it's more than obvious he played me like a fiddle.

He played me *again.*

When Ace left in disbelief, Miles won, and the game ended.

I'm so flipping stupid.

A few steps later, Coffee breaks into a jog, and Cream hustles to keep pace, dragging me along.

Probably for the best. There's no point in endlessly rehashing this.

There's no undoing it.

The dogs know our route by this point. They drag me past the beach. I'm so stuck in my head I can't even register its beauty today.

This is why I don't do relationships—or much of anything with guys.

Pippa's near disaster proved how messy love gets, and my life is crazy enough with an inheritance I'm not sure I can keep and two giant dogs who need me.

No matter how rough it gets, I don't want to sell the inn.

But I have to keep in mind the town's richest, most toxic resident is also my only neighbor.

Maybe I should reconsider if I can't get the tourists.

I'll take refuge in one thing, though. The fact that I don't do much kissing or even dating is probably why that joke of a make-out scene felt like such a big deal.

It has nothing to do with Miles Cromwell.

Nothing.

I'm just starved for male attention, and I can find that with someone else.

Anyone.

Especially if Ace doesn't think I'm an absolute bitch for what I did to him.

Believe me, I *know* I am.

My thoughts never settle before we've turned and made our way back to Bee Harbor.

My mood must rub off. Coffee isn't done with his walk, and Cream follows his lead as usual, both of them restlessly making their trademark Doberman grumbles when I start for the back door.

So we wind through Grandma's gardens instead, taking the paths slowly.

When I say gardens, I mean what's left of them.

I'm sad that they're a season out of shape, overgrown and erratic, even though I've made myself come out here once a week for basic weeding.

Truthfully, they were starting to fade a little even before her health began failing. She couldn't keep up with everything. Some of the flower beds are at least a full year wild.

But the plants must have strong roots to keep thriving like this.

They just need shaping and more attention than I've been giving them. I need to get a better look and take some notes for later.

So I unleash the dogs and leave them to run, keeping a close watch to make sure they don't Houdini their way past the wooden fence again.

While I'm strolling my own meandering path through the property, inspecting the flowers, I come to the old bee boxes.

My heart flutters.

They're the inn's namesake and they've been dormant for a while now, ever since Gram couldn't manage them the last year or two.

The bees have had a rough time lately with plummeting colony numbers, plus the constant threat of murder hornet intrusions all over Washington. A single armored monster can take out a whole colony of honeybees all too easy.

It's sad.

The breeze picks up and the wind chime hanging in the hemlock tree above the bee box draws my attention upward. The brilliant blue wind chime spins, throwing rainbow streaks of sunlight everywhere.

A few leaves are already turning yellow as summer grinds on. The blue sea glass stands out even more against the green and gold.

I smile so hard I'm woozy.

I was with Gram the day she got that glass.

A bittersweet memory turned memorial to love.

We were a few miles outside of Pinnacle Pointe, the lonely place where the ocean cliffs turn more rugged. The beach there is almost hidden, pristine, and the water so blue it sparkles.

A rare oasis of color and smooth sand by Washington beach standards. So many others are darker, murky and piled high with rocks that haven't sat long enough to be worn down by centuries of waves.

Even better, this area never gets enough traffic to litter the beach like other areas do. It seems like it's still a secret, even among some locals, and that's why we come here.

Laughing, I wade into the water until it brushes my knees.

I'm not allowed to go farther, but I don't need to.

In a few seconds, an unexpected wave will bowl me over onto the wet sand, and I'll giggle and stand up again.

"Jennifer, time for lunch!" Gram calls, looking over with sparkling eyes.

I run back up the dry sand and drop down on the blue checkerboard picnic blanket spread over the sand.

Gram puts half a turkey sandwich and a huge slice of watermelon on a plate and passes it to me. Grandpa already has his plate loaded, ready to eat.

"Hang on, Lottie. Be right back." Grandpa stands and walks away into the distance.

"What is it?" Gram calls, concern lining her face.

He doesn't answer until he's back at the picnic blanket, one hand tucked behind his back.

"A present for my girls. Sea glass," he says proudly, passing it to Gram. Her lips curl with genuine joy. "You'll make something beautiful from it like you always do. That's what you do with old things." He chuckles knowingly. "You're still doing it with me, sweetheart."

"Oh, you. I didn't have to try. You were already perfect down to your soul," Gram says, leaning in for a kiss that's as lazy and sweet as the summer evening.

Be still, my heart.

I was only nine or ten years old, but I decided then that's what I wanted for my life. What my grandparents had.

If I learned anything from watching my grandparents hand in hand at family reunions and holidays, taking care of each other as they aged, and Gram loyally mourning Grandpa for so long it swallowed her up, it's that I'd rather be single than settle for anything less than a love like theirs.

A love so real it consumes you.

I try to picture myself on the beach with Ace and a small child.

Not a serious wish, of course.

He's just a placeholder for Anyman, a kindhearted guy who has his crap together and wants to settle down and share dreams.

Somehow, I can't see him taking the time to collect sea glass. The picnic would be pleasant enough, but I don't think I'd ever look at him with the kind of breathless awe Gram had for Grandpa, or the endless sparkle Grandpa had for her.

I just can't see it.

But my phone rings, dashing my thoughts.

I swipe the green icon absently, hoping it's not a stupid robocall.

"Hello?"

"Jennifer—"

The hairs on the back of my neck stand up the second I hear his voice.

"I'm Jennifer now?"

He clears his throat.

"Miss Landers." His voice hardens to cold professionalism. "I think you should come over, if you're free, so we can discuss your comments about the campaign in person."

"Considering how things went the last time we were alone? No. *Hell no.*"

"I crossed lines I shouldn't have. I know. Unfortunately, there's no way around our contractual obligations, so I suggest we try to put it aside like civilized people and—"

He must hear my teeth grit and stops mid-sentence.

Oh, I'll show him civilized.

"Let's get one thing straight," I say. "I'm not your pawn. I don't mind telling you your creative team lacks creativity, or that you suck, because I'm providing a service until my contract expires. That's it."

He's quiet for a minute.

147

I wonder if I've caught him off guard.

"I just want you to understand it shouldn't have happened. That's not what I typically do with—"

I laugh out loud. "With what? Contractors? Or did you mean women like me? Look, I know I'm good enough to stage your photo shoots and help your video editors. But if you think it should end there..."

"Are you through?"

I bite my lip. "Actually, Miles, I'm just getting started."

"I was going to say that's not what I do with employees."

"Well, I'm not your employee. Technically, I'm a free agent."

"Technically, we still have a close working relationship. You know what I mean, just like you know it was highly improper."

"Whatever. You want feedback? Here it is. The team rocks at piecing together commercial-grade videos. The problem is, a social media campaign isn't supposed to look so polished. You're running into the same problem we had at Winthrope before we brought Pippa on board. If you want to reach the younger, trendier crowds, you *need* flaws. You need honesty. People don't like being sold to. Millennials were over it, and Gen Z thinks commercials are Boomer relics. I know you're trying to sell this little town, not ad space on your stations, but it's the same thing. This campaign has to be organic. Things like old bee boxes and honey and homey Irish pubs are what Pinnacle Pointe is all about. So are walking trails and the quiet little shops in town. This is as picturesque as the Pacific Northwest gets. Small-town bliss meets windswept beaches. Sailboats and solitude. Good company, when you actually want it. That's it. That's the whole town. No one walks around looking like a sun-kissed model here and there are no luxury resorts worth thirty one-second slides thrown together in a collage that's so fast, it hurts to look at."

He's quiet for a moment, taking it all in.

"Well?" I press him.

"You're right. Painfully right. That's why you should be in

Seattle. You need to coach them, lay this all out for the team as clearly as you did for me. Without that insight in their faces, I think we both know we're doomed for a lackluster finish." He sighs. "I'll have them clear their schedules tomorrow for you. This is top priority."

"Tomorrow? Um, I do have a life here, you know? I can't just pack up and leave."

Frick.

Maybe I should have just agreed to his office sit-down. Dealing with the devil in person has to be better than being sent to Seattle on a whim.

"Since you were so good about reminding me you're a contractor, you're contractually obligated to be in my offices at my request, Miss Landers. You leave *tonight*."

The world starts spinning.

"But—"

"Don't worry, I won't leave you stranded to figure out arrangements. I'll have Benson take care of whatever you need, whether it's paying Mr. Fix-It to continue his renovations or a dog sitter for your lovely hounds." His words are sincere. Like he actually cares he's making my life insane on such short notice.

Like he actually cares about me.

I almost smile, but I remember he's the reason I'm being exiled from paradise in the first place. And after the last two incidents, I know better than to smile—or believe anything Miles Cromwell says.

"Just give me some time to think about this," I say, finding my voice. But the line has gone weirdly silent and I look at the screen. "Hello?"

The screen blinks.

Disconnected.

Holy hell.

If I hadn't agreed to his terms, I'd fly through his door and curse him out. But he's right about one thing—I only have myself to blame.

Looks like I'm going to go to Seattle after all, and I'm getting this horrible job done.

At least if this torture session drives more visitors to Pinnacle Pointe, I might be able to ride the coattails and snag a few guests for Bee Harbor.

Only, I can't stand the thought of leaving my dogs here alone with some rando stranger.

So, after an hour-long session over the phone with a lot of begging and IOUs, I get my parents to agree to put us up for a few days.

This should be fun. Especially when my parental units are into the whole white everything modern style and the dogs love puddles.

I get packed, convince Coffee and Cream to get in the car, and head for the small airport that's only for private planes and cargo two towns over. We wait there for hours since the plane doesn't come in until after ten o'clock.

Getting them on the sleek private jet Cromwell sends takes time and a hundred treats.

Thankfully, they're exhausted from all the fussing and sleep through the flight. I'm able to enjoy forty minutes of riding in a flying hotel on wheels, complete with a Bloody Mary snuck to me from a sympathetic attendant.

Once we land, I have to lure the dogs in the car that picks us up.

It's almost two a.m. by the time I get settled in Seattle, and I should be at the office at seven o'clock sharp according to the team chat.

I sleep like the dead and I don't think the weird dreams start until near dawn.

I'm on the secret beach again.

The same oasis of swirling waters and sapphire blue that matches the spotless sky seamlessly.

It looks like that memorable day with my grandparents, except my whole perspective has shifted.

I'm not a little girl anymore, laughing and wading through the water.

I'm on a picnic blanket with a dark-haired man, and we're watching a tiny girl with long dark hair wade knee-deep in the ocean.

"Rose, time for lunch!" I call. My heart swells when she looks at me.

Wow. The girl has the most beautiful blue-grey eyes.

"Five more minutes, Mommy?" Her adorable smile cuts me in two, especially when Coffee and Cream come bounding over, splashing like overcaffeinated gazelles in the tide.

"Two," I say, holding up two fingers.

"Two!" She mirrors me, sticking up her chubby hand.

The man I still haven't looked at twines his fingers through mine. "We're negotiating now, huh?"

"She's too cute not to."

"Which doesn't mean she gets to decide."

"Maybe so." I grin. "But that gives us two more minutes."

He unlaces our fingers and draws an invisible heart on the top of my hand. "Not enough time for what I'll do to you, kitten."

Time blurs in the sweetest kiss.

I giggle. "Rose, your two minutes is up. Come on, and bring the dogs!"

She totters over with the Dobermans protectively flanking her. They all fall down on the picnic blanket with us. I hand her half a turkey sandwich and some watermelon spears.

"Hang on," the dark-haired man says. He gets up and walks away without explanation.

I frown.

It's not until he comes back to the picnic blanket and hands me a long, twisted piece of sea glass that I realize who he is.

But before he can tell me it's mine now because I'm so good at making things beautiful, I look down at the object in my hand.

It's bigger, sharper, muddier—and much redder—than the piece of glass Gram turned into a lovely ornament.

And I think that redness is blood.

I jerk awake, gasping so loudly the dogs perk up on the floor.

"What the hell was that?" I mutter.

So much for keeping my dreams free from vampire bosses. Apparently, I can see the future so clearly it hurts, right down to the kid named Rose.

But that bloody dagger-like glass...

Is it just a subconscious warning? I'm definitely due for one of those.

But I realize something else, too.

I've never been one to create things out of nothing the way Gram did. I won't be making a sea glass wind chime anytime soon, but I do know how to showcase other people's creativity.

Miles recognized that talent pretty fast. It took me years to figure it out, and I still don't think my parents agree, always so sure I'm destined for bigger and better things in the safe, stuffy corporate world.

Whatever.

"Just a dream," I whisper.

Dreams don't mean anything. Do they?

They're figments of stress and that frozen zucchini-Alfredo pizza I regret stuffing my face with before I turned in for the night.

I glance at my phone. Almost five thirty.

Since I'm not going back to sleep after that...

I need to forget about it.

I also desperately need coffee.

My other Coffee paces back and forth in front of my bedroom door, up and alert and anxious to explore his new digs.

"Okay, okay, boy. Just a minute." I yawn, stretching my arms.

His head whips from the closed door to where I sit in bed. I can see him getting ready to jump into bed with me.

"No!" Before I can get the words out, there's a big pile of dog licking my face. I stroke his long back with an exasperated groan, and Cream is right behind him in a flash. "You can't do that here, guys. If my mom sees you on the furniture, you're stew meat."

They don't care.

They don't follow me off the bed until I'm up and moving.

There's just enough time to take them for a walk before going into the office. They'll need to go to the bathroom anyhow.

Being dragged around a Seattle street by two hulking Dobermans is worse than any walk in Pinnacle Pointe. The traffic is scarier, too.

It's the city noise that excites them, the increasing morning activity, strangers and huge delivery trucks and birds darting this way and that.

I have to feed them right away when we come back just to calm them down. Then I shower and head to the office, saying a prayer for my parents as they're left alone with two anxious dogs for the day.

The only good thing about being sent here on a whim is that I'm alone. There's no raging bosshole and the dark kisses he clearly regrets.

I don't want to be here, but I'm almost back in my element during the Winthrope days when I'd power walk into the office bright and early.

This, I can manage, especially if it's Miles free.

With any luck, I'll get the creatives on the right track and be back at Bee Harbor before Miles comes back to Seattle.

As I walk into the lobby, though, my phone vibrates in my purse.

Are you settled in?

Guess who.

One minute on the floor and I'm already scowling.

I don't bother responding. He knows I'm from Seattle and shouldn't have any problem getting "settled in."

I'm not sure what he's trying to accomplish, but I'm a hundred percent *through* with his mind games.

If only my dreams agreed.

X: NO ONE'S FOOL (MILES)

The minute I told her to come over for a meeting, I knew she'd say no.

It gave me the perfect excuse to banish her instead.

Still, I shouldn't have shipped her off to Seattle on such short notice. It fucking eats at me, along with the glaring fact that lately everything I do with this girl is *wrong.*

But I needed distance.

So did she.

Space is the only cure before my lips pounce on hers again— let alone something worse. I'm goddamned lucky Jenn's instincts are better than mine.

If she'd actually shown up at my place when I asked, I know what would've happened.

I can see it so clearly my blood becomes magma.

The sweetest forbidden fuckery of my life.

It would've happened like lightning splitting the sky, intense and unstoppable.

Multiple times.

Against the wall.

On my desk.

In my bed.

Hell, anywhere I could flatten her and enter her. Anywhere I could redefine our relationship with hard, deep strokes and bruising kisses.

Jennifer Landers is a sex kitten wrapped in a fearless, man-eating smile.

Everything I thought I was immune to.

Just the type of woman who could strike me blind, encouraging my dick to ruin me *again*.

That's not even touching the fact that she's forbidden by Cromwell-Narada company rules older than I am.

A fling with an employee—contractor or not—is almost as disastrous as the last time I let my cock do the thinking, and that destroyed me.

Benson comes in with a shot glass and a worried glance. He knows better than to play my shrink, and he's been around long enough to give me the only medicine I'll take for my waking mindfuck.

"Your scotch, sir." He sets the thick glass neatly on my desk, one large ice cube rattling inside.

"Thanks. How was her trip? You arranged for someone to show her around the office, yes?"

"Sarah Valencia was happy to oblige, and so is Louise. From what I've gathered, there was some trouble getting the dogs on the plane. They've never flown private either. Once that was settled, the rest was smooth sailing. No need to worry. This is just a trip home for her. She's settling in just fine."

Are you? The unspoken question hangs in the air.

"I'm not worried, Benson. I'm being mindful of a difficult time in her life."

"Of course." I can tell by his tone he's just agreeing with me to be polite.

Taking a long sip of my drink, I glance at him over the edge of the glass.

"You made sure she has everything she needs?"

Benson chuckles. "Miss Landers is fine, Mr. Cromwell. A

town car took her to her parents' from the airport and picked her up this morning."

I'm relieved she's staying with her folks rather than some impersonal hotel, even if she has Winthrope connections and could've surely landed a spot in one of Seattle's finest properties —minus the dogs.

Fuck, I miss them already.

Without the usual commotion of the dogs running, occasionally creating mayhem along our border when they escape Lottie's old wooden fence and dig under my wrought iron, life is extra lonely.

"May I ask if you're any closer to securing the property next door?" Benson asks.

His question plunges me back into reality like an ice bath.

"No," I throw back.

Fuck no.

After the smoking kiss I stole from her, I'm sure she's invented new ways to despise my dumb ass.

Benson definitely doesn't need to find out about that.

It's just between us—and yeah, the clown wrapped in flannel who was there to witness me stealing his girl.

I only wish like hell I'd stolen her for good.

Just like I wish I had a different answer.

I wish the land was her only good asset.

"Your father's nurse called requesting espresso," Benson says, smiling as I raise an eyebrow. "It seems he remembered a trip to Rome with your mother, and suddenly his mint breakfast tea wasn't good enough."

"Do it. Fly the shit in from Italy overnight if you have to," I clip.

My grip is too tight on the glass. Benson notices as the ice rattles.

"I assumed as much. It's already done," he says affably, taking that as his cue to exit.

Thank God.

I'll pay through the nose for anything that helps Dad remember, to keep that love for my mother he lived for alive just a little while longer.

It's a hopeless battle, sure, like trying to keep a candle burning through a bone-stripping winter night.

And I have to shoulder this fight alone because Mother isn't here anymore.

All because I let a stupid slip of passion tear her away from loving her fading husband just a little while longer. Because I couldn't *save her.*

That's why I have to get a fucking grip, no matter the cost.

That's why I can never taste Jenn again.

* * *

THE NEXT DAY, I sit at my desk, using a wide brush to swipe blue streaks across a fresh canvas.

Gradually, I move on to shades of black, brown, grey.

No idea what I'm painting yet, I'm letting the scene decide what it wants to be.

Soon, an animal's head starts to take shape. He has the body of a man.

Weird, but whatever.

I'll roll with it.

A few hours later, I hover over a scene that leaves me ambivalent.

My work isn't usually so erotic.

An Egyptian goddess with fiery streaks in her hair whose face is eerily familiar lays on a hammock made from palm leaves.

Her white dress flutters open in the wind, revealing a length of rosy skin up her thigh.

An Anubis-headed protector flanks her with the same rigid stance you always see in Egyptian art. When the hell did I start painting hieroglyphics? The beast is matched by another white-headed Anubis guard on the other side.

Too on the nose. I know.

It's not hard to figure out where this came from.

I rake a hand through my hair, pissed that I can't pry her out of my subconscious.

She's showing up in my damn art now—the *one* refuge I have where nothing else bothers me—and it feels like something else is off.

The longer I stare at the scene, it's not anything wrong with the dreamscape I've created from pure lust.

What's off is me.

Snarling, I throw my brush down on my palette.

Is this what it feels like when a man slowly loses his mind?

When he flirts with losing everything?

Ridiculous.

I don't know why, but it reminds me of another time in my life when my head was too screwed up to think.

*** * ***

Years Ago

"MILES, *come down for breakfast. You're going to be late again," Dad says gently.*

He's such a tall man, this giant shadow in my doorway, and it hurts to see him worried as hell. Both my parents, really.

The panic attacks started not long after my grandmother died. Maybe it had something to do with my bully, too, that pig-faced little shit named Ralphie who wouldn't let me live it down when I lost it, crying in the library after finishing the last book Grandmom ever gave me.

For three weeks, I took his crap while the other kids laughed.

For three weeks, he made squealing noises in my face, pushed me around in the hall, and did his damnedest to break me down into a teary mess again.

Children are cruel.

Rich boys at expensive academies are so much crueler.

One day, Ralphie overplayed his hand. When he whipped that dodgeball at my face and missed giving me a black eye by two inches, I had it.

Something snapped.

Something made of fists and bared teeth, boyish growls, and a grown-up rage.

By the time they pulled me off him, Ralphie needed immediate attention for his busted nose and I needed to wash his blood off my hands.

So much blood.

The other kids avoided me after that, though a few came creeping up with a quiet respect, telling me how Ralphie had it coming when he'd had a long reign of terror, insulting their fathers and ripping up their papers just for fun.

The attacks intensified—especially at night when I'd wake up stiff with nightmares—so much that I'd be drained by morning.

"Dad, no. Go away. I'm tired." I pull the blankets up over my head.

"Miles, you've got school. You can't stand too many absences. Get up."

"I'm sick." Not exactly a lie. But it's my soul, not my body.

"Sick or tired?" Dad demands. "There's a difference."

Is there, though?

All I know is I'm boneless. Literally.

Why should I leave this warm bed for another day where half the teachers stare at me like I'm a hand grenade and the others try to be my best friend?

I don't have the energy. The rest of the world sucks.

"I'm sick and tired," I finally say.

"Is that what I should say when I call the school?"

"Sure." I'm past caring, and no lecture about my future slipping away will bring me around.

With a heavy sigh, Dad drags himself across the room. I feel the bed sink with his weight as he sits.

"This is hard for me, too, little man. She was my mom. But I'm still going to work every day for you and your mother."

"I'm not grown like you, Dad. I don't have to run a whole company."

"Someday, you will. And being a grown-up doesn't make it hurt any less." The edge in his voice surprises me.

"I miss her like hell. She used to drive me to school when I was your age," he says with a wry smile.

"I know." My throat tightens, filled with hot lead.

My parents manage to bring me my homework for a solid week.

Every day becomes the same conversation, but my will to stay in bed is always stronger than his will to get me out of bed.

Eventually, I'm placed in a temporary homeschool program so absences don't count.

In fairness, Dad tries hard to help me find some joy that none of the therapists can.

He takes me to playgrounds and amusement parks.

Mom makes me help her cook. A near disaster every time since I was born without the chef gene, but I try.

We sail the Puget Sound, visit the zoo, take road trips to California when their schedule allows, and wherever else they can think of.

Nothing matters.

It won't bring Grandmom back or help me relate to people like less of a little psycho.

Then one day, Dad walks into my room with a big box. I watch, somewhat annoyed, as he opens it and pulls out a white square.

"What's this? More homework?" I ask.

"It is. But not from your teacher."

"Huh?" I blink as he pulls out another small box of what looks like paints. "I don't get it."

"You will, Miles. Painting was an old hobby of mine through

college. Your grandmother paid for a lot of classes when I was young, but I haven't had time to paint in a good long while. I was thinking of going outside and trying to paint a tree. It's been a long time. I'm not sure how good I'll be. Do you want to come with?"

I hate that I'm intrigued.

Will the canvas help empty the black abyss inside my head?

I'd never been much of a writer, but I wouldn't have to write for this.

What if all the dark and red swirling through my thoughts could stop? What if I could clear my head and be myself again?

I feign disinterest as I follow my father outside and get set up.

The first few pictures we work on are just blobs of color.

Then, slowly, my mother's favorite rosebush takes shape.

Present

PAINTING SAVED MY LIFE ONCE.

With a brush, I could create new worlds. Better places without any pain or sadness or a hundred million dollars going up in flames during the depths of a recession.

And until the holes opened in Dad's memory, painting was this special thing we shared.

Until I let down the man who showed me this heavenly world existed.

Until I let a snake of a woman upend everything.

And now, there's another woman crowding my head so much I can't even find my muse without her.

"Fuck," I mutter, not paying attention as I hoist up the canvas and hurl it across the room.

She can't take this part of me.

Tap. Tap.

Benson again, knocking at the door so lightly I'm sure he knows I'm in a mood.

"Come!" I belt out.

He strolls in holding a white envelope, his face tight.

I don't bother asking before I walk over and rip it out of his hands.

"I didn't know if you'd want to see it or if I should feed it straight into the fireplace. But given her recent... token at your mother's graveside, plus the proposal she sent to Louise, I thought you should decide, sir."

Anger lashes my veins.

I haven't read the return address on the envelope yet, but I know who it's from.

"Bring me another scotch. Hell, this time bring the bottle," I growl.

"Right away." He takes my empty glass with him.

I sit there in grim silence, staring at the envelope burning my fingers until he returns with the drink.

What the hell does Simone want?

Is she so fucking stupid she thinks I'll ever do business with her again?

He returns with the bottle and an extra glass. "I thought you might need more than one. You don't have to do this, you know. We can just throw it in the fire."

"No, you were right. I need to know what she's after." I drain the glass and wait for the burn in my gut before I open the letter.

DEAREST MILES,

Where does the time go?

Was it only yesterday when I was more than your mortal enemy? So much more.

. . .

FUCK HER SO MUCH. I pause, exhaling fire from my lungs before I read on.

I UNDERSTAND YOU WERE ANGRY. If I ever knew the tragic outcome that night, I swear I would have let you go. I wouldn't have tried so hard to make you relax. But that's water under the bridge.

Let me cut to the chase. We work in the same industry. We're both powerhouses. Once, we were so close to becoming allies, friends, lovers.

Do you still think being bitter rivals over something so personal benefits either of us?

Her stocks must be down or new investments aren't paying off. That's the only reason she'd ever be stupid enough to come crawling back with this half-hearted direct appeal.

Seriously. Can't we start over, purely for business?

A little cooperation. Mutually beneficial and respectful, just like we had years ago.

Woman, you are the last person breathing I will ever respect.

After what we shared—

Shared is an interesting way to put it, but I force myself to finish.

A mutual respect is the very least we should have. Even after all these years, I can't stand the way we parted, but I understand your grief.

Let's talk. Anytime.

Simone

I'VE BEEN TELLING her to fuck off for years.

Why is she still sniffing around?

It can't just be the charity magnet for good press Louise mentioned. Simone wouldn't be so bold.

The witch wants something. I just don't know what.

Balling her letter up, I toss it across the room like an abandoned wasp's nest. It stops on top of my discarded canvas.

"Mr. Cromwell," Benson starts, "if there's anything I can do—"

"Is she coming to Seattle?" I ask sharply.

"That depends," he answers slowly. "Any hint what she wants?"

"She didn't say. Only that we should forget the past and cooperate."

Benson frowns, his silver hair duller in the evening light.

"With all due respect, this is above my pay grade. Do what feels right."

Good advice, except for the fact that everything involving Simone Niehaus always feels wrong.

"I need to know if I should watch my back," I say, turning my glass.

"It sounds like you've made up your mind, but for the record, suspicion is warranted where she's concerned." He pauses. "And as a bonus, the sooner you return to the city, the faster you'll see a certain redhead."

I glare at him until he smiles.

"Get the yacht ready. It's due for servicing over there soon, anyway. We'll return by sea tonight," I say.

"On it."

He leaves me alone with my thoughts, something I've had too much of lately.

I fire another text to Jenn asking for a status update on the project.

It's the last thing that should be on my mind, but the way she tastes undid me. I'm not really expecting a response.

The way her leg crept over mine.

The way her hands gripped my hair.

Everything about that moment—until the fucking Playing Card ruined it—was perfect.

My phone pings. I smile when her name flashes in the notification.

Jenn: You'll get an update when there's something new. Now let me work.

Yep, she's still pissed, and she has every right to be.

My fingers move to the screen and type.

Miles: Daily updates.

Jenn: Noted.

Miles: Do you put a lid on updates for all your clients?

Jenn: Yes, actually.

Damn. Her cold responses are driving me mad.

Miles: Elaborate.

Jenn: It's best to set expectations up front, and chasing micro-managing emails eats up time that could be used on the project.

Miles: This isn't an hourly project. You know that.

Jenn: My rates reflect your estimate.

Miles: $150K should ensure all the time required to complete the project and update the CEO.

Jenn: Should. I'm happy to reimburse you and terminate the contract so you can find a better option if I'm not a good fit for you.

Fucking hell.

She's not playing around.

Miles: Put your claws away, kitten. That's not what I'm saying at all.

You're doing a great job. I'm just saying I'd like to hear from you more.

Jenn: And I'm saying I agreed to get the job done, not entertain you.

Miles: And I agreed to your outrageous premium for having to deal with me.

Jenn: My bad. It's not nearly enough.

How the fuck am I smiling?

Normally, I like to dole out punishment, not take it until I'm turning blue.

Before I can respond, my phone pings again.

Jenn: You don't dictate how I work.

Miles: And you dictate too much. If I didn't know better, I'd think you're an aspiring CEO yourself.

Jenn: And you're just a dick. No sane person would ever want your job.

That last line almost seems like things are back to normal with the feisty exchanges we've had before.

Almost.

Then another text lands.

Jenn: You know what really sucks, though? I see you as a person now. I'm less willing to sell you my property than I was the first day you came knocking.

Miles: For the last time, after everything that's happened, I don't care about the damn land anymore. I try to delete it, but it's too late and my finger slips.

Sent.

Fuck.

No one else makes me lose my head like this. How does she do it?

Jenn: Then why the games? What do you want?

Miles: What games?

Jenn: Never mind. How about you just let it go and let me get these videos your team butchered unedited enough so they're usable?

Miles: Because I told you I don't want your land? Is that the game you think I'm playing?

Jenn: Then you won't mind me talking to a realtor.

My blood heats.

Miles: What realtor? You got another offer? When did that happen?

I don't even care that she's breaching contract.

Jenn: See my point? I'm turning my phone off. Goodbye, Dracula.

Miles: Wtf? And you tell me I'm playing games?

When she doesn't answer, I call her, but she wasn't bluffing. It goes straight to voicemail.

I barely refrain from whipping my phone at the wall.

* * *

LATER, on the yacht, I ask Benson, "How do you win a woman back after you've pissed her off?"

"You're asking the wrong man. I'm thirty-five years out of the dating game and after my Millie passed, I'm not interested." He smiles out at the calm water.

Loyal to the end.

It's respectable and disgustingly sweet and entirely Benson.

"From what I remember, it depends on what you did to piss her off, sir."

"Dammit, I don't know." I'm pretty sure I have an idea.

"Somehow, I doubt that."

I throw up my hands and storm over to the wet bar. "Do you want a drink?"

"Sure."

I pour him a brandy.

"Shouldn't this be the other way around?"

"Not tonight. I need to control something." It's obviously not my life right now, spinning its way into a mountain like a falling jet.

We clink glasses and down our drinks in silence. Then I pour us another round.

Benson holds a hand up. "I'm done. I still have to drive when we arrive."

"Don't worry, old man. I'll hire a driver."

He chuckles. "You're replacing me on duty?"

"Tonight, you're designated drinking buddy." I pour another round and we share a knowing look.

The last time this happened was years ago, and Dad was the one pouring the drinks.

He takes half the shot.

"Miles?"

167

"Yes?"

"Gifts tend to ease a woman's wrath. But only meaningful ones. That doesn't mean she'll forgive you just because you bought her something nice—but she may quit throwing things long enough to let you speak."

It sounds too easy.

"It hasn't come to that yet—throwing things, I mean."

He laughs. "My late wife had an arm like a Seattle Pilot."

"I'm sure you deserved it."

He smiles. "Maybe, but I'll tell you what. There's nothing I wouldn't give to have a pillow thrown at me one more time."

I laugh. "Never knew your wife was that intense, Benson. Not the sort of woman I picture you with."

"Ah, only just one," he whispers.

His eyes mist with a longing I'm afraid I'm beginning to understand.

XI: NO BONES ABOUT IT (JENN)

I swallow past the lump in my throat and stare up at the mammoth tower stabbing the sky.

Jesus.

I thought this part of my life was over when I moved to Bee Harbor.

If Winthrope International's old headquarters was an oversized sugar rush of luxury that made you feel small to enter —*and it was*—this place is a palace.

I square my shoulders and walk into Cromwell-Narada headquarters. I'm not the same woman who left Winthrope and Corporate America behind, even if it hasn't been that long.

So begins day two of dragging these creatives into modern marketing practices, hopefully without too much kicking and screaming.

Louise waits outside the elevator when the door opens. She's a pleasant middle-aged woman with greying hair and an appreciation for high-end, but subtle designer brand clothing.

"Good morning. Your office is ready, Miss Landers, and I apologize for the delay yesterday. I'll show you over," she says.

"Office? Will I need one? This isn't supposed to be long term."

She casts a glance over her shoulder. "Mr. Cromwell insisted. He wants to make sure you have adequate privacy during your time here."

How kind.

I almost wouldn't put it past him to install a hidden camera somewhere so he can enjoy my suffering.

Louise walks briskly and it's a struggle to keep up in these heels. She leads me to a corner office with a wall of solid glass.

My resistance dies right there, struck down by a view stolen from heaven.

This is the good part about the city and its soaring towers.

"Isn't it lovely?" Louise flashes a cheery smile.

"Gorgeous. You can see half of Bainbridge from here." But this doesn't look like a temporary consultant's desk. "Are you sure this is necessary?"

"This office has been vacant for a while. Mr. Cromwell suggested you use it—" She pauses. "I trust it's to your liking?"

"Absolutely." No joke. I'd like to meet the person not capable of liking this desk.

"If you don't require anything else, I'll get out of your hair."

I turn to answer, but she's already gone. The view is breathtaking, capturing the busy silver waters below.

But I probably shouldn't waste more time standing around.

So I move to the sizable mahogany desk in the middle of the room and free my laptop from its bag. As I'm setting it down, I notice a crisp white envelope.

I'm instantly winded, reminded of my first encounter with Miles.

Especially when I see my name scrolled across the front.

Jennifer.

Oh, God. Do I want to know?

Curiosity killed the cat and I'm not immune, kitten puns aside.

Inside, there's a dull black greeting card with a Bloomingdale's gift card still in its cardboard container, $2000 printed on the back.

A tiny note scrawled inside the card says, *For office attire. Make yourself pretty—or should I say prettier?*

My heart leaps.

He ordered me to Seattle so he could send me on a shopping spree? I can't decide if I should be offended or grateful.

This man is maddening. Nothing he does makes any sense.

I pick up my phone and punch in a text. **Is something wrong with my office attire?**

His response is immediate. *I'm not there to check, am I?*

Jenn: But you needed to send me shopping.

Miles: I need to dress you up. Consider it compensation for exiling you to help my team.

I'm mad.

Furious, really, and mostly at myself for blushing when I know full well this is more of his assholery.

Jenn: I had no idea you spent so much time thinking about what I'm wearing.

The three dots pop up on the screen like he's typing. Then they disappear.

I wait for a comeback that never arrives.

Probably for the best, considering the direction this conversation is taking.

Sorry if I caught you off guard, I send.

I settle back at my computer, reviewing videos and concepts until my phone dings over an hour later.

Miles: You know what? I have too much self-control to dignify that with an answer.

Jenn: The fact that you need self-control proves I'm right, Crankyface.

Miles: Show me what you pick out.

The next day, when I come in, the coffee station is filled with a Wired Cup campfire brew. "Nice. I'm normally a Sweeter Grind girl, but I like their s'mores coffee. This is pretty close."

Louise reaches around me to grab a cup. "Mr. Cromwell said you would."

How did he know?

More importantly, why were they discussing it?

"You talked about it?"

She waves her hand. "He asked me to order it. He wants you to be comfortable here."

The coffee is so delicious it's hard to be annoyed, but we need to talk.

I head to my lavish temporary office and sink into the high-back Italian leather power chair. It's so comfy it's hard to remember why I ever hated being chained to a desk at Winthrope.

I pull out my phone and type.

Jenn: Now you're just showing off. Also, your human side is showing, but you can quit groveling. I'm never selling the inn.

Miles: Cromwells don't grovel. I'm a good host. Learn the difference.

How's the coffee?

Jenn: Delicious. And unnecessary.

Miles: I'm sure there are a thousand studies proving caffeine helps focus.

Jenn: You weren't concerned about my comfort or my 'focus' the last time we saw each other...

I know, I know.

I shouldn't go there, but I already did.

And that's it.

That's all it takes to shut the conversation down. I didn't even mention the kiss that's still living in my head rent free. A single hint causes radio silence.

Yeah, I'm *this* close to tearing my hair out.

Maybe I should add a wig to my shopping list.

I'm so effing sick of this man and his guessing games.

* * *

AFTER LUNCH, I come back to the office to find a huge dog gift basket on my desk. And when I say huge, it's so large it takes up most of the desk, filled to the brim with high-end dog food, baked doggy treats, chew toys, and a couple stylish collars sized just for my twin brats.

My face screws up as I grab my phone.

Jenn: Didn't I tell you to quit groveling?

Miles: I've been friends with the dogs longer than I've known you. They aren't used to traveling and I'm sure they miss their quiet beaches.

Holy shit.

Now he's killing my dogs with kindness too?

I want to tell him Coffee and Cream are the only ones who'll ever put up with his attitude.

But he's right.

The Dobermans light up for him the way they only do with their favorite people.

My phone buzzes again.

Miles: Make sure they get their bones. Power chewers learn to relax with something in their mouths.

I glare at the screen. It's a known trick he only could've learned from Gram.

Jenn: I'm not sure they need your bones. They're well fed and my mother made a pet store run today.

Miles: Everyone wants my bone, Jenn. Get over it.

Heat surges under my face. I rack my brain for a good response and decide I'm better off if we just quit talking about bones.

Jenn: Your attachment to the dogs is cute, I'll give you that. Be careful, though. A few people noticed the basket. Keep it up, and they'll start thinking you have a heart.

Miles: I'm simply proving I can be a good boss.

Jenn: By showering my dogs with gifts?

Again, no answer.

173

I'm tempted to tell him I've never had a boss give me his bone before, but I'd like to stay alive.

* * *

I'm sitting at my parents' table, replaying my latest conversation with Miles about his damn bone.

"Ready for dessert? The chocolate olive oil torte at the bakery today was too decadent to pass up." Mom stands and races across the kitchen for the cake.

"It's nice having you home, honey. The house is a lot less boring with you—and those two bruisers," Dad says neutrally.

I smile, seriously grateful the dogs haven't destroyed anything yet. I also think they're growing on him.

"Thanks." But it feels so high school.

I moved out of here my freshman year and I haven't been back under their roof for more than a summer since.

Breathe. It's just a few weeks.

Mom returns with a giant chocolate pancake and a bowl of whipped cream to slather on top, placing them in the center of the table. "What did I miss?"

"I was just saying it's nice having Jennifer back."

"Oh, yes." She cuts the cake and starts serving it up. "I just wish you'd stayed more local, dear. We could do this more often."

Dad looks at Mom. "She can move back in anytime. Did you see the new condos going up in Bellevue? They've been advertising them as perfect for single professionals—and *dog friendly.*" He stresses the last part.

"Guys, I'm right here. And thanks, but not interested."

Slowly, Dad meets my eyes. "Jenn, with your experience, there's more opportunity out here than being stuck in the boonies. And it won't be hard to bring your favorite part of your inheritance with you."

Coffee barks upstairs in loud agreement.

"See? Even he agrees." Dad chuckles, stuffing a bite of cake in his mouth.

"I'm still not sure those are indoor dogs," Mom says.

"They're fine as long as they get their daily run in," I say.

She sets her fork down and folds her hands, leveling a look at me. "Well, now that you're home, I want to talk about this. I've been trying not to touch the subject on the phone because we know you have a mind of your own. You're a smart girl, Jennifer, but really, there's no point in letting that old dump in Pinnacle Pointe bleed you dry—"

Two bites into the cake and it's already ruined. My fork clatters against my plate.

"It's *not* a dump."

She gives me her biggest Mom eyes.

"Sweetie... the place wasn't easy to manage in its heyday, and now it's ancient. We always did fine financially, but sometimes, I don't know how my parents managed. There was always another big, unexpected expense looming. They were constantly fishing for cash, fighting through dry spells for customers when the economy was bad. And back then, the place had a lot less wear and tear. I don't know how you can look at me and claim you haven't inherited a money pit."

I fold my arms, trying not to lose my shit.

My parents mean well.

Just because I'm living with them again doesn't mean I can't prove I'm an adult.

"This is my decision." I look at her and then Dad. "With my assignment back here, I'm making enough bacon to get the place renovated. I'm also avoiding Seattle rent increases, and in this environment, that's *a lot* of money saved."

"Except you don't have your Seattle income anymore," Dad points out.

"Homer—" Mom starts.

"No, it's okay." I hold my father's gaze. "Actually, I'm making more freelancing than I ever made working full-time. My consulting won't always bring in big money like this, but when it does, I'm pretty well set."

He's silent for a minute, turning it over in his head like he isn't sure whether or not he believes me.

"You have to keep the money coming in somehow to run that place and plan for your future," Mom says. "It's not just the inn. If you want to start planning for retirement, for *children*—"

"Whoa, whoa." I hold up my hands. "I'd kinda need a man for that first and I'm not shopping."

My mother's face falls. I think she's about to launch into her usual I-need-grandchildren guilt trip, but Coffee saves me.

He must be as tired as I am of this conversation because he lets out a deafening bark that tells me he's not in my room anymore.

I turn my head and stare up at the open railing behind me, seeing a huge black shape.

Sure enough, his coal-shaped nose pokes between two spindles.

I laugh. "The grown-ups are talking. Go back to my room, boy!"

Another bark rips through the place, and Cream adds a few feral yips.

"They *can't* be indoor dogs," Mom says, aghast.

Coffee spins around and takes a few steps.

I assume he's heading back to my room, so I tuck into my cake again. The sooner I'm done with dinner, the faster I'll get away from this table and this judgy conversation.

"Jennifer, get that dog!" Mom screams.

I follow her eyes up.

Coffee's front paws hit the top of the second-story banister as he stands, shoving his weight forward.

Oh, no.

"Coffee, down!" I stand and scream, right before he—

Too late.

His front paws are stretched out like he's diving as he goes over.

Sweet Jesus. Please don't break a bone!

A whimpering pup and a four-figure vet bill flash before my eyes.

Until he lands on the couch in front of us with his limbs stretched in all directions.

There's a breathless second before he bounces up. He barks playfully, bounds off the couch, and comes over to sniff my hand.

Oh, thank God.

"That's enough, get that mutt out of here!" Dad growls.

Another round of barking comes from above. Not to be outdone, Cream prances down the stairs like the drama queen she is, a lot more gracefully than her brother.

I laugh.

"Not funny," Mom snaps. "He could have broken a leg."

"He's used to poking his head through the spindles at the inn, but he can't do that with your modern layout. I think it confused him. Guess I didn't think to dog proof your house," I explain.

My parents share a look that tells me they aren't looking for excuses.

So I stand and put my hand under Coffee's collar. I'll have to physically lead him away from the table. He's not easily deterred when he's hyper.

I look at Dad over my shoulder. "Now do you see why I like Bee Harbor? How could I ever move 'my favorite inheritance' to the city?"

Cream stands beside me now.

"Take them on another walk and calm them down," he counters. "They need to run off that energy."

"They've been out three times today. They just need space to roam and play. It's what they do," I say with a shrug.

But I guess a few more laps around the block couldn't hurt. I move to the key peg where I've hung their leashes.

"It rained earlier. Be sure to wipe their feet when you bring them in!" Mom yells after me.

"Wendy, calm down. I'll take care of it if they muddy the floors," he says, flashing a sympathetic look.

He's trying to stay on my good side, hoping I'll reconsider their plea to give up on having a life and anchor myself to this city.

With a leash in each hand, I bring the dogs out in good order and let them try to acclimate to the Seattle streets again.

It's getting better—*I think.*

Today I've only had to yank on their leashes a couple times to get them to turn at the corners. They're still not quite used to our treks through a busy subdivision with kids on scooters.

God willing, we won't be here long enough for them to adapt.

Being home isn't easy.

Jogging along at a brisker pace, I realize it's not because I don't love my parents.

It's just that I love not having to answer to anyone. I'm also more at ease in a more open, more chill environment.

Seattle is a vibrant rush, all young energy, which comes with anxiety and adrenaline and uncertainty. Everything here is hustle and bustle, and it's everything I want to escape.

Bizarrely, I miss the inn like it's home now.

This homecoming tells me my parents haven't changed, and that's the problem.

I have.

And I really don't belong here anymore, living on borrowed dreams, trying to please everyone over myself.

The insight makes me lighter as we start back. Coffee and Cream seem oddly quiet now, up in their own doggy brains.

About a block from my parents' place, a sleek black car rolls up beside us and slows to a crawl.

I'm insta-pissed as my eyes flick to the dark windows.

What the hell? Miles Cromwell is going full stalker now?

But the car stops on the curb.

Sigh.

This is going too far. It's high past time to give this man a lesson in boundaries.

As the door opens, I'm gathering all my firepower, putting the dogs in a heel so I can give the bossman a biting piece of my mind. If he thinks I'm intimidated, he can think—

Oh.

A woman climbs out of the back seat. The very definition of the word statuesque.

She's so tall I have to look up, lean and angled like a human greyhound. She's wearing a pinstriped tailored suit with a purple blouse.

I can't decide if she just stepped off Project Runway or Wall Street.

I bend over and peer into the car, just in case, but I can't see the jackass. She also doesn't look like one of his minions.

Then Coffee barks and pulls on his leash, knocking me off-balance. As always, Cream follows her naughty brother, unleashing defensive yips.

I yank both leashes.

"Guys, stop!" I've never been so annoyed with them, but I want to know what the hell is going on, and I can't have my dogs knocking down a total stranger.

Thankfully, they back down.

Coffee hangs his big black head and Cream lets out a soft whine.

"I hope this isn't a bad time?" The platinum-blonde shuts the door behind her with a smile that seems too wide for her face. "You seem to have your hands full."

"If he sent you, tell him it can wait until tomorrow." I give her a tense smile. "He should know me better by now."

Coffee's nose drops to the sidewalk.

All of a sudden, he's very interested in sniffing the ground, ambling as close as I allow to the mystery woman's shoes.

A second later, his head whips back and he looks at me with big brown eyes.

It's an alert face, his ears pinned back.

He yawns loudly, warning me he's stressed.

But why?

It's like he knows better than to break into an all-out warning growl, but feels like he should.

Cream shuffles in front of me with the same blank face, the white hair on her neck raised.

God, what's gotten into them?

The stranger just raises a hand. I notice a long, thin vape pen hanging out of it. She brings it to her lips and lets out a puff of minty smoke as casually as if we're in a hookah bar.

"I sincerely don't know who 'he' is. I assure you I'm my own woman," she says, her voice like steel.

But as soon as she blows a puff of smoke, Coffee's lips peel back and he growls.

"Coffee!" I pull the leash firmly.

Behave, boy, before you wind up with animal control.

It takes a few seconds as I struggle to move him behind me and Cream, where he finally melts into a sit with one more grumble.

"I'm so sorry. He doesn't usually growl." I stop, wondering if it's the vape machine weirding them out. He's never seen one before.

"Dogs will be dogs. I'm here to talk about your newly acquired property."

The inn? But if she isn't with Miles...

I don't understand.

What kind of hyper-aggressive realtor follows you on the street?

She takes another drag off her vape pen before she says, "I have a keen interest in that beautiful space of yours. I'm terribly sorry to barge in on you like this, but I just missed you before you left and figured I'd just wait for you. I also owe you another apology, Miss Landers."

"For what?" I ask.

Maybe the dogs are right. This whole thing feels weird.

"I allowed my realty firm to make the initial offer a little while ago when I should have paid you a visit in person," she says. "I also regret allowing them to send you a lowball offer."

Realty firm? Offer?

Oh, the letter in the mailbox. So she's with them?

"I'm sure such an impersonal offer—and perhaps the amount —was an insult to a cherished Pinnacle Pointe institution. I've come to remedy that today." She reaches into the black leather designer purse hanging from one shoulder, pulls out a cream envelope, and passes it to me. "Go ahead. Kindly have a look."

I open it, and my jaw drops.

When I look up to see if this is a joke, she's smiling, but her face is as blank as a wall.

"Take your time. I'm sure you'll want time to consider it with a lawyer, but I'll be ready for your call. To be clear, I wouldn't ever dream of flipping The Bee Harbor Inn or turning it into a corporate creation. My card is inside. I trust you'll be in touch."

I'm speechless.

If it wasn't for the dogs standing defensively as she turns her back, I might just fall over.

She climbs back into her car and the driver pulls away the instant the door shuts.

Coffee lets out a repressed *woof!*

"...she was intense, huh?"

He tries to pull me the way we came and Cream trots after him. I have to steer them around quickly, ignoring their sad black eyes and whines as their tails wag.

"Not right now, guys. We're not going back to the park. I need some time to think."

But when my eyes land on a second black car, I know I might as well wish for a unicorn while I'm at it.

Because Miles Cromwell steps out and marches toward me, his face set like granite.

It wasn't the park or the woman that set them off after all.

It was the most annoying man alive, and whether I like it or not, he's about to complicate my world for the thousandth time.

XII: NO BAD BLOOD (MILES)

*T*he stink of that mint-tinged smoke clings to the air like sulfur trailing a demon.

I knew I came back early for a reason. I just didn't expect to find a monster whispering God only knows what in Jenn's ear.

If Simone was ten seconds later stepping back in her car, I would've ended this shit right here.

Instead, I'm confronted with Jenn the second she spins around to calm the dogs, and judging from her look, they're the only ones happy to see me.

I fight down a laugh.

It's weirdly adorable when she goes from graceful to bumbling mess in the blink of an eye.

She's atrociously cute when she's mad, the usual warmth in her eyes turning to a stormy sea green. All of her sweetness gone in a flash of lightning, and I'm the fucking idiot-rod pulling it down from the sky.

"What are you doing here?" she bites off.

"Nice to see you, too."

"You scared my dogs."

"This is scared?" I hold out my hand.

Coffee lets out an excited yip and licks my fingers. I pull a morsel of beef jerky out of my pocket, pull the wrapper down, and hold it above his nose. "Sit."

The beast obeys, and I give him a large bite before I offer the same to his sister.

Jenn's eyes flick from the dogs to me and back again.

"You never answered my question. What are you doing here?" Her throat ticks like every word is some poison thing leaving her mouth.

"The same as you, I imagine," I tell her, deliberately cryptic.

"My parents live one block over. I bet you can't say the same. My family does well, but they're not billionaires."

"My status bothers you, doesn't it?" I drill through her icy expression, daring her to tell the truth.

"It's not my business. It doesn't matter," she flings back.

"It must if you made a point to mention it."

"Miles, what do you want?" The fight goes out of her voice as she pulls on her cheeks.

"I want whatever *she* wanted." It's a struggle to keep my tone from instantly curdling.

Jenn looks down slowly at the envelope in her hand. "Nothing that concerns you."

"What is it?"

I'm goddamned tempted to snatch it right out of her hand and see for myself. If only it wouldn't win me a well-deserved slap across the cheek and possibly bite marks from two huge guard dogs.

But if that witch threatened her—

"Miss Landers—Jenn, this does concern me. I need to know," I step forward.

"Back off," she hisses, veering back.

I shake my head.

Damn, how do I get her to listen without exposing every sordid detail? Everything that made me the hollowed-out creature I am today, the thing she finds so despicable.

184

"Trust me, you have no clue who she is or what you're dealing with—"

"And you do?" She blinks harshly, her cheeks burning raw. "*Trust.* That's pretty rich, coming from you."

"I deserved that," I say gruffly, stepping up and laying a hand on her shoulder. "Look, you owe me a heaping spoonful of hell for the way I kissed and ran and sent you here."

She jerks her head away, refusing to look at me. A deepening flush on her face betrays her confusion.

"Miles, for the last time..."

"This isn't about us, kitten. If you'll forget my shit—if only for the briefest second—I need you to *listen.* That woman, she's a scorpion. She never made a deal she liked without an ulterior motive. Stay the fuck away from her, and tell me what she said."

"No!" She rips herself out of my grasp.

"Jenn—"

"No, how about you *listen?* I don't clear my conversations with you, especially when it's not even work related. You don't get to do that, Miles. You have no right."

"And I wasn't asking as your boss." My voice gentles. Heat sears my throat.

Goddamn, I'm shitting the bed with this, and I know it.

If I could just make her understand, but this is a public street.

Hardly the time or place.

She steps closer, jutting her chin out defiantly as she looks up at me.

"Then what are you asking as? The coward who plays me like a drum? The man who kisses me like cupid put ten arrows in his ass? The man who can't answer simple questions and ignores my texts for days?"

Fuck.

If this wasn't already hellishly complicated, I'd show her there's nothing cowardly in these lips. I'd claim her right now and turn that gasping fury in every breath into grateful moans.

"What did she say to you?" I press her again.

She doesn't answer.

We both look down at the envelope clutched in her hand.

"What does it say?" I'm trying to keep my voice neutral and failing, hoping against hope that maybe she'll crack. Maybe she'll answer me, despite every reason not to.

Of course, she refuses.

I have to know.

Darting forward, I snatch the envelope from her hand and pull out the paper inside.

"Stop! You have no right—"

I don't, but my eyes are glued to that paper.

It's worse than I feared.

"Give it back right now," she says again, sweeping forward in a desperate attempt to steal it that doesn't work. I'm holding it up too high.

"Miles, Jesus. This is flipping ridiculous!"

It is, and I wish like hell my guilt overrode my need to protect her from—this sick fucking offer that's meant to humiliate me.

"Fucking outrageous. That's almost *four* times the market value," I snarl, still skimming. "Christ, she really will do anything to get to me."

Jenn's breath catches loudly. This time, I don't fight her as she rushes forward, stealing the letter away.

"To get to you? Right. Because the sun, the moon, and the stars revolve around Miles Cromwell. You're the most conceited man I've ever met."

My eyes snap to her, searching her eyes through the hurt.

"Tell me I'm wrong," she says sharply. "Someone offers to buy a gorgeous property that you offered above market value on, and suddenly it's all about you and your demented idea of paradise?"

"Simone Niehaus has a history of strong-arm tactics and hidden clauses in her contracts like bear traps. She'll stop at nothing to get what she wants and you won't get what you expect. She never acts in good faith. She couldn't care less about the inn, Jenn. This *is* about me, whether you choose to believe me or not. I'm telling you again, kitten, stay the fuck away from her."

"Why are you in Seattle, anyway? Stalking me to my parents' house?" She inhales shakily. "Do you even know how inappropriate you're being right now?"

I cock my head, trying to assess how pissed she really is on the rip-your-face-off scale. "In case you haven't figured it out, we've never *been* appropriate."

"...I can't deny that, but whose fault is that?" Her words are quiet, then louder when she says, "Coffee, Cream. Let's go."

She leads them forward.

I start to follow, taking long strides to keep up with her as she damn near bolts away from me.

"You're *still* following me?" Her mouth drops.

"We have business to discuss."

"I have a phone and email for that. Learn to use them," she spits back.

In all my infinite asshole wisdom, I deserve that.

"Just tell me you'll avoid Niehaus?"

She doesn't answer, just shoots me a scathing look.

Then she turns toward an ornate two-story house like the other grand homes on this street and heads up the steps to the front door.

I'm undeterred, stopping at the base of the stairs.

She freezes and looks back at me over her shoulder.

"You're not coming in. Leave me the hell alone."

The second my foot touches the first step, Coffee spins around so fast the leash flies out of Jenn's hands. Cream is right behind him.

The dogs stand between us like a wall of canine muscle, their eyes heavy with promises they don't want to act on if I don't take the hint.

"Jenn—" One more step forward.

Coffee's spine stiffens.

Cream yawns widely, a stress signal that finally registers in my madhouse of a brain.

She looks back at me one more time over the dogs, her eyes still hot with rage.

"I'll go," I say, backing up and turning around.

The damn dogs have effectively ended any conversation, any understanding, we might've had tonight. Still, I'm glad she has them.

While a couple of large dogs won't be enough to deter Simone's bullshit, she's safer by far with them.

Benson waits patiently at the curb. He's pulled up a few blocks from where we stopped and I ran out.

I get in the car and immediately sink into the seat, wishing the leather could bury me alive.

"I'm sorry it didn't go better," he tells me.

A simple cutting glance is all he needs.

"She has no idea who she's dealing with," I say bitterly. "She doesn't *understand*."

"Sir, in my experience, a woman who's already miffed at you is unlikely to take your advice. Explanations are usually pretty helpful, too."

I glare at him in the mirror.

But he knows me too well.

"Thank you, doctor. If we were dealing with anyone besides the bride of Satan herself, I'd agree. But when you have something Simone Niehaus wants, she comes up with the sickest shit. You know it as well as I do. She's after Jenn's property because of me. I'm not subjecting Jenn to collateral damage because I was stupid enough to dance with the devil once upon a fucked up time."

"I only know what you've told me. However, you may want to temper the devil references if you decide to be a little more honest."

Classic Benson, doling out good advice I never asked for.

"I remember too well what Miss Niehaus is capable of," he continues. "I'm just not sure Miss Landers will get over whatever it is you did to upset her."

"Probably not," I agree.

"Then if you want to communicate the danger, perhaps you'd better get past your damage first. No one wants more collateral damage," Benson says.

He doesn't need to remind me.

"Don't worry. If I can't get through to her, I'll find another way to deal with it."

Unfortunately, I know what scaring Simone off means.

I'm going to have to break my vow of silence and talk to that soulless, throat-slashing bitch.

* * *

I FINISH REPLYING to an email from Legal and pick up my phone to check my messages.

It feels like a solid brick today.

One missed voicemail from Louise.

No new texts.

Jenn hasn't so much as sworn at me since the night that vulture of a woman showed up.

I keep thinking she'll call or send some snarky-ass message eventually. Then I can cough up a real apology and maybe we can get back to normal.

Yeah.

Wishful fucking thinking.

Still, I don't want to call her.

Not when she needs time to cool down at her own pace and an honest break from the bullshit I regret inflicting on her.

I'm also sorry as hell I'm not talking to Jenn right now.

I've dreaded this conversation like a cancer diagnosis. It's been years, and if Simone hadn't invaded my life again, I'd continue sending her notes by high-paid pigeons—lawyers who charge extortionate hourly rates to deal with the human shit I can't stand to touch.

Only, I've lost that luxury.

If I want to keep her the hell away from Jennifer Landers, I have to roll up my sleeves and get my hands filthy.

I punch the number into my office phone, put the receiver to my ear, and stare out the window.

Focusing on the view from my high-rise office might avert my heart from clawing its way up my throat.

Might.

"That took longer than I expected," Simone answers with the same cheery lilt in her voice I remember, barely changed by years of chronic smoking and age.

"You're pathetic," I growl.

"Really, Miles? It's been years and you can't say hello before launching into a guessing game? I have no earthly idea what you're mad about now."

Yes, you do.

Yes, you fucking do.

"You don't know you're going after my neighbor's property to twist my arm? Spare me. You don't want it. You don't need it. You never even heard of Pinnacle Pointe before you came after me. If you're that hellbent on forcing me into a corporate partnership that's never happening, you can't go dragging innocent parties into this. And you'd better hope I never spot any detectives you put up my ass. I'll press charges for harassment and private espionage."

"Oh, sweetie," she croons. "Don't flatter yourself. It's just business... But I guess you always *did* have trouble with making everything so personal."

My fingers pinch the phone until they hurt, wanting to crush it.

"Stay the fuck out of Pinnacle Pointe," I rasp.

Stay the fuck away from her is what I mean, but I know it'll make this a hundred times worse.

She scoffs loudly. "Miles, Miles. I may never understand what you see in that little hole-in-the-wall place. However—"

"You just said it. Your offer on the inn is pointless."

"Can I get a word in?" She clears her throat loudly. "My offer was far from pointless, and I think you'll agree 'generous' is a far better description. You should've seen the way her mouth dropped when she saw the number. I suppose it is a lot of money for a twenty-five-year-old—"

"She's twenty-six."

Fuck, I shouldn't have said that.

"Well, at least now I know why this has you so twisted up." Simone's giggle comes out like a harsh rattle. "Honestly, I'm proud of you. A part of me was worried you'd never totally move on, but look at you. Dating an employee? How deliciously scandalous."

She's so goddamned patronizing I could puke.

"What's the matter? You don't want to be neighbors? I'm sure you could just move your new girlfriend in, and she'd be a lot richer. No harm, no foul."

"I'd rather catch Ebola from a monkey bite to the face than wind up your neighbor."

She sighs so slowly I can feel her nails raking down my neck, setting every hair on end.

"Always so dramatic. Same old Miles. Anyhow, I've gotten wind that you're very interested in the same property, but for some odd reason, you aren't making much progress. Are you just upset I made a better offer? I'd be happy to turn around and sell it to you—maybe at a loss, provided you're willing to make other accommodations."

"Fuck you entirely, Simone," I snap. "If you want to keep your roost at a functioning company and an endless supply of that imported shit that's killing your lungs, you'll listen very closely. Stay away from me. Stay away from my property. Most of all, stay the fuck away from Miss Landers."

So much for focusing on the big picture and not letting her get to me.

I wish I was above this right now, not struggling to keep my head above the quicksand.

She's quiet for a minute.

"Wow. You really do hate me, don't you?"

I don't answer.

"Miles, you know what happened wasn't my fault, right? You can't keep blaming me forever. Your mother—that's not fair. If I had any inkling what was happening, I never would've kept you that night when you could've—"

"Enough," I grind out. "Shut your lying mouth."

I can't believe she dared to bring it up just to deny responsibility again.

"You're a piece of fucking work. Even if the worst didn't happen, what you did was a stark warning of how you do business. You're reckless," I grind out. "Reckless and self-serving."

I hate that I can see her smile in my head, dark and red and carnivorous.

"A quality people find admirable in men," she says pointedly.

"Nothing you do is admirable. Don't act so wounded."

"Tomato, to-mah-to. Enemy, partner. What's in a word besides the meaning we give it?"

"I told you once, any relationship we'll ever have is over. Respect it or don't and see what happens. If you want hardball, I'll have every major law firm in Washington on you like—"

"Except for the ones on my payroll, you mean," she cuts in, adding a loud yawn. "Really, I'm not worried about facing you in court. You're twice my size and still a big drama queen."

My jaw clenches, so ready to show her some drama she can't ignore.

"But it doesn't matter. You're a businessman above all else, Miles Cromwell. You know how absurd this is, even if you won't admit it."

"That you offered the moon for a property you don't want just to get to me? Yeah, it's fucking outlandish."

She breathes a long sigh into the phone.

"We're CEOs, whatever our history. We have companies to grow and people to look out for. If you won't do it for yourself, will you do it for them? This is so sad. You're letting bad blood come before honest business. No one operates at our level that way if they're smart. You know that. We basically own the Pacific Northwest media space. We're both titans. If we just put this drama behind us and extended a hand—"

"Titans don't need a hand, Simone."

"Well, I tried. But you can't tell me being a player in bigger markets like LA has never crossed your mind..."

Fuck, I barely care about the Seattle market anymore. Why would I want to expand, inviting new headaches and double the bloodthirsty sharks just like her?

"To think you used to tell me your dreams," she whispers.

I wince, holding my breath.

I fucking hate that she's right.

There was a time when I would have jumped at the chance to take the world by its tail with the devil's own daughter by my side, but it's not just the prospect of business with this treacherous snake that's stopping me now.

"You know I won't give up easy, Miles. I still have my pride. So I'm offering you one last chance, and I won't let you squander it—"

Let me? She's not going to let me?

Who the fuck does she think she is?

"I don't need your permission to do jack shit."

"By working together, we can—"

"Never. *Never.* Get it through your fucking head now so we can avoid having this conversation a thousand more times."

Icy silence.

"You pretend you're a force of nature, Miles, but sooner or later, you'll reap the whirlwind."

"What?" I snort. "Is that a threat?"

"I don't think you understand. If I want an alliance, we'll have one, and you'll change your mind sooner or later. The only sure thing about emotions is that they aren't fixed. They're shifting constantly," she says matter-of-factly.

"You're psychotic."

"I prefer determined."

"Is your company in trouble?" I press the phone to my ear. "Is that why you're doing this?"

"Oh, please. Why would you even ask? I'm sure you have spies combing over my revenue reports. They've never been stronger."

"Why are you so desperate to work with a man who hates your fucking guts then?"

"I'm *not* desperate," she clips, the first time she's sounded angry. "I just know my own worth, my dreams, and maybe I know yours better than you do. You can't turn that down based on some accident a million years ago in business terms."

I wish it was that long.

I wish a cosmic timescale would heal the scars she left behind.

"Simone, it's not the history. I just know what a conniving, two-faced bitch queen of knives you are."

I hang up.

There's nothing gained in continuing this call, a circular firing squad that never reaches any understanding.

I look at the clock on my computer.

Shit.

It's not even ten a.m.

I finally understand why everyone hates Mondays.

I pick up my office phone and dial Louise.

"Yes, Mr. Cromwell?"

"Start digging into Simone Niehaus' company and all her recent ventures."

She goes quiet. "I haven't heard you use that name in a while—"

"And I thought I'd never have that pebble in my shoe again. I want to know how their business is trending and as much about their debts and assets as you can find out." She's been quiet for years. If she wants something now this bad, there must be a deeper reason for it.

Maybe if I can figure out what it is, and find her soft underbelly, I can be done with this madness once and for all.

"I'll get started right away and send you what I find," she promises.

"Thank you, Louise."

I slump back in my chair, swiping a hand over my face.

I need a contingency plan in case this doesn't work out. My next call is to my personal attorney, Martin.

He picks up on the first ring. "To what do I owe the pleasure, Cromwell?"

"What does it take to get a restraining order?"

"...from a disgruntled former employee?"

"More like a psychotic ex-partner," I snap.

He chuckles with surprise.

"Well, we've all been there, haven't we? What's she doing?"

"Trying to buy the property next door to mine, for one," I grind out.

He clears his throat and takes his sweet time answering.

"Regrettably, buying real estate next to yours isn't illegal or threatening, and the standard for a restraining order that would restrict that activity can be rather intense. Courts don't like to limit people's freedoms, so without a real threat, you're unlikely to get one. I'm sure there must be more going on?"

Where do I fucking start? I'm not even sure what to tell him.

The harder I rack my brain, the less I come up with that's illegal. That's the sickening part.

No court in the world would hold her responsible for what

she did, taking something precious I can never get back. If she did more—if she drugged me like I always suspected—I was too blasted out of my mind with shock and grief to get proof.

I must take too long to answer because he says, "Miles...are you okay?"

"I'm fine."

"Has she done anything else besides pursue this property deal?"

"She left a note at my mother's grave—"

"Wait. She was buried in Pinnacle Pointe, right?"

"Yes."

"Is she a local there?"

"No, it's Simone Niehaus."

Again, that gaping silence that makes me feel like a crazy man.

Hell, maybe I am.

"If there was no valid reason for her to be in the same town besides wanting to harass you and making a claim on the neighboring property... Now, we're getting somewhere. Send me a full account of what happened, and if you still have the note, that's better."

"I'll work on it, Martin."

I hang up, already drumming my fingers on my desk and hating what an absolute joke my life has become.

Even after all these years, the bad blood with Simone still costs me everything—or nearly enough.

Can I really afford more bad blood with Jennifer Landers?

XIII: NO TURNING AWAY (JENN)

*J*effing hate Mondays, and knowing the bosshole is back in town isn't helping anything.

Seriously.

What kind of elephant prick just shows up out of the blue and tells me I can't even entertain an offer for *my* property? And all because he has some beef with the person who made it.

Of course, I agreed to the contract when I took the job.

I have to give him first option. But still, a girl can look, and she can certainly dig deeper to find out why people keep offering so much freaking money for an old inn on a scenic slice of land that's seen better days.

What does this Simone really want, and what did he do to her?

It's typical Miles Cromwell.

He just comes barreling in, all snarls and bared teeth, and then he disappears. To be fair, I haven't made any effort to reach out since the dogs ran him off my parents' porch.

Still.

I'm so sick of it I could scream—and knowing I have to deal with him for at least the next eight hours is enough to make me want to break this contract and run off to the other side of the country. I hear Maine is nice for an ocean view.

But I can't honor Gram or myself in Maine.

Like it or not, Bee Harbor is quickly becoming home.

The sooner you suck it up and finish the job, the faster you'll be home with the dogs, I tell myself, clinging to that nugget of hope.

So I sit in my office, reviewing one short video after the next, hoping my face doesn't get stuck from cringing too hard. I tap my glasses against the edge of my desk.

I haven't worn them since my Winthrope days, but if I'm marooned in Seattle playing girlboss, I'll look the part.

Just how? How did they do this?

Some of this content feels so comically inauthentic I don't know how they botched it.

It's almost like someone said, 'Hey, this looks too real. Let's cheese it up.'

Ugh.

I drop my head to my desk with a *thunk!* It'll be easier finding the unedited footage and starting all over than explaining how to fix some of this mess.

It's time for a break anyway, and I need to get word to Miles that he needs to step in and let me have full production control of the Pinnacle Pointe videos.

So I push my glasses on and step out of my office, heading for the private elevator to the executive floor.

For a polished corporate heart, there are more people working in cubicles than you'd think, and they all like to chatter. Louise's desk is right in front of Cromwell's office.

She's on the phone when I walk up and doesn't see me. "Yes, that's right. Everything you have on Miss Niehaus, including any recent interest in new personal acquisitions."

Oh my God.

He's really not letting this go, is he?

I tell myself I don't care, but that's a lie.

Whatever.

If he wants the inn that stinking bad, he can make a better offer. Not that I'd actually sell Gram's pride and joy off to either one of them.

I don't have anything against Niehaus personally, though. She just doesn't seem right for Bee Harbor, and I'm not sure I trust her promise to keep the property undeveloped.

On the other hand, I hate Miles more than a jellyfish sting—and I hate him even more for turning my own lips against me.

No matter how awful he is in my heart, the rest of me can't resist another kiss.

Confusing much? Pathetic?

Yes.

But whatever.

"Can I help you, Miss Landers?" Louise peers over her spectacles once she realizes I'm standing there.

I shake my head like I'm clearing my thoughts.

"Can you please email Mr. Cromwell and have him notify the entire creative team not to make any more changes without my approval? I thought a note from the big boss versus little old contractor me might go a long way."

"Certainly," she says cheerfully, already typing.

Then I notice the chatter from the surrounding cubicles has stopped.

The room is so quiet you could hear a pin drop.

"Um, did something happen?" I whisper.

The silence is so intense just using a normal voice feels deafening.

"He's been holed up in a meeting for the past hour and a half. He must have just stepped out. They tend to get quiet when he's out on the floor." Louise doesn't whisper.

She's used to this. Mr. Iron Fist and his choke hold on this office so tight it curdles the whole atmosphere.

At least I'm not the only one who hates working for him.

I scoff to myself, but Louise must hear me.

She glances up. "What's wrong, Miss Landers? I sincerely

hope creative hasn't been causing you too much grief—or a certain curmudgeonly boss."

I blink, unsure what to say. For all I know, she's testing me and he put her up to this.

"It's no big deal, Louise. Just send the message, please?"

For a second, I wonder if he had another motive for chasing me down the other evening.

If Simone Niehaus hadn't been there, and the dogs hadn't lost their cool, maybe things would have gone very differently.

Maybe we could have sat down and had a conversation like normal human beings.

Not two crazies torn between peeling each other's faces off, or tearing off our clothes instead.

Yeah, no.

I never should have kissed a boss-client in the first place. Stupid me.

I definitely shouldn't be holding on to this vague hope that we could ever reach a normal understanding.

One where he sets his own greedy ambitions aside and explains why it's the end of the world if I even dare to entertain another offer on my place.

But unless I know the ins and outs of the inn's real value, I'll never understand it, will I? It's time to do some digging.

Back in my office, I call Waldo, Gram's old attorney.

"Pinnacle Pointe Legal. This is Waldo. How can I help?"

I smile. This is why I love Pinnacle Pointe. In Seattle, no attorney answers their own phone during business hours.

"Hey, Waldo, it's Jennifer Landers. Lottie Risa's granddaughter?"

"I remember you, Miss Landers. What can I do for you today?" he says pleasantly.

"I've had two offers on the inn recently. One is twice the amount of the other offer—"

"Ah, that's news, all right. We're talking a range just north of two million then? I know the Pointe can't claim SeaTac area charms or its market values, but it's still a huge house and a lot of land with an ocean view. Glad to hear any potential buyers are taking that seriously. How about the competing offer?"

"Above three," I whisper.

"Three million?" He lets out a long whistle.

"Yes. I know it's a lot, but I kind of wondered what I'd be looking at after taxes..."

"I'd have to crunch some numbers, but it would certainly still be a very nice chunk of change. Wow. I'm sure we can minimize the tax bill, if you're moving forward with a sale. There's also a structured settlement option where the money comes in over time, if the buyer is interested."

I can't help grinning, even if actually signing off on any sale feels as strange and unthinkable as getting married.

"I'm glad Gram hired the right attorney," I say.

"I do what I can. It's been a little while since the estate was settled, so I'll also need to research the provisions in your grandmother's will about when you can sell."

"When?" I'm not sure what he's getting at.

He clears his throat. "I don't remember anything off the top of my head specifically, but sometimes with inherited properties, there are clauses about when you can sell and who you're allowed to sell to. It's rather common out here, where some folks get awfully attached to their old houses. Just give me a few days and I'll get right back to you."

My stomach twists oddly.

I never imagined Gram herself writing any restrictions into her will.

"No problem. Thank you, Waldo." I end the call there.

Great timing since my cell buzzes.

Miles: I received Louise's message. I'll have a note out to creative this afternoon. We're still not talking?

I don't respond.

The whole point of not talking to someone is to *not talk to them.*

But he's persistent, and my phone vibrates again an hour later.

Miles: I've instructed the team they need your approval for any additional edits. Satisfied?

Nope.

No insult.

No backhanded compliment.

No smartass remark dripping with innuendo.

I'm honestly surprised—and a little disappointed.

I never expected Normal Miles to feel so dull.

So I start typing back several times, but snark seeps out in every message. I go back and delete them, frowning at the screen.

Eventually, I decide to check my inner bitch and send him a simple **thank you.**

So, this is progress.

Resisting Miles Cromwell in all of his stupid sex-charged glory.

But why does it feel like two steps back and less than a half step forward?

* * *

IT'S ALMOST nine o'clock and you can stick a fork in me, I'm done.

My eyes are red and bleary, watering from way too much screen time with Sarah, piecing together one new video short after the next.

I should have left hours ago, but putting in more time now means this hell ends sooner. I'll pull an all-nighter if it means being through with this.

With him.

If I'm lucky, maybe Waldo will turn up some clause that says the inn can't be sold for the next century, and the grumpiest boss alive can go pound sand.

I grab my coffee cup and take a swig.

It's gone cold and gross, just like my life.

I'm about to sign out of the company chat and drag myself home when my chat window pings.

I don't need to look at the message to know who it is.

Who else has to message me after nine?

My office. Now.

I bite my lip.

Who does he think he is?

I should just ignore it and escape while I can. The well-behaved Miles I spoke with earlier is gone, but tearing into him feels weirdly satisfying right now.

So I pack up, throw my bag over my shoulder, and march to the executive elevator.

This time, when the elevator stops, the floor is empty.

A couple of security lights are still on, illuminating the way to the brighter hazy glow of his office.

Onward I go, my knees pulsing with every step.

I swing open the door without knocking.

"What do you want?" I'm trying to sound brave, but the fight goes out of me the instant I step inside and he overwhelms my senses.

Everything about this office screams Miles Cromwell.

It's imposing and sleek and it smells just like him.

Earth and pine and obscene masculinity. Testosterone so thick I feel the hairs on my neck standing up.

It may look like a lavish office, but it feels like walking into a cave bear's den.

The floor-to-ceiling window dwarfs the one in my office. His desk dominates the center of the room, white marble and walnut, and the landscape paintings on the walls demand respect.

And at the center of this universe, standing too wide, is its ruler.

Silver-blue eyes razor through me.

His lip curls slightly and his nostrils flare. If you blink, you'd miss it, but I can practically hear him *inhaling* me.

Oh, God.

All that's missing is his spear of a tongue flicking over his lips to complete the predator look.

"Well?" I force out, throwing my hands on my hips.

"We need to talk about the unprofessional turn this work relationship has taken."

"Oh, is that all? It's only like the hundredth time that's happened. For a minute, I thought you might've summoned me here to talk about *work*."

He opens his mouth, but I don't give him time to fire back.

"Dude, if you want to give me a lecture, save it. Our relation-ship—*work relationship*—" Dammit. "—it's never been profes-sional. How could it be? You're obsessed with my land and you think just because you're a billionaire and you knew my grand-mother, you're somehow entitled to everything. But you aren't. Everything you've done since we met was a calculated move to convince me to sell the place. The only thing you've succeeded in doing is making me hate you more."

He's quiet for a heavy second that shreds me.

"You hate me?" His question comes out raw.

Vulnerable.

Oh.

Maybe I've been too harsh, laying the sarcasm on thick.

"...well... how would you feel if every interaction with you was so mechanical? A means to an end, and nothing more."

"That's fucking absurd," he growls, his eyes flaring. "Mechan-ical? Nothing could be further from the truth. Was it mechanical when you moaned in my mouth?"

Crap.

He just had to go there.

I want to laugh like the crazy woman he makes me, but there are tears in my eyes.

He kissed me—*really kissed me*—and that was still about the freaking inn.

...wasn't it?

"But last time, when you ambushed me on the street... That was about Bee Harbor. You were afraid she'd buy it, or I'd find a way around this stupid rule giving you first dibs."

With a low sound that's more animalistic frustration than sigh, he steps around his desk, moving closer, cornering me.

"Goddammit, Jenn, that had nothing to do with your land and everything to do with the woman trying to sink her claws into it. If you won't believe me, I'll sign an amendment waiving my option on Bee Harbor now. I don't care if you sell it to Paul fucking Bunyan the handyman for a dollar or even the fucking tooth fairy. That's not what this is about anymore. I just can't have you selling to *her*."

I'm so blindsided it takes real effort to find words.

"No? I just... I don't understand. If you're not hellbent on buying it, what's the problem? What are you keeping from me—or keeping me *from?*"

He stalks closer like the panther he is, his massive shoulders squared and his eyes riveted to me.

I swallow thickly.

He's so tall, so broad, a boulder chiseled into manly elegance.

Something about the feral way he watches me brings me back to that messy, soul-branding kiss.

But that's not what this is.

That's not what I should care about.

That's not what I'm aching for in my core, hollow and pleading, asking him with everything but words to let me *feel him* just one more time.

What the frick is wrong with me?

"Miles? What is this about?"

"You," he answers. His steely eyes soften, and so does his voice. The tender edge leaves me bristling. "What else could it ever be about, Jenn? I still can't get that kiss out of my head—and woman, I've *tried.*"

I'm floating.

On the verge of leaving my body.

My tongue skims my lips, which suddenly feel so parched. "The kiss you ran away from like it was poison, you mean? The one you never mentioned again?"

His eyes sharpen, turning back into razors.

"The kiss I dream about every damn night? The kiss that keeps invading my head every damn hour, leaving me so brainless I can barely function?" With his teeth bared, he closes in, stopping with his lips just inches from mine. "The kiss I've stroked myself off to twenty times this past week, every orgasm coming like a fever, so impossible to break I can't even breathe?"

Oh God Oh God Oh God.

My lungs won't work.

"Yeah, kitten. I remember that kiss," he whispers. "It's hard-wired into my head so deeply I'll take that shit to my grave." His words fall against my mouth in hot waves. "For the record, I tried to apologize."

"Y-yeah. And maybe I just didn't want an apology," I whisper.

I didn't want that kiss to end, especially not the way it did.

"I owed you one. It was inappropriate as hell and you work for me. I just don't regret that it happened—even if we weren't alone. I regret that I tore myself away."

"I still work with you, Miles—" I swallow harshly.

"And now we're alone and I still want to taste you."

He's. Killing. Me.

Especially when he closes his eyes and releases a slow breath so hot it burns my skin.

"Aren't you tired of this song and dance, kitten? This lie? I can't keep away from you. The jaws of life couldn't pry these thoughts out of my head, everything I'm aching to do to you. Simone may have brought me back to Seattle—but you're the real reason. I had to see you again."

My toes scrunch in my shoes and my knees work overtime to hold me up.

"Big words for a big man who only has one real passion." I nod at the paintings hanging over his desk.

His eyes move in the direction of my nod.

"Yeah, and you're the reason I can't even do that anymore. If I'm the scary, single-minded asshole you think I am—I've made my choice, Jenn. I choose *this.*"

I'm so completely gone as he bends, his breath more teasing than ever. My head dips back as my body tilts toward him with this wild magnetism I still can't comprehend.

But it rules me.

It makes me his prisoner.

Before I can mewl out another word of protest, he's reaching for my glasses, jerking them off my nose, and staring straight into my eyes.

"I like this better, kitten. Nothing in the way," he whispers.

For a split second, I shudder, right down to my toes.

Then his lips bury me alive.

He clasps my waist, pulling me closer, ravishing me.

He's all man, this brazen bull, backing me against the wall.

The next time I breathe, I'm trapped between the surface and muscle I can't resist digging my fingers into.

I hold on so tight as he robs the air from my lungs.

As he burns me down with lust.

As he turns me into trembling ash.

As each growling kiss makes me delirious.

My fingers tremble, tracing his jawline, admiring him like I've always wanted to.

My leg curls around his, refusing to let go, overriding the last snapping denial in my head.

"Kitten, fuck," he whispers, moving a possessive hand from my waist.

He takes my chin, gently but firmly, holding my face up to meet his eyes.

His whole gaze is an invisible thrust, splitting me open, naked and wet and fully surrendered.

Sighing, I wrap my arms around his neck and brush my other leg against his. I curl my ankle around his shin and slide it up his leg.

His hand falls to my bare thigh, and he hikes up my skirt in one rough jerk. His hands find my ass and his fingers dig in, holding me up, quickening the wet heat in my core.

This is my new reality.

Up against the wall with a boss I'm supposed to hate, tangled and clinging to him for dear life. A man who always soothes my dogs, who I also work for, and who still wants my land.

It's as ludicrous as it sounds, and yet, there's nowhere else I'd rather be.

Even through our layered clothes, the hard, thick ridge moving against my softness is an invitation to heaven.

But he breaks our kiss with a ragged breath a second later.

"Jenn, if you don't listen to anything else I say tonight—" His lips sear my chin and then my lips again. "Stay away from her." His lips press mine again and his teeth come out before his tongue dips into my mouth, angry and searching. "Stay the fuck away from Simone Niehaus. You have no idea what you're getting into. Please trust me."

I try to nod, but I can't.

"Promise me," he commands, pulling back, laying his forehead against mine.

Holy hell.

I think I'd promise him the Taj Mahal right now.

"Y-yes. I promise," I stammer, sliding my hands from the back of his neck and then down his chest.

Miles ripples under my hands, all defined strength and corded muscle. My fingers dip under his jacket, pushing it off his shoulders.

He shifts his weight, allowing me to remove the jacket one arm at a time.

Then he's on me again, speaking new orders in new biting kisses against my throat.

"Oh. Oh, Miles," I whimper.

He licks up my neck, teasing with his teeth like the vampire hero he is. "Pace yourself, woman. There's a lot more catnip where that came from."

I sigh softly, answering by working his top button open.

He rolls his head back.

I pop the next button.

"You're playing with fire now, kitten." His mouth crushes mine again, more eager than before.

His tongue thrusts against mine with carnal delight.

Shaking, I undo the whole row of buttons and work the shirt off.

"Miles?"

He releases my mouth, almost gasping for air. "Yeah?"

"You said I'm playing with fire?"

"Damn right." He thrusts his pelvis against mine. "Tell me it doesn't burn."

"God." I instinctively move in closer, deepening the friction, the sweetness. "As long as it's a slow burn..."

But part of me hopes for a wildfire.

Too much of me asks for no mercy.

He makes quick work of pulling my dress over my head, unclasping my bra with one hand, and I shrug out of it.

My hands move to his slacks, opening them as I'm lifted away from the wall.

"What—"

He silences me.

His lips are on mine.

His tongue is in my mouth.

He's taking my all, everything I am in one growling kiss.

And I realize there's no place for words here.

Not when I'm submerged in one electric wave of sensation.

And the rumble in his throat comes like thunder as he carries me to his desk, swiping everything off it with a single sweep of his arm.

I'm tumbling down on dark wood a second later, my eyes fused to his, two storms of pure lust melting together.

This time, when he presses his lips against mine, it's tender and sweet.

"Last chance to turn back. Tell me you want this," he whispers.

I nod until my neck stings.

"But here? Like this? If you want to wait—"

It's sweet that he's containing himself—barely—just for me. But I lean up, taking his lips with mine.

"No way. I can't."

With a rough smile, Miles climbs over me, grabbing my wrists as he drapes me over his desk with long, slow, carnivorous kisses.

Forget the slow burn.

I *am* the fire as I arch up against him, his hand against my panties, his thumb digging into my clit.

He releases my mouth and trails kisses down my neck and clavicle, opening his mouth over one breast.

When his tongue flicks my nipple, I'm obliterated.

Closer to coming in a way I never even knew I could.

"Miles!"

Snarling, he covers my other breast with his hand, running circles over the hard peak. His other thumb strokes my clit again, faster than before, a hypnotic friction I don't have a prayer of ignoring.

So close.

So flipping close it hurts.

And just when I'm about to *scream*, he stops, pulling away and dragging his lips lower, lower, oh God, *lower*.

He kisses my belly, dropping down to the sweet spot, leaving me squirming.

His lips move below my stomach until he finds the satin of

my panties. It doesn't deter him for a second. He just jerks them down, rips them off my ankles, and his tongue finds my pearl.

Everything goes white-hot.

Blind.

Electric.

"Oh, Miles!"

Going.

Going.

Gone!

His mouth comes in waves of pleasure, lifting me up and slamming me down until I'm a twitching mess.

I don't even know when he pushes his free hand into my mouth, or when I start biting down.

When the pleasure stops racking my body, I'm too spent to care about leaving marks.

I'll worry later.

Because I already know I'm in trouble, and I've barely begun to burn when he looks at me with lidded eyes and a guttural laugh, stroking a hand down my bare hip.

"You asked for a slow burn, kitten. We're just getting started."

XIV: NO BAD PUBLICITY (MILES)

J'm one long heartbeat, my pulse roaring in my ears, drowning out everything.

I can finally taste her, and goddamn, I'll never want for anything else except more of Jennifer Landers.

We've traded places now. I'm backed against my desk, wearing my pants around my ankles.

She's on her knees like a supplicant worshipping her god.

I watch her small, nimble fingers hook beneath the elastic of my boxers and pull. They've been damn near cutting off my circulation for a while.

I barely breathe as she strips me naked, her green eyes twinkling as she stares up at me.

My ego loves the small gasp that slips out of her when she sees what I'm packing.

"Holy...hell." Her small tongue darts across her lips, her eyes wide with delight.

"Yeah. I come by the attitude honestly, kitten. Let's see some respect."

I think I'm my usual cocksure self—*pun intended*—until her hands wrap around my girth, squeezing me so tight.

My breath stalls, turning to cement.

I'm jolted, my head snapped back, a willing hostage to every lashing of pleasure as she strokes me up and down.

Slowly and loudly.

Her every breath torn with lust.

"Fuck, kitten. If this is payback for what I just did to you, then—"

I never finish that thought.

The second I look down, her mouth parts, engulfing the angry tip of my cock.

I almost lose my nut right there, gripping the edge of my desk behind me for support.

Of all the enchanting and maddening things she does with her mouth, I never imagined she could suck like this.

I'm speechless, one with the motionless growl boiling out of me as I watch her small mouth struggle down my length. Her eyes are lit with desire and so many filthy promises I almost break.

Damn.

God fucking damn.

She's too good at this—lethally skilled.

Grabbing her hair with one hand, I twine it around my fingers for more control, before she delivers death by tongue.

And fuck, what a tongue.

She knows when to tease, when to torment, when to bring me so close my jaw clenches, when to steal the air from my lungs.

This shouldn't be happening.

I shouldn't be this obsessed—this close to letting her wring my balls dry—and I'm actually *leaning* slightly against my desk so my knees don't buckle.

My fingers pull her hair harder the closer she drags me to the edge, and I'm rasping down at her, my eyes locked on this auburn-haired angel sucking the life from me.

"Fucking hell, kitten," I groan. "If you came here to murder me, there are easier ways."

Murder, you say? The look she gives back says it all.

A buttery moan spills out of her around my cock, adding to the sensation.

"Shit, woman. You keep that up, I *will* come down your throat. Careful."

The warning doesn't stop her.

If anything, it just makes her more merciless, more eager to see me undone. I'm drowning in green-eyed sweetness until her eyes flutter shut, and I see she's pushed one hand between her legs.

"Don't stop. Play with your clit. Make yourself come while you choke on me," I growl, driving my hips forward, giving her more, everything I instinctively know she can take.

Then all I see is white.

Heaven and hell melt into one.

My balls strain, in sync with my fingers in her hair.

The instant she feels my cock ballooning against her tongue, turning to steel, she drives herself down with a fierce, muffled sound, so intent on ruining me I think she gags.

I'm a dead man—and I've never been happier.

Lightning explodes up my spine, hurling thick ropes of come, so intense it's blinding.

I'm no monk.

I've had my fair share of women, and more blow jobs than I could ever count.

But this—*this* can't compare.

Imagine comparing a cherry bomb to a thermonuclear blast.

That's what rips through me right now and douses me in flames.

I'm roaring so loud I'm sure anyone outside can hear us. I forget what time the night crew comes in to clean.

Regardless, we're both way past caring.

I exist in this moment to ruin Jennifer Landers the same way she's taking me apart, worshipping me, desperately catching everything I give her even when she loses so much down her chin.

She's a beautiful mess by the time I pull my throbbing cock out of her mouth, still hard in my hands.

Hell, so am I.

I pull her up, wiping my remnants off her face, then meld my mouth to hers with a kiss that says I'm proud of her wearing me.

I couldn't guess how long we kiss, how long I run my fingers through her hair, how long she drags her fingers up and down my hard abs, my thigh, both of us locked in admiration.

All I know is I'm still hard, and hellbent on marking her again.

But first, I need to check in.

"Am I scaring you yet?" I whisper, stamping a kiss on her neck. "If you want to call it here, run off and do some thinking, I'll understand."

She looks at me, anger and amusement dancing in her eyes.

"Miles, I swear to God, if you don't make love to me tonight—"

"I don't make love, kitten," I correct sharply, kissing her as I cup her ass and twist her around, pushing her naked perfection back down on my desk. "However, I will fuck you within an inch of your life."

The rough moan falling out of her before I even push into her, while I'm fumbling in my wallet for a condom, tells me she's willing to take any punishment.

Any sweet madness I dole out.

And I bring it in droves, growling as I thrust into the tightest pussy I've ever had a few seconds later, my arms under her head with both hands fisting her hair, pinning her down.

Air drags into my lungs in a slow, vicious pull.

I stop when I'm almost fully in, afraid I'll hurt her, knowing my own size and manic strength.

She's trembling, this creature of soft curves and copper hair, as fragile as blown glass.

215

All too breakable and endlessly lovable because she's at my mercy.

The long pause deepens our connection and—oh, goddamn —*what is this?*

This feeling.

More than the fury scalding my balls, hounding me to fuck her soul out, to mark her from the inside out.

"What is it?" I whisper, tilting her face up to mine and sucking her bottom lip with my teeth.

"I've always been afraid you'll hurt me, Miles. So hurt me *now*," she finishes her sentence on a barbed breath and a defiant jade-green look. "Show me what it's like when you wreck me so I finally know. Please. Don't hold back."

Damn, does she *hear* herself?

Her legs wind around my waist and lock.

She does.

Her lips are so mine, and when her mouth opens, I meet her strawberry tongue with violent, needy slashes.

My hips go to work, answering her prayers.

I struggle to keep each stroke inside of her long and sweet, a wanton antidote to the poison needling our veins.

I want her to feel me, and nothing else.

I want her to come so hard she realizes I'm telling her the truth, that this shit may have started with the land, but it's ending only God knows where.

Right now, I don't want her to think this is about her land or the tourism project or those stupid videos or *anything* besides the way she makes me batshit deranged.

And my encroaching madness comes out in every stroke.

Every slash of my hips.

Every curse I groan into her mouth, and then, the first orgasm my dick loots from her body.

I crash down on her, sweeping so low her nipples drag against my chest.

I bite her throat—softly at first and then not soft at all—

turning her climax into a controlled demolition that nearly ends her.

Her fingers frantically grab at my hair, slide down my back.

Her hips valiantly drive up at mine, meeting my thrusts as I fuck her right through this fit of rebel ecstasy.

Her nails graze my skin—hard enough to hurt—and goddamn, do I love it.

"Miles. *Miles!*" Her hips arch up, taking me in deeper, capturing me in clenching silk and slick animal movements.

I can't last.

I don't want to.

It's her mantra-like plea that undoes me in the end.

"Oh, Miles. Oh, God. *OhmyGod!*"

I move in her faster, harder, desperation building until I'm—

Fuck!

If the cleaning crew is here, they'll hear this scandal.

So I push my tongue in her mouth again, devouring my kitten, all I can do to muffle us.

Her fingers push through my hair, holding my head in place.

Her legs shake as they pinch my waist, her ankles digging into my ass, so desperate to hold on.

Goddamn, Jennifer.

You're making this hard.

And when she calls my name so sweetly and her body clenches again, I'm gone.

My release tears me apart like a sword, and I'm in fucking pieces when she spasms around my dick again.

We go off together, sharing the fireworks, all teeth and tongues and flaming breaths.

All breathless flames.

When the fever breaks, 'spent' is the only word that comes to mind.

Spent and awestruck.

We both lie there for God knows how long, boneless, willing our lungs to remember how they work.

"Hey, Miles?"

I kiss her cheek. "Yeah, kitten?"

"Is there a security camera?"

I chuckle, shaking my head. "That worried about an audience, huh? And I would've proudly shown that to the entire world."

"Miles!" She swats my chest like the kitten she is.

"Kidding, obviously. There's no camera in this office. As for the one on the floor outside, I'll delete the footage before we leave so one sees you leaving with sex hair."

The way she bites her lip when she smiles kills me again.

"Thank you."

I kiss her forehead. "No worries. There's no sense in inviting more trouble right now."

"Yeah, about that—"

I don't let her finish and ruin this beautiful moment, pressing a finger to her lips.

"Not now, Jenn. I'm enjoying this too much."

"What?" she whispers, her eyes soft.

"You not hating me."

Her mouth drops, but I press a gentle finger against her lips.

"Mainly because you're so fucking—" I catch myself before I say *mine.* "Beautiful."

Twirling a strand of auburn hair around my finger for emphasis, I dip my face to inhale her one more time before we start putting ourselves back together.

Once we're dressed, I slide an arm around her. "Benson's waiting downstairs. Come on."

"But I have my dad's car parked here..."

"It'll still be here in the morning. I'll save you a drive home on sore legs," I say.

She giggles. "Right, but then how will I get here without people wondering?"

I smile. "Benson will pick us up again at my place and drop us off again. Easy."

"Your place? *Us?*" Her voice catches. "Have you lost your mind?"

My gaze sharpens. "You're telling me you'd rather spend the night alone after that?"

Her teeth toy with her lip, betraying her true feelings.

"...it's just, my parents will worry. It's already so late. Plus, the dogs need to be walked, and they get stir-crazy if I'm gone too long. I can't do that to them."

"So text your parents and tell them we're working late. We'll swing by and pick up the dogs."

"Oh my God, no. I'm not ruining whatever multimillion-dollar penthouse you live in with fur and Doberman drool."

"That's why I have housekeeping," I tell her. "And if you get your cute ass in the car right now, it's not too late to have someone drop by and bring them a few new bones to keep them busy. Now *move*, kitten."

She giggles. I win this round.

My hand swats her ass, ushering her out the door.

* * *

I CAN'T BELIEVE I was so worried about leaving Jenn sore.

I wake up stiff as a board and aching the next morning, but every bit of pain was worth it.

Proud new memories of the way I savaged her for hours come back to me, wrecking her with one stormy orgasm after the next.

The night ended with her bouncing on my cock while I pulled her hair like reins.

Fuck.

Fuck.

Even as every muscle below my waist protests, there's one that's still ready for more.

And there's one more beating with a strange, irregular rhythm that alarms me every time I look at her.

She could be a pinup model, hand to God.

The light seeps in through my bedroom window the next morning, framing the angel lying next to me in a halo of morning.

It's almost too magical, and I'm not a man who gets easily bewitched.

Her cinnamon-red hair glows around her face.

The rest of her could slay me a thousand different ways with her softness, her creamy skin, her unearthly shudders when she comes apart, impaled on me.

My comforter is pulled over one side of her, but one arm and leg stick out adorably.

I kiss her on the forehead, get up, throw our clothes in the wash, and start to ponder breakfast as my stomach growls like a bear. There wasn't much appetite for dinner last night during our six-hour sex marathon.

Hell, I'm not even sure what she likes. Though if the late Lottie Risa's cooking was any clue, I'm sure scones have been a normal part of her breakfasts since she was knee-high.

I pull up an old recipe for blueberry scones I have book-marked on my phone and set to work.

Thirty minutes later, soft footsteps announce her arrival.

"Miles?" Her voice is soft and high-pitched, almost nervous as she wanders down the hall.

"I'm in the kitchen." Right. We didn't exactly stop for a tour last night. "Just keep walking straight. It's on your next right."

She greets me with a kiss on the cheek, wrapped up in a throw blanket.

Perfect timing.

I pop the scones in the oven and turn to face her, throwing my arms around her before I drink her lips again.

"Good morning, kitten. You sleep all right?"

"Yeah." Her face turns crimson. She bites her bottom lip and looks down. "But I—I can't find my clothes."

"Everything's in the washer."

"Huh? You do laundry?" I answer with a shrug as she cocks her head, tossing back a bashful grin. "I guess I'll have to stay wrapped in a blanket?"

"You don't have to. I'm more than willing to have you enjoy the morning naked."

Her blush deepens.

"No way! I just meant—well—maybe I should stay in bed until my clothes are dried?"

"Bed. I like that idea." Growling, I pick her up, carry her to my room, and lay her down on my bed. "I set a timer. We've got twenty minutes before breakfast is served."

"But it's already daylight! We'll be late."

"I'll let the boss know. He's a hard-assed prick, but I think he'll understand a little downtime with a pretty lady."

The way she giggles carries me to heaven.

I stretch her out on the bed slowly, taking my sweet time kissing every inch of her. "You're not too sore for this? We went hard last night."

"No." She blushes again. "Not much."

Thank God.

My lips work long and slow, then I untuck the blanket around her, baring her to me in all her naked glory.

She smiles. "What are you doing?"

"The hell does it look like?" I kiss down her neck to her tits, pausing to suck each pert nipple soft. "This is your wake-up call. The coffee can wait."

She laughs and strokes my face with her hand.

"You're such a dork, but I'm glad you approve..."

Approve?

I could take the next week off and spend every waking minute deep inside her. It's only my last frayed thread of sanity that keeps me from actually doing it.

Turning my attention back to her nipples, I suck harder and she sighs.

I fucking love how responsive she is to every touch. Her

body makes the most exquisite music, this song of pleasure I jealously write all over her.

Soon, her sighs become moans.

One lazy moment is all it takes for her to go from innocent angel to the sexiest hellcat I've ever hauled into bed.

My lips roam low, skimming her soft belly, dipping down to the sweetness between her legs. I only stop to inhale her, to fill my lungs with Jennifer Landers until I can't.

When she moves her thighs together shyly, I push them apart again and dart her a look.

"No. There's nothing to pull off with my teeth today and I'm not fucking waiting," I growl.

With the way her face heats, I almost skip straight to plunging my cock inside her again, but I won't miss the opportunity to taste her again.

"Miles... what are you doing?" she whispers when I stop too long, admiring the scene as my hands rub her thighs.

"Massaging you, kitten. Soothing sore muscles the best way possible." My tongue flicks up her opening then.

I lick her, suck her, and breathe her in, working my face against her opening until she's smothering my senses.

Yes.

Goddammit, yes.

I know what a greedy fuck I am, but this pussy is straight black magic.

I'm spellbound as I wear her down, already drunk on her taste, lashing my tongue against her clit and holding it with my teeth. My fingers delve inside her, finding the soft spot on her wall that makes her tense and hold her breath, hold on until a whimper slips out.

Let go, kitten.

Give it all up for me.

The fight goes out of her as her legs fall open, wider than before.

I don't have to fight her this time.

My tongue brushes over her in maddening circles, both of us hypnotized.

My body grows harder with every noise she makes, every cry spilling out of her, but I won't take her like I did last night.

The morning is too gentle, and the long day ahead makes me want to savor this woman, to try to do the impossible and get my fill.

When she's close, I let up, teasing her with feather-light kisses down her opening. Right before I part her legs and plunge my tongue in her depths.

"Ohh, Miles! Oh—God."

Even as her nails spear my shoulders, I lavish and soothe her.

I was too rough last night, and this is my apology made flesh.

This is also how I lie to myself, pretending I'm not already hopelessly addicted to this pussy and the alluring siren it's attached to.

Fuck her for taking over my life.

But fuck me entirely.

I'm the dolt who invited her in, and right now, I can't fathom ever regretting it.

With a messy whimper, she slings her legs over my shoulders and arches into my strokes. Her breath comes faster, like she only needs the slightest friction.

I'm happy as hell to oblige.

Her fingers tangle in my thick hair, pulling my head closer, begging me to finish her.

Come for me, kitten, I ask without words.

I write my name over her clit with my tongue just as her hips start thrashing.

Then I'm snarling, claiming her with my mouth so fully her scream rips through my house.

We'll calm the dogs later, who run up to the shut door, barking up a storm and whining.

A brickbat to the face couldn't tear me off her right now.

And nothing will stop her from being blown to the seven winds.

I've never enjoyed watching a woman come apart this much before.

Her legs convulse for an eternity as I pull her to my face, making her ride my mouth, my dusting of a beard, holding her prisoner until she's gasping and limp.

When I'm finally sure she's completely spent, I come up and kiss her, hovering over her.

She takes the slow, deep kiss I offer.

"Taste yourself, woman. Only way you'll ever understand what you do to me," I whisper.

She's too flushed, breathing too hard to answer.

I smile like the madman I've become.

We kiss in heady silence until the oven dings.

"Breakfast." I stand up with a knowing look over my shoulder, loving how she laughs. I point to a door on the other side of the room. "My closet is over there. Wear whatever you want until the clothes are dry. I'll feed the dogs and throw your stuff in the dryer once the scones are out."

When she walks into the kitchen a few minutes later, this time she's wearing my old USMC t-shirt. I'm not sure who looks more surprised, me or the Dobermans, who look up from the small antlers they've been gnawing.

"How do you take your coffee?" I ask.

"White."

"White? That's a new one. Are you fucking with me?"

"Um, we already did that, but... It's easy. Just pour heavy cream until it turns white and add sugar."

"Okay, one glass of sugar-milk with a dab of coffee coming right up." I wink at her.

"Dick. But I love the way you don't hide your art here." She turns her breakfast stool, studying the paintings on the walls like we're at a museum.

I follow her gaze to where it stops on the Celtic owl painting beside the breakfast bar. One of the few creations I'm genuinely proud of, once a gift for my mother's sixtieth birthday.

"Oh, wait. Isn't this like the one on your shoulder?"

Nothing slips past her, the little minx.

I grin. "Good eye. They're similar designs. I did the painting first and liked it so much I took a picture and asked for a recreation at the tattoo shop. Celtic designs get pretty intricate because of all of the knots, but the artist pulled it off."

She blushes and smiles. "I agree. I thoroughly examined you. I noticed the eagle tattoo on your other shoulder. Is that from your paintings, too?"

For a second, I hesitate, working on the coffee.

"No. It's from my days in the Marine Corps. Played a big role in making me the man I am today," I tell her, unsure why I'm even thinking about revealing the other part. "My late mother, she loved owls. I keep them around for the same reason you have your grandmother's gardens and bee boxes."

Her eyes gleam with sympathy as she nods. "Oh. Oh, right. I'm sorry, Miles."

"It was a long time ago."

And still just like yesterday, I think bitterly.

I pry the dark thoughts off my mind and set the scones down to cool, then quickly whip up my take on honey butter.

"These won't be Lottie good, but they're nothing to sneeze at."

She smiles, drawing a happy breath. "Smells amazing. If we all had to live up to Gram's cooking, we'd be so screwed."

The way she bites into the scone a minute later and chews so intently says I did the job.

"I have to say, you don't seem like a Marine," she tells me.

"What does a Marine seem like?"

She doesn't say anything, just picks up her scone and slathers it with more honey butter.

"I don't know. Tough. Street smart."

I snort. "You think I'm not?"

Again, she laughs.

"You're scary. You paint landscapes and make property deals. You manage a multibillion-dollar media company and you look like you could knock down a linebacker. Also, you're so rich—and a good cook—it's just hard to imagine you sleeping in tents, scraping dehydrated food out of bags."

"Tents are for officers. Everyone else sleeps on the ground like real jarheads. You'd be surprised how many CEOs in this town have done their four to eight years with Uncle Sam."

She chews thoughtfully and swallows, sipping her sugar-milk.

"I suppose you're right. Pippa said Brock did some time in the Air Force, and I know Lincoln Burns and Cole Lancaster also served."

"Yeah. Veterans everywhere in the ranks. Discipline gets you a whole lot further than money ever will. War is business. It teaches you how to survive on no sleep and gut-rot coffee. You go forty-eight hours if you need to and you make your bed before you leave the house. It's better training than any MBA degree for frat boys." I shrug. "Grit's worth its weight in gold."

"Lucky you," she whispers. "Yeah, if I hadn't slept in two days, I'd just lie down on the ground and pass out."

"You'd be court-martialed in no time."

"But I didn't leave. I just needed sleep..."

"I suppose beauty sleep is extra important for you, kitten."

She looks up and sticks her tongue out.

"I hate you for making me like that stupid nickname." She takes a bite of scone.

"As long as you hate me enough to keep fucking me like last night," I growl, grabbing her hand and squeezing.

The lopsided smile she throws back says that's a *yes*.

"So how long have you been painting?" she asks.

"Since I was a kid."

"Impressive. The owl is definitely cool, but the paintings in the living room of my grandma's house and your office are my favorite."

I nod.

"The Narada Falls set—the ones in my office—that was my dad's work. I had them put up after I became CEO. My father got me into painting originally. I can't deny his style rubbed off on me."

I stuff my face with scone so I don't have to see the surprised look on her face. I don't tell her Narada Falls was also my mother's namesake and a contender for her favorite place on Earth, the spot where my father proposed when they were young.

"Pretty amazing. You're both very talented."

I nod my thanks.

"Is your Dad still around?"

"For now." She looks at me like she's expecting more, but I don't elaborate, especially when I've already said too much. The words also come out more clipped than intended.

Fortunately, the distant dryer buzzes, sending the dogs skittering with excitement and giving me the distraction I need.

I throw back the rest of my coffee and scrounge up Jenn's clothes.

As adorable as she is in my old t-shirt that hangs off her like a garbage bag, we both need to get to work at some point.

"Maybe I should Uber," she says.

I throw her a look.

"Don't be ridiculous. Benson has to take me in anyhow. You'd might as well come with."

"Miles, if people see us get out of the car and walk into the office together, they're going to talk."

I shrug. "It's just one night. We needed to get it out of our system, don't you think?"

"One night. Sure." She doesn't look up from her second scone, and something about her tone rings hollow.

My gut clenches.

Is this dumbass honesty too much?

I clear my throat. "Obviously, we won't make it a habit. But it's stupid for us to go to work in separate cars. If anyone says anything, they can take it up with me, and I'll tell them we had an early morning business meeting."

Yep.

Definitely dumb. Definitely too honest.

She barely speaks to me during the ride in, and I'm annoyed as hell with myself for trying to quit her cold turkey when I can already feel my hunger building again.

* * *

OF ALL THE STUPID, *shit-for-brains things you could've said...*

By evening, I keep thinking I should call Jenn and try to smooth over my idiocy this morning, but when she mentioned people talking if we showed up in the same car, it was like a bucket of ice water being dumped on my head.

It woke me up from a dream I never knew I wanted, not before we—

Fuck.

There's no denying I lose my mind when she's around. My brain transfers all thought control to my dick.

And last night, nothing made it through my head except how fatally gorgeous she is, how right she feels in my arms, how magnificently she lights up with every kiss.

What people might say about me—or more importantly, *her* —was the furthest thing from my mind.

The worst part is, I know there's no hiding this thing we've started, if we decide to keep it going.

How could I ever have her in the same meeting room without people noticing how starved I am every time I look at her?

"Mr. Cromwell?"

The knocking doesn't wait for me to answer before my office door swings open.

Bradley's face is red and pinched tight, but that isn't what screams there's something wrong.

The bearish head of my company's public relations and my personal reputation manager never blows into my office announced.

What now?

"What's the matter? Don't tell me, the charity gala in Medina tonight?" I ask, my mind snapping to the first thing that springs to mind. "We already have two teams covering it and plenty of freelancers for support. Our stations will be the first to report a nipple slip or drunken insult, so you don't have to worry."

Bradley just stands there, shifting his bulk uncomfortably.

Not good.

Whatever he's here to tell me is bad news, the kind with no easy fix.

"It's your side project and—ahem, Miss Unmentionable."

Miss Unmentionable?

Is Jenn right? Has the talk about us already started right under my nose?

Damnation.

I'm going to be in damage control very soon, if that's the case, and I'm not sure even Bradley can help me with that.

"Cut the shit. What side project?"

"Your Pinnacle Pointe tourism project," he says nervously, bowing his head.

Fuck.

"And Miss Landers has done something to warrant a visit from PR?"

He quirks a brow. "Miss Landers? No. I'm sorry, sir, I should be more specific. Pacific-Resolute just released an exclusive story on Pinnacle Pointe around noon. It's all over their major channels, and it'll be trickling into the papers tomorrow for sure."

Disaster.

I'm just not sure what form it's taking.

"Damn. I wish we'd beat them to the punch, but any extra coverage for the town will only increase their tourism prospects. Unless..."

It clicks in my head before Bradley meets my gaze and clears his throat.

"Their exclusive trashed the entire town, Mr. Cromwell. Their affiliates are playing up a string of small-scale burglaries this summer, painting it as a second-rate, crime-ridden place to live with crumbling infrastructure and dilapidated houses."

Shock knifes through me.

For such a tiny community looking for more revenue from outsiders, that's devastating news.

Hell, with small-time fishing in decline, the mayor believes tourism is the only way forward to avoid the fate of so many other little island towns in Washington.

If Simone cuts them off at the balls, I'm not sure how Pinnacle Pointe survives.

Still, it doesn't warrant a visit from the head of PR, unless he's the only senior officer with the balls to tell me to my face.

"That's grave news for our plans with the town. However—"

"What does it have to do with you? Or this company? Yeah, I'll get to that," he promises. "Mr. Cromwell, this is a five-alarm emergency. You either release your content *now* and say a Hail Mary it outshines Pacific-Resolute's bullshit exposé—or you wait, and you don't release it at all."

My gut sinks.

"What? Why?"

"Because, sir. There's no reasonable way your content will come across as authentic once her story gains steam. After folks hear about the robberies and see one shot of algae growing on roofs and fishing shacks falling down... well, you know what they say. There's no second crack at a first impression."

"Go on." I tap my pen on my desk like a cat flicking its tail in irritation.

"The Pacific-Resolute people already interviewed one old

woman whose house was broken into last spring. She didn't have much to steal, so they took her CPAP machine. The lady saw it as attempted murder since she can't breathe at night without it with her sleep apnea and all. How can you publish a story about this charming little town that belongs in a Hallmark movie if Granny goes viral talking about how someone tried to suffocate her in her sleep?"

My hand curls into a fist.

"They were still talking about it at Murphy's," I bite off. "Mrs. Smith way overplayed it, but why? The fuck did steal her CPAP. Then someone from the local church put up a fundraiser in no time and it was replaced the next day. Attempted murder? Christ, that's dramatic. The thief was caught a few weeks later when he tried to sell it on eBay. Some dipshit college kid visiting on spring break. He partied too hard and didn't have the money for the bus ticket home."

Bradley goes quiet for a minute, stroking his greying beard. "You're serious? Fucking aye."

I nod.

"But what's the one truth in media?" he asks.

I wait for him to tell me.

"You're only worth as much as your reputation, sir. The truth doesn't matter nearly as much as how believably you can sell it. Once you've lost your audience's trust, you've lost your audience. Period. No audience means no ad sales, and no ad sales—"

"Means no revenue. I know that much."

"So, we're looking at the same problem. Either your tourism project goes viral before Suffocating Grandma, or it's a total loss."

"I'll take care of it, Bradley. Thanks."

"Please keep us in the loop," he says as he stands. "My department needs to be ahead of this, whatever you decide. I'm telling everybody to stand by for a late night."

"Absolutely. On your way out, tell Louise to assemble

creative in the conference room right now. I'll call Miss Landers."

"Will do. I'll be there too," he promises.

Then he's gone, leaving me alone with this unexpected dumpster fire.

What the absolute shit?

What am I dealing with?

What does psychobitch possibly think she has to gain by trashing Pinnacle Pointe?

Does she know I've already scuttled her from buying Bee Harbor, and now she's nuking the whole place?

We're *not* shelving the project. Besides being a sunk cost, I'm a man of my word, and I promised the mayor and the council I'd come through for them.

This is personal now.

I'm the first and last reason Simone is going after the town, and I'm not fucking having it.

I just need to figure out her game plan.

Is the inn still a factor?

If tourism tanks and Jenn winds up left with a bed and breakfast in a dead little town no one visits, that'll definitely hurt her own prospects. It'll hamper her ability to make repairs, too, and the place has a list of those a nautical mile long.

I pick up my phone and hit Jenn's contact, the mess I made this morning already a distant memory.

"Hey," she answers cautiously. "If this is about earlier—"

"I need you in the executive conference room in ten minutes."

The long pause tells me she's blindsided.

"Is something *else* wrong?"

"I'll explain once we're settled. For now, help round up everyone from creative you can."

"Miles—"

"Mr. Cromwell in the office. In front of others, I'm still the CEO, and you'd be wise to—hello?"

She hung up on me.

Fuck!

I slam the phone down in its cradle.

I know, I know.

I'm being an ice-cold bastard and I probably deserved it, but I have an entire town and a lot of livelihoods depending on me right now.

I have to get in front of this ASAP, personal consequences be damned.

XV: NO EXCEPTION (JENN)

"What were you thinking?" I ask myself as soon as I end the call and drop the phone on my desk.

I knew who he was all along.

But I still slept with him.

Multiple times.

More orgasms than I can count.

Screaming, breathless, bone-rattling finishes I thought only happened in spicy novels and never real life.

This isn't exactly a new pattern for him, or us—and I have to remind myself there isn't an us.

This is exactly what he did after he kissed me.

A huge flapping red flag I just straight-up ignored as soon as I saw him in his office with that hangdog look and a few rough words inviting sin.

You know it's bad when you don't even wait for a real bed with a man you shouldn't be screwing.

God help me, I'm the dumbest woman alive.

Waldo, please call me today. I need to be done with this man and his company.

Tell me there's some magic clause where I can sell to the realtor after all and get on with my life.

Yep. I'm at the point of thinking about pulling up stakes and asking Gram for forgiveness for the rest of my life.

But not really.

Sigh.

I glance at the computer screen.

Six more minutes to make it to the conference room without the world's hottest mistake tearing my face off.

At least the dogs made it home okay, though, courtesy of Benson. Unlike me, they'll have sweet memories of their time in his palace looking over Lake Washington.

After wasting a couple more minutes browsing cottages in Pinnacle Pointe I don't have the gumption to rent with my make-believe money from an imaginary sale, I take the private elevator up.

Maybe he's so pissed at what we did that he's going to terminate my contract, and we can just be done.

Yeah, no.

Or he'll just berate me about how unprofessional it was, like it was all my fault, and send me off on my merry heartbroken way.

He's right about one thing—it *won't* happen again.

Not unless he gets bored and I get a lobotomy. *Or horny.*

Or whatever blow to the head made him say the crap he said yesterday.

Ugh.

He'd better hope he has Louise in the room if he even so much as makes a snide comment. Otherwise, I'm going to knee him square in the balls.

I swing the door to the conference room open and storm in a few minutes later. It's dead silent.

Huh?

"Hey, Jenn. How you holding up?" Smokey Dave sounds weirdly depressed.

"Fine, you?" I take the first empty seat I find, more weirded out than ever when he just shrugs.

235

Soon, the entire creative team from Pinnacle Pointe is gathered there, but the room is giving me serious funeral vibes.

Then I spot Miles and a couple of other suits at the back of the room, talking among themselves. The way his hands slash through the air sharpens my nerves.

Whatever this is, it's big.

Miles moves to the front of the room a minute later, clasping his hands in front of him and donning his best calm face.

"I'll keep this short and to the point. I need all Pinnacle Pointe content edited, polished, and published in under forty-eight hours. We've lost the luxury of time." He barely pauses while a few shocked gasps and whispers fly around the room. "We can no longer afford to treat this like a side project. I need the main push ASAP."

Whatever I expected, it wasn't this.

What the hell is going on?

This was always a nonprofit side project. It can't be about money.

"If you have any questions, email the department head, and if they don't answer, you come to me. Go get started. Dismissed." He claps his hands like he's talking to a pack of dogs.

People start filing out with rumors darting back and forth.

I stay behind, hoping for a chance to ask Miles what happened.

Why the sudden urgency?

And holy shit, does he know what he's truly asking?

I'm not sure I could have everything ready for prime time in two days if you held a gun to my head.

He notices me standing there, glares, and says, "I don't have time for games or personal affairs, Miss Landers. Go. Help them."

Games? Miss Landers?

What the fuck.

"That's pretty rich coming from you." I can't help it.

"What do you mean?"

"Gee, I don't know. You've completely changed the scope of my project without a word of explanation. What's changed? You owe me that much."

His lips thin and his eyes gleam like blades.

"You really want to know? Fine. You have more of a vested interest in the town's tourism than anyone else in this room, minus yours truly. If we don't move our asses and bury some devastating bad press, Pinnacle Pointe may never recover."

Bad press? What?

Who could have anything bad to say about Pinnacle Pointe?

It's a portrait of serenity.

There isn't much there in modern conveniences, sure, but there isn't much to complain about either.

"Experience tells me if this garbage proliferates unchecked, long-term opinions will harden in under a week. That's the news cycle. If people hear attacks repeated every day about this town with nothing to counter it, eventually they'll believe it. And once they've bought the lie, the truth no longer matters. The attacks have to be combated with positive press or we don't have a fighting chance. Your inn will be worthless. The general store and the bar will shut down. The few jobs left there will dry up in no time. So, Jenn, if you don't want a ghost town, kindly put our bickering aside and get on board."

What flipping attacks?

"I don't understand. Who would come after Pinnacle Pointe?"

He sighs. "Jenn, just go help the team. We don't have time for this now, I promise you."

I glare at him.

"I'll explain everything later." His voice softens. "If you have any issues with the project, come straight to me, okay? Time is critical."

The heavy weight in his eyes is the only thing that makes me bite my tongue until it hurts, spin around, and march out his door.

On the elevator ride down, all I can think about is how this makes no sense.

The only person I know who doesn't like Pinnacle Pointe is my dad, and that's because he's a city boy who's allergic to fresh air and wild salmon.

What happened?

There's only one way to find out.

* * *

I DON'T HEAR from Miles the rest of the day.

He has no intention of talking about what happened.

Big surprise.

Chalk it up to one more broken promise. But the fact that he won't explain what the hell is going on worries me more.

Where are these attacks coming from? And why?

Despite being buried under a mountain of work, I can't resist some sleuthing.

I don't leave the office until after eleven. Forty-eight hours isn't enough time to clean up the mess, but a girl has to sleep sometime. Thankfully, Dad took the dogs out on his evening jog, and they're still content with their bones by the time I drag through the door with a burrito for dinner.

Lying on my bed, I open my laptop and Google Pinnacle Pointe.

The first hit in the news is an article about drugs and crime.

Um, what?

I'm instantly annoyed.

I've only lived there for a couple months, but Gram would have been the first to notice if anything was turning shady there.

Still, I click the link, holding my breath as my eyes scan over the title.

Pinnacle Pointe: The Peak of The Opioid Crisis

AT FIRST GLANCE, *Pinnacle Pointe seems like another idyllic small town nestled on an island along the Olympic Peninsula. Tourists usually stick to the main strip or The Bee Harbor Inn, a long-time favorite until its recent closure.*

Just past miles of sandy beachfront with picturesque shorelines, you'll find the town's general store, an Irish pub, and a diner that's only open through lunch.

That's it. That's Pinnacle Pointe, a place that looks too honest for secrets.

Or is it?

Two blocks up Blakely Street, a different story begins to unfold.

AN IMAGE FILLS THE SCREEN. It's a residential neighborhood.

I recognize a few of the houses, most of them are in various stages of disrepair. Some of them look like they might blow over with a strong enough wind. The caption reads, 'The Real Pinnacle Pointe.'

THERE'S *an old neighborhood in need of repair. Then there's two more up the street. The same grim chapter of old-world Washington in decline that's played out a hundred times, except here, it's the entire story.*

ANOTHER BUSTED-UP NEIGHBORHOOD fills the screen. I scroll past pictures of homes with worn, dislodged siding and greenish algae on the roofs.

UNTIL *2001, Pinnacle Pointe's poverty rate was steady. Then the fishing industry went into a downward spiral, faced with fierce competition from larger corporate mergers and foreign suppliers.*

With job loss came peril, and soon, destitution.

Now with only a handful of local businesses left, job opportunities are scarcer than ever.

Anyone who can, plans their escape. The town's negative population growth just keeps diving as young people exit for better opportunities.

ANOTHER IMAGE POPS UP. A tiny brunette woman with lines carved by stress on her cheeks, holding a microphone in front of a waitress I think I recognize from Murphy's.

JESSICA KING SAYS, "I can't wait to leave this town! The pub is the only work in town, and so many customers don't even tip. Try living on minimum wage with guys getting grabby. And sometimes, when the tips do come in from the summer crowd, you'll see another customer trying to swipe the cash from the table. It's awful."

Jessica's desire to leave for greener pastures is clear, so I ask what keeps her here.

An elderly mother with bills piling up.

A grandmother at the only retirement home in town.

An uncle who hasn't managed to stay sober, but who never stops trying.

With ample obligations and little money, Jessica reckons it will be a while before she has enough to leave this city.

Like so many others mired in the town's economic abyss, she's effectively trapped. Time and hope are both running thin.

I roll my eyes. These situations are hardly unique to Pinnacle Pointe, sad as they may be, so why write about it?

And what's it got to do with drugs?

I keep reading.

IF JESSICA'S despair seems shocking, it isn't the absolute bottom.

One candid townsperson went on record anonymously.

"There's money to be made in the Pointe, right or wrong," he said. "You just gotta know where to find it. I've had my own business since eighth grade. Used to be a lumber factory in town. Then my old man got sick and got laid off. We couldn't afford his medicine. I had to help the family out."

THIS SOUNDS LIKE A GOOD KID. He'll set things straight, right?

"I STARTED off selling uppers on the docks as a side thing. It was enough to buy us food for a week. Soon, it was adding up to three thousand bucks a month. The summer crowd went nuts for the pills, especially the college kids. But everyone wanted them, and I only had like sixty pills a month with my own prescription and the ones I could pull from my friends."

At this point, the young man pauses and grins.

"I started making runs to Portland and hooked up with suppliers. But some dude in a leather jacket showed up a few months later at the drop site. He told me they were watching to make sure they got their cut, and if I started stiffing them, I'd be 'done.' Don't think he just meant cut off. So I freaked. I got paranoid. I tracked every pill I sold religiously, and paid them extra just so we were good."

The young man hesitates. His eyes flick over his shoulder. It doesn't matter that we're in a closed office, he's that nervous about who could be listening.

"My Portland guy wanted to recruit me for more. He promoted me."

Our anonymous source now sells prescription painkillers and other illicit goods all over town at meeting sites we agreed not to highlight.

"Tourists always pay the most," he says. "Everybody wants to have a good time away from home—but the people who buy at church are steady customers in the slow season. Plus, they can't rat you out without going down with you."

The young man gives us a calculated smile.

. . .

GOD.

My heart thrums in my chest, shell-shocked that anything like this was going on there. And apparently for years?

It just keeps getting better as I read on.

The next section rattles off five "robberies" that happened in Pinnacle Pointe over the summer. But from the descriptions, they seem more like trumped-up petty thefts.

The last paragraph catches my attention.

THE QUIET MIDDLE-CLASS neighborhood on the edge of town is the only place insulated from the burglaries. Two founding families of the oldest church rest on one side of the road. Farther up the street is the once bright and beautiful Bee Harbor Inn—and the town's only billionaire.

You might be tempted to think protection comes from the billionaire, who's made his slice of Pinnacle Pointe his own private fortress.

You'd be wrong.

Rather, it's the well-kept, well-lit inn that shelters this side of town from the quiet anarchy pulsing through the streets. Even vacant, Bee Harbor's peaceful legacy lives on.

For some in Pinnacle Pointe, the porch light is always on.

WHAT THE—? THAT WAS MY GRANDPARENTS' old slogan.

Seriously.

Who the hell is behind this, and why are they painting the inn like it's some special safe space?

It's like they knew our tourism campaign was coming, and now they want to trash the town before it gets off the ground.

My stomach knots.

Could it be an insider? Who else knew about the tourism project?

When this crap gains traction, everyone in Pinnacle Pointe will hate me for having the only kind word in the entire hit piece.

But they have to know I wouldn't have agreed to this.

I wonder how far its reach already is.

I go back to the search results page. The next hit has the same journalist holding the microphone for an old lady who looks like she belongs in a Medicare commercial. It's a video.

"Didn't you say your home got broken into this summer?" the brunette asks.

"They did! One of those rats broke into my house and stole—*get this*—my CPAP machine of all the things!"

The other woman makes a face like she's sucking a lime and pulls the mic back. "What could they want with a medical device?"

"Crank money! What else? The kids who come boating in the spring and summer are always high on something. It's all over town," the old woman snaps, shaking her head.

My heart drops into my gut.

Okay. Yeah. Miles is right.

I see the urgency now.

We have to dump some good press, pronto, if we want any hope of burying this dreck.

And with creative still plodding along, trying to come up with content that doesn't suck, that means it's up to me.

I don't get much sleep.

The nightmares come fast and furious.

Bee Harbor, up on the auction block because I can't afford the property taxes anymore.

An arson attempt that kills my business and wipes out my savings.

Then the new owner, leveling the place and selling off the land to some investor who turns it into a strip mall.

Only, my alarm clock saves me from more punishment.

On my way to the office, my phone rings. Pinnacle Pointe Legal flashes across my screen. "Hello?"

"Miss Landers, it's Waldo. Is this a good time?"

"I'm almost at work, but what did you find?"

There's a moment of silence.

Oh, boy.

"I researched your grandmother's will extensively, diving deep into the property records," he begins.

"Let me guess. I can't sell, can I?" I whisper.

"You can. In three years."

"Great. Maybe I'll still have a good offer then." *And if miracles still happen, maybe Pinnacle Pointe won't be a ghost town with a bad reputation.*

"There is one exception," Waldo says quietly.

"What's that? And why didn't you mention any of this when you first explained the will?"

"There's a confidentiality clause. I was only supposed to mention it if you directly asked. Miss Landers, it was months ago, and I do a lot of wills in an aging town like this. That's why I had to go back and reread everything, especially with a property of this size. But the confidentiality clause stopped me from explaining it up front."

I sigh. "Okay. What's the exception?"

"Your grandmother specified a potential buyer. If an offer appears from this specific buyer before the three-year holding period is up, then you're welcome to sell to Lottie's preferred buyer at any time of your choosing."

My stomach drops. "Preferred buyer?"

"Yes, it's—"

Don't say it.

Don't say his name.

I already know.

"Mr. Miles Cromwell. The man who owns the neighboring property. If you're interested in selling, I could certainly reach out to him for you."

Wouldn't that be lovely?

"That won't be necessary," I rush out. I should end the call now when I have a million things to do and not enough time. I think Waldo has told me what he knows, but I don't hang up just yet.

"Is there anything else I can do for you?" he asks.

"I just don't understand. Why would she do this?"

"The conditions? Well, sometimes when you're leaving something with significant value to a younger heir, it helps them make informed decisions. Your grandmother probably believed she was protecting you."

"But the one buyer—*why him?*"

He laughs. "That part, I don't know. I've seen very few cases like this involving a neighbor, and in my experience, when it happens, the surviving family usually understands the whys better than I do. But Lottie always was eccentric, bless her heart."

That's a freaking understatement.

Just how close was Miles to my grandmother? How did she ever *stand* him?

"Okay, well, I'm glad that's cleared up," I lie. "Thank you."

Now I cut the call.

Wow.

Wowww.

I don't know whether to be touched or freaked out that Gram basically wanted to force the prince of arrogance into my life.

For what?

It's like some quirky rom-com setup, but without the effort a man makes to win the leading lady over and fix everything.

Sighing, I push the button for the elevator and step inside.

So, I'll admit he might have good intentions—*sometimes? Maybe?*—but he's no romantic. How did Gram think he was someone worth—worth what?

Worth knowing?

We can check that one off the list.

Besides some quick cash, I'm not sure what I've gained by knowing him.

Befriending? After some of the stunts he's pulled, I don't want to be friends.

Becoming more?

Yeah, no. That ended with the gravity-defying sex I hate that I still have stuck in my head.

He flat-out told me it was a mistake, and honestly, he was right.

I'm still seething at the thought and snickering bitterly to myself when the elevator doors open and I step out.

It's a hard truth to choke down, but at least I know where we stand.

My choices are either keep living next to him, or abandon ship and sell, giving Miles Cromwell what he's been angling for this whole time.

My phone dings.

Speak of the literal devil.

Miles: Status update, please. I need to know where we're at.

My fingers fly over the screen, typing.

I sent it to Louise on my way in. Ask her.

A few more texts ping, but I ignore them, diving into my work instead. The sooner this gets done, the faster I'll be through with him.

About an hour later, though, he starts blowing up my Inbox.

JENN,

Are we not speaking again?

Can you write two pillar articles rebutting the claims in the Pacific-Resolute piece? I'm confident you've read it by now.

Once you've done that, have it posted immediately. I'll have creative structure all their social media posts around it.

Yours,

M. Cromwell

. . .

"IGNORE HIM," I hiss to myself.

And I do for the next half hour, reading over the article draft from our writers, which Sarah spent all night tightening up in edits.

I happily send back my approval before I respond to Dracula.

IT'S on its way to publication as we speak.

We're still talking, but only about business. I'm not so petty I'd freeze you out when we're in crisis mode, Miles.

I'm earning my keep with the company. Just not with you.

Never yours again,

Jennifer

BUT AS THE email goes out, there's no relief.

As soon as the panic push ends, we're right back to square one.

I'm more confused than ever, and I can't help wondering how much more he'll destroy my life before he's gone.

XVI: NO BACKING DOWN (MILES)

*M*ission accomplished.

If there was an award for slinging great content under a mountain of crushing pressure, my team would have it.

Before the hefty bonuses arrive on their next paycheck, I start showing my gratitude with a catered breakfast in the conference room from the finest café in town.

But first, they deserve a few words.

A few more than the rundown I sent everyone by email this morning, explaining the plot against Pinnacle Pointe without directly calling out Pacific-Resolute.

I walk to the front of the room and clear my throat.

"I want to thank you, everyone, on behalf of myself and Mayor Johnson of Pinnacle Pointe. The content you've posted may well save this town from years of distress. You crushed every turnaround time and exceeded all expectations. You're the heroes of Cromwell-Narada. So go ahead. Stand tall and be proud of this company, and prouder of your work." I pause while applause rattles around me. "There's also one woman I have to thank individually. Without her, I doubt we would've pulled this miracle off on the same grand scale. We'll get to that in a moment, though.

"You'll be pleased to know I had several reports commissioned addressing the real crime situation in Pinnacle Pointe. Real facts, not fluff. The hit piece was worse than dishonest. It was entirely circumstantial. Our rebuttal focuses on genuine problems and solutions, with input from the local mayor and sheriff. Another interesting fact we learned in our research—there's no record of Jessica King anywhere in Pinnacle Pointe. The attack article shamelessly used a fabricated source."

A few gasps ring out.

Smokey Dave swears under his breath. "Dude. *Not cool.*"

"There'll be a time to address that later. For now, Jennifer Landers, will you please stand up? You saved a lot of asses, and I'd like to lead the next round of applause."

She stands, wearing snug black slacks and a blouse with a slit in each arm.

Goddamn.

This woman could show up decked out like a rodeo clown and I'd still be captivated.

My eyes are riveted, undoubtedly shining with hunger and a guilt I can't hide.

My latest blunders haven't left my brain for a single second through this mess.

And I'm reminded of that again as she turns, nodding her thanks to the crowd without ever meeting my eyes.

"Thanks, guys, but I should get back to work." She starts walking toward the door, waving at smiling faces.

I expect her to look back, to show me the slightest acknowledgement.

Nothing.

Damn, I've really fucked this up.

LATER, when I'm ready to sign off for the day and get some well-earned rest, she's still logged into the crisis team chat, her icon lit green.

Since I know she's here, I take the elevator down one floor and walk into her office, stopping in the doorway.

"When you're here this late, you should shut your door. Any psycho could barge in."

She looks up and rolls her eyes.

"Too late. One already did."

I smile like the idiot I am, knowing I set myself up for that.

That gets her moving, though, packing up her things as she stands.

When she reaches the doorway, I'm still standing there unmoving.

"It's too late for this. Miles, I'm exhausted." Her words are clipped and ice-cold.

"How are you really? Beyond the big fire we just extinguished, I mean."

She scoffs, wrinkling her nose like I'm drenched in gasoline.

"I'm dandy. How do you *think* I am?" She pushes past me—rather, she tries.

After a second of fight, I think better of it and let her pass, holding in a sigh.

Still.

I can't leave this festering.

So I chase her to the elevator, calling, "Jenn, wait. Let's share a ride home."

She whips her head around, scowling.

"Let's not. I don't share car rides or anything else with dudes who just use me to get their rocks off." She pauses. "Or guys who charm their way into my grandmother's will. Screw you, Miles."

The acid in her voice shocks me.

"Will? What the fuck?"

"You heard me."

"Wait, you have to explain that last part. Jenn, I didn't know.

What about the will?" I follow her into the elevator, standing at her side with a glare that could scratch diamond.

"Go away."

"Tell me what happened."

She jerks her face up to meet my eyes. "Maybe I would, if you hadn't kept the whole Pinnacle Pointe hack job as tight as a drum. It would've been nice knowing what we were dealing with, instead of hearing it from Google or waiting until you decided we deserved an explanation."

"Tit for tat, huh?" I snort. "Fair, I suppose. For the record, I never used you. I'd take a scalpel to my own balls before I —Jennifer!"

The elevator chimes and the doors open. She doesn't wait a nanosecond before storming out.

"Scalpel sounds like a great choice, Dr. Dickhead."

I race in front of her, holding out my hands. To any bystander, I'm sure I look like a desperate fucking mess. The fact that she turned me into such a depraved creature should end this right there.

"Don't make me push you," she warns, knowing full well she'd have the same chance of moving me as Mount Rainier. "Miles, will you move?"

"Come home with me," I snarl, grabbing her hand.

For a second, she twists sharply. The hate glowing in her eyes spears me, and still I hold on.

"Let go," she spits.

"No. Not until you understand I never meant to hurt you, kitten. Curse me. Scratch my face. Call me every filthy name in the book. I know I deserve it. Hell, have me arrested. I'll suffer it all—whatever the fuck you want—if you'll just hear me out."

Her glare never softens.

The sigh I hold in burns my lungs. "Jenn, I'll explain every-thing as soon as we're somewhere more private."

I release her arm, expecting her to bolt, but she just stands there glaring at me.

"Nope. You should've done that days ago, and I don't have the time or synapses left now. I have dinner with my parents and two giants who need some love. I'm not your plaything anymore."

"If you won't make time, I will. I'm coming with you." The words are out of my mouth before I comprehend what that means.

The rancor on her face vanishes, replaced by shock. "You're what?"

"I'm coming, I said. We need to talk about this tonight."

"*About what?*" she hisses.

"Everything," I whisper, leaning closer until we can't help but breathe each other. "Everything I wish I could stop fucking up."

"...you can't be serious," she says quietly.

"Tell me I look like I'm joking," I growl.

Then I lunge forward, throwing the massive glass door open, holding it for her. She stalks past me, guarded, but doesn't run.

I follow her outside into the soft nighttime rush of traffic.

"Wrong way. Benson's parked over there." I point to the curb.

"I'm *not* going home with you. I'm never making that mistake again."

Fuck.

That castration I promised her would be less harsh.

"I already told you I'm coming home with you," I say, watching as her eyes flash with uncertainty again.

"My car's here." She turns toward the parking garage.

"It's late and you're exhausted. I'll pay any overnight fees and I'll have Benson swing by for you in the morning. You shouldn't be driving in this state."

She turns her nose up. "What state is that? Chronic exhaustion from arguing with an overgrown dick who never learned to take 'no' for an answer?"

My brows pull together like thunderheads.

"I'd call it stubbornness. From shutting this dick out when he's trying to help you," I venture, watching as her face falls.

"If you wanted to help, you should've stocked up on tissues."

"Excuse me?"

She sighs. "You could've saved us both a metric ton of energy and stress by just jerking off—and you would've had an easier time tossing it in the trash than with me."

She has a way with words.

I don't let it paralyze me, though, reaching for the car door and holding it open.

"Get in. Don't make me beg, kitten," I breathe, my voice torched.

I think it's my tone that makes her hesitate.

She doesn't climb in right away, but she's not walking away. Her gaze drifts to the cool, dark interior, considering it.

"Sending Benson to pick you up isn't scandalous, if that's your concern. I've done it for other employees when they needed it, like you do now."

"You're serious?" She studies my eyes.

I nod.

The fight seeps out of her as her eyelids flutter shut.

With a draining sigh, she slides into the vehicle. "This is just because I'm too tired to drive. I still don't want to argue with you tonight or hear more excuses."

"I'll take it," I say warmly.

"Whatevs."

The drive to her parents' house isn't far, less than twenty minutes. In front of the curb, I step out first and hold the door for her again.

She darts past me without a word or a second glance.

I can sense Benson smiling from behind the wheel, even with the privacy screen up. I follow her to the front door.

She spins around. "What the hell are you doing? I'm home."

"Having dinner with you. How many times do I need to say it?"

"You weren't invited," she points out.

"And I'm not leaving until we talk this out, Jenn. If that

means eating with your folks and a couple dogs who could eat me if I piss you off enough—"

"Pssh! Coffee would rather lick you to death, and you know it."

I smile. "Maybe. Can't say the same for Cream. Women are wildcats when they step in to defend their friends from a man who's pissing them off."

Shaking her head, she stabs a finger at the dark vehicle behind me. "Go home, Miles. Don't be ridiculous."

"Only if you come with me."

"Never."

"Right. Looks like I'm staying the night then."

"Go home. Go home. *Go home!*"

She's shouting now.

There's this weird roughness in her voice, and I almost give up before I cause a nervous breakdown. Only, that's not rage or distress in her eyes, I realize a second later.

She's laughing.

Even if she wants to tear me limb from limb on her parents' doorstep, she still finds my antics entertaining.

For a heated second, our eyes lock, and we're stranded in uncertainty.

Then the Dobermans bark loudly from inside the house.

A slender blonde who looks a lot like Jenn in the face opens the door. "Jennifer, what are you doing out here in the dark? Come inside. The dogs saw you and they're already in a frenzy!" Her eyes fall on me. "Oh, you brought a date home? Why didn't you tell me you were with Ryan Reynolds?"

"Mom!" she hisses.

I offer her mother my hand. "Hello, Mrs. Landers. Miles Cromwell. Jenn was helping me with a very important media project and it ran rather late."

She shakes my hand, beaming at me like I really am a heart-throb actor.

"Mr. Cromwell, of course! Wow. I guess all those years she

spent glued to her phone paid off. She was always so persistent with her homework and it's the same with her work ethic."

"Your daughter has impeccable discipline," I agree.

And I enjoy watching a red-faced Jenn, who won't dare look at me.

"You didn't save her a trip home, did you? You should stay for dinner, Mr. Cromwell."

"Call me Miles, Mrs. Landers, and I'd be delighted. Jenn already invited me, but I didn't want to impose."

"Did not!" she whispers from one corner of her mouth.

"With your approval, I think I will. A good home-cooked meal is hard to come by in my business. Devil's hours and all that."

"Bring your appetite and come on in!" Her mother motions us inside with a bright grin.

Jenn's look daggers me.

"Your mother asked. It would be rude to say no," I say with a shrug.

We follow her mom inside. Jenn stays a few steps back, lingering in the entryway.

"Mom, could you give us a minute?"

"Of course." Her mother starts down the hall.

The second she's out of sight, Jenn grabs my arm and digs her little nails into my skin.

"What's wrong, kitten? I'll take off my shoes."

"Don't you *dare* leave this foyer. What do you think you're doing?"

"I told you. I'm staying until we've talked this out, and right now, it looks like I'm having dinner with your generous parents."

Her eyes drift up to the ceiling, begging for help from above that'll never come. I'm sure God is on my side.

"This is harassment, you—"

"Harassment implies motive, and I laid mine out very clearly from the start. Besides, just because I'm a billionaire doesn't mean I'll turn down free food."

"You know what? Fine. *Fine.* Stay all night if you have to. After the crap you've pulled, I'm not speaking to you. I'm stuffing my face and going to bed. *Alone,*" she stresses.

I smile like she's just agreed to two weeks in Maui with me.

I've seen her glare a hundred times, but never this viciously.

Progress.

The only thing worse than molten contempt from a woman you're trying like hell to win back is when she feels nothing at all.

"Sweetheart, can you show Miles to the table? We're almost ready!" her mother calls from the kitchen.

I give the air an exaggerated sniff, smiling like I've just walked into a busy steakhouse. I don't have to pretend I'm hungry when my stomach rumbles.

"You heard the lady. Dinner's ready and I'm hungry as hell tonight."

"I'm going to murder you in your sleep," she vows under her breath.

"Lovely. That implies you'll be with me when I'm sleeping tonight," I whisper in her ear. "Careful. I might risk an untimely death if it means watching you come your little brains out for me five more times."

Her face could rival a Carolina Reaper.

"You might want to cool down first, Jenn. Drink some water. Otherwise, your parents will wonder what in the world we've been discussing," I advise.

And I laugh like it's the funniest damned thing, even before she kicks me in the shin and stomps off.

* * *

"Despite her contractor status—sorry, Jenn always reminds me she's not my employee—she's the best person I've had on payroll for years. She rescued our latest project on a brutal deadline." I cut into my pork roast and take a bite, chewing happily as her mother beams at me. "Divine, Mrs. Landers. Are all the women in your family food magicians? Lottie was the best cook in Pinnacle Pointe, hands down. Ask anyone."

"Ohhh, so you're *that* Miles? You lived next door to my mother-in-law?"

"Guilty as charged."

"I wish we could have met you sooner. Mom always spoke so fondly of you on the phone," Mrs. Landers gushes between bites of potato. "Jenn, how did you not mention this?"

I look over and my kitten shrugs, staring numbly at her plate. "He had Grandma charmed. That's for sure."

She's barely eating, just scattering food around. Her jaw is clenched, and even though she's visibly pissed, I can't help but remember the last time I had her in my arms.

She stabs a crispy potato with a fork and glares up at me. "What are you grinning at?"

Damn.

Am I grinning?

"Just enjoying our sit-down over this fantastic spread," I say.

She rolls her eyes. "Right. My mistake. Honesty never was your strong point."

I don't look away, still chewing my food.

Both of her parents flash her a disapproving look.

"What?" She sets her fork down and looks up. "We're not at work. I don't have to play nice."

"Jennifer, he's a guest in this home, and yes, you do," her father says sternly. "Now, why do I get the feeling we're not talking about work?"

"Oh, God," Jenn groans. "Can you just treat him like you treated my prom date?"

"Date?" Her father blinks. "I thought he was your boss..."

She looks like she's about to start breathing fire. "Well, yeah, he is. But technically, he's—"

"I am her boss, but she's very much a free agent," I cut in. "That's what makes her efforts so admirable. No other consultant puts in more effort than ten new hires. With her, I got damn lucky."

Her father looks between us and nods slowly.

"You hear that, hon? You've got a war chest of recommendations if you ever get tired of island life."

"Yeah, Dad. I'll get right on that, whenever my big city allergy miraculously goes away." Jenn returns his impressed smile with a yawn.

Fuck.

Tough crowd.

Then Coffee trots into the room carrying a rubber chew toy, a ball with rabbit ears, adding his two cents as it thuds on the floor.

Her mother gasps. "Jennifer, get them out of here!"

There's my cue.

I reach into my inner coat pocket. "Coffee, sit."

He saunters over to me and sits next to my chair. Everyone stares in shock as I drop a treat on the ground. Cream noses in on my other side, her curly tail wagging, and I feed her one as well.

"He's a dog whisperer too?" her mom says, leaning toward Jenn and whispering, "*Hold on* to this one."

"He's very good at bribes. Kind of his specialty." She reluctantly meets my eyes.

"I prefer the term 'negotiator,' but touché. Dobermans are very cooperative if you offer them the right motivation," I say, digging a few more treats from my pocket.

I had them stuffed into the side console of the town car for a reason and fetched them when Jenn wasn't looking. If I can win over her dogs, maybe she won't be far behind.

Mr. Landers looks at his daughter. "Nice touch, but, uh, should we give you two a minute?"

"Don't bother, he's just—"

"Would you?" I cut her off, giving her old man my best disarming you-can-trust-me grin.

Jenn rolls her eyes as her parents start picking up their plates and head for the kitchen. "You won't charm him like Gram. He's too much like you, and sooner or later, he'll see right through your BS."

"Let him. Every Landers deserves nothing less than total transparency going forward," I say.

"A little late for that." She sighs. "But the dogs need to go out. Are you coming?"

"Sure." Maybe she's ready to talk, though I won't get my hopes up.

Five minutes later, we're sitting on an outdoor sofa while Coffee and Cream run back and forth across the small well-tended lawn.

"Are you ready to tell me what atrocity I've supposedly committed with your grandmother's will?"

She folds her arms. "I'm not accusing you of anything, Miles. Gram was a stubborn woman and her decisions only made sense to her sometimes. She wouldn't have done anything she didn't damn well want to. That doesn't mean I'll ever understand."

"Neither do I, kitten. What did Lottie do?"

She meets my eyes. "She put a clause in her will. There's only one buyer I can sell her land to for the first three years of my inheritance. Otherwise, it reverts back to the executor who will sell it to her one acceptable buyer and give me the funds."

I wonder if the sky just came loose and dropped on my head.

I draw in a deep breath as the news sinks in.

"Me? I'm Lottie's preferred buyer?"

She nods like she's just gotten a terminal diagnosis.

"That kind, chaotic, wonderful woman," I say, laughing. "I give you my word I never asked to be included in her will. She knew I was interested in the land, of course. I made her a generous offer once, about a year before she passed. She told me she thought you'd be interested in selling if I could hold on a little while longer. I certainly wasn't planning on displacing her."

"Because you're such a gentleman, right?" She huffs out a breath.

I smile. "If she put that in the will, there must be a reason. Lottie knew I'm the only one who'd offer you a small fortune for Bee Harbor—the only buyer without an ulterior motive," I add, fighting back the harshness trying to creep into my tone when I remember Simone. "Your grandmother was simply trying to do what she always did best. Take care of you."

She looks down, too crestfallen for more venom.

"Then why, Miles? Why put a three-year moratorium on the sale?"

I mull it over before saying, "Three years is a long time, kitten. She might have thought you'd decide against selling it at all, or that you'd have it up and running in that time if you wanted to stay."

"Well, if I sink more into it with upgrades, that's less profit no matter how much I ever sell it for. Wouldn't she be more worried about me getting a good offer?"

I shrug.

"Once people invest sweat equity, they're less likely to take a bad deal. I want the land, sure, but I'm done trying to charm it away from you. You're content there. I damn sure wouldn't be if you decided to give it up without putting in your best effort there first. If I ever buy it from you now, it'll be a legitimate offer that you want. Wholeheartedly."

She stares at me. "I want to believe you, but this doesn't sound like the Miles Cromwell I know."

"Because I'm admitting defeat? You don't know me, kitten."

"Because you're finally being real with me," she whispers, adding, "*I hope.*"

"My dumbassery reached new heights this week, I'll admit," I tell her. "I think I owe you an explanation about everything that went down this week, and the real reason I wanted you to stay the hell away from any offer from Simone Niehaus."

"You owed me that before I went hunting on Google."

"You found the hit pieces. It runs deeper than that," I say darkly.

The edge in my voice softens her gaze.

"I have to tell you now. Everything. Will you come to my place for a nightcap?"

"You could just tell me here."

I look over my shoulder at the back door of the house, making sure there's no one in earshot. "I could, but I'd rather do it alone."

"Liar. We're alone now." She draws a tired breath. "I'm twenty-six, Miles, and it's not Victorian England. My parents won't surprise us. You think they'll pop in to check on me?"

"They've left you outside with a bloodthirsty beast who wants to drag you back to his lair. Frankly, they *should* check on you, kitten."

That wins me a wan smile.

"You said it this time. Not me." She leans in with a longing glance. "If I come to your place, will you make me regret it again?"

I lean forward, my nostrils flaring as lemon sweetness invades my nose.

"Hell no. You've made your point, and this old dog can learn a few new tricks."

Smiling warmly now, she tilts her face back.

An open invitation.

I grab her chin gently, meeting her lips with my own, pressing my tongue softly into her mouth.

Goddamn, I've missed this.

She matches my urgency, my passion, gasping before she pulls away and takes a worn breath. "You're making this hard. Now I wonder if I'll regret it if I *don't* go."

I chuckle and kiss her forehead. "So, you'll come?"

"Only if the dogs are with us. The more I can keep them out of Mom's hair, the better."

"They're well behaved. It's not a chore."

She shrugs. "I don't think they've dealt with this much change before coming here. Strange homes, the city smells, the noise... it's all new and it upsets them. Especially poor Coffee."

"He's a growing boy, aren't you, Coffee?" I pitch my voice up and slap my leg loudly.

He and Cream come running over.

"Jenn says we have to go inside. You guys ready for a sleepover?" I scratch between his ears, then lean over and pet Cream the same way.

Jenn's smile lingers, and she finally looks at me again like I'm not debris stuck to her shoe.

"You too." I look at her sharply. "I don't know why you think they're such a struggle. They do exactly what they're told."

She laughs. "No, they do what *you* say, and it's very annoying."

I fish around in my pocket again for more salmon snacks. "You just need to invest in the right bribes."

"Why do you walk around with dog treats in your coat pocket anyhow? It's weird."

"I had to get to you somehow, didn't I?" I raise an eyebrow, watching as she blushes but doesn't answer. "I learned their favorites after Coffee dug his way over to my house a couple of times."

Later, in the town car, Jenn makes no effort to free herself when I pull her onto my lap.

I told her we needed to get the sex out of our system.

That's what I thought our first night was all about.

Now, I know there's no fucking her out of my system, and I'm not sure what to do about it.

But I know how to figure it out.

Yeah, fuck, I'm probably heading down another highway to

hell with heartbreak strewn along it like shrapnel. The trouble is, I'm past caring.

In the elevator at my house, she slips her warm hand in mine and looks up at me with such trusting eyes, I want to kick my own ass for the way I shredded her before.

This is definitely the wrong path.

Definitely guaranteed to complicate everything so much more.

Still, it's happening, and it's going to be a long damn while before we talk about any other touchy subjects with words.

XVII: NO ONE BUT YOU (JENN)

I'm trembling all over.

He's moving inside me, shaking me to the core, all muscle and masculinity and punishing strokes.

"How fucking bad did you miss me, kitten?" he rasps between breaths.

His silver-blue eyes are sharpened knives, deadly instruments that pierce me to my core with every animalistic glance.

His cock bottoms out in me again as our hips collide, and he holds it there, waiting for an answer.

"B-bad, Miles. *God!*"

I'm panting, on the edge, completely held hostage to his movements.

"Grab hold, Jenn."

"W-what?"

"Hold the fuck on. As hard as you can," he orders, waiting until he feels my nails in his neck.

My blood could burn through my veins as he deepens his strokes, his eyes still holding mine.

Every thrust comes harder, crashing down like he wants to break me—and I can't say I'd mind in the slightest.

His pubic bone grinds against my clit each time he hits my depths.

Faster.

Faster.

So fast, so furious, so unrelenting.

Soon, he offers up a forearm. I sink my teeth in, clinging to him, hot pleasure turning me into confetti.

"Let go, woman. Come for me."

Holy hell, do I ever.

The instant my pussy clenches, greedily riding his thrusts, I feel him swelling. The muscles on his throat work, ticking with pleasure, his teeth bared.

New heat hurls into me a second later from the condom we forgot in our frenzy.

His head snaps back in total reverie, his face slick with sweat like a blessing.

He's a portrait of scandal as he empties himself inside me, low growls erupting from his throat with every pump, all the molten fire he floods me with.

I'm boneless ecstasy forever.

Time has no meaning when your release rips you apart.

I'm happily blind, deaf, and dumb for this vampire man and his whip of a body, launched into a paradise that only lets me glide back down long after he's finished exploding.

He still stares at me, though.

So intense I smile, watching his pleasure, loving how he holds his cock inside me like he knows how much I enjoy having his seed buried deep.

It takes an eternity before he collapses beside me, pulling me into his arms.

"You regret it, kitten?"

I look at him, my mouth forming a question.

"The condom. I wasn't thinking. Fuck, when we burst through that door, I only had one thing on my brain."

His kiss sears me with a naked reminder of what that obsession was.

"No. It was glorious, and I've got an IUD."

He grins back.

Yeah, I don't think anything could make me regret what we just did.

But I've been here with him before. Who knows what I'll regret tomorrow if he becomes an evasive prick again.

For now, I just relax in his arms, dozing before I startle awake and realize I didn't agree to come here for this—the hottest sex of my life was just a bonus.

"Mister, you still have some explaining to do. Remember?" I kiss him on the cheek, playfully sliding my nails down his chest.

With a guarded smile, he turns, staring up at the ceiling and its dark wooden beams like he's gathering his words.

"As fucked up as things are now, Simone Niehaus and I were on friendly terms once."

My mouth drops open.

I wasn't expecting that.

"I know. Another time, another life. We both came from corporate royalty, me with Cromwell-Narada, and her with the publishing empire her grandfather left behind. She turned it into Pacific-Resolute in no time. We were always bumping heads at conferences, but the public swipes at each other gave way to talking ideas. Eventually, she had me convinced we could do the impossible, and corner roughly a fourth of the entire US media market."

"Holy crap," I whisper, batting my eyes.

"Big dreams, I know." He smiles bitterly, something sad and sharp in his eyes. "For a time, I thought that was all Simone was. Harmless. One more driven career freak with ambitions a thousand feet taller than her. I didn't see the danger—or the dagger, not until it was in my back. Once she shattered my trust—along with any faith in humanity I ever had—I called the deal off. She's been bitter as hell ever since, thinking I'm the reason she never clawed her way to the heights she was hellbent on achieving."

"But wait. If she backstabbed you, then why would she be bitter about you canceling the merger? She had to expect it would happen."

His expression darkens.

Why do I feel like I'm getting the truth, but not all of it? What else is he holding back?

"The knife was almost a mortal wound, though I don't think she intended it to be. She still imagines I'll get over it someday, everything she fucking *took* from me."

He goes quiet.

I want to know what that means so bad, but the edge in his voice, the pain, it scares me.

What I really want more than anything right now is for Miles to stop suffering.

So I grab his hand gently, bring it to my lips, and just hold it against my cheek until his breathing softens.

"She's been scheming to force her way back into my good graces," he says finally. "Obviously, that's never going to happen. I can't do business with someone I can't trust, no matter how solid their company seems. If she thinks she can't get a piece of my business, I think she'll do everything in her power to destroy it, and she doesn't give a damn who or what she hurts along the way."

"What?" My breath catches. "We can't let that happen. I'll do whatever I can to help. What you did for Pinnacle Pointe...even if you had your own reasons, it was a huge plus for the whole town. No good deed should be rewarded with a crazy stalker coming after you, let alone anyone caught in the crossfire."

He picks up my hand, brings my wrist to his lips, and kisses it.

"That's sweet, kitten, but I'm not sure there's much we can do beyond what we just did. Fend off her bullshit. We have to wait until she slips up, and that could take years. Her moves are hard to predict. She's cunning and meticulous." He locks his arms around me and plants a kiss on top of my head. "I think this might be our last chance for this—" He motions at our intertwined bodies with his hand. "At least for a while. Not because I want it to stop, but because the project wrapped up early. There's no reason for you to stick around Seattle."

I smile.

"There's no good reason for you to stay here either." Unless he's changed his mind again.

I hold my breath until his mouth crushes mine.

He kisses me so hard, his tongue searching, chasing mine until we both ripple.

"Fuck, you're hard to argue with. I suppose I could go back to the Pointe once I'm sure morale has improved at home."

"Yes, please. Come back with me." I lean up and kiss him again.

Smiling, he pulls away.

"If I do, there's no escape then." He stops and turns us so I'm flat against his bed and he's climbing over me, eclipsing me with his delicious weight.

"This will—" He comes in for a kiss. "Keep happening." Kiss. "Again."

I close my eyes, relishing his warmth, his taste, and his pine scent that reaches down inside me and strokes me like the kitten I've resisted being until I couldn't.

Miles Cromwell transforms me.

"I'd like that, Miles," I whisper, barely audible. "Just don't make me say it twice," I add.

He exhales sharply, his massive length pressed against my opening. I release a slow breath at the way it makes me tingle.

"Goddammit, you're so warm. You know I can't say no to this sweet little pussy."

I push my hips up, tempting him, daring him not to.

"Kitten." He sighs as he sinks into me, anchoring himself

deep. "Shit! You already know I'm going to come inside you again. Hell, every time I'm in you. I can't go back to rubber."

"Don't you dare," I whimper back.

His eyes hold mine.

I can tell he's barely holding back, aching to tear me to pieces again.

My lips attack his, begging for a beautiful ruin.

The second he drives deep and his teeth catch my bottom lip, I'm on my way to paradise.

* * *

"THE INN IS A FLAGSHIP. Anyone who lives in Pinnacle Pointe or even passes through knows Bee Harbor. With the amount of business she sends your way, you should be paying *her* for using your paint," Miles says.

The man behind the counter laughs. "If only business worked that way."

"It works that way when you give me a better deal."

The man adjusts his glasses and throws up his hands. "All right! I'll give you a ten-cent-a-gallon discount. With the amount of paint you need, that will add up."

I lean into Miles' ear and pull out my debit card for the business account. "Thank you."

Miles puts his hand over mine and pushes the card back at me. "No. I've got this."

"But it's for my property..."

"And I'm the only person you can sell it to for three years, right? The least I can do is help put a fresh coat of paint on it."

I smile so hard I almost break, trying to play it cool.

I fail miserably.

"But I'm not selling. Plus, she left me a business account for repairs and incidentals. I'm not even spending my own money yet..."

Miles won't be moved, though, and I look over and see the hardware store owner passing his black credit card back.

"Way to distract me."

Hiding a smile, he says a few more words to the store owner about setting up a delivery, then slips his arm around me and ushers me out of the store.

"You know, the longer you're away from the city, the sweeter you are, Mr. Cromwell."

"Don't go getting emotional on me, kitten. I wasn't in the city when we met and you thought I was an absolute bastard then."

"I *know*. Now, I'm starting to think you have a heart."

The exaggerated look of horror he throws back makes me giggle.

He opens the passenger door of his SUV for me.

I step forward to climb in, but Miles leans in, keeping one hand on top of the car.

"Miss Landers, if I've grown a damn heart, I'm sad to say you own a significant chunk of the real estate. I wonder what you owe me in return?"

Oh, no.

Why does he have to go and—

Heat drums under my cheeks.

Just like that, his arms are around me, and his mouth moves to mine for a steaming kiss.

I break away from him before I melt into a moan.

"You should take me home. ASAP."

"I should, shouldn't I?" He helps me in the car and then gets behind the wheel himself. "What else is on your mind, Jenn? Felt like you were somewhere else while we were deciding on colors."

"Maybe. My most lucrative contract ended recently," I say, side-eyeing him.

"Sorry to hear. You should reach out to the boss. I'm sure he'd be interested in keeping you on in a consulting role for future projects."

"Well, I'm actually glad it's expired."

He looks at me.

"There were too many rules," I say with a smile.

"Rules?"

"You know. About not kissing or the world might end. That kind of thing." My heart flutters like mad. "Not that I didn't enjoy a little sneaking around. But only to a point. After a while it's just complicated. Y'know?"

He reaches over and takes my hand.

"I understand completely. I lost the best damn marketing contractor I've ever had recently, though her new role is irreplaceable. She works long hours under me, listening to my every demand, and every time I think she can't possibly take on more, she surprises me."

I laugh until my sides hurt. A delicious heat curls through me when he tangles his fingers in mine.

"Will I surprise you again tonight, Mr. Cromwell?" I whisper.

"Only if you last more than five minutes riding my face, kitten," he growls, looking over as the vehicle stops at a quiet four-way intersection. "And if you can't do that, you'll come your pretty little auburn head off for me three more times."

My pulse quickens.

"You're more honest here than you are in Seattle, too. And definitely more demanding."

His eyes flash as he looks at me, hungry quicksilver. The raw magnetism makes me fall a little more stupidly in love with this terrible man.

"Woman, you have no clue, but I promise, you're about to get one," he whispers, taking my hand.

By the time we pull up to the inn, he's breathing through clenched teeth while my hands work, rubbing him through his slacks.

* * *

A FEW DAYS LATER, I'm sitting on the sandy beach and smiling, pleasantly sore from three nights straight of being kissed, licked, bitten, and fucked into oblivion and back.

If Miles Cromwell sprouted a heart, he's also made mine completely ravenous.

The quickie this morning before he went off to review his latest reports barely holds me over until evening. It's just after lunch, and I'm thinking about tonight so much it's pathetic.

A loud bark yanks my brain off sex.

Long enough to look up and see Coffee and Cream chasing each other into the low tide in wild circles that make me laugh.

The white dog has a piece of driftwood in her mouth. Her brother closes in to steal it away from her, both of them splashing around with every bounce.

They're thrilled to be home. No question.

Honestly, so am I.

"Jenn, can we talk?"

I turn around to find Ace standing over me. He looks sullen and his hands are stuffed in his pockets.

Well, crap.

I've been expecting this for a while. Best to just get it over with, I guess.

"Sure." I pivot to face him.

He drops to the sand beside me, his face oddly guarded.

"I wasn't sure if I should do this, but hell. I need to come clean about something." His voice is strained.

My heart skips with worry.

The guy is usually so laid-back, and he's been a saint after the way Miles stole me right out from under him.

Unless...unless it's about that and he's been bottling it up?

"Ace, no worries. If you need to chew me out, go ahead. I deserve it. I kissed a guy while we were on a house date and never really got a chance to apologize. I'm deeply sorry for that. Whatever you want to say, it can't be as bad as what I did."

"You sure?" He laughs awkwardly. "And thanks, but everything else... that's water under the bridge. You made your choice. I'm not gonna try to compete with a billionaire."

I give him a friendly nod, trying to make him feel at ease. "So if it's not that, then..."

I wait.

He scratches the back of his neck and slowly looks at me.

"Okay. A few weeks back, this woman—kind of a bold, freaky tall blonde—came up to me one evening at Murphy's. She said she was with a media crew, looking to do a story on the Pointe. I thought she was with your tourism group, so I was happy to help. I even asked her if she was. She told me yes." He pauses, frowning before he continues. "At the time, some of the questions didn't sit quite right with me. But I knew if you were in on the project, it had to be fine."

"What kind of questions?"

If Simone was up in his business, this poor man was like a lamb to the slaughter.

"All negative shit. She kept asking me about the burglaries we'd had, but other than the CPAP machine and Mrs. Smith, I didn't know much. Then she started poking around at you and Miss Lottie and the whole history of Bee Harbor. Your grandparents never had no enemies. I didn't see how anyone could spin it negatively. So I might've blabbed on about the past more than I meant to, and she acted interested enough, even if I think she was angling for more. But..."

I nod. "But?"

"Once that article dropped and everybody started talking about that hit piece, I realized it was probably connected to her. I felt like a damn heel, afraid I helped her trash the town. I said a few things about Cromwell I regretted later, but when they didn't show up in the slime pieces, I figured there was another motive. They wanted to hurt Pinnacle Pointe. At least they didn't go after the inn, and I'm glad as hell you and Cromwell buried it."

That's one mystery solved.

I guess we know how Simone found out about the tourism piece. Ace told her.

Then something else hits me.

"Wait. You don't know anything about the anonymous kid entrepreneur who got his start selling prescription drugs, do you?"

He throws his hand up. "Nope. No idea who that was, and everybody grilling their son in this town can't come up with an answer. Some folks think it's another fabrication, and that's how I lean, too."

I smile. "I hope you're right. I want to believe this place is full of good people."

"That's half-true. But I already tried to dirty up your man for no good reason besides my damn ego, and it didn't feel right. And personal stuff aside, I can see how Cromwell must not be such a rat bastard after all. If he hadn't commissioned all those puff pieces, well, we'd be done for." Ace grins at me. "You two saved the day."

"He's a good guy. You just have to get to know him."

Ace nods. "I'm sure he is—"

I can tell he's not done, but he's stopped talking.

"Is there something else?"

"It's just—frankly, lady, I can't comprehend dating a dude like that. You could do a lot better, media hero or not. But that's none of my business. All Lottie ever wanted was for her granddaughter to be happy. She must've told me a hundred times over the years."

"That's all Lottie wanted—first, second, and third." Miles sits down beside me and slips an arm around me.

"I should go." Ace gets to his feet.

"Bye," Miles says, waving him away dismissively.

I elbow him in the side as Ace walks away.

"What? He's trespassing on my turf," Miles rumbles.

I might be mortified, but I'm laughing.

"What? What's so damn funny?"

"You. He actually said you're not so bad, and you just had to go caveman, didn't you?"

"I had to make a point. You're mine, Jenn Landers, and the man blew his chance, no matter how much smoke he blows up my ass." He pauses. "Is he still pissed he lost?"

"No, he's a grown-up. But he said I could do better. Might have something to do with your overall demeanor."

"Eh, feedback is useless unless it's specific. I can tell you he doesn't deserve you because he's never fought for you. Hell, if another man barged in on my date with a beautiful woman, I'd send him packing right away. Not leave her in a room *alone* with him."

"He trusted me, Miles." I smile, still feeling a little bad about it.

"With a woman like you, there's always somebody else waiting with their dick in hand, drooling at their chance. If this guy's too stupid to realize that or care, he never deserved you. And you were never that interested."

My face heats.

I hate how I can't argue with his Neanderthal logic.

"He's a nice guy," I insist. "He'll find somebody and he'll make her very happy."

"Well, what the fuck was Prince Charming doing here anyway, gracing us with his presence?"

"I think he told Simone about the tourism piece."

"Of course, he did," he bites off.

"Miles, he didn't know. Honest. He even asked her if she was working with us and she lied through her teeth."

"So, he's gullible, too. Figures."

I swat his chest—*I try.*

But Miles catches my hand in midair, leans over, and snuffs out my insult with a kiss.

"Behave," I whisper, as soon as he lets me come up for air. "Do you really think you still have anything to worry about? I couldn't *make* myself think of anyone but you, crankyface. I've given up trying."

He pulls me into his lap with a warmth in his eyes that slays me.

"Truth be told, kitten, the idiot may be right. Sometimes I'm not sure I deserve you."

"Sucks for you. You're stuck with me anyway."

* * *

LATER, WE'RE SITTING IN MILES' office, working or at least pretending to try.

I'm hunched over my laptop, cobbling together breakfast ideas for the inn, and he's at his desk doing who knows what. But he has my dogs in thrall.

Coffee lies at his feet, loudly snoring, while Cream rests on the other side, curled into a doughnut and drowsily watching me type.

Her curly tail wags when I pump my fist in the air.

"What's the word?" Miles looks up from his screen.

"Ten people. Ten people have asked to stay at the inn as soon as it reopens! One couple might even want their wedding here, but I'm not sure we're ready for that yet. Today I even got a tech startup in Tacoma poking me about a corporate retreat next spring."

Miles smiles. "I always knew."

"What? Weren't you the one who thought I'd want to pull up stakes?"

"That was before I figured out you got the lion's share of Lottie Risa's blood, and claws sharp enough to hold on for as long as you'd like."

This man.

I don't dare look up and let him see that he's touching my soul, so I nod my thanks and return to my screen. I need to fire off a response to the couple looking for a wedding venue on my doorstep.

We both go back to work, but when I look up a minute later, Miles is still staring at me intently. But his hands are moving.

There's a huge calendar on his desk and he keeps pushing something under it.

"What are you doing?" I ask.

"Nothing," he throws back.

"You sound like a guilty child. Miles?"

"I didn't do it. Not yet."

"Oh, so you're definitely guilty."

"Of what?"

"Nothing good." I return to my email and let them know I'll be happy to provide a quote closer to the formal reopening, if I think we can manage it by then.

Once I've sent the email, I glance over at Miles again. He keeps looking at me, glancing down and shifting whatever it is he's hiding under that calendar.

"Okay. What are you doing?" I demand.

"Solving the world's energy problems," he lies.

"Somehow I doubt that."

"I'm offended you don't believe in me."

I roll my eyes. "What are you actually doing? What are you hiding under there?"

"Cookies."

"You're still lying." I wish he'd just tell me.

Enough of this.

Fighting back a smile, I push my chair out and stand.

He hunches over his desk, guarding his secret closer.

I walk up behind him, snake my arms around his neck, and try to pull him up, but he's too strong. I can't move him an inch.

But I slip my hand under his collar and start drawing tiny hearts over his bare skin. At first he holds steady, but it isn't long before I find a ticklish spot just under his ear, and he relaxes into the back of his chair.

"Not fair," he growls. "You'll pay for this later."

"Make me," I whisper.

Now that he's out of the way, I can see he's propped the bottom of his desk calendar up and there's—a small canvas under it?

Red-brown waves crawl to the edge of the painting, and it takes me a second to decipher it.

No way.

No flipping way.

It's—

A beautiful woman.

Emerald-green eyes.

Hair bursting around her like it's part of the sunset.

She stares up at me like my best self looking back from the mirror.

I can't help the gasp that slips out of me.

"Miles, you—oh my God."

"Told you not to look. You ruined the surprise."

"You're painting me," I finish.

With a wonderful chuckle, he spins his chair and pulls me into his lap.

"Hope you don't mind—and if you do, I'm not sorry. I've wanted to touch you with my brush since the first time I saw you. You gave me the perfect opportunity, working your sweet little ass off in the corner. You're beautiful in profile, woman. Fuck, I—"

I don't let him finish.

I just press my lips to his, overwhelmed with butterflies I can't even describe. If I'm lost in heady emotions, he must feel it too.

He kisses me so thoroughly my lips feel raw.

"You like it?" he whispers, this adorable hint of uncertainty in his voice.

"Are you joking? I *love* it." I find his lips again.

His tongue caresses mine.

Then a throat clears loudly at the open door and a hand knocks.

"Mr. Cromwell, the dinner you ordered has arrived. Your ice cream and carrot cake are in the fridge. Should I leave the rest outside if you're working late?" Benson asks with a knowing smile that almost makes me faint.

In his usual sleek black livery, he looks like the world's best put together DoorDasher. He's carrying a box of nachos and a pepperoni pizza as wide as Miles' chest from the pub. The entire junk food feast I insisted on tonight.

He's a nice enough guy, but I want to tell Miles to put a freaking bell around his neck.

Miles releases my mouth. "On my desk is fine."

Benson walks over, gently sets the food down, and asks about plates and silverware. Miles waves him off since it's all finger food.

"Enjoy. Also... I'm glad to see you happy again," he adds, making his way to the door without a glance back.

"Good night, Benson."

After sunset and eating half my body weight in pepperoni and the stringiest mozzarella sticks known to mankind, I give Miles a tired look. "Oh, man. The dogs will need to go out soon."

"Night run on the beach? It'll help you feel human again."

"Only if you're taking Coffee. No way I'll keep up with him tonight."

"This speedy boy? He's just full of energy."

Coffee lifts his head up and lays it on Miles' knee, winning himself a head pat.

"He's a good boy, aren't you, Coffee?"

Coffee groans his agreement tiredly.

I burst out laughing again.

He's very good at that.

Once I settle my stomach enough to trick my legs into working, Miles leads Coffee ahead on a leash while I hang back with Cream.

He's right about the walk. It helps shake off the pizza coma, even if I don't admit it. We wind up going farther than planned.

When I look up while Cream darts at a little frog diving under a rock, we're on the stretch of beach leading into town, roughly behind the general store. He hands me Coffee's leash.

"Your turn."

I take it, winding it around my hand with Cream's. "You're wimping out on me now?"

"I need a bottle of water. Do you want a drink?"

"Nope, your water will be fine," I tease.

"Greedy kitten. I'll get two." He leans in and kisses me.

"Fine, but since I've got the dogs, you can carry them both. The whole point of drinking your water is so I don't have to carry the bottle."

He plants a kiss on the top of my head. "You're lucky I'm smitten."

While Miles runs inside the store, I walk ahead and set the dogs free so they can play in the sand.

As I smile up at the night sky above, offering a hint of my happiness to the rolling darkness, I wonder how long this fairy tale can last.

From everything he's said about Simone Niehaus—everything he was willing to share—swatting down her attack piece on this town won't be the end of it.

And when she comes for him again, will I be ready?

Will he?

If there's going to be an us, will we face down whatever she throws at us?

I want to believe it so badly.

Just like I want to be the reason Miles Cromwell always smiles.

XVIII: NO SETTING SUN (MILES)

*T*he sunlight splashes over us in Jenn's room, making it all too easy to believe the world is at ease.

We keep doing this, alternating between her place and mine. I never imagined how much good a simple change of scenery could do me until now.

The view beyond the glass door to her balcony is so frigging beautiful it turns me inside out.

The sun just started to hang low in the sky, and the light bounds off the ocean, casting silver shards everywhere.

"You know, I'm torn. It's hard to decide if I should keep this for my room or use it as a luxury suite. The rental income would be amazing." She places a decorative pillow on the settee we've just brought up to the master suite.

"Speaking of income, have you given any thought to renewing your contract? I can't let my creatives get lazy again with the cutting-edge platforms. You're too good at keeping them in shape," I say.

She beams me a weary smile.

"Maybe later on after the inn reopens. But it can't be as intense as last time."

"When it comes to you, kitten, there's nothing too intense." I sweep her into my arms, inhaling her lemon sweetness.

She giggles. "Seriously, I need time for this place. We're just a few months away from the big relaunch."

"I'll make sure of it. You can work remotely for the most part, though I might require office visits every now and then, especially when I'm stuck in Seattle this fall for the year-end push."

"I'm okay with reporting to my more-than-boss."

"You'd better be," I whisper.

She closes the space between us, stretching up on her toes. "Do you like it more against the wall or on your desk?"

Damn. She knows how to drive me crazy.

"Right now, I'd enjoy it most in your bed," I whisper, catching her bottom lip with my teeth.

My hand cups her ass and squeezes.

She turns cherry-red, but she still tries like hell to pretend she's not flustered.

Little minx.

I pinch her peach of an ass harder.

She grins and bites her lip. "Maybe later."

I drop my arms around her waist and pull her closer. "Your desk this time. It's only fair we defile it after we've done it to mine."

"How about your bed when we're finished here?" she whispers.

"That means waiting and I'm *not* a patient man today. That's your fault, Jenn."

She exhales slowly and sweetly.

"That's what I like about you most," I whisper. "Keep this room for yourself. You deserve a sanctuary. The cottage could be revamped as a higher-end luxury suite, perfect for honeymooners." I point at the wall beside her bedroom door. "Don't put anything there, either. That's my wall."

She blinks at me. "Why do you need a wall in my room?"

"If you won't let me take you on the desk or your bed, that's where I'll fuck your soul out." I push every scalding word against her lips, loving how she shudders.

She slides her fingers inside the waist of my trousers. "If you keep teasing me, you won't sleep at all tonight."

I cup her face, tilt her head back, and kiss her deeply.

"Promise me you'll make good on that threat."

She licks my bottom lip, all the invitation I need to drag my tongue against hers.

With a soft whimper, her leg curls around mine and I lift her up, carrying her over to the bed without resistance.

"It's later now," I say.

She nods slowly, worn down by the lust spell I've worked on her with every seething kiss.

And not a second too soon.

I'm fucking bristling to be inside her, to mark her again from the inside out.

I lean in and my lips storm hers, fierce brushstrokes, painting her with the intensity of my desire.

I trail down her neck to the top of her low neckline and stop, sliding a finger between the satin of her shirt, feeling her delicate skin.

As I unzip her blouse, I'm hit with how marvelous this is.

No matter how many times I strip her naked, unwrapping Jennifer Landers will always feel like Christmas morning.

She leans up, too, working at the first couple buttons on my shirt.

One more kiss.

One more moan.

One more minute closer to the hard, sating rhythm we need.

Then she yanks my shirt off before she's finished freeing me, sending a few other buttons flying. She goes for my jeans and when they don't fall fast enough, she shoves them down.

I'm laughing darkly as she slides my boxers down next, curling her hand around my length the instant I'm free.

I let out a breath that's searing my lungs, grab her wrist, and move it away.

"You don't like it?" Her voice is so timid there's nothing to do but kiss her.

"You're interfering with my plans."

"Your plans? What—"

My tongue never lets her finish, working over hers, speaking the unspeakable without a single word.

When I release her, she whines and kicks her legs.

There's my cue.

I kiss down her neck and keep going until I have her nipple pulled between my teeth, fully at my mouth's mercy.

"Oh!"

My cock jerks with the moans spilling out of her.

It's like I'm taking her apart with every flick of my tongue. Every fluttering circle around her nipple makes her tremble, and soon she thrusts her hips toward me.

Deliciously greedy.

I stay stoic.

"*Miles, please,*" she whispers.

Not yet, kitten.

Not fucking yet.

A few more harsh tongue strokes tell her who's in control.

"But...but I need..."

I silence her, sucking her other tit, turning her pleas into moans like honey.

Goddamn, I revel in this.

"Miles!" she hisses, that sharpness in her voice telling me it won't take much to drive her over.

So I kiss my way to her stomach, running my tongue along her waistline, arching through that thin strip of hair to this kitten's pussy.

She's on the bed now, her hips writhing, pleading with everything she's worth.

I run my tongue down her seam, but I don't fuck her yet.

I don't suck her clit.

When I bring her off, I want her to feel it in her bones.

"Damn—Miles!" My name slips out of her so ragged.

She sighs with denial, locking her legs around me as I decide to truly mark her. I grab her hips and sweep her into my mouth, pushing my tongue into her delectable cunt and holding it there, barely breathing.

This is how I burn her down.

This is how I make her my living canvas.

I'll paint every letter of my name inside her. My tongue goes to work, delicate at first, and then all hunger.

M-I-L-E-S

"Oh, God!" Her thighs pinch my head.

I growl with satisfaction. Her hands fumble at my hair, my scalp, so desperate I'd grin like a fool inside her if I wasn't already occupied.

M-I-L-E-S again.

"Oh! Oh, *gawd.*" Her voice cracks on the last word, and I know she's not begging for divine intervention.

She's asking me for total corruption, and I'll happily oblige.

She's down here with me, ready to spend a year in purgatory if that's what I ask to finish her.

She's lucky I'm a kind man—and I'm also very fucking hungry—and I know it's time to bring her *home.*

C-R-O-M I start.

"Miles. *Miles!* I-I need you now."

Fuck.

You'd better believe I almost give in, but I'm in too deep not to deliver the fireworks she's earned.

She's such a good, good girl, and she's all fucking mine.

Her legs are shaking, restlessly hugging my head.

The soft sounds spilling out of her can't be called words, just violent breaths, and that's where she finds her end.

W-E-L-L

I can't breathe as she goes off, but I'd rather suffocate than stop.

Snarling, my orderly marking becomes incoherent tongue lashes.

Her clit pulls into my mouth.

Only three sweeps before her legs grip my head so hard it hurts. But it's nothing like the ache in my cock.

The deprivation I happily suffer just to blow her to smithereens, to send her to the screaming stars and back, to make Jenn Landers come like she never has before.

I'm rewarded with a wet heat against my face.

I *knew* she could squirt, and I lick shamelessly, devouring her orgasm like it's top-shelf bourbon.

She's panting when I finally come up for oxygen.

My lungs protest, but my dick has full control, and it won't be denied another second.

Before she's even floated back into herself, I slide into her, pushing my cock in to the hilt.

I'm a creature of pure light and heat with the sun glowing on my back, giving me this wicked energy to throw myself into her with everything I have.

Wild abandon.

Devil strokes.

Animal rutting.

My hands slide under her ass, hoisting her up off the bed, holding her open while my cock slams into her and our hips collide hard enough to bruise.

It brings her off again—if her first orgasm ever even ended—turning her into this glorious thing of breathless sighs and convulsions and fluttering eyelids that still scream my name when her open mouth can't.

Miles, Miles!

It echoes in my soul even though I've rendered her silent and breathless.

And it's all I hear a second later as the sunlight burning my naked skin hits the fire in my blood and ignites, exploding up my spine, collecting in my brain and balls before everything I am billows up and goes nova.

"Jennifer! *Goddamn.*"

My voice is more like a book tearing in two than a man forming words.

That's the sound of me coming more undone than I've ever been in my life, my cock swelling in her depths, splitting open with one more hell-thrust.

Fuck!

I come so hard my eyes stick to the back of my head.

Muscles I didn't know I had strain, heaving machines, all for the single-minded purpose of spilling myself inside her, claiming her in the most primal way possible.

Good thing she's got her protection, or she'd walk away from this with triplets.

Hell, the fact that it doesn't freak me out in this heated, clenching moment where ecstasy grips like a brute and wrings us out says everything.

It proves I'm dependent on this high, this woman.

This beautifully fucked up thing with a thousand complications that's impossible to quit.

And when we start breathing again and I seal our insanity with a kiss, I know.

I know I don't want this to end.

"I marked you," I say brokenly, as soon as we're nestled together, bathing in the sun and the slick afterglow of our own sweat.

Her mouth drops open in amusement. "You—what?"

"Did you feel it? I wrote my name inside you, Jenn." I reach down between her legs and cup her mound, leaking my nut. I close my palm against her pussy and hold the rest in. "Call it cheesy or whatever the fuck. Don't care. You're mine now. Head to toe, inside and out. Finders fucking keepers."

She laughs louder, making this whole vibe more dreamlike

than it already is, and it's so damn erotic I'm already getting hard again.

"You're a crazy man. You know that, right?"

I swat her thigh and she jumps.

"Whatever. Just as long as you know you belong to that madman."

We spend some time sunbathing before its cleanup time.

Then we hit the shower together, and after I bring us off again with her pressed up against the wall, I find a couple robes and take her hand.

We walk outside on the newly repaired balcony, just in time to finish watching the sunset. I sit on the outdoor chaise she's put outside and she curls up next to me.

"It's so beautiful. People would pay dearly for evenings here."

I pull her into my lap.

"But you'd miss this view," I growl, pressing my forehead to hers.

Not that it's the end of the world.

If I have anything to say about it, she'll spend more time next door at my place which has a majestic view that's pretty close.

My phone rings, and I fish it out of my pocket, glancing at the screen.

"Louise. I'd better take this," I tell her.

She leans closer to me and stares out at the setting sun.

"Cromwell."

"Hi, I have news from Legal—"

"About time. Report."

She hesitates, though. "I'm afraid you won't like this, sir. We have no good options legally against Pacific-Resolute."

"How?" I clip.

"The content was all original, so we can't claim losses due to anything stolen. And it seems the claims that you were 'bribed' to portray the town in a positive light weren't salacious enough to warrant any action for libel since they weren't really public."

"Shouldn't I be the judge of that?"

"You're welcome to consult Bradley yourself, of course. I'm just the messenger," she reminds me tactfully. "But Legal says if you file, it'll likely be thrown out in under a month. If it's tossed, then you have to pay her attorney fees."

"Fuck. It won't stop if that whore gets away with this," I snarl. "This can't be the end of it. Simone won't quit until I fold. Until I'm dead, just like—" I stop, nearly biting my tongue.

Beside me, Jenn stiffens.

I don't need to look at her to know her eyes are fixed on me.

"Louise, I have to go." I cut the call and slide my arm around my girl again with a sigh.

"Miles?"

I don't look at her, keeping my gaze on the sunset over the ocean, where any woes are unimaginable.

"What did you mean?" she asks again.

"What?"

"You said Niehaus wouldn't quit until you were dead. You think she wants to kill you?"

"No. Not exactly." I look at her, hating the worry glistening in her pretty green eyes. "And you need to not scare yourself sick, kitten."

She stands, hands balled into fists.

"I will worry! If someone wanted me dead, would you just be so chill? And why didn't you tell me before? You can tell Louise, but you can't tell me?"

I stand and move closer to her.

"I shouldn't have said that. I wasn't serious. She's a monster bitch but she's not a serial killer."

No, there's only one death I'm sure she had a hand in.

"Shouldn't have said *what?* Telling me to calm down or that this horrible woman won't quit until you're dead?"

"Both," I say flatly.

She snorts. "Did she kill someone you know?"

Fuck.

I've never hated my big mouth more than I do right now.

"I was upset and I overreacted. That's all." I guess I can't avoid lying because I'm not sure I truly overreacted. "If the witch doesn't stop, I'll be a corpse of a CEO. That's what I was getting at."

"Were you?" She puts her hand on her hip. "I've never heard that expression before in my life."

"I made it up."

She glares at me, her eyes swirling with suspicion.

"Miles..."

I throw my hands up. "Kitten, lay off. I told you I overreacted. End of fucking story."

"Is it?" Her eyes narrow. "I want to believe you."

"I promise."

I'm lying, and it guts me, but no fucking good will ever come from giving her the truth, the whole truth, and nothing but.

"What upset you then?" She slips her hands into mine.

"What do you mean?"

"You said you were upset and overreacted. What made you so upset?"

"It isn't obvious? Legal says I can't go after Pacific-Resolute for slandering Pinnacle Pointe. It pisses me off, but it's not going to stop me from enjoying this sunset with you."

Slowly, she nods and lets me lead her back to our seat.

Once she's nestled against me again, she sighs hard enough to rattle her frame. "Miles, if anything happens to you—"

"It won't. I told you, I'm all right. It's under control. There has to be another way to push back at her for this shit, and I'll find it."

For a moment, she's quiet.

Then she says, "Are *we* all right?"

My jaw tightens.

If she has to ask, I wonder if we are.

"Yeah. Is there a reason you don't think we are?"

"...it just feels like you're comfortable discussing whatever it is with Louise, but not me."

"Sweetheart, I've told you what's going on. Louise just reports what Legal says, and they say it'll take more effort to shred her." I pick up her hand and rub my thumb over the top. "We're fine."

"And you've told me everything about Niehaus?"

"Yeah."

"So you were just old friends who discussed a business merger until one day you weren't?"

I stare at her, hating the doubt in her eyes. "Is that so hard to believe?"

"Not necessarily, but... this whole thing seems a little too intense, if it was all business. It feels personal."

A low bitter laugh burns my throat. "Welcome to Corporate America, where we jagoff CEOs care so much about business and the almighty dollar that there's no distinction with our personal lives."

If only that was the truth.

If only Jenn wasn't too close to my waking nightmare.

If only every smile didn't feel like a cut to my face the rest of the night, where I pretend to forget about Niehaus and convince Jennifer there's absolutely nothing to worry about.

* * *

A FEW DAYS LATER, Jenn sets three plates on the table in front of me. "Try these."

I look up from a pile of breakfast food.

"Since you're in the scone game, I need your input," she explains. "First up, my grandma's orange zest scone recipe—"

My nostrils flare as I inhale citrus heaven. "I can already tell you that's a winner. Your grandma made the best scones."

She laughs. "I'm not worried about the recipe. It's more the execution—*my execution*. There's also a homemade cinnamon roll and a strawberry French toast."

I pick up the scone and take a bite. "Tastes awesome. It's just missing Lottie's honey butter." Using a fork, I cut a piece of the cinnamon roll off. "Why are we doing this again?"

"I'm trying out breakfast recipes for the grand reopening. Ace said the painting should be finished today."

"How often do you talk to that guy?" I growl between bites.

"Um, often enough to know what's going on with my own inn? Don't worry, if he ever makes another pass, you'll be the first to know."

"Woman, if he so much as *sniffs* you..." I don't finish that sentence.

I just stuff the rest of the scone in my mouth and make a show of chewing like the jealous wolf I am.

"God, you're ridiculous." She slaps her thighs, but she laughs brightly. "Take your time with the roll."

I take a bite of the cinnamon roll next after rinsing my mouth with water.

"Decent. It's not quite Sweeter Grind Regis roll tier, but it's not bad at all. Nice and sticky." I finish devouring the spread, saving the French toast for last. "Yep. You're Lottie's granddaughter. No question."

"What was your favorite?" She beams.

"The scone. You did her old cookbook justice and the flavor pops with coffee. Bet they'd pair well with anything. Your guests will leap out of bed if their morning starts with those."

She gives me a kiss of gratitude as I refill my coffee, then head to my office.

A few hours later, I'm working on reports, not so patiently waiting for more on Simone when Jenn blows through the door. "It's ready!"

"What?" I look up.

"The painting's done. Ace just texted. Let's go look."

I need to finish this expense report, but the place is next door, and she's so giddy I can't stand to tell her no. "Coming."

The dogs follow us over, bounding along behind us, always thrilled to be back on their home stomping grounds.

"Damn," I whisper, taking her hand as we stop in front of the old building.

I've never seen Bee Harbor look so good. The fresh burst of colorful paint really livened the place up, giving it some soul. "Do you think this is what it originally looked like?"

I know she tried to stick with the original colors she found sifting through her grandmother's things.

"I think so. I've seen the old photos, but they were black and white. The building is ready, though, but I'll need to find some help if I'm going to open this year. If I can find a few good people, I could be open in time for the Christmas stragglers."

Paul Bunyan steps out from behind the inn, carrying empty paint buckets he tosses in the back of his truck. "It came out looking pretty good, don't you think? All set except for a little touch-up."

"Amazing," she gushes.

I know it's just business.

I know who won the girl.

But damn if I'm not glaring anyway, wishing I could send him to the cornfield like that brat in the old *Twilight Zone* series.

Lifting a hand, I give the handyman an exaggerated wave. "Bye, Ace."

With a rough nod, my gaze follows him until he gets in his truck and drives off.

Jenn's hand grips my arm and she looks up at me with her lips pursed. "You jealous freak. You realize if you run him off, you have to do the touch up work, right?"

"I know my paints," I bite off, trying not to laugh as she rolls her eyes. "Also, if you need a few part-timers, just put up a sign at Murphy's. If you don't find someone there, there's a staffing company in Seattle. They wouldn't work long term, but they could help fill in the gaps."

"That's for cleaning and helping me with check-ins, though. I don't have the budget for a new handyman, hint-hint."

"If he quits, I'll cover you. And I'll find you the best damn handywoman who ever swung a hammer."

"Oh my God! Stop. The inn came with a handyman."

I snort loudly. "He only works so cheap because you're pretty. You're taken now, too."

"Yeah, well... until the inn is back on its feet, I kind of need discount labor."

My fingers lace through hers, pulling tight. She knows I'd rather run him off, but for her sake, I'll behave.

I lean over and brush her lips against mine, loving how she gasps lightly against my mouth, melting into the kiss. Before she pulls away, I add teeth, seizing her bottom lip until she shudders.

"What was that for?"

"Sealing the deal. I'll leave your handyman alone, but I'll also mark my territory," I whisper.

She laughs. "You really are crazy, Mr. Cromwell."

I pull her closer, running a hand down her back.

"About you? Yeah."

Goddamn.

How is it the light moments with this woman are almost as good as the hot and heavy ones?

"It's also pretty crazy to think I can actually do this. I'm going to run an actual hotel," she says breathlessly.

"It's not. You're more capable than you give yourself credit for."

She looks at me. "But part of me hates totally walking away from marketing..."

"You don't have to. My team needs you and I'll keep you on at a relaxed schedule, wherever you'd help my people the most," I say, kissing her again.

She nods. "I'm not sure I can balance opening an inn and the work you'd be paying me for."

"I'll give you a raise then, and you'll hire more help."

"You have an answer for everything."

"No. Just a burning desire to keep that smile on your face." I rest my forehead on hers, tracing her cheek with my finger. "You can't give up here, and my creative team can't afford to lose you."

Neither can I, I think darkly.

"Will you keep the name?" I ask.

She cocks her head at me.

"The Bee Harbor. It's solid branding and has a history, but you don't harbor bees anymore." I nod toward the back near the gardens, where the faded bee boxes sit vacant.

She smiles softly. "Give it time. Come next year, you—or Benson, I guess—are going to be up to your ears in honey."

"Real cute, kitten," I rasp against her throat before engraving it with my kiss. "Somehow, you must think you haven't already delivered all the sugar I'll ever need."

XIX: NO HIDDEN TRUTHS (JENN)

"It's so crazy I'm just crashing in my own bed for the first time in a week!" I adjust the pillow behind my head, throwing it down behind me as Coffee noses at the corner.

"Dare I ask?" Pippa teases.

"Don't you know? I've been staying with Miles while the inn was being repaired."

"Oh, wow. So it's weeklong sleepover serious now." She gives me a thumbs-up.

I throw back a numb look.

She shrugs. "You know it's a big deal when you've got a billionaire so thirsty you're tearing him away from his work."

"He's staying busy. He's hosting some meeting today. I could have stayed upstairs, but I've missed being home, and so have the dogs."

"Are the repairs done?"

"Yeah, pretty much, everything important. You already know about my winter opening plans. God, Pippa. I never thought I'd own a hotel after doing so much time at Winthrope, but—here I am."

She smiles. "I'm proud of you, girl. And I don't mean any

crap, but... are you sure you're ready? Do you think it'll be too much?"

"It's a ton of work," I admit. "But if Gram managed all these years, so can I."

"Oh, yeah. You're a certified girlboss. But you've gone through some sweeping changes recently with your grandma dying, moving here, taking the gig with Cromwell, and falling head over heart for him." She smiles sweetly as I flip her off. "Just know, you don't have to decide everything right now. You can reopen, then decide if you want to keep hacking at some marketing work on the side, whether it's for him or somebody else."

"Yeah," I say wistfully.

I miss this easy chatter.

I needed this.

You'll never get a better steaming shot of courage than the kind you get from your best friend.

"I knew I missed you for a reason," I say. "Are you guys coming out on the boat with us tonight?"

"Totally. It's been too long since you spent an evening with me and Brock."

I smile. It really hasn't been that long since her last visit, and even less time since I returned from seeing her in Seattle.

It's the distance, I think. The way Pinnacle Pointe swallows everything up and sucks you into its own dreamy little world.

"I'm just pumped you're following in my footsteps. You have your own billionaire bad boy and he'll wife you up soon enough."

"Pippa!" I hiss, hating that I almost add *don't jinx it.* "Did it ever feel too good to be true with Brock? I'm still waiting for the other shoe to drop."

"Wait, why? Did he do something wrong?"

"Do you remember the second crazy offer I got on the inn?"

"Yep. Still can't believe you didn't take it, honestly."

"You know I couldn't."

"Right. Grammy's ghost and all—and I guess I don't blame you. Lottie might haunt your ass forever."

I laugh. "Actually, she doesn't need to show up in a mirror or rattle any chains. Gram had this weird clause written into her will that the only person I could sell to for the first few years is Miles. I can't take the crazy offer even if I want to."

"Well, damn. Way to play cupid from the afterlife, Granny Risa."

I laugh again.

"That's a stretch. But anyhow, the woman who made the offer, she's some crazy he used to work with who backstabbed him..." I fill her in on what little I know about his history with Simone and the smear campaign against the town.

Talking it out, I can't help noticing the strange, incomplete picture he's left me with.

By the end of it, Pippa shakes her head.

"Man. I know how uptight CEOs get about their little business secrets. You don't have to tell me."

"He said he couldn't trust her to do business. And seeing how she went after Pinnacle Pointe, I can't blame him, but still... I wonder what I'm missing. There's something else going on with this woman."

"Hold up. When you say something's going on, you think he's playing you?"

I hesitate. "I'm not sure what to think, Pippa. He got so mad when his assistant called to say he couldn't sue her I thought he might chuck his phone off the balcony. He told me she wouldn't stop until he was dead, then he tried to walk it back. But I know what I heard. I just don't know why he won't be honest about the rest."

"That's odd for sure. Maybe he just didn't want to worry you, or maybe he told his assistant because he thinks the whole thing started over a bad business deal. Men are weird."

I stare at her. "You don't think this is *just* about business either, do you?"

She's quiet.

"Hard to say. Guys like Miles do go nuts over their deals, and they turn into lions when they're facing down a real threat. So, yeah. That doesn't mean Cromwell is lying to you, necessarily, but he's probably holding something back."

Just like I suspected.

I knew it, but hearing her agree makes my heart sink.

"He swore they were just friends who were looking at a merger once, but why would it make him so bitter? I don't understand."

"Well, don't overthink it too much. She's probably an ex or a bad hookup, and he's just afraid to tell you."

"That's kinda what I'm worried about," I say.

"Why? He had a life before he met you."

"Oh, for sure. I'm not jealous or whatever." Cream groans next to me in her sleep and I stroke behind her ears. "That's what bothers me about this whole thing. Not that he had a girl-friend before he knew me or whatever. It's that he thinks it's better to hide it than just give me the whole ugly truth."

The silence hangs heavy between us.

"Hmm. That's a tough one. But I'll try to get a better read on him tonight," she promises.

"You don't have to."

"Yes, I do. I'm not letting any stupid man and his secrets hurt you, Jenn. But I don't think you have anything to worry about. If she's an ex of some sort, he probably thinks telling you would upset you."

I hope that's all it is.

I want to believe her so bad.

I don't want my stomach turning over, but my instincts don't care about hope or excuses.

They keep screaming there's more.

* * *

LATER, we're all laughing at the table, picking over the remains of dinner on Miles' yacht while he refills our wineglasses.

Piper looks at Miles as he sits down.

"Truth or dare time." She takes a big sip of wine.

His eyes flick to me and back to Pippa. "Are we in middle school?"

"Yep," she answers quickly. "No grown-ups fear truth or dare. They pick truth and answer."

"Okay, I'll indulge you." Miles' jaw clenches with a smile. "Let's do truth."

"How many girlfriends have you had?" she asks without skipping a beat.

He glances at me and looks across the table to Brock Winthrope, who shrugs, slugging down half his wine.

"A few. Like any man my age," Miles says thoughtfully.

"What's a few? Three? Ten? *Thirty?*" Piper presses.

"Definitely on the lower end," he answers. "I think it's my turn now."

Piper shakes her head. "Not so fast! You didn't answer the whole question. You have to name a number or it's a partial truth at best. No points for that."

Miles doesn't respond.

"You know the consequence for lying on a truth means accepting a dare, right?" Pippa quirks an eyebrow.

"Piper," Brock cuts in, his eyes glowing warmly with warning.

She looks at her husband and rolls her eyes.

"Oh, *fine.*" She turns to Miles, holding her fork up. "Look, I'll just say it. I like you, but if you hurt my friend, I'll neuter you."

Miles stares back blankly. "Is there a reason we're behaving like pirates?"

Holy hell.

The downside with having a friend who pulls no punches is that I have a friend who *pulls no punches.*

I'm so mortified the blood drains from my face. But I knew this was coming.

I've known Piper Renee-now-Winthrope long enough to know how defensive she is, especially after her own heart-stompy misadventure with the man next to her.

She smiles sweetly and cuts another piece off her steak. "Sorry. I'm just giving you the Winthrope welcome. We look out for our friends and nobody more than Jenn."

"Sweetheart, maybe you should tone it down," Brock whispers, running his hand over hers.

"Oh, Brock, it's a simple statement. I don't understand what everyone's getting so worked up over."

I do.

Miles sends me a curious look and I smile apologetically.

After dinner, Pippa and Brock move to the far end of the deck. She's wearing his coat. His arms are wrapped around her waist, inseparable as ever.

I move to the railing across the deck so they can have their privacy.

They're so cute together, and they're still basically newly-weds. It's a relief to see a couple where the passion never fades.

The night is beautiful and bright with late summer stars.

Even the air feels crisp and cool without being frigid. The water shines blue against the boat in the sparkling moonlight.

I'm a little punch-drunk that this is actually my life.

Outside work, I never pictured myself chilling on yachts, but now I wouldn't trade it for the world.

Miles approaches, his heavy footsteps filling the stillness. "How do you do it, kitten? You're more beautiful tonight than you were the first time I saw you on this boat."

I smile at him. "Thank you."

"Your friend is hardcore. I like anyone who's willing to speak their mind, though."

I laugh awkwardly. "I'm so sorry. I didn't know she was going to get all overprotective. I didn't ask her to."

He reaches for my hands and twines his fingers through mine.

"No. I'm glad you have someone willing to throw down for you. That's hardly a bad thing." He pulls me into his arms. "Fortunately for Mrs. Winthrope, I have no intention of *ever* hurting you. I hope you know that."

"I do." I nod slowly like his embrace leaves no room for doubt.

"Come to the master suite with me? I want to show you something."

I turn slowly, side-eyeing him. "Isn't it rude to run away from our guests?"

"Tease. They won't even notice we're gone."

"How can you be sure?"

Miles gently flattens his palms on my head and turns it so I can see the other side of the boat. Brock stands against the railing, tangled in his wife. Their faces are connected and Pippa's eyelids flutter, lost in a starry night of kisses that's theirs, and no one else's.

I sigh happily. "I mean... I guess they won't miss us."

Miles laces his fingers through mine and leads the way to the main quarters.

"I know you didn't tell her to, but is there a reason Piper asked about who I dated before you?" he asks.

"I don't know," I say.

Although, I'm fairly sure I do.

"If there's something you want to know, ask me yourself. I'm not hiding anything."

My fingers tighten around his, wishing it could all be just that easy.

"I hope not. Obviously, I won't hold anything that happened before you knew me against you."

I wait for something.

Anything.

But he doesn't speak, and our fingers stay twined as he pulls me closer.

Does that mean he's truly not hiding anything—or he is, but doesn't know how to admit it?

We take the stairs below deck to the personal cabins.

Once we reach the master suite, he opens the door for me and I step through. He follows me inside, hugging me to offer support.

I need it as my eyes dance around the exquisite room until my knees buckle.

It's that beautiful.

A canopy bed occupies the center, dressed in rich French brocades. There's a glass wall across from us with a desk in the corner and a full wet bar with a mini fridge beside it.

Of course, the ocean view is absolute perfection through the spotless sliding door leading to a private balcony. Even in the dark, the water shines like a mirror, capturing the stars beautifully.

"Another place that inspires you to paint?" I ask, turning in his arms to face him.

His lips turn up. "You know me too well. Since you brought it up, that's half the reason we're here. Look up, kitten."

He turns me around again and places his finger under my chin, tilting my head back.

What he has to show me hangs on the wall above the bed in a heavy golden frame.

It's a lifelike portrait of a girl with windswept red hair on the rocks, and—*holy hell*—I'm not wearing any clothes.

"You didn't," I whisper, almost winded.

But he did.

I can't stop looking at the painting.

My hair blows around me in ribboning sweeps. I stand tall, way more confident than I'll ever be naked in real life.

I don't know whether to be flattered or horrified.

"When did you—I mean how—"

His embrace tightens, cutting me off.

"From memory, sweetheart."

"I didn't know you painted like that." The day he painted me in his office, he was using me as a model.

But then I remember the tiger. He certainly didn't need a model for that.

"When you're etched into my soul, it's easy," he says.

As much as I fight it, I'm shaking, frozen in place and staring at the picture.

He didn't miss any detail.

My hair is brilliant, glowing like embers in the evening sun. I've seen the same shy smile painted me is wearing a thousand times in the mirror.

I swallow thickly. "Miles, it's crazy realistic. You know I'll die if someone sees this, right?"

He pulls my face up firmly, stamping his lips against my throat.

"They won't. This is for my eyes only. No one else will ever see it. Only you. I had to show you my real muse, and it's not this ship. You're looking at her, Jenn."

Yep.

He's trying to leave my heart a pile of shattered glass tonight.

"I'm glad, but it's right there on the wall. Um, how will you make sure no one else sees it?"

Smiling, he steps away and moves to the dresser on the opposite wall of the desk. He picks up a remote and points it at the painting.

"You're going to... turn it off?"

"Watch me."

With the flick of a button, a thick burgundy curtain closes over it.

"I won't have the cleaning crew ogling you. With you, kitten, I don't fucking share." His silvery eyes flash.

Presto, I'm smiling again like the lovestruck little fool I am.

"You thought of everything." I lean up on my toes impulsively and kiss him again, loving how his teeth rake my bottom lip.

"How long do you think we can be gone without being noticed?"

"We have the whole night. I'd bet ten million Brock is taking his wife straight to their room, and they won't be coming out again."

"Their room is—"

"The farthest from ours."

"Oh. Oh, thank God."

He presses his lips to my forehead. "Don't thank me. I'd never miss a chance to be alone with my girl."

He picks me up and sets me on the bed then, kissing me down against the mattress. His hand slides between my legs, searching and hungry and hot, but I slide out from under him and stand.

"Turn around, Miles. Cover your eyes," I whisper.

He tilts his head, questioning.

"Just do it. Trust me."

He turns, lying so his back is to me, and I go to work undressing myself.

I can't believe I'm going to do this. It takes every ounce of courage I have.

But he painted it, didn't he?

I try to strike the pose in the picture, but there's no wind in my hair. Even if there were, it still wouldn't look anywhere near that good windblown, and I'm sure I'm nowhere close to the radiantly confident girl in the picture, but still.

I try.

For him, I try to look like a freaking knockout.

"Okay. Go ahead and look." I strain out the words.

He rolls over, and his face tightens.

Eep.

Not as good as the painting?

But his eyes linger, shields of metallic blue light, intense and impassable.

"Um, I know it's not quite as neat as the picture, but—"

"Kitten, shut it. Right the fuck now. I could paint you a thousand times and I still wouldn't come close to capturing how gorgeous you are right now." He sits up on his knees, stretches to take my wrist, and pulls me in.

I go down on the bed, overheated and laughing with relief.

Holy hell, I really am his.

The way he stares at me combined with his words makes me a lot less self-conscious, too.

"What will I do with you?" he asks, his hot breath falling against my skin.

Heat throbs through my body. I close my eyes.

"Anything you want."

Growling, he hovers over me, grabbing one breast.

I close my eyes, savoring the warmth and worshipful strokes of his tongue. He sucks until I'm in my glory, panting, my legs open and pleading.

I can't wait.

I reach up, desperately unbuttoning his shirt.

He stops touching me just long enough to help.

And he's not half-bad himself—*not bad at all*—as his nude chiseled body falls against mine.

He takes my hand and holds it over his heart. It's beating so furiously under his ribs.

"There. Feel it. That's all yours, woman. Tonight and tomorrow and forever."

My breath catches.

I'm dead.

Slayed by a single animalistic look and words too sweet for life.

I can't stop smiling as his heart drums under my palm. After a minute I ask, "Just your heart, Miles? Nothing else?"

"Slide your hand down, kitten, and see."

I do, and I take my sweet time, tracing his rock-hard body until I find his cock and squeeze.

"Fuck," he rasps, lapping at my breast as I stroke him.

When I circle my thumb over his swollen tip, he stops licking me, his focus broken.

"Jennifer," he sighs. His fingers work, pushing my legs apart and finding the nub above my opening that's almost gone electric.

I'm breathless at the first sweep of his thumb.

"Oh, God. Miles!"

His hand slips downward and a finger dips in.

My mouth pulls open in one long moan.

He climbs over me then, leans down, and our mouths meet.

I don't want the way his tongue moves over mine to end, but I need more. So I lock my legs around his waist and rub my body against his.

He deepens our kiss, slurring it into a growl as he thrusts into me.

This is what I love about this man.

His greed.

He always makes sure every inch of my body is pressed to his as he moves inside me. So close, but never close enough.

His intensity floods me with emotion, and soon, I'm overloaded.

I come so hard I see stars without glancing at the window.

His chest swells as his breath quickens, thrusting hard and deep, and when he groans and empties inside me, my vision blanks out and the rest of my senses go with it.

Heat.

Heart.

Miles.

Why does he make it so heartbreakingly easy to love him?

When it's over, I collapse in his arms, and he still doesn't allow any space between us.

"What are you thinking about?" I whisper in the darkness.

"That I should have done this the first time you were on this boat with me."

I laugh. "C'mon. What are you really thinking about?"

"Mostly what it'll take to tie you down and spend a whole damn week like this. You?" His eyes are smiling so sweetly when he looks at me.

"How safe I feel when I'm in your arms."

"You are," he whispers. "I'll never let anything hurt you, kitten."

I believe him.

I'm also more tired than I thought because before I know it, I'm dozing off in his arms. Though this has happened a hundred times, when I wake up next to him in the morning with the sunlight spilling in, it's euphoric.

I've fallen asleep before with Miles in my head and every emotion that comes with him, happy and angry and just confused.

I've fallen asleep in his arms after making love many times.

But last night was different.

There was something too raw. Too real.

After a lazy brunch on the main deck with Pippa and Brock, the yacht docks again at the marina and we say our goodbyes to the Winthropes.

Miles doesn't let me out of his sight for the rest of the day.

When night falls, the passion we trade in his bed is just as intense, and I'm so high on this strange billionaire painter man that I might just float away.

But if and when I do, I hope it's gently.

I hope he won't let me fall even harder than I already have.

XX: NO GOOD DEED (MILES)

I'm at my mother's grave, clutching a bouquet of purple roses to my chest.

There's a woman crying over her tombstone. I'm not sure who she is when I can only see her back.

She's definitely in mourning, though, wearing a sweeping black dress that almost scrapes the ground and a black hat with a silk scarf poking out behind it.

I wait for what feels like forever with a face-ripping wind cutting into my cheek.

One minute.

Five.

Ten.

Sighing, I march forward, clearing my throat loudly to get her attention.

It's like she's one more cemetery statue here, this dead, life-less thing rooted to the ground. No movement except for the slow, shaking slump of her shoulders.

Is she crying?

As much as I sympathize, I can't wait all day.

"Miss, are you okay?" I reach out and tap her shoulder gently.

NICOLE SNOW

Before I can blink as another biting gust of wind slams me in the face, she pivots around in a violent, startled movement.

But the expression on Simone's face has no fear.

She's laughing. Not crying at all.

"I'm fabulous, Miles. Mommy dearest won't be lonely for long."

My chest constricts like I'm being crushed by five hundred pounds. My vision blurs red.

I'm goddamned suffocating before I lunge at her, before I pick all six feet of her up and evict her slimy, murdering ass off this hallowed ground and—

Why do I hear bees? That droning noise in my ears can't just be the hot rush of my own blood.

Then this spot on my arm goes ice-cold and I tear awake, gasping for air.

"Fucking nightmare," I mutter to myself.

Thankfully, my fit didn't wake Jenn.

She snoozes next to me, and when I look down, Coffee has his cold, wet nose pressed against my arm. His big brown eyes are huge and fixed on mine.

That explains one thing.

"I get it, buddy. Give me a second and I'll take you out," I tell him.

The big Doberman perks his ears as he looks at my night-stand and barks. That's when I realize the buzzing wasn't bees, but my phone.

Bradley's name flashes across the screen.

Shit, what now?

PR doesn't call at five in the morning, but these aren't ordinary times.

Grabbing the phone, I pad through the house quietly to let the dogs out for a bathroom break.

"Cromwell."

"Mr. Cromwell, hope you'll excuse the early hour, but this

couldn't wait. We have a new problem. I thought you should hear it from me."

Fuck, what else is new?

The only person who's worked for me longer than Bradley is Benson himself. If he's dancing around disastrous news, it must be catastrophic.

"Go ahead."

"When I logged in this morning, I received a request for comment from a freelance reporter assigned to a story involving two former employees. A couple of women who worked for the company years ago—"

"The correct comment is always none," I snarl, raking a hand through my messy bed hair.

"Normally, yes, but this time, that would only fan the flames. These women worked under Royal Cromwell, and the story seems to be about him. Not you."

My father?

My teeth pinch together like a vise.

"What kind of story?" I ask.

Bradley clears his throat. "There's no easy way to say this. They're alleging sex scandals, saying he offered to promote them if they'd sleep with him."

"What?"

It takes me a minute to register what he just said. I physically rock back, my legs scrambling to hold my weight like I've just stepped into a sinkhole.

"Names—do we have names?" I'm so fucking shell-shocked I'm stammering. "It has to be Simone. She's fucking disgraceful."

"That was my first thought as well," he says carefully. "Should we talk to Legal?"

I'm torn.

I don't know what to do.

Sure, I have the resources and legal weight to quash these stories at the snap of my fingers. If I decide to go that route, no one will ever hear them, at least not for years.

Every instinct I have screams at me to give the order.

It can't be true—it fucking can't—not when they're accusing a man who loved my mother with his entire soul of living a lie.

But what if he did?

You always hear it, a tale as old as time in this sick slaughter-house of a world.

How refusing to believe women who come forward is the reason women *don't* come forward. If there's the slightest chance Simone didn't put them up to this, I don't want to be that man who silences them.

My head throbs, ready to pop right off.

My father was a good man. I don't want his name dragged through the mud, even if he's too sick to understand the allegations.

I also can't stand the thought of this shit hitting the news, or how his nurses will look at him. They might be the finest professionals money can buy, but if there's any hint of truth—if there's even the slightest doubt he lived a life that was predatory and abusive—they'll never look at him the same way again.

My gut twists. I choke back bile, racing to the faucet in the kitchen to clear the taste from my mouth.

"Mr. Cromwell?" Bradley tries again. "Would you like me to have Legal work on blocking the piece? We can tie it up in court for months and weigh our other options."

Oh, now Legal can help? Fucking wonderful.

Too bad they wouldn't get off their asses with Simone before it came to this, when the victim was Pinnacle Pointe.

"No. Don't do anything until I get there. I'm heading to the office immediately. In the meantime, contact Pacific-Resolute and tell Simone to get her ass here from Portland, then forward me the accusers' personnel files. I want to know who I'm dealing with."

"Will do."

"Bradley, who else knows about this?"

"Right now, it's you, me, and the intern who received the

request for comment and escalated it to me. But if Legal doesn't hit the publication with a gag order ASAP, I don't think we'll keep things quiet for long."

After waving the dogs back inside, I go to my room and start packing. No clue how long I'll be away, so I just dump several days of clothes in my suitcase.

Jenn stirs awake from the noise.

I glance over and find her still peacefully snuggled in my bed.

"Sorry. I would've waited, but something came up that can't," I whisper, almost too low for her to hear me.

She sits up in bed and looks at me, her brows knit together.

Shit, shit.

What do I even say? I can't get her mixed up in this more than she already is.

So I just turn my back and head into the closet, retrieving a small pile of boxers for my bag.

"Miles?" Her voice draws my eyes to her. "Miles, what's wrong?"

"There's been a PR incident. I need to get to Seattle right now."

"Incident? Are you okay?"

Goddamn. This is not the rabbit hole I need to go down right now.

"I'm fine. We're fine. Everyone's fine. The man on the moon is fine," I growl, checking over what I've packed.

"Jeez. Why are you snapping at me?"

"Because. I don't have time for twenty questions today. I promise I'll explain more after I get to the office and see what I'm dealing with."

"Well, if it's that serious..." She climbs out of bed and walks around me into the closet. She opens the drawer she uses for her overnight things and starts tossing clothes into my suitcase.

Fuck.

Here comes the part of the conversation I didn't even know I'd have to dread.

I dive into my luggage, pluck her clothes out, and set them gently on the bed.

"But why?" Then her mouth pulls into a thin line. "Oh. You don't want me to come."

It's half question, half statement.

All heartbreak.

"There's been another problem with—fuck it, you already know."

"Simone?" Her eyes are saucers.

"Yeah. And I don't want you mixed up in more of her crap. It's better this way. Safer. Jenn, she wants to get to me, so let her deal with me alone."

I swore I'd protect her. What kind of man would I be if I risk letting her get dragged further through the mud?

"You're still hiding something," she says weakly.

"What?" I fold my arms, throwing her a look. "Jennifer, please. I don't have time for drama. Not today."

"So, you don't want to risk me being hurt by her because she's already done something horrible you won't tell me about?"

I can't decide if there's more hurt or anger in her eyes.

Damn.

"It's not your problem. It's mine, kitten, and you shouldn't be involved. Hell, you already rose to the occasion so beautifully once. You're the reason Pinnacle Pointe came out of that on the other side. It's fucking unfair to ask you to deal with that again, especially when it's not even work related."

I wish like hell it was. But this time, it's personal.

"That wasn't just for you, you know? I love this town."

"You're missing my point. The town wouldn't have *been* in trouble without my history with this vampire bat. The latest crisis is my fault, too."

"Your fault? Yeah, right. How?"

"She won't give up. She's a ruthless fucking empire builder. If she can't strong-arm me into reconsidering working with her— and I never will—she'll do her damnedest to take me down.

Simone Niehaus doesn't give a single solitary shit who gets caught in the crossfire."

"I'm technically still part of your creative team. And even if I'm not, I'm part of your life...aren't I?" She swallows thickly. "Look, whatever this crisis is, I should come. Let me be there for you."

The sadness hanging in her eyes makes this agonizing.

"You have Bee Harbor and a life here. I'm not disrupting that when you're reaching a critical stage with the reopening plans, let alone putting you in her sights."

"Miles, I don't care. I want to support you. I just—I don't want you to have to go through this alone. That isn't fair." Her voice hitches and she swipes at the corner of her eye.

Fuck, she's going to be the death of me.

That's my kitten. Such a sweet, gentle girl who cares too much for a man who doesn't deserve her.

There's nothing I can say here that doesn't make me sound like a coldhearted jackass.

All the more reason why I'll never forgive myself if I let her waltz into becoming one more target for Simone's machinations.

"The answer's still no. I'm sorry. I'd rather risk having you hate me than risk fucking up your life," I growl, searching her eyes.

"How noble." Sarcasm drips from her voice.

My lip curls.

I don't blame her for being upset.

I'm such a flaming hypocrite I don't know how I'll stand to look at myself in the mirror.

If this were the other way around—if someone hurt Jenn and she wouldn't tell me who or let me fix it—I'd be volcanic with rage.

I'm her partner.

My place is right beside her.

But what she thinks doesn't matter, and neither does my hypocrisy.

Protecting her from any sneak attacks is sacrosanct.

"You have to understand, this isn't easy. I'm dealing with a sociopath."

"And I'm dealing with a control freak," she throws back.

I grit my teeth. "Jenn, I'm leaving either way, but this control freak would rather do it knowing you're on my side. Don't fight me."

I move in to kiss her, but she whips around, blocking me.

I'm stranded, waiting in freezing silence too much like my nightmare until she turns.

For a second, she looks at me harshly. Then her eyes soften.

"When have I *not* been on your side?"

I smile. "I'd rather do this knowing we're okay."

"I want to be, Miles." She sighs, and her lip quivers. "Except... I don't think we are."

But this time when I bring my lips to hers, she lets me kiss her.

She doesn't fight when I deepen it.

Her soft arms wind around my neck and cling tightly.

I break away so reluctantly my bones hurt, drawing a frayed breath.

"I'm going to miss this."

"Take me with you," she counters.

"Against the wall?"

She slaps my chest. "To Seattle, you donkey."

At least she's smiling again, and so am I.

Somehow, I have a feeling it'll be the last time I do that for a good long while.

"Can't do that, kitten. I need a favor from you."

She raises a brow. "I'm not sure you're in good enough graces for that."

"Just keep your head down. Stay here as much as possible," I growl. "If anything gets weird, you call me."

"Don't tell me you're that worried about Ace? God, Miles, if that's why you're asking—"

"Paul Bunyan hadn't crossed my mind," I say, cutting her off. "This is serious, woman. I don't want you to be a sitting duck for every sneaky little shit with a camera, if Simone decides to make my problems yours. If you need anything else, tell Benson."

Her lips thin.

"I really don't understand."

And I don't elaborate with more that will only stress her to hell and back.

She throws her head back and stares at the ceiling, worry and frustration mingling on her face. "For the record, I don't need a babysitter. I've lived alone for years. I'll watch your house, but don't be a dickhead."

I grab her then.

She tries to squirm away, but I hold her so tight until she stops. Like I'm wishing my heart wasn't a weathered boulder, and I could believe laying out the truth would only do us good.

With Simone, I know better.

"Dickhead or not, you haven't been on Simone's radar before. Let me go, trust me, and you never will be again."

* * *

REVIEWING the old personnel files on the flight to Seattle doesn't help me wrap my mind around any of this fuckery.

I wish something added up.

Both women coming after my father had stellar records with the company and never filed a complaint about anything. During their employment, they were both married.

Which makes this shit even more gut-wrenching if there's the tiniest rice grain of truth.

When he still had his mind, Dad was a principled man.

I go through his old records for good measure, looking for a whiff of any complaint.

Nothing.

But if you were strong-armed into unimaginable favors by your CEO, you wouldn't report it in those days.

If you were the CEO doing the strong-arming, you could hush it up all too easily.

The lack of intel in the files doesn't offer any answers.

It fucking hurts.

I'm not just looking for proof that my old man was a quiet monster, a snake in the grass—but evidence that my entire family, everything I thought I knew, was nothing but an epic lie.

Still, I know women who are being abused have to be believed to come forward.

I can't let drag on without turning over every rock.

When I get to headquarters, the first thing I do is go straight to Bradley's office.

"You really did come right away." He sits up in his seat, blinking at the clock.

"Yeah."

A quick glance at his desk shows he's got both women's files open. "Frankly, sir, I'm inclined to dismiss this all as a fabricated lie."

"Because you liked my dad?"

He purses his lips. "Because there's zero evidence in either personnel file to support their allegations. I've contacted Judith in HR. She's running reports now to see if there were any anonymous complaints during the time they worked here. Your father was responsible for that anonymous tip box on the main floor before everything went digital."

I didn't even think about anonymous complaints, but he's right.

Dad rolled out the incognito complaint system in the mid-nineties after a friend's daughter drove to our house one night and asked how to advise a friend who was being sexually harassed by her manager. Then she admitted the manager worked for him, and she was the *friend*.

Dad was her godfather, though, and he was happy to step in. Most of the women who worked for Cromwell-Narada didn't have that kind of backing.

"Let's see what HR finds before we decide what to do."

"The other thing is you've been CEO for years, and they haven't worked here in ages. Why now? Right in the middle of all this trouble with Pacific-Resolute? They could have filed a complaint, launched a lawsuit, outed it on Facebook or Twitter or anywhere else." Bradley scratches his beard, trying to make sense of it.

"That also crossed my mind. Being CEO is all about making the best decisions when there's no clear 'right' decision. This might be the first time I've had no clue what to do with a company issue. These ladies did their jobs well and they left without issue. One received a recommendation from her manager. No sign anyone here ever had an axe to grind with them. Still, I don't want them discredited publicly. I'm not destroying their lives if there's even a hint it could be true."

"But?" He looks at me expectantly.

"I don't believe it is. I don't *want* to believe it. And if it isn't, we need to prove that, too."

"Well, you're right that we can't just sweep it under the rug and hope for the best. From a PR standpoint, and as your father's friend, I'd personally like to see the story quashed—"

"Which I won't do, Bradley. Not until we know what the hell happened. There's also a legal blind spot. What if they go after my father?"

"Oh, no." Bradley's eyes widen. "No judge would ever waste much time with anyone going after Royal. He'd be deemed unfit for a trial rather fast."

"Not fast enough to avoid being dragged in front of doctors and psychologists who aren't there to help him, just to analyze his state of mind," I grind out. "In the meantime, he could be pushed off to die in a mental hospital."

Bradley looks down at his hands.

He knows I'm right.

"I trust it won't come to that, sir."

"Look, can we get a meeting with Legal set up ASAP? I want all options on deck. I'm not gagging the journalist, but if there's a way to delay it without dragging anyone into court, I want to know that too."

"I'll set up a meeting now. In the meantime, I'll put out a statement the instant any of this starts showing up on Twitter feeds. We believe in a victim's right to come forward, and we're taking this matter seriously. We'll put out an updated statement when we have a better understanding of the situation."

"Perfect," I say, even though it's anything but.

"Miles?"

"Yeah?"

"I don't mean to overstep, but..." He doesn't finish the sentence.

"But?"

"There are other rumors around the office. About you and Miss Landers."

"From who?" I bite off.

"Not sure, sir, but it's been going up the chain. I don't think either of you are exactly secretive," he says.

"Meaning what, exactly? I've never mentioned her to anyone." No one who isn't named Benson, anyway.

"Maybe so, but these matters take on a life of their own. With your father's accusations, you certainly don't want anyone getting the wrong idea. Would you consider bringing on another consultant or—"

He trails off.

Or ending things, he means.

"She decides where she wants to work, Bradley. Not me. Right now, she's mulling more consulting for us on the side."

"Then for the sake of both you and this company, I hope you figure out where she's needed most," he says with a nod.

"I have a lot of work to do. Let me know when Legal responds." I leave his office with hornets under my skin.

I head for my office and check my cell.

Jenn hasn't called or texted since I left in a huff, and I don't blame her.

Annoyed with myself, I hit Benson's contact.

"How is she?"

"Hard to say. She left shortly after you did."

"What? I asked her to stay there."

"She said you were clear about her having a life, so she decided she'd better live it. Lord knows there's plenty to do at the inn," he tells me, but he's holding something back.

"Benson, spit it out," I growl.

"And it seems you still haven't told her everything about Miss Niehaus."

"Is she mad at me?"

"Seething. In the nicest way, of course. There's one more thing, though."

"What?"

"She was so upset I didn't want to ask, but she took a box of clothes home with her."

Oh.

Oh, fuck.

He has to mean the stuff she kept at my place.

"Thanks for the update. I'll talk to her." I kill the call, then throw my phone down and dig my nails into my scalp.

Fuck Simone and the cactus broomstick she rode in on.

Later, I'm still up in my head, racking my brain, trying to figure out how to start unfucking this damage, when there's a knock at my door.

"Come."

Bradley walks in with the heads of Legal and HR.

"Have a seat," I say.

They each take a chair.

"We'll start with our legal options, then you can tell me your recommendation," Bradley says.

Truman from Legal clears his throat, his foot tapping the floor nervously. "I have very limited information to go on, Mr. Cromwell. All I know is that two women told someone your father offered to promote them in exchange for sex years ago. If true, that constitutes criminal sexual harassment. Of course, we have no information to confirm this at the moment. Given what I have available at this time, the options are suing for slander, ignoring it until one of the women sue us and mounting a defense at that time, or launching our own investigation."

Everyone stares at me, their eyes drilling through my skin like they can see the headache eating me alive. I hold in a sigh and steeple my fingers.

"What do you recommend?" I ask drearily.

XXI: NO DRY EYE (JENN)

I know, I know, *I know.*

I shouldn't have let him leave alone when there's clearly more to this weird half story than what he's telling me.

Not when he's freezing me out.

Not when he's a mess who thinks the apocalypse will strike the moment he ever shows the slightest real emotion.

I know all that, and it still stings my heart, just knowing he's going through it alone.

Worried is a ginormous understatement.

It took ages to get any real feeling out of him. If he starts thinking those cracks in his armor are some kind of weakness— if he shuts down completely—what then?

I ponder it until my head hurts, my chin propped on my hand, when Coffee flies at Miles' office, thunks his big head on the door, and barks up a storm.

"Seriously, boy? It hasn't even been a day," I whisper, scratching his neck.

I get the feeling, though.

When he doesn't see Miles, he runs around the house in circles, snorting at the ground and launching into a tirade at the slightest sound outside.

I open the office door for the dogs and let them sniff around.

Coffee circles the room with Cream in tow before they trot back out, retracing the last steps Miles ever took in this house.

I'm not even sure why I'm here after taking my things, but I promised to look after his place, didn't I?

Cream heels next to me and whimpers, looking up with the whiniest puppy dog eyes.

"I miss him, too. He'll be home soon."

Never one to let go easily, Coffee paces to the bedroom again. When he doesn't find Miles waiting for him with a treat, he throws his head back and lets out a grumbling, distinctly Doberman howl. I follow him to the room with Cream behind me.

"Dude, you're not a wolf." Even through the melancholy, I laugh.

Coffee stomps his feet and barks at me again.

Yeah, the dogs can't handle this confusion either.

After a lazy day where I pretend to do some work on the inn's pilot plans and a sleepless night, I hit my limit.

At four a.m. I crawl out of the bed, clean up, pack my stuff, and kennel the dogs before I send a quick message to Benson.

The valet helps me load the car just before sunset.

"For the record, ma'am, this is a bad idea," he tells me.

"Why?"

What does he know that I don't?

"Mr. Cromwell, he's a stickler for rules. He may not welcome your help—or even your presence—if you're certain you want to surprise him in Seattle." His face is unreadable.

"Thanks for the warning, Benson, but it's my decision. I'll take the blame if that's what you're worried about."

He hesitates. "No, ma'am. It's just, well, he's a very reserved man. And you've gotten rather good at bringing out his human side. It would be tragic if he falls back into old habits. I don't want to see him push you away."

The honest worry in his voice makes my heart race.

"That's his move, but I appreciate your concern." I nod at him and he gives back a ghostly smile.

Then he walks off to get Cream's kennel situated in the back and secured next to Coffee's.

I shut the door and move to my driver's seat.

I have to wait almost an hour for the first private ferry to load up at the docks, saying a quiet prayer that they still have space for one more car and their cargo hold isn't booked up today.

Fortunately, I'm in luck.

As the ship chugs across the Sound, I feed the dogs treats through the kennels to keep them calm.

The despairing look on Benson's face replays in my head.

Am I doing the right thing?

I don't know, but we're about to find out.

* * *

As soon as I've unloaded my stuff and two sleepy Dobermans at my parents' house, I start calling old contacts.

When Sarah doesn't answer, I try Dave and a couple other people from creative content. But all their lines go straight to voicemail.

That sets my mind racing when it could mean anything.

If the entire office is that slammed trying to put out the mystery fire that pulled Miles back here, it must be bad. Or he instructed his staff not to talk to me.

Yikes.

All the possibilities are bad. A few hours later over coffee at a Wired Cup down the street, I try again.

The only person who picks up their phone is a junior copywriter, Ericka, and she's vague as hell.

I can't decide if she really doesn't know what's going on or if she just doesn't want to tell me. Either way, hounding the staff gets me nowhere.

After dinner, I have my keys in my hand and I'm headed to the door.

"Where are you off to, Jenn?" Dad asks. "You haven't sat down since you got here."

I look at the keys in my hand and pause before answering.

Honestly, I have no idea. I just know Miles is determined to keep me from finding out how serious this is.

Going to his place feels pointless. He either won't answer, or he'll only open the door long enough to yell at me for intruding on his secrecy.

With a deflated sigh, I hang my keys back on the wall and pull down the leashes instead. "You know what, you're right. I was thinking about some gas, but it can wait. I'll take the dogs for a walk instead."

"Are you sure?" Dad asks. His voice contains none of his usual judgment for my choices.

Actually, I haven't heard him sound so gentle since I broke my arm going across the monkey bars in the fourth grade.

"Yep. They should be waking up from their naps." I force a smile and then whistle. "Coffee, Cream! Let's go, guys."

The beasts come bounding downstairs, tails wagging as I leash them.

As they drag me along, losing their wits in the city smells, I realize I should just get my butt to the office.

It's neutral ground, and Miles won't make a scene at work.

If he still slams the door in my face, at least it'll be easier to suss out what's going on in person.

I'm technically still a contractor, even if I'm between active contracts with Cromwell-Narada. It wouldn't be unusual for me to visit.

It's something.

Knowing my next step makes the jog home lighter. Even when the dogs go crazy, barking at a tourist packed pedal pub that goes by with people laughing loudly into their beers.

* * *

IN THE MORNING, I stand in front of the elevator to Cromwell's C-level floor.

The moment of truth.

He forbade me from coming here.

He hasn't called or texted since he left.

None of my company contacts have been eager to return my calls, except Sarah, who texted me so late I wasn't awake to text her back.

Holding my breath, I wave my badge in front of the door, hoping my credentials still work.

The reader makes a clicking sound and the light turns green.

A minute later, I'm stepping off the elevator and walking past Louise's desk in no time without acknowledging her.

I don't register her face until I've already passed her.

"Miss Landers? He's in a meeting," Louise calls out behind me.

I stop and whirl slowly on my heel.

"What meeting?" I ask neutrally.

"I don't know. He told me to cancel his morning because he had a meeting outside the office that couldn't wait."

"Where?"

She looks at the floor. "I—I don't know."

"Louise?"

Again, no answer. I watch her swallow, her throat working like she's trying to find room for a lie.

"Do you know what the one drawback of being a fairly honest person is?" I ask flatly.

She looks up and blinks. "No?"

"It tends to make you a pretty crappy liar, and you're too nice for that, Louise. Now, where's this meeting? Don't tell me you don't know."

"I'm sorry. Mr. Cromwell instructed me not to tell—"

"You're not telling *anyone*. You're telling me. Big difference."

She squeezes her eyes shut and grimaces.

"You didn't let me finish. Especially you, he said." It's barely audible.

"What?" It's like a knife going through my heart. "Especially me? He said that?"

She slowly opens her eyes.

"Miss Landers, forgive me—I don't think it has anything to do with you personally. From what I gathered, he thinks he's protecting you."

Holy shit.

I'm torn between turning into a human icicle or slugging Miles Cromwell in his stupid, secretive, overprotective face.

Don't I get to decide if I need protection from—whatever the big bad is?

"Louise, I'm worried about him," I say honestly. "Where is he?"

"...I'm sorry. I didn't ask to be involved with this. I know Miles thinks he's doing the right thing and—"

"And?"

She doesn't answer.

"You don't think he is? Well, that makes two of us."

She still doesn't answer, staring down at her nails.

"Why doesn't he want me to know what's going on? I know it's that Niehaus creeper again. Nothing else would get him this upset."

"I've already said too much," she strains out.

"Louise..."

"Jenn." She looks up slowly, her eyes set like steel. "Don't make me call security. I'd never forgive myself."

Jaw, meet floor.

I stagger back a step and throw my hands up.

"Whatever. I'll go." I have no intention, but I have to disarm her somehow.

I start walking away slowly, holding my breath.

"Miss Landers? You're not going to say anything, are you?" Louise waits until I look at her.

I shake my head slowly.

"Then if I told you he was at the Sweeter Grind a few blocks away..." She pauses.

"I'll do my best to help. Thank you, Louise."

"Please do," she whispers, guilt written all over her face. "I've already said too much."

I pull my phone out of my purse and search the nearest Sweeter Grind.

It's a three-minute walk.

Perfect.

I head for the elevator and dart through people in the lobby, bursting out of the building and sprinting toward the coffee shop.

My shoe catches on something rubbery—a blown out bit of tire or a discarded boot—and next thing I know, I'm spinning.

Shit!

I barely land on my feet in the tumble without falling, but my ankle twists with a sickening crunch.

It hurts like hell.

Groaning, I lift my foot and shake it out.

I can still move it, thank God, so I know I can keep going, limping through the pain.

"Yo, you need to be more careful! People throw crap everywhere around here." A tall guy with shaggy blond hair snaps.

What's his deal?

He bends down and picks up a rubbery violin case from the sidewalk where I stand.

The object I tripped over. *Oops.*

"Sorry!" I mutter without stopping.

I'm almost there.

A minute later, I yank the door open, expecting to find a wall of scowling suits that looks like a typical corporate shakedown with mafia vibes.

But Miles isn't here with an entourage.

He and Bradley are perched in an overstuffed leather booth, and across from him—Simone Niehaus. Tall and carnivorous, wearing a navy-blue pantsuit that makes her look more like a mob capo than a media mogul.

What the actual hell is going on?

I slide into a chair at a two-seat table in the corner, hoping to observe from a safe distance.

But Simone takes a drink of her coffee, sets it down on the table, and turns her head like a snake sensing something small and furry and edible.

The way she looks at me feels nastier than any rattlesnake, especially that weird, gleeful smile.

With my heart in my throat, she points at me.

Oh God Oh God.

So much for cover.

Dread consumes me as I stand, cringe, and approach the table.

There's no point in hiding now.

"Oh, Miles," she says. "I'm so glad to see your little girlfriend showed up to spy. Maybe *she* can talk some sense into you."

His head whips around in a fury I've never seen.

Cold, cutting eyes slice me open.

His mouth twists like he wants to say something—or like it takes all his effort not to.

But he hasn't gotten a word out when Simone's smile widens and she says, "Have a seat, missy. You're just in time to help him come to terms with his dearest father's antics."

"Antics? What do you mean?" Every word comes out tasting metallic.

Like copper.

Like blood.

Like I totally shouldn't be here.

With a hissing snicker, her focus shifts to Miles. "You never told her? You didn't tell her about your recent family revelations? My, my Miles... Did you even tell her about *our* history?"

The color washes out of his face.

I need to do something, but I'm at a total loss.

"He said you two were friends—hard to imagine," I force out.

"Friends?" She stares at him. "*Friends?* Is that what you call it?"

"Simone!" Her name flies out of his mouth like a shotgun blast.

She meets my eyes with a dark look.

"Lovers. Paramours. Friends with benefits. Fuck buddies. There are so many words for the same thing on a scale of eloquence to gutter rubbish, I suppose, though I'm not sure any of those fit. I'd like to think we were soulmates, Jennifer. Perhaps we still are. We were certainly heavy before—well, did Miles tell you that, or should I spill the beans?"

My heart rabbits so hard I fidget my hands together, digging my nails into my skin.

I'm not sure how I'm still standing against the rancor in his eyes.

"Simone, shut it," he snaps.

Bradley lifts a hand like he wants to lay it on Miles' shoulder, but he flinches back at the last second.

"I see some things never change." She releases an exaggerated yawn. "Really, I doubt we would have broken up if the merger hadn't fallen through—"

"Like hell. I called it off because I knew you were nothing but a conniving, two-faced, greedy goddamned banshee. After what you did..." His voice cuts off, silenced by raw fury.

His shoulders tremble like he's about to detonate.

Holy hell.

I'm not even listening to whatever sickening, smartassed thing Simone spews out next.

I need to get out of here.

Before I'm the one who explodes so violently I'm not sure I'll ever pull myself together.

The big revelation here shouldn't kill me.

I suspected it.

Deep down, *I knew.*

But I gave him so many chances to tell me what really happened, to explain, to help me understand why he ever fell in love with such a sinister mockery of a woman.

And he lied.

He dodged the truth, and I let him.

God, I'm such an idiot.

My head knew better, but my heart didn't care.

I start for the door, but my ankle is still tender from the fall. My foot wobbles over the heel I'm wearing and I twist my foot again.

This really is the best day ever.

This time, my ass smacks the cold hard tile. Several baristas spin around, calling out and asking if I need help, if I need—

No.

No, dammit. There's nothing anyone can say or do or offer to help me right now.

Because ambushing Miles and being scolded by the viper he couldn't be honest about wasn't humiliating enough. Now, I have to fall on my face in front of both of them.

"Jenn, can you walk?"

When I look up, he's standing over me, speaking through the fury still storming in his eyes.

Jerking my head from side to side, I peel myself up off the ground, fighting the pain just long enough to shoot out the door.

I haven't made it two steps when I realize he's behind me, calling "Jenn, wait! Wait, goddammit."

I can't.

I can't even feel myself think.

I'm all instinct, limping away as fast as I can and hating how a drunken snail could beat this pace.

When I find a tiny side alley beside the coffee shop, I drag myself down it.

Of course, it's a typical Seattle dead end with a rank smelling dumpster at the end.

My stomach heaves.

I have to fight down bile.

"It's not what you think," he says coldly as he catches up.

"How would I know that, Miles? You haven't told me shit."

"And you shouldn't have interrupted," he growls. "You have no fucking clue what you just walked into."

My stare hardens. "Yeah? It sure looked like I walked into you and the ex you couldn't be honest about plotting to murder each other."

"Jenn—"

"It's true, isn't it? What she said? You were lovers. You lied every time I asked you."

"She's nothing now. Just the biggest regret of my fucked up life."

I turn away. I can't look at him anymore through the burning haze of tears.

"You lied about her, about—do I even want to know?" I suck in a deep breath, hating that *I do.* "Why, Miles? Why couldn't you just tell me about Simone and whatever's going on with your father?"

"She wants to *kill* my father, the same way she did with—" His voice booms through the alley. "When I told you to stay the fuck away from her, I had good reason, Jenn. Why couldn't you just listen?"

I'm so confused, so hurt my brain isn't working.

Did he mean that literally?

The snake-woman in the coffee shop is sleek and cold, yeah. But she doesn't look like a murderer.

I also have a hard time seeing her overpowering any Cromwell man.

But Miles' emotion is real and raw and explosive. It's

palpable on his face, the muscle twitching above one silver-blue eye.

There's no doubting the venom in his voice.

Why couldn't you just listen?

"I'm listening now, aren't I?" I force out, refraining from adding *jackass.*

He sighs and pinches the bridge of his nose.

"I'm sorry. This shit's coming out wrong. Years ago, she wanted a merger. She got close to me, gained my trust. She was so fucking desperate to pull a deal out of me that she dragged me off to Miami. She seduced me and shut down my phone. Pulled the battery right out sometime after we left the airport, before we even got to the hotel, and—and hell, I've always wondered if she drugged my drink while she was at it—all so she could convince me to sign the damn agreement she brought along. It was supposed to be our big celebration."

He collapses against the wall, drawing a ragged breath while I wait.

"I wasn't quite drunk enough to sign her bullshit without discussing it with my legal team, but I missed a handful of calls while my phone was disabled. All from my dad. His mind, it isn't good—dementia, Alzheimer's, whatever the fuck. It wasn't then either, but back then he still had enough sense to call me when my mother collapsed."

He pauses again.

I don't even know what's coming next, but I do.

Hot tears flare down my face, my heart breaking for him, for us, simultaneously.

"Miles..."

"For reasons I'll never understand, Dad knew enough to call me on their landline, but not to call 9-1-1. He didn't even understand what was happening. Every voicemail was worse than the last, asking why she went to sleep. Why she wouldn't wake the fuck up." He inhales like he's breathing nails. "My mother was still breathing for over an hour. Then she wasn't. By the time I got the voicemails the next day, the police found them. He was sleeping next to her, holding her like they were just taking a nap. Mom, she was—you already know. So there. There's the whole ugly fucking truth that turned me into this. Happy now?"

His eyes glint with a stabbing pain I'm not sure I'll ever understand.

And I'm sobbing so hard I haven't formed a response when he starts talking again.

"And now...now, the bitch-queen responsible for my mother's death wants to obliterate my father's reputation from beyond the grave and tear apart his company—his legacy."

I don't know what that means.

I don't care.

I'm beyond broken.

"God!" I step closer. "Miles, I'm sorry. So sorry. I wouldn't have interrupted if I'd known. The way you left, you scared me."

He holds up a hand to stop me.

"We couldn't have talked this out with Simone anyway. Still, you ruined my last chance to warn her off before this escalates. I need you to go back to Pinnacle Pointe, and this time, stay there."

I'm speechless.

Hurting or not, he's never been this frigid with me. This empty, unloving thing I'm struggling to recognize.

"I get that you're hurting, but you... you don't own me. I'm not some little minion you can order around. If you can't understand that—"

"If you can't wrap your head around what I need to do, then you should definitely go. Stay there, Jenn, and stay away from me."

Gutted.

I barely wipe my eyes with my sleeve before I whip around, stepping down on my foot exploding with a thousand tiny pinprick knives that stab up my heel.

"Ow!" I throw my arms out, trying to hold my balance so I don't fall over.

"Damn. You're hurt." His voice softens, far too close to me. "Let me give you a ride."

"No!" I shake my head until I can't see.

"Jenn, you can't walk on that foot. You'll just make it worse."

He's totally right and I still ignore him.

I just stumble along in halting steps, feeling what's left of my shattered heart crunching underfoot.

"Jenn, please. Let me get you home safe, or at least call you a car."

He's just a blurry silhouette when I look back through tears, hissing, "Don't bother, asshole. Go finish your meeting and sort out your life. You don't have time for me."

"I'll make time," he growls. "Let me get you to your parents' house. You can figure out the rest from there."

"Jesus, it's too late, okay?" My voice breaks.

"Too late?"

How can he not understand?

There's no coming back from this.

I wipe the tears from my eyes, still slurring my words. "I... I have no idea what you want, Miles, but it's not me. And I'm... I'm better than that. I deserve more than a man who can't decide, who can't make up his fucking mind—"

"You knew I had a fucked up past," he bites off.

"And you let it define you. You never trusted me. You just left me behind. Then you—*only you*—turned me away."

His mouth opens, but he closes it again.

If I ever thought I'd take any joy rendering Miles Cromwell speechless, it dies on the spot.

"You don't trust me, and you think you're better off alone—and maybe you are. You don't love me." My voice catches on that shredded L-word.

I need to leave.

Get out of here right flipping now.

336

"That's not true, and you know it," he says finally, his voice so raw.

"What's true is that you don't trust me enough to care about you in spite of your mistakes. You won't trust me when you're hurting. You couldn't tell me the truth until you chased me out of a coffee shop in a rage."

"Jenn—"

"S-sorry. I shouldn't have been stupid enough to fall for a man too afraid to show me who he really is and who thinks he can order me around."

"Jenn," he growls louder, dragging himself forward like he's been shot.

"Miles, stop. Let me go. Let me give you what you want one last time—I'm going, and you'll never speak to me again."

He's quiet as I limp away, this time with no looking back.

I'm too pummeled, black and blue down to my soul.

But that's the problem.

I'm not overreacting.

This is the reaction I should have had sooner.

Then tearing myself away from him wouldn't have to hurt like this.

Whatever else I do, I can't look back.

A single glance might catch my tattered heart on thorns of doubt.

My foot feels like it's covered in a fire ant colony by the time I hobble a block or two and find an Uber. I practically throw myself in the back seat, swallowing another rattling sob.

The driver confirms my parents' address and we're off.

I try not to look, but I catch one last glimpse of a miserable, deflated Miles sulking by the alley. His eyes are red as he stares after the car.

Then he raises his fist and slams it into solid brick. My voice hitches, thinking of him breaking his hand.

"Miss? Everything okay back there?" the driver asks.

"Y-yeah. Just a rough day."

And I wipe my eyes for the hundredth time, but the tears keep coming.

How do you make them stop?

How do you stop mourning something that was never meant to be?

XXII: NO TIME FOR REGRETS
(MILES)

*P*ain vibrates through my shoulder from the impact.
Not enough.

Not one iota of the hell I deserve for ramming a knife through her chest, yanking her heart out, and leaving her literally limping away from me.

The woman I love—the woman I'm still too fucking stupid to tell—left crying and ruined and it's all my fault.

I shouldn't have cornered her in the alley with my brain an armed minefield.

I should have just let her leave and left it alone.

All the shouldas don't matter now, though.

Because we're here now.

I've already destroyed something more fragile and beautiful than anything I'll ever deserve.

My kitten will never speak to me again.

I throw my arms up, yelling a few incoherent curses at the sky.

If there's a God up there, he isn't in my corner today.

He just makes me watch helplessly as her Uber vanishes with a destroyed look that hurts vastly more than my ruined hand.

I release a breath.

At least she's safe now.

Safe from *me.*

She'll be okay and I won't have to cut my own tongue out to protect her anymore.

I also still have a fire-breathing bitch to finish dealing with.

To be fair, Bradley warned me.

Any face-to-face meeting with Lilith incarnate was bound to be cursed from the second we sat down.

Still, I never imagined this.

I never expected to drag myself back to Sweeter Grind, hoping for a chance to save my father from more hellish stress and legal interrogations he'll never understand, and all after I obliterated the woman of my dreams.

I throw the door open and glance over at the booth where we were sitting.

As expected, the biggest murdering whore in the universe is gone. Was she watching my entire meltdown the whole time, getting her fucking jollies off?

I slouch down across from Bradley, swiping a hand down my face.

"Miss Niehaus left a message," he says cautiously.

"What?" I ask miserably.

"'Don't do anything stupid.' Her words."

What the fuck?

It's too late for that.

The big fat fucking idiot line was crossed the day I had my people set this meeting up.

"I think that's what she's waiting for, honestly," Bradley continues.

"Waiting for what?"

"For you to pop off and do something reckless. She's a master manipulator, Mr. Cromwell—not that I need to tell you. That's why she had you meet here, and that's why she called Jennifer over. She's hoping if she pushes your buttons, you'll lose it in public. You'll do something truly damaging."

The awkward way he shrugs tells me I already did.

Goddamn.

I shake my head like it weighs a metric ton. "I had to talk to Jenn."

"Certainly, you did nothing legally actionable. Our security specialist made sure there were no cameras around. Um, how did that go, by the way?"

I shrug. "About like walking into a petting zoo full of rabid llamas."

Bradley winces, his bald head reddening.

"Is Miss Landers okay? I noticed she was limping when she left..."

I nod. "She took an Uber to her parents' place. She's strong. She'll get over."

I fucking hope.

"Are you okay, Mr. Cromwell?" he adds.

"I'm peachy, Bradley, considering Simone will stop at nothing to make every new day on this rock a fresh stage of hell."

"So, I don't know what you did to her, but the woman holds quite a grudge."

"I didn't *do* anything. Besides torpedoing the merger after she got my mother killed."

He goes quiet. I don't blame him.

There's no polite response to that.

"Why are we still here? Let's get back to work," I growl, already standing.

At least at the office, I can stay busy. I don't have to dwell on the fact that Jenn hates me forever and I don't even have a way to thwart a dangerous sociopath from shredding my life.

I go through every anonymous HR complaint that's ever been filed over the last twenty years for what feels like the millionth time.

I'm looking for a needle in a fucking haystack that likely doesn't exist.

Something to corroborate either woman's story, or something to clear Dad beyond all doubt.

You can guess what I find.

Jack shit.

Nothing.

There are vanishingly few complaints. In fact, the ones that turn up have more to do with benefits and compensation than anyone's bad behavior in the office.

I regret lying to Jenn and pulverizing her heart, but now that it's over, there's nothing to distract me from getting to the bottom of this abyss.

I pick up Jillian Oakes' file and call every number listed. When she doesn't answer, I try sending a text, and then I try numbers I find on Google supposedly associated with her.

No response.

Ava Wickes is next, the other accuser. Several different numbers are listed in her file. The first one seems disconnected, and there's no answer at the second number. It's probably useless, but I try the third anyway, a more recent one added from my own quick data digging.

"Hello?" She picks up on the third ring.

"Ava Wickes?"

"Speaking."

I inhale slowly. "Mrs. Wickes, this is Miles Cromwell."

Her breath catches loudly.

"Miles Crom—oh." She pauses. "Yes, what do you want?"

I sigh.

Fuck, I wasn't actually expecting to have this conversation.

"I just wanted to apologize to you on behalf of my family and my company if—" Hell, I don't even want to say it, much less open the doors to more hell legally. "—*if* my father ever did anything underhanded or unethical. He hasn't been well for several years and his mind is basically gone. So the most I can offer is a heartfelt apology on his behalf." I draw a deep breath. "But if he ever wronged you in any way... I need to know."

She's dead silent for a minute.

When she speaks again, her voice is much softer, almost weak. "Yes, I'm—I'm aware of Royal's condition. I hate bad-mouthing him to his own son, but he... he just had another side. I'm sure you don't want to hear the gory details."

I grit my teeth.

If only she knew how very badly I do. I need the truth, no matter how many sharp teeth it comes with.

"Mrs. Wickes, just give me your version, please. Off the record, we don't need lawyers for this."

Again, that choking silence.

"I'm not sure I'm ready to discuss this with you, Mr. Cromwell. All I can say is everybody has another side. I'm sorry his actions dragged you into this. We've all done things we aren't proud of, and I'm sure it's the same for your father."

Isn't that the fucking truth?

An image of myself lying nude on silk sheets while Simone licked up the inside of my thigh pops into my head.

We all do things we don't want anyone knowing about. But I didn't drug myself and pull the battery out of my phone—even after I mentioned my father's problems to Simone, and she laughed sympathetically when I told her my mother was too stubborn to hire a full-time nurse.

I can't believe Dad would ever betray her like that with some bullshit fling.

I can't believe he'd ever pressure anyone to sleep with him, much less women who work for him.

Did he?

"Mrs. Wickes, that's fine. Just tell me this—did my father ever do anything unethical?"

"Your father worked so hard the decade before he stepped aside. With so many changes, with the internet coming into play, I think he lived there half the time. He said he was lonely—" She stops.

That much is true.

He hated being away from us, especially my mother.

"Eventually, he just went about taking care of his loneliness the wrong way. The promises he made, well..." She trails off. "When he asked for the unthinkable, he promised a promotion and told me I'd make twice my salary. I wasn't thinking then. How could I say no?"

"The unthinkable," I repeat coldly.

Damn.

Again, icy silence.

"He asked me to—I mean, he wanted us to—I'm sorry. I don't want to have this conversation right now, okay? My attorney will be in touch."

"I understand. You've already spoken to a reporter, though."

"Yes, and it would probably be better if we kept this between our counsels, wouldn't it?"

"I just want your story," I say.

"He asked me to sleep with him," she snaps, almost too quickly. "There. Is that what you needed? As for the rest, you can read the article."

My gut hardens.

Goddammit, no.

On so many levels, I don't want the bitter truth.

I could care less about my dementia-stricken father's sex life.

I just need to know why he left this open sore, ripe for Simone to come along and pick it open to fuel her stupid war on me.

"Mrs. Wickes, listen—"

There's a muffled click.

"Mrs. Wickes? Ava?" I pull the phone away from my face and look at the screen, flashing my worst fears.

She disconnected, leaving me alone with this flaming wreck of a scandal and zero answers.

"Fuck!" I shout, slamming my hand on my desk and swearing again.

Of course, it's my inflamed hand with bruises already

fanning out from the knuckles. I rip my hand back, biting at the pain.

Was she telling me the truth?

Was my father a predator?

Was he ever as madly in love with my mother as I believed before she died?

Hell, did I even *know* the man?

Has my whole goddamned life been an illusion?

* * *

A FEW DAYS LATER, I'm stuck in another meeting with Bradley and Lucas Truman, the head of Legal.

"I've reconsidered sitting on our asses. Why wait for someone else to make a move?" I tell them. "Just make sure the asshole reporters Pacific-Resolute put up to it drop the stories before they're published."

The attorney nods and scribbles something in his notebook. "I'll have to investigate, but I can take care of that. If we can't stop them indefinitely, there's probably sufficient cause for delay."

Bradley shakes his head. "Don't do it, Truman."

Truman looks from Bradley to me and then down at his notebook.

"Why the hell not?" I ask.

"It's a bad move when it's public. There are already whispers on Twitter from the reporter assigned to this. If you'd tried to gag her from the beginning, maybe it wouldn't look so bad. But the allegations have lingered, the rumors are swirling, and you've only half-heartedly investigated the rest."

I stand, stopping him mid-sentence.

"Excuse me? I didn't half-heartedly do anything. There's nothing concrete *to* investigate. I'm chasing fucking ghosts."

"Absolutely, sir. Frustrating. Be that as it may, if you squelch these stories now, it's going to look like you're silencing legitimate accusations. Especially with no evidence to disprove them."

I sigh. "How the hell am I supposed to prove a negative? Isn't my father innocent until proven guilty?"

"Yes," Truman answers.

At the same time, Bradley says, "No."

I glare at him.

"I mean, Truman's right about the legal system. But that's not how the court of public opinion works," Bradley says.

Shit.

I don't like it, but he's right.

I have to let this catastrophe play out publicly, or I'm so completely screwed I'd need to pull a direct confession out of Simone's ass to ever set things right.

By then, it won't matter.

Not if a court wrestles with the case for years, deciding whether or not the claims are scandalous.

Once Royal Cromwell gets pegged as a womanizing predator, the story will stick.

It will tarnish the whole company.

It may even mean he's ripped out of his cozy little nursing home and thrown into a state mental hospital, where he'll spend his dying days.

"Have you managed to speak to either woman?" Bradley asks.

"Wickes. I can't get Oakes on the phone."

"You probably won't," Truman says. "Any attorney worth their salt will advise them not to take any off the cuff calls."

"What did Wickes have to say?" Bradley asks.

"Nothing useful. All she said was that my dad was a lonely man and he tried to fix it the wrong way," I say.

"We need a PI," Truman says. "Otherwise, we're going to be limping along with our shields down."

"If you think it will help, do it," I say.

He nods. "I'll have one ready to go by end of day."

"In the meantime, what do I do?"

"Legally? Or are you asking what's best for the company?" Truman asks.

"The second." *I guess.*

"Until we've gotten to the bottom of these accusations, there isn't much we can do," Bradley tells me. "If it's Royal's legacy you're worried about, you could start a content campaign focusing on all the good he did during his life. Though that could backfire once stories start circulating. Regardless, I'd advise you to increase brand awareness campaigns to spotlight Cromwell-Narada's accomplishments. It's damage control at this point. The company is likely to have a PR stain for a while no matter what we do, even when the allegations are disproven."

When. He said when, not if.

Bradley doesn't believe it'll amount to anything, but I can't be so sure Ava Wickes was lying either.

She never trashed him on the phone, though.

That doesn't sound like a woman with an axe to grind, or someone who would've seen my father as a monster.

When the meeting ends, I follow them to the door and close it behind them.

Goddamn.

I don't know what to think anymore.

I'm certainly not thinking as I storm across the room, grab Dad's paintings from the wall, and hurl them on the floor.

"Did you do it or not? Don't make me hate you." I catch myself, flattening my wounded hand against my desk for balance.

If my father really was a cheating, predatory fuck, I'll never forgive him.

But the only person in the room I can't forgive right now stares back when I turn, catching my reflection in the window.

My father hurting women is only hypothetical.

I already did.

I refuse to let her face crystalize in my head as I throw myself

347

back behind my computer, sign in, and pretend to be productive.

If only I could lie to myself as easily as I bullshitted Jenn.

Every worn second I'm wasting my life without her brings back her teary, red face and the look of shocked betrayal after I forced her heart through a meatgrinder.

If only I could be the man I still hope my father is, I might have had a life with Jennifer Landers.

XXIII: NO SWEET DREAMS (JENN)

*I*t's been weeks since the whole incident at the coffee shop with Miles and the ugly past that ruined a future I didn't know I desperately wanted.

Weeks since I tasted his kiss and shuddered underneath him.

Weeks without him here, watching summer give up its warmth to autumn with the first brilliant ribbons of color in the trees, the crispness in the air, the rains coming more often.

Weeks, weeks, and only a lifetime left to go.

Sigh.

As soon as I came back to Pinnacle Pointe, I threw myself into the inn. I've hired a few part-timers and decided to do a limited test reopening before winter. Just a few rooms at a time.

It's kept me busy and shaves a few minutes off dwelling on Miles every day. It also helps that he hasn't been back at his place since the sky started falling.

"Jenn, we have a problem," Maria says, peeking into the old storage closet Gram converted into a back office in the main building. She's a pleasant young lady who greets everyone with a grin.

I close the article I'm reading on a famous little inn in Heart's Edge, Montana, and look up from my laptop. "What's up?"

Her cheeks redden when she grins. "I can't believe it, but... I may have overbooked a room. I'm so sorry."

"Don't apologize! I'm not even sure it's your mistake. That spreadsheet doesn't always save right in the cloud. That's the point of a soft opening, right? So we can work these kinks out before we bite off more than we can chew. Do we have any other rooms?"

She looks down, fidgeting her skinny fingers together.

"Of the three you said were ready right now? No."

I puff out my cheeks and slowly blow the tension out, trying to decide what to do. "What's the situation?"

"I gave the key to the woman who came in earlier. Now there's an older man at the front desk. He really wants this room. He says it's been his for every stay the past twenty years."

"Twenty years?" I blink at her. "Is there any chance the woman would be open to me putting her up at the new Airbnb in town?"

"Maybe, but I don't think she'll like it. She kept saying the windows and light here made it a perfect place to work on her scrapbooking. The new place is pretty dark and woodsy."

"Of course." Maybe Dad was right and I've taken on more than I can chew. I stand. "Where are they now?"

"He's still waiting downstairs. I think she's in her room on the second floor."

Since the lady already checked in, I'll start with the man downstairs.

He's an older guy in flannel with a bit of a belly, wearing a worn fishing cap. He stands in the small lobby with his arms folded over his chest.

"Hi, are you the new manager?"

I give my most charming smile. "At your service."

"Wonderful. Lottie would have never overbooked my room."

His room? He owns it now?

"I'm sorry, sir. My grandmother left some large shoes to fill, but I'll get there one day—"

"Oh." His eyebrows dart up. "So you're the famous grand-daughter?"

"I don't know about famous, but yeah. Lottie Risa was my grandmother."

"She was awful proud of you." He nods briskly.

I get the feeling he wonders if she should have been. "Thanks. Anyway, I'm terribly sorry for the inconvenience. We're still getting set up here for the reopening and things are a bit messy."

"No need to fret, doll. I just need my room, so if you'll get that cleared up, I'll buzz right out of your hair."

I smile. "Any chance you'd be willing to take another room in town at my expense? It's a small duplex rental owned by a friend. I'd still have breakfast sent over and would also comp you two free days in the future."

He frowns. "Can't you offer that to whoever you booked my room to? I've been staying here for years. I don't mean to be a mule. I'm just used to *my* room."

Oof.

I hold in a sigh.

"Let me see what I can come up with."

But the woman on the second floor isn't much more willing to budge than the man who knew my grandmother. Eventually, I'm able to sacrifice my own bedroom in the house to get her out of the room this guy keeps insisting is his personal haven.

Thank God.

I end up staying outside in the cottage that's still undergoing some renovations.

It's drafty, but it's only for a few days.

I'll survive.

Later that afternoon, I'm taking a break in Gram's garden with a steaming latte and a blanket, scanning over a new gossip blog piece about Royal Cromwell.

In the last week or so, the news has been coming fast and furious. He was apparently a very generous man, and his charities funded the largest art education program in Seattle, putting the recipients in a difficult position with the headlines.

CROMWELL'S ROYAL SCANDAL

Not one, but two previous employees have come forward accusing former Cromwell-Narada chief and Seattle art benefactor Royal Cromwell of sexual harassment during his tenure as CEO. Cromwell, who now resides in an assisted living facility due to neurological deterioration, is expected to face examinations soon to determine his fitness for trial.

Awful.

I don't know where the truth begins or ends, but either way, Miles must be reeling.

It's not my problem. But I can't resist scrolling through the blog's fine print and—

Wait.

It's a Pacific-Resolute publication?

Of flipping course it is.

But if it's true, the women have a right to complain and seek justice, and so far there's nothing to indicate it's a setup...

"Ah, there you are. Sorry I gave you such a hard time earlier."

I glance up from my phone to find the old man with the one-room obsession.

"No problem. Did you get settled in?"

"Oh, yes. That view is always one in a million. Like I said, I've been coming here for decades. There were times when we looked forward to this place all year." A whimsical smile crosses his face.

"We?"

He sits on the bench next to me with a rolling sigh.

"My wife and I came to the Pointe every year. Almost since the time we were newlyweds." He chuckles. "I was broke back then, but she married me anyway, bless her. We couldn't even afford a proper honeymoon till her friend got us a weekend package at Bee Harbor. We wound up moving to Boise, but we loved it so much we came back every year to revisit our roots, so to speak. Until she got too sick to travel. I lost her a few years ago."

My heart snags.

"I'm sorry to hear that..."

"Well, I'm just glad the old place is open for business again. Old Lottie's spirit is still here, no question."

At least that explains why Gram would have made sure he got his special room. The man was an early customer and a love-bird too.

I don't notice he's glancing at my screen until he says, "Reading about Royal Cromwell, huh?"

I nod.

"It's a damn shame. Call me out of touch, but I don't believe a word of that junk."

"You don't?"

"Nah. I remember the good old days. Royal used to stay here with his wife, too. We met them more than once. About fifteen years ago, we were all holed up here during a mean storm and a power outage. Royal's room was the only one with a wood-burning fireplace. There was a family here with a sick little girl and the place was booked up. He and Colleen gave up their room to keep the kid warm. They spent the night crashing together in the lobby on the sofa. Lottie had that little old couch in those days—the one with the ugly green plaid like pea soup—and his wife liked to stretch out. In the morning when I came down for coffee, I found him on the floor, curled up next to her like a dog." He shakes his head.

A laugh slips out of me, remembering the old cramped plaid couch he's talking about.

"Oh, wow. Yeah, Gram didn't want to give up that old sofa until it was threadbare."

Grandpa must've reupholstered it five times over the years and she just wouldn't let it go.

"Back in my day, folks didn't wait to point fingers when a man's in no condition to defend himself. Not that it ain't worth looking at with so many bad apples and all, but hell. If Royal was that sort of man, he fooled everybody with the way he always loved Colleen."

Painful.

Giving up his room for a sick child is consistent with everything else I've read about him, too.

At least until this article, but too many older men who looked like saints to the world had the souls of absolute devils.

He could've gone through life with two faces.

The nicest guy in the world and the brute.

There's no reason why both can't be true.

Miles showed another face I'll never forget. But why do I still care?

"It's odd. I just hope the truth comes out eventually for everybody's sake," I say neutrally.

"I'm thinking it's about the son, one way or another, but what do I know? The kid was always just as generous as his folks."

"You know Miles?" I ask. It's weird hearing him referred to as a 'kid.'

"A little. We met a couple times, mostly when he was younger and he'd tag along. I've always donated to Cromwell charities, and I know he took them over when his old man passed the torch. If these women had a problem, I'm sure the kid would've done the right thing in a heartbeat."

Maybe.

Probably.

But what if they just didn't feel safe coming forward until they knew he couldn't retaliate or shut them down before it ever got to a judge?

Then again, I can't picture Gram hanging out with a man who harassed women. I shake my head.

"I know the feeling. These cases are damn frustrating," the old man says. "Bet his boy is all knotted up over it. They were always so close."

"I should check on him," I say absently.

But as soon as the words are out, I remember why I shouldn't.

He doesn't want my help with this.

He made that crystal clear when he told me to *stay out.*

And if he had any change of heart, I think I would've heard from him by now.

The old man smiles. "That would be nice. Well, I should finish my walk."

He stands, stretches, and walks off, leaving me alone with the wind kicking up.

I stay there a little while longer with the dinging wind chime until my cheeks are numb, trapped in bittersweet thoughts and picturing a future that's dull, grey, and glacial.

* * *

WHATEVER ELSE ANYONE can say about him, Royal Cromwell brings out strong reactions.

Miles is convinced Simone wants to hurt his father to hurt him.

Some random old man who was a Bee Harbor regular is outraged on Royal's behalf.

Meanwhile, two hurt women who worked under him years ago swear he coerced them into the kind of gross, horrible affairs you hear about every month now with politicians, businessmen, and Hollywood big shots.

My brain is Swiss cheese.

Nothing about any of this makes freaking sense.

But every time I get confused, I just hear the old man saying, *Bet his boy is all knotted up.*

Miles is a heartless jackass and a human hand grenade, but he doesn't deserve to go through this alone.

No one does.

That's not why I'm here, though.

I'm too curious.

Finding out the Cromwells had a history with Gram long before Miles had his fancy house built next door is a total shock.

So I walk into Gram's old home office, where she keeps the old records that overflowed from the inn. I'm not sure what I'm looking for as I start sleuthing.

But there are boxes.

So many boxes.

It takes over two hours to dig through a stack just to get a handle on how the records are arranged. She kept everything on paper right up until the end.

"Jeez, Gram! You really wanted to make sure whoever inherited the inn earned their keep," I say out loud.

Finally, I find a box marked 2005-2015 and pop the lid off.

Seems like a good place to start.

There's a file folder for each month of the year. At least she was organized, but since I'm not sure what I'm looking for, it might not matter.

My directionless treasure hunt burns up the evening.

It's past midnight and my third cup of coffee when I take the dogs out. I still haven't found anything useful.

Royal Cromwell and Colleen Narada-Cromwell did stay here a few times every year for weeks at a time, but there isn't much more in the file than old credit card receipts and reservation details.

If I had any fantasies I'd find something useful, they're snuffed out fast.

Whatever.

It was a long shot anyhow, but as a bonus, I'm learning a lot about the inn's operations going back years. Gram even collected email addresses on old paper cards.

I laugh at that. The inn would be doing a lot better if she'd done something with all the email addresses she collected.

Better late than never, I guess.

I start logging them on a spreadsheet as I go, building a makeshift email list.

I'm up to 2013 in an hour, cruising from one month's manila folder to the next.

March must be the cursed month.

Every March folder has a pile of receipts for high-ticket repairs.

When I get to June, I find Royal and Colleen Cromwell were at the inn most of the month. It's just another set of dates at first, and his name comes up multiple times through these folders.

Why does it matter?

I tap the side of my head like I'm hoping it'll shake something loose. It seems important.

Sighing, I grab my phone and pull up another article I read earlier today.

Halfway down the page, it's there.

"It's hard to talk about this even now. Royal wasn't an open tyrant, just a lonely old man who worked too much and went about solving his problems the wrong way. His advances started a few months after I went to work for him and lasted until the last time I saw him," Ava Wickes stated.

When I asked her to tell me about the last time she saw Royal Cromwell she said, "It's obviously been a while. He's been gone for years—the last time was back in mid-June of 2013, I think," she said. "I remember because I'd just left my niece's pool party. He was already making noise about stepping down as CEO. I needed a reference for a new job. I knew the only way I was ever going to be able to put this mess behind me was going to be a fresh start. I owed it to my family and myself, so I lined up a new opportunity. But I needed a reference letter from him. He called me over to his mansion on Bainbridge Island so I could pick it up in person. His wife was gone for some conservation thing in Canada, and well, you can guess what he wanted."

I wrinkle my nose.

If that's true, it couldn't be more disgusting.

Still, I flip back to the file and—*wait.*

Gram's records show he checked in on June 7th, 2013 and checked out on June 30th. Roughly a three-week stay *with* Colleen.

There are even daily receipts where they paid for incidentals like a sunset cruise Gram partnered with in town, plus laundry service. The receipts are all in order and stapled to the final bill, clear as day.

I flip through them three times.

"Holy crap," I whisper, my hand fluttering to my mouth.

Royal Cromwell wasn't in Seattle anytime in mid-June that year.

He was here.

But maybe Wickes just mixed up the dates?

Then again, maybe she didn't, and there's something terribly wrong with everything.

I pick up my phone and open my camera app, switching to its document scan function. These receipts are old and a little faded, but the scanner produces clearer images than a photo.

I capture all the Cromwells' requests and transactions across their stay that month.

Receipts don't lie.

There is no way he was in Seattle on the days in question. It's just not possible.

Ava Wickes' story doesn't add up, which means—

I swallow a rock of pure tension in my throat, wiping my brow.

Asshat or not, I have to tell him what I've found.

So I open a fresh email and pull up a contact I'm glad I didn't delete.

MILES,

Ava Wickes is either seriously off about the dates she claimed your father met her for the last time, or she's outright lying.

Royal Cromwell wasn't in Seattle any time after the first week of June, 2013. He was here at Bee Harbor with your mother. I have receipts to prove it.

I ATTACH the receipts and stare at the email, willing myself to hit Send.

But if I do, what am I inviting?

It doesn't take back the scorched earth way we left things.

It could also make me a party to a mountain of legal action.

Worst of all, Miles still doesn't trust me with his problems. I'm never going to be important enough to matter to him.

Ugh.

I want to send it, but I don't.

What the hell is wrong with me?

Why am I even playing detective for a man I can't stand?

The last time I tried to help, we saw where that ended.

My head drops lightly against Gram's old desk and I keep it there, fighting back a blinding headache.

I may loathe that man with a vengeance, but I miss him.

I miss him with every last frayed irrational fiber of my being.

A tear like napalm slides down my cheek.

Yeah.

I've got to get out of here before someone wanders in and sees me crying.

So I pack up and flee to the cottage, fling myself on the bed, and burst into tears. The dogs hop up and burrow in next to me like my bodyguards.

He never loved me, and I was a fool for thinking he ever would.

Walking away was the right decision for both of us.

I know it, but I'm just not ready to let go, and this hint of proof shows it.

I cry until my head hurts and my nose is gross. I pop two pain pills, bury my head under my pillows, and try to force my mind to blank out enough so sleep finds me.

Even if I hate Miles Cromwell, if it's Simone behind this and Royal Cromwell is innocent, none of them deserve this.

I can't hang on to what I've found forever.

But whether I send it or not, it still feels circumstantial. If I'm going to step in, I need more.

Come morning, I'll figure it out.

But morning is a long way off.

I spend the night tossing and turning through fever dreams where a man with the most mesmerizing silver-blue eyes wipes the bruises off my soul, one smoldering kiss at a time.

And those eyes are so pleading, even as he's silent, swirling with the same question over and over.

Can you ever forgive me, kitten?

Sometime near sunrise, I wake up with Cream licking her paw and catching the edge of my ear with her tongue. Plus, the terrible knowledge that this is the closest I'll ever get to Miles Cromwell taking away my pain, begging for forgiveness.

Only in my dreams.

XXIV: NO WATERWORKS (MILES)

I've officially hit a fucking wall headfirst.

Dead end.

Nothing indicates my father ever had an inappropriate relationship with either woman, but nothing disproves it either.

With Pacific-Resolute's stories out in the world now, the gossip mill is spinning like a jet engine.

Hell, the whole company has turned into a rumor mill.

Morale couldn't be more abysmal, and I'm too damned distracted at the center of this mess to do anything about it.

Forget it.

Live in the moment.

Focus.

I've been struggling with this painting for two goddamned weeks, every time I find a second to step away from the fray and try to re-center myself in my art.

There's an outline of an older home in the background.

I know the color scheme is red, blue, and yellow, but I can't decide where to start filling in the colors.

The foreground is an intricate summer garden. With each brushstroke, it's becoming increasingly obvious someone is lying in that garden, small and supple.

People aren't my thing.

And yet I'm painting them a lot lately—one person in particular.

My phone pings and I throw my brush down on the palette, spattering paint.

It's a news notification from Pinnacle Pointe. A closeup of Bee Harbor Inn fills the screen, the headline photo of a new travel piece.

Suddenly, I know exactly how to color the building.

Apparently, the inn is picking up some buzz.

After a successful soft opening, they've announced a larger reopening just before winter. The locals are excited for fresh blood, especially in a slow season.

If I weren't a raging dick, I'd be there in person.

I'd congratulate Jenn on turning the place around, proving her abilities beyond her wildest dreams.

But I won't be there.

Not after the way I ran her out of my life.

I'm here with this crushing darkness that has no answers, and it's what I deserve.

I set the phone down and pick up the brush again.

Coloring the building only gets me so far, and soon I'm slipping past the neat lines of walls and sky, my focus tripping over my frustrations.

"Goddamn," I mutter.

It's not what I want to be painting.

Stabbing the brush back through the water, I dip it in a white oval on the palette.

The woman lying in the garden wears a fluffy white dress. I add some blue, layering tiny dots over the fluffy dress. They're tiny diamonds, I decide, immaculately sewn into the dress.

They'll make her sparkle beautifully when she stands, though she'd do that anyway.

I know what I'm doing.

My next strokes add rust brown—*auburn*—around her head like a halo of hair.

Fuck, so much for losing my woes on the canvas.

Why did I ever push her away?

Her words from that day come back to me like a drill to my skull.

"You'll never speak to me again."

The memory alone leaves my heart roadkill.

I'm about to push the canvas on the floor when the door to my office swings open and Benson walks in. He looks at me intently.

"Put it away."

I look up, startled at his gruffness. "What, the painting?"

He folds his arms in front of his chest. "Do you see anything else on your desk?"

"No. I'm just working on—"

"What you're doing is straining yourself. Put it away and focus on the real issue."

"I didn't know you volunteered to be my shrink," I snap, stabbing the brush in the water anyway.

I move the painting to the sideboard, stand, and begin cleaning up the paints and brushes.

"Happy? While you're here, why don't you enlighten me on what you think the 'real issue' is. If you're here, there's no one in Pinnacle Pointe making sure Jenn's okay if Simone strikes."

"No need. She's already hitting you where it hurts, sir," he says confidently.

I turn, gritting my teeth, wishing that weren't the bitter fucking truth.

"The inn is doing well. I'm sure you've seen the news?" he asks.

"I read. That still doesn't explain what you're doing here."

"The dogs are as rambunctious as ever." His knowing smile reminds me how well he reads my mind.

Deep down, Benson knows I care about Jenn and her over-grown monsters, whether or not I ask.

"Glad to hear it, but I didn't ask about those barking noodles. What if—"

"What if, sir? What is it you're worried about Simone doing if she's no longer on your payroll or in your life?"

That's a heavy question. I don't know the answer.

"You're just driving yourself crazy with worry," he says.

"Wrong. The lawyers are doing a fine job of that all on their own. Plus, those visits with Dad..." I don't say more.

I had to fight like hell to be there with my attorney while the first of many court-appointed specialists raked him over the coals.

My old man didn't even realize what he was answering, or why.

Did you know Ava Wickes? Can you explain your past relationship, Mr. Cromwell?

What about Jillian Oakes? Surely, you remember her?

Both times, he turned to look at me with the same rheumy eyes, like he's waiting for me to hand him the right answers.

Both times, he answered yes.

And then he told them about neighbors and friends of my mother's I barely remember, confusing them with his accusers.

"It isn't fair, Benson," I snarl, turning and resting my hand on my desk. "I screamed at Truman today, wondering how long they'll keep at it. I almost wonder if they're on Simone's payroll. Any normal shrink could spend an hour with the man and deem him unfit for a courtroom."

Benson's face pulls tight with sympathy.

I'm not looking for pity, and I don't need an answer.

I just wish this shit was happening to me, and not my father, whatever he did or didn't do.

"The woman is vindictive. Insane. But that's partly why I'm here. I'm not the best person to look after Miss Landers for you," he says.

I stare at him.

"Why not?" He's rarely bucked me over the years when he's paid well to be loyal.

"She won't speak to me, for one. I even tried to let her know I wasn't just reporting back to you. She said she didn't want anything to do with you or anyone associated with you."

"Damn." I can picture Jenn warning him off, her eyes still glinting with the anger and heartbreak I put there.

I really have shit everything up beyond repair.

"Is Paul Bunyan still around?" I try not to sound pissed.

Benson shrugs. "Somewhat. Mostly during the day, working at repairs in places that won't bother the guests. Frankly, I might feel better if he was around more often so she has an extra set of eyes."

Protection? From him?

That makes me snort.

The clown left her alone in the room with me, didn't he?

"If it's security she needs, I'll send someone out."

Benson chuckles. "I'm sure you know that's not what I meant."

I sigh. It's time to be blunt while he's here.

Benson might be the only man I can ask about this without getting a canned answer from someone with esquire behind their name.

"I need to ask you something, and I need the truth."

His brows go up. "I'm honest to a fault, even when I give you crap."

"And I appreciate it, but I'm going to ask you a hard question. Don't sugarcoat anything."

"Understood."

I finish cleaning up and putting my stuff away before I return to my desk chair.

"Do you believe anything Wickes and Oakes are saying? Could it be true? You've been around so long you're practically family. If anyone knew my father's secret affairs—hell, if they were there carting him around to live a double life—it would be you."

Benson hesitates.

For a second, my heart sticks in my throat.

"I don't, sir. I haven't believed any of this since the second it started, but of course, this kind of allegation has to be fully investigated. I'm sorry." He catches himself, drawing a deep breath as his face reddens. "Frankly, it makes me angry, Miles. I'd bet my last ten years salary that Royal never cheated on Colleen. Not once. The man had ample opportunity when he was younger—women threw themselves at him at every party, every lounge, every hotel. He never *once* took them into the back of my car."

Damn.

He's definitely upset when he's slipped out of his usual cheerful formality and he's throwing around first names.

"Forgive me. No point in catalyzing your stress by going off like this."

"No, Benson. Vent. You're the only one who comes close to understanding it. It's so damn hard to prove a negative."

"I know, but if you don't, everyone will start assuming it's true. When I said it had to be fully investigated, I don't mean just for the accusers' sakes. That's part of it. I have a grown daughter myself, and I'd go to prison if any big shot ever lured her into his bedroom. Women need to be believed when they come forward. But being public like this, it's so damaging to Royal, too. If he's as innocent as we think. Without a full investigation, if this goes on for years, you'll never clear his legacy."

"I know." I fall back in my chair.

I reach into my bottom desk drawer and pull out a bottle of bourbon with two glasses.

Before he takes his first sip, I look at him seriously.

"You swear on your life you never saw Dad do anything?"

"In all my years of service, if he ever had a secret affair, a liaison, I never knew. You have my word. Even when you kept him at home for a couple years with those nurses, before he was too far gone... he'd wake up crying for her. Then he'd call me up and demand I take him straight to Pinnacle Pointe." He swallows his bourbon and sets the glass down sharply. "Royal always forgot where we were going, or why, until we made it into town. Then he always remembered. And I had to practically drag him away from her graveside with his nurse, still clutching flowers because he couldn't hug your mother. Sometimes multiple times in one day."

My throat burns like there's some small, angry animal trying to erupt from inside me, clawing its way out.

"I worried about him. Even with that fog over his brain, he was almost obsessed whenever he remembered what happened to her. I never had the heart to stop him or talk him out of his trips. Who was I to decide when grief turned into obsession?"

Fuck.

I asked for this gut punch, though.

I'm almost winded when I say, "I never knew he visited her so often, Benson. Obviously, I checked in with his nurses and knew when he traveled. Didn't think he spent all that time at the cemetery."

"He liked to go alone—or at least as alone as he could be with us standing by for him."

My eyes pinch shut.

"Fuck." It's barely audible.

"I know. The doctors don't think he had the capacity by then, but I think he didn't want you or anyone else to see him grieving. When your mother was alive, they always had their special moments away from the world. If he ever betrayed that in dark, ugly ways, I never knew about it. It could've only happened when I wasn't around—" He stops talking abruptly.

I get the feeling he's not done.

"What? Did you remember something?"

He shakes his head. "The only thing I remember now is how much pain Royal was in after Colleen. After he understood she was truly *gone*. He loved her with his whole heart right up until he couldn't. I doubt he noticed other women existed while he had his mind. Sometimes in the car, after we left the cemetery, he used to say, 'one of these days, I'll get my ticket.' He meant his ticket to the other side. I'd always say, 'you don't mean that.' And he'd just tell me, 'Miles is a good boy. He'll be okay with you, Benson. I just need to see my wife again.'"

So, this is what it feels like to be torn open by a hungry lion.

Whatever the hell happened, my parents had something special that will always escape me.

Something I could've had with Jenn if I wasn't such a fucking dumpling.

I don't say anything, just refill our glasses.

"Thanks again, Benson." I try to give my words the finality they usually have when I'm dismissing him, but I don't have the energy.

Not after what he told me.

"Are you going to be okay?" he asks as he stands.

"Yeah. I just need to think."

He nods. "I'll be in my suite downstairs if you need anything, sir."

I watch him as he walks to the door but doesn't open it.

"Yes?" I look at him.

"If that kicked puppy look has anything to do with Miss Landers... I doubt it would hurt to call her."

My lips pull tight.

"She's not speaking to me. Not after what I pulled."

"Women usually say that until you offer them a good reason to listen." He winks at me and walks out the door.

Yeah. Benson speaking from experience with his own dead wife just brings back more memories.

My parents were separated by death for years, and Dad never quit loving her. That's a hard pill to swallow.

What would he have given for one more day with Mom?

A memory pops into my head.

Jenn and I in bed with the dogs, the sun spilling in, layering everything in golden light.

She's still asleep and softly snoring.

To anyone else, she's the portrait of pure innocence.

Her whole body is tucked under the fluffy white duvet on my bed and her auburn hair coils like the halo of untamable hair I tried to paint.

I don't deserve her.

I never did.

My father worshipped every step my mom took for the forty-eight years they were together.

Me, I didn't even make it to six months before I pushed the woman I loved into the damned gutter and left her there to rot.

THE NEXT DAY at the office, after dragging myself in late, I sit down to a new email.

The weekly content report from Sarah Valencia and Smokey Dave.

I'm not sure I want to see it, but I open it anyway. It's my job to know how fast we're sinking.

Views are dogshit across all platforms, TikTok being the worst. No surprise.

Without my top consultant steering them to make steady improvements, the whole team seems rudderless, just running off sheer inertia.

The reports tell me everything I already suspected.

Engagement is down.

Subscriptions are down.

Ad dollars, down.

The only thing saving this company from a total meltdown right now is years of leveraged goodwill and recurring clients on ironclad contracts.

If I had to match last year's revenue in new business or die, I'd be digging my grave.

My phone vibrates with a news notification set to my interests.

There's a new mafia film shooting in West Vancouver, and a Pacific-Resolute funded blog about pop culture has the exclusive scoop.

The comments stretch into thousands from eager fans who love their crime flicks.

For the past few weeks, Pacific-Resolute has been dominating every entertainment market from Bellingham to Eureka.

I walk away from my desk and move to the massive window.

I can't handle more reports, more proof of our impending fall staring me in the face.

Gazing down at the tranquil, rainy city below, I'm frozen. A feeling that's becoming way too familiar.

I have to do something.

How did Simone Niehaus get this much control over my life?

Hell, not just my life but my company.

"Is everything okay, Mr. Cromwell?" Louise asks, standing in the doorway.

Her words shake me from my thoughts. I didn't even hear her come in.

"No, it's not."

"What's wrong?"

"You really want to know? I'm a drunk goddamned sloth who's forgotten how to get up off his ass," I snarl.

"Mr. Cromwell...even people who think that still choose to work here. You're being too hard on yourself."

"I'm not being hard enough, Louise. Truman hired three investigators weeks ago, and so far, nothing. I want you to reach out to them again, and have them send reports directly to me. Hell, find me a list of new PIs. The guys we have aren't cutting it."

She nods slowly. "I'll get on it right away." But she doesn't move to leave.

"Is there something else?" I bark.

"Well, I'm not part of Legal, but aren't there risks to breaking the usual procedures? I thought you said the investigators were reporting to Truman for a reason."

"There are risks to doing nothing, and they're compounding daily."

Her eyes swell with sympathy.

"I sincerely hope this won't be the case, but... what if the investigation goes the wrong way?"

"You mean, what if I wind up proving my father's a monster? Do you think he's guilty?"

"I can't say. I wasn't in this role during Royal's tenure."

"Have you heard anything?"

Her weight shifts lightly.

There's something she's obviously uncomfortable telling me.

"Be blunt with me, Louise."

She meets my gaze. "Your father was from a different generation. It's possible it happened, and the predatory nature of the relationship was only clear in hindsight. That's a story that's played out over and over, so it's entirely possible you set out to prove innocence and find something dark. But once your investigator finds it, there will be no going back for this company."

Theoretically, she's right.

In reality, Benson's story about Dad's visit to the grave tells me there's no way.

Not fucking possible.

It didn't happen, because he'll love my mother until the day he dies.

"I'm skeptical that happens, but on the off chance it does, of course we'll make a formal apology to the victims with a generous cash settlement. I'll hire an outside firm to form a plan to keep that kind of thing from ever happening again. Sexual harassment of any sort will never be tolerated at Cromwell-Narada, I promise you."

She smiles. "I believe you—and I believe in you, Mr. Cromwell. Oh, and I appreciate the fact that you vetoed any layoff projections if things continue like they are. Sorry. I couldn't resist peeking at that report with HR."

I scoff. "Louise, that was never a question. I'll take the hit to my own net worth before I put people out on the street over some shit that happened years ago. Are people that worried about losing their jobs?"

She shrugs. "Metrics are down in every measurable way since the story broke. I know more about what's going on than most. I understood why you weren't fighting the story, but even I questioned it. I think a lot of people saw the silence as an admission of guilt."

"With ad dollars tanked, they're worried a lawsuit will bankrupt the company?"

Louise nods.

I sigh. "No wonder morale is in the toilet."

It's not just that my senior staff think they spent part of their time working for a predator when they didn't. They're all worried about job security.

"Until I've heard from the investigators, I'm not sure what I can ask for besides patience, which is already the official line."

"Just ride it out until you know something," she agrees. "I doubt you're going to lose anyone before then."

Fuck.

"People are talking about quitting?"

"I mean, nothing definite. Some folks are shopping around casually for backups. But let me reach out to those guys for you so there's one less thing to worry about."

I nod my thanks.

Screw this, I should have just hired the PIs myself.

Less than an hour later, Louise returns. "I have two lists of fresh candidates. The short list has the five highest ranked PIs in the state. The longer list contains every active PI in the state. I didn't know how many you'd want to contact or what their availability is like, and I'm assuming you want this done quickly. I thought more options would be helpful."

I take both lists and thank her.

Once she's gone, I turn to face the soaring glass window again that shows me the city, fading behind the fall rain like a dream that never existed.

Behind it, the Puget Sound is even more obscured in the fog.

The dismal weather doesn't stop my eyes from wandering where they can't see.

I miss Jenn.

I miss Bee Harbor.

I miss every slobbering happy lick from those dumb dogs.

No matter how this ends, I'll miss what I demolished as it becomes as distant and unreachable as the sun in the weeping cityscape outside.

I'll always mourn our stillborn future, and even if she forgives me one day, I can't imagine ever giving myself the same reprieve.

XXV: NO EASY LOVE (JENN)

"More coffee?" the waitress asks.

"Yes, please," I say.

"Please, please!" Pippa chimes in, flicking her hair over her ear.

She fills our cups and walks away.

"I still can't believe you loaned me Fyodor and Ekaterina. Thank you so much. This is the first time I've been out of the house in a week besides walking the dogs ever since we started renting rooms. I would've been toast with Maria out at a debate tournament this weekend."

I smile, sincerely grateful my bestie loaned out her hubby's valet and his wife. They're this cute Russian couple and they both work like mad.

"No big!" Pippa sips her coffee and waves a hand. "Honestly, they've been bored since Brock's life got a little less exciting in the danger department. His lovely wife jumped at the idea when I said the words 'cozy little inn on a secret island.' Plus, if that crazy lady sends anyone after you, now you've got a Russian badass who can snip a man in half with one steely-eyed look."

She grins.

I laugh. "He's quite the charmer if you give him a chance. I'm pretty sure my old scrapbooking lady wanted to flirt if his wife wasn't there. Anyhow, you're a lifesaver, again. Coffee's on me."

She holds up her paper cup in salute and I push mine against it.

"So, any word from Captain McHeartsmashy since he showed his true craptacular colors?"

I shake my head.

"Dick. You're better off, I think. Any guy who goes nuclear doesn't deserve you. I told Brock the dirt about Cromwell would be a perfect excuse to take ad dollars elsewhere, too, but he's a big professional party pooper." She purses her lips in a pout.

"Miles is—" I stop. For some unholy reason, I want to defend him, but I shouldn't. "He's in a confusing place. Not that I'd forgive him easily after the crap he said, but I get why he might not be rushing in to apologize with everything else going on."

"No excuses for bad behavior, lady."

"Yeah, well, there was more going on that day than just meeting with someone he can't stand. And now that I see how she's trying to sink him, a part of me gets why he went off."

Pippa takes a slow, thoughtful sip of coffee before she says, "It's not your problem anymore. He made sure of that. And you can't just dismiss the claims if you don't really know whether or not the psycho ex-girlfriend really put them up to it."

"No, but I have my doubts. Especially about Ava Wickes."

"Wickes?" She squints at me. "Oh, right. The lady who said daddy dearest couldn't keep it in his pants. You think she's lying?"

"Depends. She says the advances went on even after he retired. Right up until the last day she saw him..."

"Just because he stepped aside for his son doesn't mean he lost all his power. Look how powerful Brock's grandparents are despite pretending to retire."

I shake my head. "Pippa, the article says the last time she said she saw him was June, 2013 at his Seattle mansion. It can't be true. Royal Cromwell and his wife were on Bee Harbor's guest roster for most of the month. I found the receipts."

"Oh. Oh, shit," she whispers, stopping mid-sip.

"Yeah." I pick up my phone and punch Ava's name into search to pull up the article just so she can see the June comments. But something else appears under recent results. "Oh, that's interesting."

"What?" Pippa asks.

"I Googled her name, thinking the articles about her allegations would come up, but here's something else..." I don't say more while I'm skimming a short piece about her daughter.

"Jenn?"

"Looks like a local news outlet did a feature story on her daughter, but they got a few comments from Ava, too."

"Why would they do a story on her daughter?"

"She has a 4.0 and near perfect SAT score. About six months ago, some organization—Rising Stars—offered her a full scholarship to the college of her choice. She's also a pretty popular teen TikTok influencer."

"Rising Stars, you said?" She stops and picks up her phone. "Huh. Must be new."

"Why do you say that?"

"Ugh, I memorized like every major Seattle scholarship by name while I was helping Maisy apply. Even Dad was pulling his hair out. She got a couple smaller ones, and a generous donation from the Bank of Pippa and Brock covered the rest. Anything for my little sis, right?" She smiles. "But I've never heard of Rising Stars."

She types on her phone for a minute and glances at the screen.

"Honestly, Miles should have put this kid on his creative team before all this shit went down. She has more followers than your travel channels."

"The younger they are, the faster they blow up these days," she says. "Hey, did you see Rising Stars was founded by

Simone Niehaus? I'll give you one guess who the corporate backer is."

"Pacific-Resolute. Jesus." A chill sweeps down my spine.

There's something eerie about this.

Either Ava is flat-out lying or she got her dates horribly mixed up for the last time she saw Royal Cromwell. Meanwhile, her daughter was just tapped for a free ride from a nonprofit controlled by Miles' mortal enemy.

There's more going on here, but what? How?

"What's the kid's name?"

"Huh?" I'm so gobsmacked I'm only half paying attention.

"Wickes' daughter?"

"Michelle."

"Michelle Wickes?"

"Yeah. What are you doing?" I ask.

"Scanning her social media. There's more coincidence here than a bad Christmas movie," Pippa says.

I sip my coffee in agreement. "But I thought Miles Cromwell wasn't my problem?"

She throws me a sour look.

"He's not. But everybody loves a good mystery and you're already in this one too deep."

I laugh. "Piper, you're bad."

She's silent while she taps furiously at the screen, then looks up with her mouth pulled into an O.

"Look at this. Michelle Wickes and her mom are on a weekend getaway to the Olympic Peninsula. Only an hour and a half from here."

My stomach flips over.

Oh, no.

Is she thinking what I think she is?

"Hold up. You went from 'we can't dismiss anything' to proposing we stake out complete strangers?"

"I mean, *you* said it and not me. But there's enough smoke hinting at a huge flipping fire here." She smiles while I fold my arms. "Aw, c'mon. You know the inn's in good hands, and do you really have anything better to do today?"

"Dogs to walk."

"Bring them with! Or Fyo will run them out a few times. Pretty sure he's already best friends with Coffee. Andouille's gonna be so jealous when we get home."

I crack up, hoping I see the day when I introduce Coffee and Cream to the Winthropes' overgrown sausage dog.

"Seriously, though, don't think you're doing this just for Miles," she says. "If Royal doesn't have any actual skeletons in his closet, you're helping clear an innocent man. If nothing else, you're satisfying your own curiosity—okay, fine, *our* curiosity. Also, if we get arrested, my husband will bail us out."

I roll my eyes. "So, we're reliving our dumb teen years."

"Works for me!" She laughs, but then she sobers up. "For the record, I think once this issue with his father clears up, you'll have a chance to talk it out with the rich idiot—if you want to."

"I don't."

That's a heaping lie.

Seeing Miles again is all I think about.

If he won't come to his senses, a little closure would be nice.

That doesn't make this healthy, though.

"If we do it, we need to be extremely careful, Pippa. We'll do it for everyone else who works there. Cromwell-Narada has been on a steady decline since the stories broke, and I don't want the junior marketers I helped losing their jobs over this."

I shudder, thinking that Smokey Dave might never leave his house again if he has too much downtime.

"Can I ask you something, Jenn? If you're so over Miles, why keep up with his company at all?"

I sigh.

She's known me too long to buy any little white lies.

She also knew how intense my feelings for the jerky grumpwad were before I did.

"I'll never be completely over him. If I can help with this, I have to. I don't want this company failing. He'll only blame himself. I know, I know it doesn't matter. It's not like he's even called me since it happened."

She reaches across the table and squeezes my hand.

"It gets better. Keep the vigil going. Brock and I went through pure hell for a while, too. Relationships are just hard, but if love was a cakewalk, it wouldn't be worth it."

* * *

"CAN we get a drink before we do this?" I ask.

"I've never said no to liquid courage," Pippa says with a smirk.

We haven't checked into our room at the little lodge just outside the Hoh Rainforest yet, but we walk past the front desk, down a long hallway of transitional style worn wood and green hues leading to the main bar.

I'm about to enter, but Pippa grabs my arm. "Wait."

"What's up?"

She holds up her phone and looks at a woman sitting alone at the corner of the bar. "That's her."

Yep.

Definitely her.

She's still wearing the same outfit, this white sweater with black stripes crisscrossing it.

"Game time," Pippa whispers eagerly.

"Whoa. I'm not sure I'm ready for this. What about the liquid courage?"

"Jenn, you can't miss the chance," she hisses eagerly.

Unfortunately, she's right.

My legs feel like cement as we move toward the classy bar and Ava Wickes comes fully into view.

She's slouched over, staring at her drink, a black espresso martini that looks like it's strong and probably not her first of the day. Her forehead creases as she rubs her face, deep lines carved by emotion rather than age.

She rubs her eyes like she's trying to banish away a weariness down to her bones.

"She looks stressed for a lady on vacation," I whisper. "Pippa, I don't know. Maybe we shouldn't bother her."

"We so *should*. Get ready," Piper whispers back.

I hold in a sigh as we sit down beside her, leaving just one seat empty between us.

We order a couple glasses of wine and pretend to talk about our dogs.

Pippa keeps nodding too sharply, jerking her head at the woman behind me, while I sputter through sips of wine and shrug every time.

So much for liquid courage.

But Pippa doesn't let me flounder for long.

While she's still laughing about Cream bringing me raw oysters from the beach last week, she turns her stool, looks over, and gasps slightly.

"Oh. Oh, hey! Don't you know Michelle Wickes?"

Ava looks up slowly and blinks like she needs a few seconds to center herself. "Yes. She's my oldest daughter. How do you know her?"

"We follow her TikTok," I say from over Pippa's shoulder. "Huge fans. Really."

"I knew it! You were in her Insta stories this morning making coffee, weren't you? Nice pumpkin latte!" Pippa gushes.

Ava pulls on a smile that doesn't look totally forced. "That's my little girl. Always posting stuff I tell her not to share with me. I'm too old to entertain the world, but you know how kids are today."

"For sure. My kid sister's the same way," Pippa says.

I smile at Ava warmly. It's easy to latch on to the one thing we might have in common.

I just wonder what her bright-eyed daughter will think if it turns out her mother's a liar who's being bribed to spread rumors about an elderly man who's mentally incapacitated.

"I can't complain," Ava continues, lifting her martini. "Michelle's social media is basically the reason we're here. The resort comped us a tourist package for her to come out and do some videos. The fall nature walks in the forest are always a huge draw."

"Nice!" Pippa holds up her wineglass in celebration. "I do some travel vlogging myself. Before I started focusing on the hidden gems—the comfy little places anyone can visit—I used to do promotions for luxury travel lines."

Ava nods respectfully, but her eyes are so tired.

"Does Michelle get to bring you out to cute little towns like these very often?" I ask.

Ava nods. "Sometimes, but only when it doesn't interfere with school. I've always said keeping her grades up comes first. She's also on her school's triathlon team, and that takes a lot of time."

"Oh, yeah. I just love small towns," I continue, trying not to babble. "After living in Seattle, I'm ready to settle down in a quiet little town like this. My last stint at Cromwell-Narada almost *killed* me."

As soon as I say the name, Ava turns away, downing her martini faster. Or else she's looking for an excuse to ignore us as she shrinks back on the barstool.

Ouch.

Not the reaction I hoped for.

"But I can't knock the benefits or the pay," I venture. "I inherited this property out in Pinnacle Pointe recently, actually. I'm trying to run a bed and breakfast, but without the pay and benefits I got at Cromwell, I don't think I'd have a fighting chance." I wait until she's looking at me, pretending to listen with a wary smile before I continue. "I even had to work with the CEO for a while. Miles Cromwell. Ever heard of him?"

Her lips thin and she shakes her head firmly.

"That was the biggest pain. He's smart and generous, but damn, he's—he's just a bit much. Demanding doesn't begin to describe it."

Ava stiffens and stares straight ahead, behind the bar at the liquor gleaming in tall bottles. Then she turns to face us.

"Are you another reporter?"

"No. Absolutely not," I rush out. "But I do want to know something."

Here we go.

The moment of truth.

I can feel Pippa trying to beam encouragement into my brain while Ava looks at me like a statue.

"How did Michelle wind up with a huge scholarship by Cromwell's main rival months before the story about Royal Cromwell broke?"

And why, in all this time, did you never mention it? I don't ask that, though. I'm being nosy enough and I don't want her shutting down completely.

"Ah, there's your punchline," she throws back bitterly. "You really want to know how my daughter got it? She's a freaking genius, that's why. And Pacific-Resolute cares about recruiting talent. They started Rising Stars to help talented youth reach their full potential. A shame Cromwell never thought of that— they never thought of *anything.*"

Before I can counter, or even defuse the tension, she slides off the barstool and storms away, muttering a few words to a waitress she passes about charging her tab to her room.

"Crap. I came on too strong," I say.

"Interesting reaction, though. She didn't say anything about the allegations," Pippa points out.

That's true. But she could've just been flustered or angry.

"She just said her daughter deserved the scholarship."

"Well, yeah. She's a mom, Jenn. But it's a little weird that she didn't launch into a defense or blow up on you for cornering her like this. She just left."

Weird? Maybe.

Smoking gun? No.

"And I blew it. We're never going to get more out of her now," I say glumly.

"Give it time," Pippa urges, waving the bartender over to order another round of wine for us. "Now, we just cool our heels and wait."

"Wait for what?" I wonder, shaking my head.

"For the guilt train. It's pretty slow, but the bigger the lie, the harder it hits eventually. Give her time and space. I'm sure we'll find out what Ava Wickes really is soon."

I wish like mad I shared her confidence.

* * *

LATER, the guilt hits, but it's not for Ava Wickes.

Hot water sprays down my neck as I try to wash the stink of what I did off me.

There's no way we're getting more out of her now, and her daughter is an influencer. I'm probably going to go viral at some point for hounding a victim, which will only make Cromwell-Narada look worse.

I wonder if Miles is going to hate me more than he already does.

But I shouldn't care about that.

I shouldn't care about what he thinks, and he shouldn't be all I ever think about when everything reminds me of him.

He's a bittersweet drug I'd give anything to kiss again, right after I whack him across the face.

But the healthiest decision is to leave that man the hell alone, including his problems.

It helps that he has no desire to talk to me either, or else he's too busy.

How did he wreck my life so fast?

I didn't even know Miles Cromwell a few months ago.

The trouble is, time changes everything, and time loves to play kickball with your heart.

I'm just rinsing shampoo away when there's a knock at the door.

"Jenn! Can you hear me in there?" Pippa screams through the door.

What now?

"Jenn!" she calls again.

I turn the water off and wring out my hair. "What's wrong? I'm almost done."

"Someone wants to talk to you," she says.

What?

The urgency in her voice makes me throw my clothes on, pull my wet hair into a ponytail, and walk out the door. But there's nobody in our room.

Pippa slips in from the open door to the balcony, waving me over. "Come on! We're out here."

Whoever I expected to find, it's definitely not Ava Wickes.

She has her back turned, but even before I see her face, I can tell she's in tears, red faced and gripping the railing for support.

"Ava?" I start softly. "What's wrong—"

"I *knew* people wouldn't buy it. I just knew it and I tried to tell her. I told her he'd worked with so many women over the years and never had a complaint. Not once. The man was a Boy Scout, and the way he always was with his wife..."

She trails off, her shoulders shaking. I stand there in companionable silence, letting her breathe, my own breath stalled in my lungs.

"God! What was I thinking?" Her hair whips her shoulders. "Someone had to call our bluff, and honestly, I'm glad it was you. But she was so insistent." Her voice cracks again.

It rips through me every time she says *she.*

I don't need to ask.

"Ava, are you okay?" I ask. "If you need to come in and sit..."

She wipes her face angrily with her hands.

"N-no. No, you shouldn't worry about me. I'm a horrible person. I should've grown a spine and told her hell no from the very start." Her face screws up as she struggles for composure. "I lied to the whole world, pretending Royal wouldn't promote me unless I slept with him. Jesus."

I don't know what to say.

If I wanted some big confession, here it is. But somehow, this doesn't feel like a win.

It's just heartbreaking.

She shakes her head again, wiping her eyes.

"Her... her name is Simone Niehaus, but I'm guessing you know that. She founded Rising Stars. She went to see Michelle at school personally one day and talked up the scholarship like it was a sure thing. Like Michelle was the only one it was meant for. It seemed too good to be true and—and it was."

"That's so underhanded," I whisper. "You didn't know."

"But I did. Nobody shows up granting magic wishes without asking for their pound of flesh. Oh, but she didn't ask me to make the allegations until later, when I was counting on the money. When I refused, she said she'd pull Michelle's scholarship if I didn't. She... she said she'd have Michelle blocked from every university she ever applied for."

She's crying so hard now she can't speak.

I pull her in for a hug.

I don't know her, but I do.

She's one more human being lured into a terrible thing, and the rights and wrongs can wait until she has a hug.

"You did what you had to for your daughter, Ava."

"Y-yeah. Michelle wants to be a doctor. She got into NYU, and I can't send her on my income. But it's not just that. My husband is sick. Bone cancer, three times, and we're always waiting for it to come back. If Simone could blacklist Michelle from college, I knew she could put the screws in me, too. She could cost me my career with her connections, and I have to be able to work." She sniffs at the air. "I'm sure she threatened that other poor woman, too. Jillian. Because when I insisted no one would believe the line of crap she gave me to sell, she promised they would. She told me she had another person lined up. I'm so sorry. Earlier, when you came at me in the bar, I panicked. But once I calmed down, I knew I couldn't let it go on like this. I had to come clean. I had to..."

I don't let her finish before I hug her again.

Over Ava's shoulder, I see Pippa, standing with a melancholy smile on her face that says *told ya.*

"Ava, listen. You're not the one who should be apologizing until you're blue in the face. You were under duress. I'm pretty sure what she did falls under criminal blackmail. But if you want to make this right, I'm not the one you should be talking to."

"I... I know," she stammers.

"I'm sure you met Miles?"

"A few times," she says, nodding shakily.

"He loves his father. What Simone did to bring down his company and trash Royal is totally personal. She's toying with him, and I bet he blames himself for it happening."

I draw a slow, deep breath and hold it.

"If you want to make this right, you have to tell him. Let Miles know what happened so he can use his resources. So he can fix this," I urge.

She looks down sheepishly.

"You think he won't hate me? Or try to put *me* in prison?"

For a split second, it's a dark uncertainty.

Miles is the type of man to go on a warpath over his family, torching anyone who'd hurt them. But I think he'll know she was a pawn, attacked and powerless.

However visceral his anger is when he finds out the truth, he'll come to his senses.

Just like you hope he'll find them again with you, I think painfully.

But this can't be about me right now.

"How would I even do that? He called me before and I hung

up on him. That was before the stories, the legal filing, all the dirt flying around... No one at Cromwell-Narada is just going to put me through to the CEO now."

I sigh because she's right.

"Hang on." I dart back into the room to grab my phone and hand it to Ava. "Put your number in my phone."

She holds my gaze.

"I'll send you Miles' cell," I explain. "If he doesn't answer, text me and I'll tell him you need to talk to him."

"Wow, thanks. You were pretty close to him, huh?"

My heart flips over.

"Yeah. You could say that."

Ava bites her lip and stares at the ground. "One problem."

"What?"

"If I do this, will Michelle lose her scholarship?"

I look at Pippa, lost for words.

She just shrugs. "You have to do the right thing, Ava. But I can tell you from experience, these things usually work themselves out. Before I got married, I worked two jobs and took care of my disabled dad and little sister. Michelle is smart and crazy good at networking with people. She'll get into NYU, and you'll find a way to make it work, one way or another. I promise."

"She's worked so hard. If she loses her chance, all thanks to my stupidity, I'll never live it down."

Pippa and I share a sad look.

"Life isn't fair. But if you don't do the right thing, how can you teach your daughter to?" I ask.

"If Michelle loses her scholarship, I'll never forgive myself," Ava says miserably.

"If she loses it, you should never forgive Simone Niehaus. She can't mess with people's lives like this. You can't let her get away with it."

"Sue her. Press charges," Pippa says sharply. "It doesn't matter if you win. The publicity alone will be bad enough to force her out of Pacific-Resolute, and they'll have every reason in the world to compensate you. And if they don't, someone else will."

She stops just short of thumbing her own chest and I smile.

If things fall through for Michelle, I'm pretty sure Brock and Pippa will be right there to help her.

It's nice to be reminded why we're besties sometimes.

Even if I'll owe her a few more drinks later.

Ava rocks back and forth on her heels a few times before moving past us. "Thank you again, but I should go. I have some unpleasant calls to make."

You and me both, lady.

Now, we just have to hope it isn't too late.

XXVI: NO MISSING ANGEL (MILES)

"Y ou're supposed to have a whole damn team working for me, and this is the best you come up with?" I whack the file down on my desk, clenching my phone.

Fucking hell.

I could have come up with more than this trifling tip about a mother-daughter trip to the Hoh Rainforest myself. It doesn't help my father's case.

"We're still working on it, Mr. Cromwell. Where there's smoke, there's fire," Ross the PI says.

"And I wish you'd find the fire before there's nothing left to salvage."

"I'll call you in two days with an update," he promises.

"You'll call tomorrow. You'll also hope there's more meat to the bones than this." I end the call, set my phone down, and look at this pathetic excuse for a report one more time.

Is it odd?

Yes.

There are a lot of bright kids in the world.

What are the chances Simone slithers out of the woodwork

to hand a scholarship to the daughter of one of the women claiming my father was a sex-crazed devil?

Slim.

But is it proof—the undeniable pants-on-fire proof—I need?

Hell no.

I'm still stuck beating my head against the wall for the thousandth time, wondering how I prove a negative.

Also, Wickes is just half the battle. We haven't turned up a damn thing that's suspicious with Jillian Oakes yet, the other woman.

It feels like the more PIs I pile onto my crack sleuthing team, the worse the results get. I'm nearing my wits' fucking end.

My phone rings. I don't recognize the number and Louise is away from screening my calls on her lunch break, but with the way things are going, I can't afford to miss out on anything that might put a dent in this hell.

"Cromwell," I snarl.

"Mr. Cromwell?" It's a woman, and—is she crying?

"This is Miles. How can I help you?"

"Um—I don't really know where to start, especially when this didn't go well last time, but first off..." She pauses and exhales heavily. "I owe you an apology, Miles."

That's not something women usually say to me.

A second later, it registers, battering my brain.

"Mrs. Wickes?"

"It's Ava, yeah, but don't hang up!"

Legal won't like this, but I listen.

Moving the phone away from my face, I slide the audio recorder on and return it to my ear. "What are you apologizing for?"

"I just... I wanted to tell you how very sorry I am for what I said about your father. I—I didn't mean for this to happen. None of it. But she was so persistent—she threatened my daughter if I didn't comply—"

"She? Simone Niehaus, you mean?"

"Yes. She threatened to take everything. She held a scholarship over my head. That's no excuse, I know, and I regret that it's gone this far. I regret it so deeply, you'll never know. I'm sorry. I let her bully me into doing something horrible. It must be so raw for you... So that's why I have to end this. I'm willing to go on record and say Royal Cromwell did nothing wrong. I'll retract my statement immediately."

I feel like I'm floating above the room, completely disembodied.

Is this real life?

I'm so shocked I don't know what to say.

"Miles? Are you still there?" she asks.

I clear my throat. "I'm sorry. I'm just processing. Have you explained this to your daughter?"

I'm not even sure why I ask, it's just the first thing that comes to mind.

"I told her what happened. She agreed I had to do the right thing. Michelle's a sweet girl. She said she'd rather go to community college and transfer than take a dime of dirty money. Really, I didn't expect her to forgive me so fast. I don't expect the same from you."

Damn.

This kid is potentially losing her chance at life, all because Simone will yank her scholarship if her mother stops playing ball and tells the truth?

I can't even be mad at the woman.

There isn't enough anger left over when it's laser-focused on the real shitworm here.

"Doing the right thing won't change anything for your daughter. I'll see to it," I snap.

"What? No. Oh, no, I can't let you do that. You've been through enough, thanks to me, and it wouldn't be right."

"What's not right is someone blackmailing you into lying for survival. I appreciate you calling me today. That took guts." I let her catch her breath before I ask, "Is there any chance you know about Jillian Oakes falling into a similar situation? I'm just trying to get to the truth and sort this mess out, but if you were blackmailed, odds are she was too."

"I contacted her this morning. We both had a good conversation and we want to make it right. The lady at the bar told me it's not my fault, whatever mess I caused. And it's not too late if I just call you."

"What lady from the bar?"

"I think her name was Jenn or Jenna? It all happened so fast, but she said she knows you. She's the one who made me realize how screwed up this is."

My jaw damn near hits my desk.

Jennifer Landers.

My Jenn.

My kitten.

I close my eyes and struggle to breathe.

Fuck me.

Even after everything I've put that woman through, she stepped up and did what the best paid investigators in the state combined couldn't pull off, and she did it *all for me.*

"She was very concerned about you. She said you'd blame yourself if anything happened to your father or the company. I knew she was right, but just telling you the truth still didn't feel like enough. That's why I went to Jillian."

I'm dizzy.

Delirious.

I don't know what part of this is more disorienting anymore.

The fact that Jenn came through for me in my darkest hour, or that my father did nothing wrong and Simone fucking blackmailed people into lying publicly.

My head is spinning, but I refocus on this moment, this conversation.

"What did Miss Oakes say?" I ask hoarsely.

"She's an attorney. From what I gathered, they threatened

her with being disbarred if she didn't cooperate and go along with this scheme."

Shit.

I'm no attorney, but I know that disbarment usually requires wrongdoing and an attorney would damn well know that. "Did she mention what Simone planned?"

"When she first got out of law school, Jillian worked as a public defender. I guess she lost a string of cases, and some of those guys went down for long sentences. She gathered them up and convinced them all to sign a complaint by promising to pay for their appeals. Then she told Jillian if she didn't cooperate, the complaints would all be turned over to the bar association and she would help the men file a class action against her. Jillian didn't feel she'd done anything wrong, but she works for a nonprofit now. She couldn't afford to fight the association and defend herself against a huge suit at the same time."

Goddamn.

That's one complicated scam, even for a woman who might be Satan's right hand.

"But I convinced her. Jillian agreed, we can't let this stand. So, we're ready to do the right thing. Just let me know what your people advise. It's pretty appalling that Simone Niehaus went after a sick man with lies like this—and I'll never get over the fact that I enabled her. Again, I'm sorry."

"You've apologized enough, Mrs. Wickes."

I mean it, too.

There's only one person with zero conscience in this shit show.

"But it's disgusting how she tried to manipulate us. I told Jillian we couldn't be scared. We just have to come forward together," Ava said.

"You're both very brave for stepping up. This whole thing is about getting even, bad blood, and it's damned deplorable she's dragged others into it. I give you my word, this won't hurt your daughter."

"You're a good man, and so is Royal. After everything else... it's a relief to know it. I don't think there's anything else I can tell you for now, but if I can do anything else to help you clear this up, please let me know. This is my fault."

"The buck stops with Simone, but thank you again for being brave." I end the call.

The fog around my brain should be gone now, but it's not.

You never expect a crisis to just end like a raging storm passing by.

Except, it hasn't. Not until I know with absolute certainty that Simone Niehaus will pay for the fuckery she started.

Now, I have the tools to make her.

I don't feel better, though. Not when there's a bigger storm hovering over me, still raining down hell.

This can't truly end until I've made things right with Jenn.

My pain broke that beautiful creature and I watched her stumble away from me wounded.

I didn't try hard enough to stop her.

After all my mistakes, she still went and proved my father's innocence.

Goddamn.

I have to make things right with her more than I need to crucify Simone.

Even if I have no idea where to start.

I just know I'm not losing my angel, my star—if she can ever find it in her to give the bumbling ass who rolled over her heart a second chance.

Louise comes into my office then, her shoulders squared. "I'm just here to remind you about your three o'clock meeting with HeronComm."

"Cancel it," I say immediately.

Her brows go up. "Should I give a reason?"

"I don't care. Mag Heron knows the mess I'm in, and he'll understand. His media buys can wait."

She nods and starts to duck out the door.

"Wait," I call.

"Yes, sir?"

"Any word from Miss Landers recently?"

She stares at me. "Not since the day she crashed your meeting with—well, I won't say her name. It's like inviting more of a curse around here."

I chuckle, and it seems to brighten her face.

"Has anyone else heard from her, Louise?"

"Not that I know of, but if I can be frank... I can tell you, if I went through what happened after she crashed the meeting, we wouldn't talk unless he called me. Preferably in person. So, if you're waiting on a phone call, Mr. Cromwell, you might be waiting a long, long time."

She has a point.

I'll find a way to settle this in person, but first, I have one meeting I need to take.

* * *

"I STILL THINK this is a bad idea, Mr. Cromwell. If you go any farther, you'll be out of sight," Truman says into my Bluetooth headset.

"Understood." I sit down on a park bench and wait.

Every breath I take feels like acid.

"If you're certain you're moving forward, good luck," he tells me. "And remember, nothing provocative."

"I'm pissed, Truman, not crazy. It's time to settle score. I'm in control," I bite off, forcing my face into a mask of cold neutrality.

He doesn't say another word as I wait.

Every second creeps by like my whole world turning to tar, slow and black and choking.

I watch a few pigeons on the ground circling a tree, posturing for scraps. One bird comes across a chunk of bread crust and flaps its wings, puffing up, but his rival is quicker.

The other swoops in, snatches the bread, and takes off, leaving the losing bird seething with shrill squeaks.

Then I hear those heels.

Just a single stiletto *click-clacking* on the pavement at first.

My head snaps up from the pigeons. I get a good, long look at greed personified into a leggy woman who only moves in power strides.

Simone strides up in a black suit and matching designer stiletto heels, a cryptic smile pulling at her face as she tries to stare me down.

My eyes never flinch.

I watch her the whole way over as her feet sink into the wet grass. She looks down and wrinkles her nose before she yanks one muddy spiked shoe out of the ground at a time.

"Did we have to meet here of all places, Miles? It's been raining for days."

"I know."

Her face sours.

"If you didn't have to dress like a vampire bat everywhere you go, it wouldn't be a problem," I say.

She throws her head back with a shrill, grating laugh.

"He still has a sense of humor! I love it." She exhales and looks at me again with frosted eyes. "I suppose that's why you wanted to meet outside in the elements at a giant dog toilet. I'm glad you came to your senses, though." She looks around and waves a hand at the great outdoors. "Even if it *is* a dog park. Your girlfriend would be proud of you, I imagine—she's turned you into a dog person, hasn't she?"

I don't answer.

I'm too busy tasting blood as my teeth pinch my cheek.

The bitch has some nerve to mention Jenn after everything she's done.

"Such a shame it had to come to this. If you'd just called me sooner, you could've avoided a lot of the carnage and time away from her and those lovely doggos." She gives me a smile as demure as a cobra's.

At one time, I might have fallen for it, but now?

I try to understand what I ever found attractive in this woman as I glare at her, my knuckles straining white in my fists.

"No matter, though, it's the destination that's important. You had to be so stubborn, Miles. Don't worry. As soon as our resources are combined, I'll make sure the story vanishes. Wickes and Oakes are quite open to an outside mediator, it'll be like it never happened."

She sits on the bench next to me, this human shadow that doesn't need any sun to make everything darker and more depressing.

"How can I believe you, Simone? You've given me a hundred reasons not to trust you. You've never given one to believe anything you say."

"I've already apologized for taking such drastic steps, didn't I? An apology I think you accept—or else we wouldn't be here."

She pauses, barely biting her lip, her eyes raking over me like she's expecting an answer.

I'm fucking granite, completely unmoving as I fix my eyes on the pigeons battling each other for food again.

"Miles, you know this isn't personal. I took no joy in going there, but it was the only way to get through to you." She pauses and sniffs. "Anyway, we'll both be better off once we're pooling our resources. And I don't expect you to agree right away, but hey—once we're running joint campaigns again, sharing world-class clients, and tearing up the California media market, maybe that merger will be back on the table."

Again, I'm silent, refusing to look at her.

"We've always been better together. I'm just sad it's taken this much time and effort to get you to a place where you realize that."

I'm not expecting her to reach for my hand.

My instinct screams to rip her fucking arm off, but when her hand sweeps over mine, I turn my fist up, grabbing her fingers.

I squeeze until it hurts.

It must be jarring.

Her eyes widen, suddenly unsure, and she swallows loudly.

"Of course, I'll... I'll make sure the stories about your father disappear. You don't have anything to worry about. We certainly can't do business without this schoolyard unpleasantry behind us, right? We're two royals squabbling over the same kingdom. Let's like it, Miles." She hesitates. "...don't you think?"

"Yeah. Let's," I clip, releasing her hand.

I leave her squirming awkwardly before I fish out my phone, pull up the live video I want her to see, and slowly pass it over.

Her eyes bounce from the screen back to me.

"What's this?"

"That's us doing business. Let's watch together."

She raises an eyebrow but stares at the screen.

"Isn't this from the PNW Herald?"

"Correct. We have a partnership with them," I tell her.

I hear her inhale sharply when the camera focuses on Ava Wickes and Jillian Oakes. The women stand in the center of the screen, a microphone in front of them.

They shift their weight nervously, but determination flashes in their eyes.

"I'd like to thank my employer, Pacific Northwest Herald, for allowing us a public platform to set the record straight. We both have something we really need to say regarding the recent accusations against Royal Cromwell," Ava says pointedly, looking at the other woman. "Jillian?"

Simone's cheeks are already turning red as she looks at me. "What the hell are they doing? I didn't know *anything* about this."

"Listen and find out," I urge, hoping Truman's getting all of this over the Bluetooth.

"Ten years ago, I worked for Cromwell-Narada's legal department as a junior attorney," Jillian begins. "My first few years with the public defender's office wasn't coming close to paying off my loans from school. I needed a corporate job with real compensation and Cromwell was the perfect fit. I rose through the ranks quickly in their Legal Affairs department. Eventually, our then-CEO, Royal Cromwell, noticed the long hours I put in and my ability to settle cases quickly and efficiently. When our director left, Royal offered me the position. However, I went into law to make a difference, not money. And in four years with the company, I paid off my student loans and found a way to support my family. I turned down the promotion and asked for a reference letter instead. Now, I'm the legal director of Pacific Conservation Defense Fund. Something I did entirely on my own merits, with a little help from Royal Cromwell that came gratefully and unconditionally. During all of my years in this field, the only person who has ever harassed me—" Jillian says, drawing a deep breath.

"Is Simone Niehaus, chief executive of Pacific-Resolute," both women say together.

"Miss Niehaus threatened my reputation and my livelihood. Her proxies convinced convicts who received life sentences during my time as a public defender that their chances of appeal would be better if they filed a suit against me and complained to the Bar. These men were caught on video committing violent acts. I did what I could, but there was video evidence. Defending a lawsuit backed by top criminal attorneys isn't cheap, even if I were to win, and the only way she promised to back off and drop it is if I made an open claim she gave me in writing against Royal Cromwell," Jillian finishes.

"Preposterous!" Simone screeches. For a second, I think she'll hurl my phone across the dog park. "How did you pull it off? We had them on *lock*."

I hold back a smile as the livestream goes on with Wickes taking the mic.

"Being a parent with a sick husband meant I had to be mom, dad, and sole provider at times. I couldn't move up into management because I would never have time for my child. I've done well enough to keep us going all these years, but only just. Now, my brilliant daughter wants to be a doctor. She was accepted to two fine medical schools and deserves an opportunity to go. I couldn't pay for that and keep up a house and medical bills not covered by insurance, but incredibly, she got a scholarship with Rising Stars."

Simone's face wrenches like she knows what's coming next.

Goddamn, I'm enjoying this.

Ava draws another breath and says, "A scholarship Simone Niehaus threatened to pull if I didn't make terrible, deceitful allegations against Royal Cromwell. I'm just sorry I let her bully me into playing along. I want to be clear—not one of the advances ever happened. Miss Niehaus also told me she'd have me blacklisted from every national news outlet, but she didn't have to go that far. All she had to do was threaten my daughter's dreams. But my Michelle is a better person than me. When she found out the truth, she told me it was okay—she *insisted* I do the right thing—and together, we worked out a backup plan. We knew what had to be done. That's why I'm up here with Jillian. The Cromwells don't deserve your scorn, but maybe I do."

They stand back from the mic then, opening the floor for questions from the gaggle of reporters assembled.

I finally turn to look at Simone. She's so colorless her face looks like a mushroom stretched over bone.

"*How?* How could you do this—this butchery—to me after everything I offered? After I did the heavy lifting to make you richer and better? After what we had, Miles?" Her eyes are black stars about to go nova. "I swear to fucking God, I'll slit your throat in broad daylight, you little idiot."

I snort, holding back a smile.

"For such a tall, bitter, miserable bitch, you're not very scary. You've taken the only two things that ever mattered to me. Letting me bleed out in the park would be a kindness, as long as it's not in front of little Jackie and her poodle over there."

I point a thumb to a girl with her dog off to the side.

"So dramatic!" she hisses. "What have I taken from you?"

"My mother and—fuck, you already know. You robbed my father of the last years he was able to remember her, to love her, the only goddamned thing he ever wanted in life."

I stand and spit at the ground, right next to her feet.

I'm dead set on keeping it together, but every man has limits.

"Disgusting." She rolls her eyes. "Again with the victim act. How was I supposed to know she'd have a heart attack that night? I'm not psychic. We were on the verge of something beautiful, Miles, and I couldn't risk distractions. I did *not* kill your mother."

"No. You stranded her to die," I growl, venom coursing through my veins.

"Oh, please." She pinches her eyes shut, glaring with utter contempt. "And the girl—you did that yourself. You can't possibly blame me. Jesus, she looked at you like you were a king. She would have believed anything you told her. Let me guess, you just couldn't be honest about your feelings, could you?"

My jaw tightens.

"See? Same old Miles. I may have added a little twist of pressure, but you drove her away, Mr. Man," she whispers bitterly.

"Doesn't matter," I snap, hating that it does and abhorring that she's right. "The fact is, you're done. Right here and now. You have no power over me or anyone else, Simone."

She doesn't say anything as she stands, this frozen wraith almost as tall as I am.

Still, the arrogant curl of her lip makes it clear she doesn't believe she's lost.

"Back down. Face the music," I say slowly. "After that conference, it's going to move like lightning. You'll spend your days in meetings with lawyers, trying to avoid criminal charges. You'll certainly be removed from Pacific-Resolute by the board. You can't deny it."

Her face screws up as she shakes her head—fuck, is she actually choking back a sob?—but she stretches her arm out, her hand flying toward my face in a blur.

She must pay her nail tech a fortune to keep her fingers sharpened into those bright claws.

I narrowly miss losing an eye and duck back, lunging for her wrist again just before she slaps me.

"Now, you're being ridiculous. Stop throwing a tantrum before someone gets hurt, Simone. It can't help you."

She throws herself against me, slapping my shoulders hard and reeling back again.

It's like wrestling a damn deer.

Only deer hooves would bruise less than her bony elbow stabbing me in the side until I'm able to pin her arms, tumbling her to the ground.

My eardrums are bleeding as she breaks into a screaming fit.

"Help! Help, help me—assault!" she bellows. "He's hurting me!"

A few distant bystanders in the park are watching now. Thankfully, the closest ones don't intervene. They saw who struck first.

"Simone."

I repeat her name a few times until she stops struggling, sticking to the ground under me.

"Shut up and turn around," I whisper.

I let her up, just enough so she can turn and sit up.

Then she sees Bradley and Louise standing outside my company car across the street from us with their phones out.

"Your people, they're—recording?" Her jaw drops in disbelief.

I grin and nod.

"This time, I came prepared. Unlike the ways you've fucked with me over the years, if you stop now, I'll let you crawl back to the wreckage of your life without slapping you with assault charges. Although, there are two separate witness records of you trying to hit me. I hope once you've stepped down from leadership, apologized to the public, and settled with the women whose lives you tried to ruin, you'll turn over a new leaf. But that's really up to you. It was never nice knowing you."

She stares at me with her mouth hanging open, utterly dumbstruck.

"God, I should have given you a lethal dose that night," she hisses. "This would have been so much easier."

All I do is smile, grateful to know she really did drug my drinks on that trip and I cheated death.

I'm not sure why I even turn around and stare at this pitiful insect long enough to add, "It's never too late to change. Until recently, I always thought that was fluff talk, but I've become a believer."

She blinks a few times and steps away from me.

Fine with me.

The more space between us, the better.

"Miles, who... who the fuck are you?" she whispers.

Her voice is softer than I've ever heard it. More like a scared little girl's than an executive who's used to machine gunning orders and getting her wishes granted on demand.

"A better man than the one you knew." I say over my shoulder.

Then I walk around her to my car without looking back.

In a few more strides, she's behind me, right where she belongs.

Marooned in the past.

"Where are we going, sir?" Benson asks as soon as I'm in the back seat.

"Take me to Jennifer," I say, feeling my gut twist.

If this showdown with Simone was nerve-racking, it's nothing like what's ahead.

There's so much more at stake with my kitten, and so many ways it could all go catastrophically wrong.

XXVII: NO FORGETTING YOU (JENN)

*M*y Facebook and Twitter feeds are blowing up.

Everywhere, there's chatter about Simone Niehaus' fall from grace and removal from leading Pacific-Resolute. The board acted swiftly to send her packing, but that's not what keeps the stunned gossip going.

Ever since Ava and Jillian came forward about her blackmail, other people have piled in, revealing years of abuse at the hands of this heartless snake-woman.

I shake my head, reading a post from someone named Melissa who knew Simone in her college days.

Simone and I interned together at Cedarwell Media in Eugene. I made the mistake of telling her about my idea for a monthly home magazine piggybacking off the work we already did for their main publication.

I put together the pitch. I spent months outlining the content. I didn't know I left my work printed out on my desk at lunch one day.

A few days later, Simone pitched a near-identical concept to the chief editor and CEO, and she was leading the company's biggest publishing success three months later.

. . .

Dirty pool.

If anyone has a date with a mid-ass collision and the karma train, it's definitely Simone.

She's on track to be sued by practically everyone she's ever worked with, and she totally deserves it.

I know it's not my problem. I shouldn't be grinning ear to ear, but I am.

And I hope Miles finds some peace watching her choke down a giant spoonful of justice.

It's a blustery night at Bee Harbor with intense waves crashing against the rocks outside.

There aren't many guests here and tourist season is basically over in Pinnacle Pointe, but I'm staying in the lobby for another half an hour or so just to make sure no one needs anything before I feed the dogs dinner and crash.

I close my social apps and open a few freelance sites.

While I'm waiting, I might as well cold pitch a couple potential marketing clients.

I'm typing a message to the owner of a San Diego based media company when a shadow falls over my laptop.

I put on my best customer service smile and look up.

"Can I help y—Miles?" My breath catches.

My stomach insta-knots.

What does he want?

He's standing on the other side of my desk, all tallness and manly angles and so Miles it hurts. His scent engulfs me, pine and testosterone wedded in an unholy fusion that strokes my brain like a kitten.

I hope he can't see me leaning against the edge of the desk. It's the only thing that keeps me standing.

"Can we talk?" His silver-blue eyes are brighter than ever, twin meteors coming to wreck me again.

Can we? I wonder cynically.

Regardless, I swallow past the rock in my throat.

"Sure. What do you want?"

"I had to thank you for everything, Jenn. You came to my rescue when I damn well didn't deserve it." The regret shadowing his eyes cuts me in half.

"Ava Wickes, you mean?"

Of course.

I should've known she'd mention me at some point, even if I hoped she wouldn't.

He nods, his gaze softening. "She said you found her at some resort and convinced her to call me and spill her guts. You accomplished more than a whole team of investigators I threw together. Hell, if you hadn't found her, this still wouldn't be resolved. My old man would be spending his last days in a state mental hospital. I owe you the universe, woman."

You lunk.

You stupid, sweet, bad-for-me man.

I can't believe you still surprise me.

I shrug, rolling my shoulders so suddenly my bones hurt.

"You don't owe me anything. It was the right thing to do, regardless of whatever happened with—well, everything."

"Jenn, you didn't have to follow her to another town and talk some sense into her. That wasn't just thoughtful. It saved my ass."

Glancing down at the desk, I sigh. "Come on. First off, half of it was Pippa's idea. She was along for the ride. Also, Simone tried to pin made up sexual abuse on your poor father, and after seeing all the bad press and the Twitter tea... It's safe to say your dad wasn't the only one she tried to screw over. If a cartoon villain like her ever came after me, I'd hope to have a hero charging in."

"Then you see why I had to protect you." His eyes search mine as he leans closer. "Not that it excuses anything. After the shit I barked at you, I'd wear a muzzle for the next ten years and it still wouldn't make it right."

I try not to snicker at the mental image that brings.

Stay strong.

Don't get his hopes up that he's winning you over because he's totally not—is he?

"How did you know Wickes was lying, anyway? Even I didn't know what to think."

"I had proof. Your parents were here when Wickes claimed she last saw Royal, and I had the records to back it up. I was, um, trying to work up the courage to send them over. But I also wanted a silver bullet first."

He looks at me silently, his eyes glowing like soft blue stars.

"Gram kept paper records for everything. I didn't plan on chasing Ava down like I did. It just sort of happened, thank God, and Pippa deserves a huge amount of credit for getting me off my butt and—"

I stop mid-sentence when his finger lands softly on my lips.

My eyebrows go up in question.

"Stop. You don't owe me an explanation. You're goddamned amazing enough."

My heart thuds so loudly it's deafening.

He's tall and handsome and too complicated for life, and now he's complimenting me with a love in his eyes I don't know what to do with.

But love doesn't just magically fix everything.

It doesn't explain anything.

And God help me, I know where this goes.

Jenn, stay strong, a voice pleads at the back of my mind.

"Is that all then?" I force out.

His face falls.

"No. Jenn, pushing you away was the biggest mistake of my life. Worse than missing my father's calls that night, and I couldn't control that, no matter how many years I beat myself over it. It isn't my fault my mother died, and it wasn't Simone that pushed you away."

He pauses.

A shaky breath fills my lungs.

"It was me," he whispers, his voice so raw. "No matter what

she pulled, I could always control the way I treated you, and I failed that test miserably. You told me you deserved better. You were right, and you do. I'm sorry as hell it took me this long to realize it, and sorrier I didn't realize what I had. That's why you've got a talking jackass barging into your work and hounding you. I want to believe this mess drilled some sense into my brain. I want to be the man you deserve."

Holy mother of—why is he doing this to me?

Why?

My eyes sting.

I blink a few times, fighting back the tears that are two seconds from spilling over. "Miles, that's really sweet, but... I'm just not sure it changes anything. What do you want?"

"A second chance."

I knew he'd say that.

My eyes flutter shut and I draw a breath.

This is the moment of truth.

We're about to find out if I've feasted on enough self-help TikToks and audiobooks to battle the addiction.

Because the truth is, Miles Cromwell is still my favorite high, and all I want is another fix.

Because none of his heartfelt apologies explain how this ever works with us, and I don't believe it can.

"Jenn? What are you thinking?" he whispers, so close to me now.

He's leaning across the desk, tormenting me with the proximity of his lips.

"Miles, I—I don't want to hurt you."

"But?"

"But I don't think that's a good idea."

I can hear his lungs heaving. I think his soul escapes in that breath.

"Because I hurt you? I'll make it right, Jenn. Whatever it takes. Anything."

His eyes search mine, pleading, but I shake my head.

"It's not just that. I've had some time to think since you were away. It's just... We're very different people. Sometimes, we're good together. Sometimes, we're *too good*, if I'm honest. But I don't know if sometimes is enough, and when it's not, our lives clash and short-circuit and nothing works." I don't dare look at him. I turn my head and pretend to stare at my computer screen. "I'm staying here in Pinnacle Pointe, no matter what happens, and I'll try to make Gram proud. Going back to Seattle pretty much confirmed how off it feels. But I don't think that's the life you want—"

"How? I own the house next door," he says.

"And you're not living there most of the time. You have other interests, a massive company to run, and traveling is almost as easy as snapping your fingers. How could you ever settle for this and... and really make a life here?" I pause. *And make a life with me,* is what I really mean, but I can't bring myself to say it.

We both draw heavy breaths at the same time.

"Deep down, you're a good man. Someday, I'm sure you'll find what you're looking for, but I don't think it's me and my little inn. If we tried to start a life together, I'd only get in your way. Our personalities would clash. You'd always be there to bail me out or try to protect me, but sooner or later, I'd just get hurt again. It doesn't mean I don't care about you. If a fish loves a bird, where do they live?"

"Am I the fish or the bird?" His smile is so sad it breaks me.

I can't help smiling back, feeling my heart turn to dust. "Whatever you want, but my point is, we've had our moment."

"Don't do this, Jenn. I know I fucked up and I'm sorry." He reaches over, clasping my hand, always so small in his palm. His fingers curl around it like a security blanket I can't stand to throw away.

God, I've missed his warmth so much.

And I'm going to miss this man forever.

The tears slide down my cheeks, but I put on a brave face.

"I know it's... it's hard. And I'm sorry, Miles. It's killing me too, but if we get back together and break up again like I'm sure we will, it'll only hurt worse later. Plus, if I hadn't found Ava Wickes by accident and followed her to get a confession, would we still be having this conversation at all?"

He doesn't answer as he releases my hand and falls back a step.

I nod. "That's what I thought. I'm sorry. It's probably best if you go..."

"It's not like that,," he whispers. "The only reason we wouldn't be talking is because I'd still be running around trying to figure out the truth about my dad to save him and save the damn company. The second that was done, I'd be here. Tell me you know that, kitten."

Kitten.

Oh my God, he's shattering me into pieces so small I'll never fit together the same way again.

"I can't live without you," he rasps, all smoldering pain.

Fumbling, I reach for a tissue at the edge of the desk and wipe my eyes. "Y-yes, you can. You were doing it just fine before me."

When I hear him sigh, I think that's it.

I'm expecting him to storm off like he should.

Instead, he reaches over and grabs my hand again.

"What are you doing?"

"Come with me. I need to show you something first, before I know I'm done."

"Miles, you should go." My voice hitches again.

"I'll leave as soon as you see it, if you still want me to."

With a sigh, I don't resist as he leads me out the back door and around to the gardens.

They're different.

A lot of Gram's old pots and worn boxes are suddenly surrounded by shiny new brass-colored urns. Some are empty and some are already occupied with vibrant cold weather perennials.

Even with winter creeping in, it's the first time since I got here that the garden looked truly green and alive.

Almost like it used to under Gram's green thumb.

I open my mouth and try to speak, but he goes first. "Just had them brought over. The empty pots have all the seeds for next year recommended by a master gardener, the same guy who landscapes my place. And that's not everything."

I follow to where he's pointing and gasp.

"What's this?" I see a neat row of new pink bee boxes tied to the tree.

"If you're keeping the name, I thought you might want honey for Bee Harbor next year. I already set up an order with a bee specialist for the spring. They'll be delivered then, unless you cancel. Otherwise, we can plan on making our breakfasts with the best local honey again."

We.

We.

This whole thing is so thoughtful, so beautiful it hurts.

Miles Cromwell, are you trying to torture me?

"It's gorgeous. Really stunning, Miles," I force out. "Everything I'd want with new plants."

"No, ma'am."

Another hot tear rolls down my cheek. He's going to argue with me now?

"Oh?"

"They're not new. They're the same plants your grandmother always had in this garden. The bee boxes aren't the same color, but you like pink, and I wasn't buying them for Lottie."

He put so much thought into this and he wants me to know it.

"I appreciate it. It's a striking gift, but how do I know you've really changed? Plants can't make up for what happened in Seattle."

His eyes narrow. "Would I be here groveling myself into a crater if I hadn't changed?"

"You sent Coffee and Cream gourmet treats once. You're just generous. I know that. The problem is, I need consistency. I need a man who wants a partnership, who can be on the same page, and we're like characters living different stories. You're high fantasy, and me, I'm—well, too silly to tame fire-breathing dragons or find forbidden treasure."

His puzzled look hardens as I shut up.

A crumpled line appears between his eyebrows.

His mouth is twisted, and for a second, I think he might lose his shit like I'm losing mine.

The tears are merciless now, drowning me in a clammy heat that's so intense I'm blind, even through the rain sprinkling from above.

This is harder than it should be.

I only get through it by remembering the way he gutted me in Seattle.

"We're neighbors, Miles, and it's probably best we're neighbors from a distance. We share a border, but there's plenty of space. We can live on this coastline without ever having to speak to each other."

"We can't even talk?" His bewildered look slays me.

It's dark and conflicted, pain dredged up from his core.

"It's just—" I have to turn away to keep from bursting into ugly tears so cruel they won't let me speak. "It's too much. Too painful. Look, I want this as bad as you do. In another life where we could merge lives, maybe it could work. But now... now, it's impossible, and one of us has to admit it."

I can't even see straight at this point. So I walk back inside alone, leaving him standing in the garden with the rain dousing his dark hair into an unruly crop against his head.

I don't get any real work done.

As soon as I head back to the cottage, I grab a bottle of wine and start upstairs, biting my bottom lip to silence the ruthless heartbreak.

I wait for Coffee and Cream to settle next to me before I pop the cork off and drink straight from the bottle.

I'm beyond giving a damn at this point.

For the first time since the inn opened, I realize it's my entire life, and I don't want it to be.

* * *

THE NEXT MORNING the doorbell rings just before we open.

I assume it's a new guest showing up to check in or a delivery. But I open the door to find a delivery man with a bouquet of roses arranged in a crystal vase.

"There's been a mistake. I didn't order any flowers."

"Someone must have sent them. You're Jennifer Landers, right? There should be a card," delivery dude says.

So begins a daily ritual that lasts for over a week.

The flowers come so often I'm on a first-name basis with the delivery driver.

Marcos.

"I'm running out of space for these and I don't want to toss them all outside," I say a few days later. "Any chance you could start dropping them off at a local church or homeless shelter or something?"

"No can do. I gotta go where the delivery gets routed, lady. Sorry."

I nod. "Okay."

He hands me another bunch of roses bigger than my head.

"At least all the guest rooms have fresh flowers, I guess."

At least I no longer have a functioning heart to worry about.

"See you tomorrow, Jenn," Marcos says with a smile.

The next day, when the doorbell rings before check-in, I just assume it's more flowers. But when I open the door, it's not Marcos the flower guy.

A man I haven't seen before shoves a bulky tablet in my face. "Hi, need you to sign for this, ma'am."

I blink. "This?"

He hooks his thumb over his shoulder and points behind him. There's a large trailer parked in my driveway. On it, a shiny new boat in Bee Harbor colors with my logo painted on the side.

I go down leaning against the wall for support, seriously convinced I'll black out for a hot second.

"No way. No flipping way. This—this is a *mistake.*"

He looks from the boat to the house and taps his tablet. "Right address. Right recipient. Seems like a pretty specific custom order. Don't tell me I screwed up?"

"But I-I didn't order a boat. I think I'd remember that."

"Well, somebody did, and I just need a signature for delivery. I'm not here to take your money. It's already paid in full."

"...but I don't have anywhere to keep it."

"I was told there's a crew restoring an old boathouse. I'm just supposed to leave it in the driveway and come move it once the work is complete." He smiles.

"I'm sorry... did you say boathouse?"

He nods.

I didn't even know I had a boathouse.

Then I remember the dilapidated structure near the beach.

Grandpa used to joke he kept his pirate treasure in there, and it looked like an accident waiting to happen. It's been rotting and falling in my whole life, and now it's so misshapen I never knew what it was actually supposed to be.

I'd planned on tearing it down and replacing it with a floating gazebo dock for weddings, maybe in the next summer or two if things go well.

"I-I can't pay a crew."

Delivery man shrugs. "Don't know anything about that, I'm afraid. I just need a signature so I can get to my next stop."

A black car pulls up behind the trailer with the boat and a man in a suit steps out.

I frown. "Now what?"

"No clue. Will you sign this or not?"

I shake my head. "No. This has something to do with my crazy ex-boyfriend."

Delivery man's brows dart up. "Whew. My crazy ex set my clothes on fire in front of my ma's house. If I ever get the kinda crazy that randomly sends boats and work crews to refurbish old buildings, I'll put a ring on that ASAP."

"Can you just go? I'm sorry, I can't keep this boat. I don't even know what to do with it."

"No offense, but it sounds like the crazy ex took care of that with the whole boathouse repair thing."

"Who hired you, anyway?"

"Says here..." He looks at the name on his tablet. "Cromwell-Narada?"

"Ugh. I knew it," I sigh out.

His jaw drops. "Hold up. Your crazy ex is *Miles Cromwell?*"

I don't answer.

The man in the suit comes up the stairs to the front porch now. "Hi, Miss Landers. I seem to have caught you at a busy time, but I'm supposed to explain the account that's been set up for you. I'm happy to wait if you'll have a minute in the next hour."

I blink. "Account? *What account?*"

Seriously.

What the hell is going on?

"I should explain. I run a business management service. Clients set up an account with my firm, and then I take care of their business needs. The account set up for you was specifically intended for up to three tour guides with a boating license—"

Okay.

Breathe.

At least now I know what I'm supposed to do with the boat.

"I'm sorry you had to come all this way. I don't want the account," I say, trying not to snap.

"Oh, are you certain? I made it clear to the man I talked to that if you changed your mind after signing the contract and funding the account, you'd lose ten percent to the cancellation fee."

He's too good at making everything so hard.

"Whatever your terms are, I didn't set up the account."

"Forgive me, but why would someone else set up an account for your business?"

"Crazy ex-boyfriend. Go figure," the delivery guy says, swirling a finger in a circle next to his head.

Suit guy blinks in confusion.

"Just take the boat back. I have to go get a crew off my land," I say before I turn and sprint off toward the pickup that's pulling up on the side of the road.

An entire week passes after that without any new fanfare.

No more truckloads of flowers, no random boats or work crews, no freaking messenger penguins like Pippa had with Brock—though that would've been adorable.

It's almost too quiet.

I think he's beginning to get it through his head.

We have to move on with our own lives.

Just not with each other.

It's bittersweet when I finally have the time and space to hear myself think.

It's what I've needed since he had his change of heart, but knowing he's given up on us rattles my head.

The finality of it stings so deep.

The next day, there's a break in the blustery winds and rain. I'm taking my dogs on a walk on our usual path along the beach and then into town.

We're about to turn around the block when Benson comes out of the general store and waves at me, holding the door.

I wave back out of instinct. But should I turn around?

Oh, no.

If Benson is here, his boss is probably close by.

I take a deep breath and suck it up.

If we're both determined to stay in this little town as neighbors, we're going to see each other. And one day, I'm bound to see him with another woman.

That will be a lot worse.

The dark thought puts a lump in my throat so big I can't breathe.

But I can't spend my life running, and seeing Miles now and then feels like good practice for what's coming.

Sure enough, I see him walking out of the general store a second later.

I almost smile before I catch myself.

His arms are bursting with canvases and art supplies. It's impressive that he just keeps painting his way through everything that's happened. Or maybe he's just starting again?

My heart sinks because I'll never find out.

There was a time when I didn't have to guess what was going on in his life.

But I made my decision, didn't I?

Still, Coffee spots him and takes off in a mad dash. Cream is right behind him, belting out loud yips.

I tighten my grip on the leashes and use my body weight to pull them back. As if I have the strength to hold almost two hundred pounds of combined Doberman insanity.

"No, no, guys—heel!"

They jerk to a stop—barely—still straining on their leashes with intense looks and wagging tails.

Miles meets my eyes. His mouth opens.

God, he's so beautiful.

He's going to say something, and whatever it is it will leave me a sobbing mess.

With the leashes still twined tightly around my hand, I yank the dogs toward me and run back the way I came.

Yep.

Still addicted.

I can't get caught up in him again.

Even if I gave in and told him I love every part of him, there's no guarantee he wouldn't change his mind again.

No promise he'd ever accept me, understand me, and try to build a life for us.

Right now, it's a chase.

A game he's losing, and billionaire beasts as driven as Miles Cromwell hate accepting defeat.

Once I've admitted I'm still in love with him, he's won.

He'll need to find a new game.

I can't take that kind of heartbreak again.

* * *

Back at home, I draw a hot bath, down some more wine—don't worry, I've started limiting myself to two glasses at a time—and doze off among the bubbles with my head propped up.

When I open my eyes, I'm back on Miles' yacht.

We're in warm waters. The high sun feels almost tropical.

He steals me away to the master cabin without uttering a word.

There's a familiar nude picture of me on the wall, but there's a curtain over it.

"Nothing will ever do you justice in the flesh," he growls before he kisses me. "Fuck, kitten. You've kept me waiting forever."

I don't resist as he pushes me against the wall and devours me, each heady stroke of his tongue reaching down inside me.

He sets me on fire like no one ever will.

When I blink, we're still in his bed, and we're not making love.

The sex is over.

Shame.

But Miles cradles me, peppering my neck with tender kisses, raking his stubble against my skin like he's marking me. The sensation makes me giggle, but the whole moment is sweeter than chocolate.

Then he places his hand over my stomach and asks, "Should we go?"

I don't understand.

Not until I take a deep breath and look down. The usual chonkyness around my belly is more like a proper balloon.

Holy shit, I'm—

"Maybe. I'm not sure," I answer.

"I vote go, kitten. If I'm wrong, they'll send us home. But I'd feel better if we went to the hospital." He helps me up.

That's when I wake up with tears in my eyes, mourning everything that might've been, and all the things that will never be.

Screw the two-glass rule.

Miles effing Cromwell, why did you have to send me away that day?

Why couldn't you have just let me in, let me help, and proved you get me?

The irony is I ended up helping anyway, and he knows how much I helped him.

How much does a good deed matter if we're both miserable?

Sometimes, I forget this is a game.

But I'm starting to wish everything that's happened ever since Gram died was just a bittersweet dream.

XXVIII: NO LAST WORD (MILES)

*B*enson helps me load poster-sized placards into my SUV one by one, side-eyeing me hard every time I grumble.

"What is it you always say, sir? Time spent second-guessing is wasted time."

"Why did I ever think this would work? If revamping her grandmother's garden, dispatching bees from Seattle, and a whole damn boat didn't seal the deal, then how will some amateur paintings do me any good?" I ask.

Benson just looks at me and smiles, his old eyes twinkling. "Somehow, I've got a feeling this is closer to what Miss Landers prefers. Speaking straight from the heart usually goes a lot further than any lavish gifts."

"That makes no sense."

He chuckles, lifting the last card into the trunk. "In case you haven't realized it yet, Mr. Cromwell, love isn't logical. If you're still expecting a consistent rhyme and a reason, well, you haven't figured it out."

Damn him, he's gone full philosopher, but he's right.

"Do *you* think this will work? Don't lie to me."

"I think you'll know for certain, one way or the other, when it's finished."

"That's what worries me," I say.

"If it doesn't work, will you just give up?"

My jaw tightens. "You know I can't. Not when she's a five-minute walk away, Benson."

"Then good luck, sir."

A few minutes later, with Benson in the passenger seat this time, I pull up in front of the inn, grab the placards from the trunk, and head for her front door.

I rap my knuckles against the cold wood and wait.

The knock echoes through the whole house and my entire soul.

A dog barks in the distance ahead of footsteps.

Then Jenn cracks the door open.

She's more beautiful than ever. Her auburn hair is messed up like she's just been outside in the wind, spilling down her neck and framing those green stars for eyes that lock on to mine.

She's not happy to see me.

Her face falls and her mouth twists as she says, "Miles—"

I put my finger in front of my mouth.

"I know. We can't keep doing this and I'm not supposed to speak to you. Since I'm a sucker for punishment, I hope you'll give me five minutes. Five minutes is all I'm asking, Jenn."

She frowns, folding her arms in front of her chest with a wary look.

She hasn't sent me packing into exile yet.

I'll take it.

I have the placards under my arm, arranged in order, and I hold the first one up.

It's a scene I painted days ago, the silhouette of a man reaching for a woman in a lush summer garden. The woman turns away, her face ghostly pale.

Between them, there's a wall of jagged words shaped like

barbed wire, an entire thesaurus of synonyms for hurt, heart-break, anger, and confusion.

"You decided we shouldn't speak to each other. Since I'll always respect your wishes, I had to find another way to say this. Here it is," I tell her.

The man can't reach through the barbed wire fence of words to his lady.

She inhales slowly and turns her head. Probably hoping I don't see her hiding a sad laugh.

I let the first placard fall to the ground at my feet.

Number two shows the silhouette of a beautiful woman flanked by two hulking black and white dogs. They're all standing just inside the very same doorway I'm looking into right now.

The man has one hand on each side of the doorframe. He's peering down at her and she's staring up at him, magnetic lines of attraction pulling them together in tiny black hearts only the dogs can see.

The caption reads, *Until I met you...*

Once I'm sure she's read it, I drop it.

The next painting has my misshapen silhouette. I'm sitting at my desk, surrounded by piles of reports and half-finished paintings.

This was my life. This was all I had, it reads.

I let go. On to the next.

Then along came you.

Our silhouettes are calmer, humanlike shadows with neat lines and soft neutrals. We're sitting together in Lottie's garden, just the way I remembered it when the old woman was still in her prime.

Jenn nods like she's urging me onward, so I drop the placard.

Life finally made sense like I never knew it could.

Her silhouette stands against the railing on the deck of my yacht. I'm behind her with my arms locked around her waist.

Yes, it's almost that goofy-ass pose from *Titanic*, but with her, it isn't silly at all.

I let go, revealing the next scene.

Life was worth its weight in gold.

Two orange silhouettes are twisted together like twin flames, locked in an intimate kiss lit by an orange sunset over the warm red ocean.

Again, I release it, and it clatters to the ground.

You became my logic.

My treasure.

My only true love.

The scene shows me sitting at the desk in my home office. She's in my lap. The ceiling above blurs into a night sky lit by a thousand little pinprick stars shaped like tiny blue-white hearts.

Next card.

Before you, my biggest regret.

In the background, there's a shadow of a man handcuffed to a bed. But the center of the picture is a vibrating cell phone with a skull flashing across the screen, and a dozen black flies circling it.

She sighs and nods slowly.

I throw this placard down harder than the others.

After you, only one.

We're strolling through Pinnacle Pointe. She's walking Cream and I have Coffee. Both of the Dobermans are painted with huge panting smiles.

The placard drops.

The next scene shows a woman's jagged silhouette limping away while a pitch-black shadow of a man stands beside her, stupidly watching.

My biggest mistake. Forever.

A tear cuts down her cheek and she twists her head to wipe it away.

Shit, am I hurting her again?

Reminding her how absolutely stupid I can be?

423

I let the card fall with a loud crash against the ground.

The next picture is my silhouette with a fractured red heart in my chest.

No caption necessary.

Down it goes.

Now, a silhouette of a woman in the center. She's wearing a cape with one hand resting on her hip. Her other arm is up in a triumphant power pose.

It's surrounded by small vignettes of the female superhero directing a creative team, corralling two massive dogs, running an inn, and finally, handing me the two shattered halves of my own heart.

You put me back together, and I still broke us.

I look at her.

Jenn's hands hang loosely at her sides now. No longer folded protectively across her chest.

Goddamn, please let that be a sign.

"M-Miles..." she stammers.

I let the painting fall and hold up the next.

Every day, you're so close.

The silhouettes stand in the lush garden again with their backs turned, a wall of night between them.

Next scene.

But so damn far away.

This painting is almost identical to the last, but the barbed wire fence of words is back.

I drop the card quickly, revealing the final scene.

My breath is molten lead in my lungs.

I don't want to give up on her. *On us.*

But I've put everything on the line here.

If she rejects me again, after this, I'm not sure when I can take another beating. I'll have no choice but to crawl back to my house with my tail between my legs.

Her eyes glisten as she blots at their corners with her finger. I give her a few seconds so she can see the next card.

Our silhouettes are still in the garden now, but she's wearing her cape. Both hands planted on her hips. I'm in front of her, on my knees, holding out my heart, a neat repair line sewn between the two halves, mending them.

Hell, I'm almost on my knees for real right now.

Almost.

But I stand there, holding the sign, too afraid to let this one drop with the grim clatter of finality.

I cling to it so fucking hard my hands hurt, but it's not the sign I care about.

I'm hanging on for life.

Desperation in every torn breath.

My last chance.

Our last hope.

Possibly my last word.

She's frozen in front of me, her bottom lip quivering, still periodically wiping her eyes.

Fuck, what was I thinking?

Have I just made it worse?

My heartbeat drums in my ears. It's like my own stupidity has a pulse.

At least I tried.

I nod tightly and look down at the mess of cards under me, signaling I'm ready to leave her alone.

I'm ready, even at the cost of the rest of my hellish life alone.

Just as I'm about to bend down to clean up the mess I've left on her porch, she shoots out the door and cannonballs into me.

"Oof!" I look down.

Jenn's arms are around my neck, shaking as she takes hold.

My arms instinctively fold around her. I steady my weight to keep us both from falling over.

Her lips brush my cheek, needy and unsure.

"God, you... you..." It's just a low moan and she still can't get it out. "Miles."

She kisses my cheek again, this time harder.

My face is wet from her tears.

Why is she crying?

What do those tears mean?

I swear, this woman will be the death of me.

Still, ever the hopeful idiot, I hug her tighter. "Jenn, it's been over two months since you were in my arms."

"Y-yeah." She moves a hand from my neck to my hair and runs her fingers through it, smiling up at me. "You were counting, huh?"

"Every damn hour. I needed you, kitten."

She closes her eyes, melting against me like it's all she's ever wanted to hear.

"Why didn't you tell me?" she whispers.

"I tried." I pull her hand from my hair, bring it to my lips, and kiss it.

"Sooner?"

"Because I'm a dumb fucking buffalo."

"You're in luck. I love buffalos," she counters, laughing. "But really, just one."

It doesn't register at first, the fact that she still *loves* me after all of this shit.

And if her words aren't enough, her eyes don't lie.

She's gazing up at me like I've plucked all the stars from the sky and I'm offering them like diamonds.

Goddamn, this woman.

I find her lips and kiss her madly, truly—fuck, I don't care —desperately.

Tasting her for the first time in months feels like windows thrown open in my soul, letting in the light after a long, cruel winter.

How did I ever let this girl go even for a second?

How did she decide to give me a second chance?

"We should go inside," she whispers.

"Sure. Let me grab the placards."

"Later." She breaks our embrace, tugging on my shirt. Then

she takes my hand and leads me in. "You won't leave me tonight, will you?"

I stop and stare at her.

There's something so hauntingly vulnerable in her words.

She still questions my commitment, of course, and that's my fault. I'll never stop trying to make up for the damage I've caused.

"The only way I'll ever be away from you again is if you lock me out," I say.

"That won't happen," she whispers.

I pull her closer and kiss her again, rebranding her lips in my memory until she pulls away, gasping.

Too soon?

"Miles, we... we should probably go upstairs. I have a couple guests downstairs tonight."

I twine my fingers through hers and nod.

She leads me up and we stop just long enough for the dogs to come flying out. Coffee immediately sits in front of me, staring up and wagging his curly tail.

With an exaggerated sigh, I give him the signal.

He shoots up on his hind legs, licking my face, and Cream is right behind him.

"They missed you like crazy!" Jenn laughs. "Almost as much as me."

After they're out of the room, we step inside and she locks the door before sitting on the bed. "God, I've missed you so effing much."

I sit down beside her, taking her hands in mine. "You were so afraid. You wouldn't talk to me."

Tears stream down her face.

"I was scared. So scared you'd change your mind again..."

I'm such a fucking idiot.

I haul her into my lap. "Jennifer, I never changed my mind, not once. Not even that day I lost my shit and said some terrible things. I didn't want you on Simone's radar. I just didn't want you getting hurt to get to me and—fuck."

I can't finish.

Not when she looks at me with green eyes so soft they reach to my depths, lighting everything in witchfire.

"And?"

"And I'm terrified of you, truth be told."

"What?" She gives me a startled laugh. "Yeah, right. Because I'm *so* scary."

I lift her hand and kiss it.

"I've lost practically everyone I've ever loved. Nothing hurt like losing you, knowing you were still *here.* Somehow, knowing it was my fault—knowing I fucked up and made it happen—seemed better than you leaving me on your own."

Her lips are on mine in a heartbeat.

Our tongues mingle until she breaks away.

"You should have just told me, Miles. There's no chance I'd ever leave you."

"I see that now," I growl, finding her lips again.

We kiss like the love starved creatures we are until we tumble backward on the bed.

Then we lie there tangled up in each other, neither of us making any effort to move.

It's languid and sweet and so intense it's almost blinding.

It isn't even sex—that's bound to come later—but goddamn, it's enough.

Her head rests on my chest where it belongs.

Her legs lock around my thigh.

Finally.

I won my kitten back.

"I love you, Jennifer Landers," I whisper, pressing my forehead to hers.

She kisses me with a fluttery moan.

This time, her nimble fingers move to the top button of my shirt.

Undressing her feels like unwrapping a present I've waited my entire lifetime for.

Sinking into her mends my soul.

Every stroke brings us to another level of heaven we never reached before.

When I release in her and she goes off gloriously in a fit of shaking ecstasy, her screams barely muffled against my shoulder, I'm fucking home.

I'm home, and they'll need an entire SWAT team to evict me from this woman again.

Waking up with her a few hours later is paradise, and this time, I won't let it slip away.

* * *

Two Months Later

I LOOK out the window at the dusting of snow, standing impatiently inside the tiny jewelry shop in Pinnacle Pointe.

My own reflection gazes back in the glass.

"Are you sure about this? You haven't been back together that long," Benson reminds me with a severe look.

I cock my head. "We're back together for good, and I'm done delaying my future. You know that."

He smiles. "I do. But you made me promise years ago to check your mental health if you ever planned on tying the knot."

"I said that?" I stare at him in silence, catching my reflection in the window again.

It stops me in my tracks.

He looks like the same Miles Cromwell, but I'm looking at a different man.

"You did. So, one more time, are you sure, Miles? And are you certain you need to do it next week?"

"Surer than I've ever been in my life." I mean it.

I want Jenn to have my name.

I want her in my house every night, eating my cooking and curling up with me and walking around in nothing but a robe.

I want her with me, wearing my ring and my t-shirts.

I even want her crazy dogs crowding up our bed and snoring in my ear.

"You could have found a better selection in Seattle," Benson says.

"Yeah, the wrong kind. I know my kitten. She'll enjoy an antique far more than something flashy."

The jeweler comes to stand behind the case I'm looking at. "Can I help you with something?"

I point at a yellow gold ring with an oval diamond centerpiece. The two teardrop diamonds are arranged to touch at the points resting on both sides of the oval. The band is carved into roses, and in the middle, something too perfect.

"Benson, what does that look like?" I turn to look at him.

He leans over to see where I'm pointing and squints. "I think I see...a bee in a rose bush?" His eyebrows dart up. "Wow. I guess it's meant to be after all."

That's all the confirmation I needed.

I'm already grinning like a sappy goddamned fool.

"Give me that one," I tell the jeweler.

The man takes it out of the case. "This ring might be a little hard to size with the intricate metal work. I can't guarantee I can make it perfect without disrupting the pattern."

"I borrowed the ring her grandmother gave her last week so I could get a size. If it's not a good fit, I'd like to have one just like it made. This *is* my wife's ring," I say matter-of-factly, taking Jenn's ring from my pocket and handing it to the jeweler.

Benson chuckles. "She hasn't said yes yet."

"And? I'm a good negotiator."

He laughs louder. "I have a feeling if you call your proposal a negotiation, Miss Landers will slap you."

"Whatever. I've got this."

And I do.

I don't tell Benson that when I say I'm good at negotiations, I mean I'll give that woman anything she wants to be mine.

She already knows I can't live without her.

"This is perfect," the jeweler says a little while later.

"It's a fit?"

"Yes. This ring is from the 1930s. I was worried it wouldn't line up, but your girlfriend has slender fingers."

I grin. "She's perfect that way."

And after this, perfectly and irrevocably mine.

I open my wallet and hand him my card.

"You sure? Most guys stop in here a few times before they commit."

I nod firmly.

I've never been more sure of anything in my life.

Well, maybe one thing.

He swipes my card and passes it back to me.

"I should have been here sooner," I mutter as he boxes the ring up and slides it over.

"Good luck," he says, waving as we turn to go.

* * *

THE NEXT WEEK Jenn and I are bundled up against the biting December wind, walking my property with the dogs.

They stay close to our sides and trot faster for extra warmth, though they seem cozy enough in their black-and-red checkered coats.

"So, why do I want to see your new storage shed again?" she asks with a curious smile.

"It's a good place to keep your boat."

"Huh? But I agreed to have the boathouse restored."

Damn. I didn't think my cover story through.

"Because. Maybe I have a surprise for you and you love me too much to tell me no."

She giggles. "I do love you. Some days."

Brat.

I pull her closer as the wind sweeps through her hair and drop a kiss on top of her head.

"What if I promise to overcompensate for my less than noble behavior tonight?"

She looks up at me and grins. "What if I don't want to wait until tonight?"

"Then I'd be happy as hell to oblige."

She blushes and laughs.

I drop an arm around her, shepherding her onward to the new shed. "I love it when you blush."

"Miles, it's freezing. Hurry."

"I'll heat you up when we get there. Don't fret," I tell her.

She giggles and elbows me.

"Speaking of the boat, did you decide when to start the tours?"

"I'm hoping for March, weather pending, but if it's still too frigid we may have to push back the date."

"That'll be a good new income stream for the inn. You could even add a few kayak rentals in the future, if you want to expand the docks."

She looks at me. "I could. But aside from you playing hero with my old boathouse, the inn is my problem, remember? I don't want to make a habit of you propping up my business."

"And I want to make your problems mine," I growl, grabbing her hand and bringing it to my lips.

She smiles softly as I kiss her skin.

Coffee and Cream run ahead of us, both of them barking impatiently.

It's like they can read my mind.

A few more steps toward the dip in elevation, and the tower comes into view, planted on a windswept cliff.

It's fifteen stories high with a winding staircase, custom built from reclaimed white stone just like a real historic lighthouse. Red bands glisten in the sun going up its length, each spaced evenly in fresh paint.

"Holy—Miles! That's no shed."

I shrug. "A little white lie for a good reason."

"It's seriously beautiful. Pinnacle Pointe hasn't had a lighthouse since the old one was torn down in the fifties. Gram used to mention it."

"Right. The original lighthouse wasn't far from here, supposedly. The builders had to make adjustments for changes in elevation. The top isn't functional like a true lighthouse either, but it does have ambient lighting, an observation deck, and an elevator. I told them to preserve the spirit of the original as much as possible. It'll bring in tourists for sure."

Her face screws up with happiness as it dawns on her.

"Totally." Then before I can get in another word, she breaks into a run. She doesn't stop until she's at the entrance, looking back at me impatiently. "We're going in, right?"

I laugh as the dogs sprint around her.

"Thought you didn't want to see my stupid shed, kitten," I call after her.

She looks back and grins. "You're lucky I don't mind you being a crappy liar when the lies are actually good. This town rarely gets new attractions."

In a couple large strides, I've closed the space between us. "It may be a tourist attraction, but I built it for the woman I love."

She stops in her tracks and turns to face me. "Thank you."

"You're welcome, Miss Landers," I say for old time's sake.

With any luck, I won't be calling her by that name again.

"Shall we?" I pull the door open and hold it for her while the Dobermans run ahead, sniffing around the smooth floor.

She looks around slowly, reverently, and then goes up the first two steps and stops. She's staring up at the winding staircase.

"That is a lot of stairs. Do you think the dogs will be okay?"

"There's always the elevator."

Grinning, she steps back down into my arms. I lead her and the dogs into the elevator.

"This is even classier than I thought," she whispers, laying her hand against the copper and custom brass finishes I had installed.

"Only the best. My kitten is demanding."

Cream lets out a loud *yip!* of agreement.

"Any chance I can use this place for wedding pictures and include it in my packages?" she asks with bated breath.

"Woman, what part of yours don't you understand? You can use this place to dance around naked in the moonlight for all I care. Hell, I might endorse that use more than anything."

"Stop!" Laughing, she smacks my chest just as the elevator stops on the top floor.

"Between the new boat tours, the fresh honey, and a flipping lighthouse... I think Bee Harbor is in for a strong year."

"Yeah," I agree as the doors slide open and I give her a minute to soak it in.

I know she'll need it.

Jenn gasps at the floor-to-ceiling view of the ocean.

"Oh. My. God." She walks straight to the window and sits down in front of it on the bench nearby. "This is straight from a dream, Miles. You've done so much for me..."

"I told you, we're partners. What's good for you is better for me. Just one problem."

Her face tenses. "What's wrong?"

"We need to formalize this partnership."

"Well, yeah. I've always told you I'd sign a contract, whatever you want, and even repay you for your investments."

I shake my head slowly, trying not to laugh at her clueless expression. "No. I have something else in mind."

She stares at me, her eyes wide with wonder even before I make my move.

I drop to one knee, retrieve the velvet box from my pocket, and flip it open.

"Oh my—oh my God! Miles!" she gasps, looking into the box. "It's a bee? *Itsabee!*"

She flies up and hugs my neck so fast it bowls me over.

I go down laughing, bracing as she stamps a dozen kisses on my neck, my lips, my everything.

I deepen the kiss as long as she lets me.

"Technically, I was supposed to ask for a yes, but if that's your answer—"

She giggles until she's red in the face. "Miles Cromwell, you know I love you."

"Enough to be Jennifer Cromwell? That was the question."

Her eyes ripple like polished jade.

"God, yes. I've wanted this forever."

I kiss her again, pushing her to the ground. The dogs are crouched behind her, and I hold up a finger in warning, asking them to stay.

"I would have asked sooner, but I couldn't chance scaring you off."

She's shaking her head fiercely as Coffee reaches his limit.

The big black dog rushes us, nosing into the action so he can lick the side of my face. Like always, Cream follows, burying Jenn in about thirty sloppy dog kisses.

I think the entire lighthouse shakes from how hard we're laughing now.

When they finally let us up, we've got two hellhounds between us.

I look at Coffee. "Not cool, dude. You made my girl move."

Jenn stands and I come up on one knee again.

"Why are you still on your knees?"

"Because there's one thing you didn't let me do." I take the ring from the box and slide it on her finger.

"Miles, it's gorgeous," she whispers.

I'm inclined to agree.

We enjoy a quiet moment, entirely lost in each other, until the elevator dings again. The unexpected flash of light makes Jenn jump and burrow her face into my chest.

"Excellent timing, you guys!" The photographer steps out of the elevator.

Jenn blinks at me in shock.

"Before you ask, yes, you can use it as promo for the wedding packages, but I wanted a few for us first." I get back on my feet, pull my fiancée tight, and slide an arm around her waist. "We're the first engagement shoot here."

She beams like the sun. "I love your insanity so much."

"Love you, too, kitten."

XXIX: NO FINAL OFFER (JENN)

Four Months Later

I'm standing in front of the full-length mirror in Gram's old room, absolutely awestruck.

My heart skips every time I do a slow turn.

Is that girl in the mirror really *me?*

With a smile so happy it breaks me, Mom adjusts the veil around my updo. "Oh, Jennifer. You've never looked prettier in your life."

"Thank you."

She hugs me, releasing a long sigh that turns into a nervous laugh. "Silly me. You're a bundle of nerves and I'm the one who's not ready for this. Promise me you'll visit as often as you can?"

"Mom, I'm fine. I'm just a few hours from Seattle, and I already lived here. Not much is changing."

"Not quite," she says gently. "My baby girl is all grown up and she's marrying a billionaire."

"You're being way too dramatic."

"One day, Jenn." Her eyes mist over as she clasps her hands. "One fine day, you'll be a mom, and then you'll understand."

Will I? We've never talked much about kids.

And for now, I'm okay with that.

Everything with Miles has always been about the journey more than the destination.

"I don't know if he even wants children," I say.

"He doesn't get a choice. You owe me grandkids—human children who aren't beasts that can knock me over."

"That's not what I meant, Mom. It just hasn't really come up yet, and I'm cool with that."

I am cool, aren't I?

She shakes her head like she knows. "Don't go down that road. Everyone gets the jitters on their wedding day, but these things always work themselves out."

I hope she's right. I hope she's—

Knock! Knock!

"Who's there?" I call. My mind is racing now with a million things that could go wrong today.

What if it's Miles?

What if he just realized he doesn't know if *I* want kids?

"What now?" Mom rolls her eyes and approaches the door. "You're fine, hon. The kind of men who build lighthouses to propose aren't the sort who'd leave their bride jilted at the altar."

"Mrs. Landers? Hi. Your husband told me I could come up for a minute. I'm Waldo Spencer, Lottie's estate attorney. Is Jenn around?"

"Yes, but... forgive me, does she really need a lawyer on her wedding day?"

"Mom, it's fine." I step forward, my curiosity piqued.

"I'll only be a moment." Waldo studies me, a slight man with perfectly round spectacles. "Miss Landers, you are stunning. I'm sure your grandmother would agree if she could see you. My sincerest congratulations."

"Thank you." I smile. "But is something wrong, Waldo?"

"Nothing at all. I just have a special delivery from your grandmother, per her instructions."

I blink. "How is that possible?"

"She left a letter and instructed me to deliver it on your wedding day. I always take care of my clients' requests, however unorthodox, so here I am. Of course, I'll stay for the reception," he says with a wink.

"Thank you." I grab the letter he holds out before he walks away.

"Wow. That was sweet of her," Mom says once she closes the door. "What does it say?"

"Let's find out." I rip the envelope open and take the letter out.

It still smells faintly like her, this bright summery scent of flowers and honey that's totally Gram and hard to pin down. I fight back a tear at the corner of my eye as I begin reading.

DEAREST JENN,

You finally did it! I hope your wedding day is as beautiful and magical as you. Most of all, I hope you're happy.

If you're reading this, then Waldo knows you've decided to marry your neighbor, Miles Cromwell.

You've probably figured out by now that I tried to give you the tiniest nudge toward destiny.

Wasn't it Shakespeare who said, 'All's well that ends well?'

I've lived my entire life like an open book and now that I'm gone, I'm not one to start keeping secrets.

Here's the truth, the whole truth, and nothing but, or may lightning strike me down (again, I guess).

I was friends with Royal and Colleen Cromwell, and later, their workaholic son.

I knew Miles had a terrible time with his mother's dreadful death, and though I never got him to admit it in words, I always felt he blamed himself.

By now, you know Miles is a good man.

Generous and kind, even if he experienced so much loss that he walled himself off from the world. I tried to set him up with a couple different girls over the years, a debutante and a farmer's daughter. He was unimpressed with both and said they told him what they thought he wanted to hear.

That's when I knew he needed a headstrong young woman with beauty and brains like my granddaughter.

That's when I knew I had to tip the scales, even from the Great Beyond, and I'm not the least bit sorry I did.

Jenn, you love so fearlessly. You're the kind of old soul who can help him learn to live and love again. But I also know that loving fearlessly doesn't come without costs. Too many men feel threatened by women with backbone. Too few could ever balance your dreams with theirs, and I couldn't bear the thought of that.

So I gave you my greatest gift, worth so much more than the inn—a good man.

He'll protect my granddaughter.

He'll be your missing piece.

You'll complement each other, and if you're still reading this through the tears, I'm certain you complete him.

Setting you two up was easy. Miles had his eye on my property for years.

I told him to make you a decent offer knowing full well it would be overly generous, so if by chance you happened to sell too soon, you'd be better off than you were before. And, of course, that stubborn man would do something marvelously stupid that would keep throwing you two together again and again.

But I didn't believe you'd sell, and I didn't think he'd walk away.

I knew you'd give him the hell he needs. Just like I knew Miles would give you his heart.

That's why I left so many instructions for poor Waldo. He assured me they weren't legal, and you could've overturned them in a heartbeat with any two-bit lawyer, but I knew you wouldn't.

You've never let your old grandmother down, dearest heart.

You never will.

Today, you've fulfilled my dying wish.

I always swore I'd leave you in good hands, and here you are.

So let Miles take care of you and my fur babies, Jenn. You'll be safe and happy and entertained with him. I'd bet my entire soul on it.

Your love is the beating heart of Bee Harbor now, and it'll forever keep you going since this old heart couldn't.

All my love,

Gram

HOLY HEARTBREAK AND A HALF.

Flaming tears roll down my cheeks by the time I finish. I'm shaking so much as Mom softly clasps my shoulders.

"Easy, sweetheart. You'll mess up your makeup." Mom pulls a cotton square from the dresser, dabs my face, and retouches everything.

"C-can you believe it?" I stammer.

"Actually, I can." She wipes a tear from her own cheek. "That was exactly the sort of harebrained scheme Mama loved to pull. Aren't you glad it worked?"

I nod vigorously.

God, yes.

When I thought Gram just left me money and a beautiful old inn that's slowly coming back to life, I thought it was her greatest inheritance.

Now, I know she delivered my entire future.

I inherited the best husband in the entire freaking world. I just have to marry him first.

If I had any lingering wedding day doubts, they're gone in a puff of teary-eyed feels.

Reading that letter made it clear and banished my worries.

This is the right move.

All the things I don't know about Miles, all we're meant to be, we'll find out. Together.

How could it be any different? The man was handpicked by Gram to be my own personal guardian angel.

I'm still smiling as Mom finishes my makeup fix until another knock at the door interrupts us.

"Now what?" I stare at the door.

"No idea. This has already been more eventful than my wedding day, and my parents brought every able-bodied horse on the island! Let me find out."

Mom answers the door again.

This time, it's Dad. He shaved off his mustache for today and he looks so adorably clean I laugh.

"The preacher man's here and the groom is in place. Everybody's ready to cry and eat their weight in appetizers. We're just waiting on the prettiest bride Pinnacle Pointe will ever have," he says with a smile just for me. "You ready, Jenn?"

"As ready as I'll ever be." Every footstep feels like I'm airborne as I walk over and take his hand.

Here we go.

Dad helps me down the stairs, and we go out the back door to the garden.

Coffee and Cream bound up from their napping spot by the door like my personal guardians, protective as always.

"Dear, you really should have let us kennel those dogs. Today of all days."

"They're family. I'm sure they'll behave," I say with a smile as Dad leashes them up for good measure.

Coffee lets out a low *woof* of agreement, moving in next to me.

Just around the corner, my whole future comes into view.

We stop and stare in awe.

A couple local girls glide down the path in front of me, throwing rose petals of every color.

With smiles flying everywhere, Dad strolls forward, guiding me down the long, winding natural aisle until we're at the new gazebo by the cliff where Miles waits.

There's an altar set up inside with Royal Cromwell's painting of this garden—basically a reflection of our surroundings—hanging in the backdrop.

My dad places my hand in Miles' hand. "Take care of her for me."

"You have my word." He smiles at me and looks at my dad.

Then it's all just a glorious blur.

Lots of words about love and fate and divine approval.

Lots of promises we make forever.

Lots and *lots* of smiles from our little audience.

But there's none bigger than Royal Cromwell's, sitting by his nurse in his wheelchair. It's just this subtle thing you might miss if you don't notice when it happens.

The old man locks eyes with me and smiles. I swear there's a flicker of recognition in his pale-blue eyes, an understanding that says, *be good to my boy. Love him like my wife loved me.*

I will, Royal.

God, will I ever.

And when the preacher says, "You may now kiss the bride," Miles surprises me again on a day with so many.

He doesn't lift my veil.

Instead, he brings my hand to his mouth, taking his time in this sweet, slow kiss.

He kisses my ring first before turning my hand over to kiss my palm.

"I love you, Jennifer Cromwell."

It's a miracle I don't go to snotty, crying chaos right there.

Several people throw "awwws" around, and I'm not sure if it's Mom or Pippa who yells it the loudest.

I'm too preoccupied by the intensity of my husband's gaze as he pulls my hand down, still holding it in his.

As he lifts my veil, places his hands possessively on my waist, holds me so close, and kisses me with the weight of his whole being.

My toes scrunch.

For a second I'm so lost in Miles that I forget we're really married now.

This is where I want to be.

This is where I want to *live* forever as I smile at him and say one last secret thanks.

Gram, wherever you are, I hope you're watching.

I hope you can see me smiling at the man of my dreams.

* * *

LATER, when the sunny reception finally ends long after nightfall, he loads me in his SUV and drives me down the street to his —*well, our*—new home.

"I still can't believe you gutted the house," I whisper.

"You wanted a modern transitional farmhouse with all the conveniences, and you're getting it. I had every contractor in a hundred miles beating down my door for this job. Everybody wins," he says, twining our fingers together.

"I know, but you're giving me a flipping castle."

"And you love it."

I giggle because he's too right.

"It has more charm than any new build I've ever seen. But you're sure you have no regrets?"

The way he side-eyes me says I'm being ridiculous in the most endearing way.

"We agreed. We both need a fresh start. Something that wasn't completely yours or mine. It had to be *ours.* Besides, the inn books solid every night, and staying there would cost you a nightly rental income when you can rent out the best room in the house. Never mind the fact that we'd have no privacy— something I was adamant about." He glances over and grins when he sees me blushing. "Go ahead and try to play it off. I'm just glad my queen adores her palace."

He's. Killing. Me.

444

I smile at him. "No denying it, but your queen loves it even more when you call her 'my wife.'"

"Get used to that, my wife, because you're mine now. Mine completely." There's an intensity in his tone that echoes through me. "You know it, don't you, kitten?"

Heat thrums under my cheeks.

"Yeah," I whisper. "But I wouldn't turn down a reminder."

Grinning, he parks the SUV in front of the door. We don't even make it to the garage as he carries me inside and up the stairs to our master suite.

I lean up and kiss his chin. "This part so isn't necessary."

"Liar. You think I'd miss my chance to carry you over the threshold?" he growls.

"Technically, we passed the threshold."

"Technically, sweetheart, there's no chance I'm turning you loose before you're down on the bed, stripped naked."

I grin. "And then?"

"Then I fucking devour you."

Sure enough, he carries me to our room, but he doesn't place me on the bed like he promised.

Instead, he sets me on my feet and nods at the virtual assistant speaker on his nightstand.

"Calista, play 'All of Me.'" He puts his hands on my hips and draws me closer as the song starts. "Dance with me, Mrs. Cromwell?"

I can't help but smile. "Of course. But haven't we danced to this song once today?"

"That was for a crowd. This one's for us."

My heart flips as I follow his lead.

Miles holds me so close I can feel his pulse, his heat. I'm delirious with his scent in no time.

My smile deepens. The last time this song played, it was our first dance at the reception.

"Will you still love me like this after the honeymoon?"

"Yes, ma'am."

Our bodies meld seamlessly, gliding across the floor.

His muscles ripple against me, and God, I've wanted to be alone with him ever since I first saw him standing in the gazebo, decked out in this navy-blue suit that accents every angle of his body.

He may be patient.

I'm not.

Grabbing his shoulders, I stand on my toes, pressing my mouth to his with a moan that embarrasses me.

He stops moving to the music in perfect precision and deepens our kiss, growling deliciously in my mouth.

His hands roam my sides, retracing my curves, coming together and stopping just below the small of my back over my butt.

His tongue delves deeper in slow, sensual strokes that leave me dizzy, breathless except for a startled, "Oh. Oh, Miles."

His grip tightens.

"You still taste like wedding cake and espresso," I say when we break.

He chuckles. "And you taste like honey stolen from heaven's pantry. Always, woman."

Grinning, I work on his tie, my cheeks flushed as I slip a few times.

He places his hand over mine, guiding me, then stops my movement.

"Pace yourself. I want this to be special," he orders.

"It's always special when I'm with you."

His mouth attacks mine again, showing me how little patience he truly has.

The kiss feels so intense it leaves me reeling, and it's a good thing I back into the edge of the bed for support.

His tie comes off and I unbutton his coat, running my hands down his chest, his chiseled abs, the bulge below his belt that's holding back the storm of a century.

I bite my lip—*I have to*—as I glide my hands back up his shoulders, tucking them under his coat.

His eyes are incandescent as he shrugs out of it, desperate to help my fingers work at his shirt buttons. It's gone in record time.

We both sigh with relief as he turns his attention to my dress. I knew I picked something easy to take off for a reason as he slides the zipper down, tracing every newly revealed inch of flesh with his tongue.

"Miles!" I shudder.

It's all detailed silk, but it's had its time to shine as it falls to the floor.

He breaks our next sultry kiss just long enough for his eyes to rake over me.

I must look funny with my body fastened into a skintight lace slip.

"More beautiful than the dress," he whispers.

I smile. I wasn't expecting that.

"How does this come off?" he growls impatiently, reaching for the zipper.

"It doesn't. Not yet." My eyes light up with anticipation.

I run my hand down his chest, digging my nails into his skin, making him feel my need.

He sighs loudly, every last bit of him bristling.

His trousers are tented, his cock pulsing angrily behind the fabric.

"You must be so uncomfortable," I whisper, reaching down to squeeze him. "Let me help."

"Goddamn. Yeah, kitten, set me free."

And I do, helping him unbutton his pants and shove them to the floor to join my dress.

They fall around his ankles, and he kicks off his shoes.

The instant he's free, I don't wait.

I pull the boxer briefs down, cupping the hard, needy length of him with my hand.

"Fuck." He sighs. "How does the slip come off? Tell me *now*."

"Down the back." I slide my fingers down his thick manhood, then let go and turn around, so we're back to front.

He's harder than stone with raw desire, hot and firm against my ass.

I've never wanted anything so bad.

It's like a fever, this lust, this animalistic need to be joined to my husband—holy shit, *my husband*—for the very first time.

He unhooks the first three brackets in slow seconds that make me so wet I can't stand it.

The slip comes loose around my breasts while I count the deepest breaths I've taken all day.

"Feels good," I purr. But it's nothing close to what he's about to make me feel.

His hands slide between the loose bra cups of the slip and my breasts. He cups them with a rumble in his throat, running his thumbs over my nipples, pressing good and hard.

I close my eyes as a moan drifts up my throat.

My ass pushes against his shaft, desperate to give him the same rush, igniting every nerve.

But he's so patient.

I hate and love that he's so flipping calm, so controlled, so Miles.

He caresses my breasts long enough to make my body ache for him before he grabs at the last few hooks.

"Go. Just rip it off," I beg.

"No, kitten. Torturing you is part of the fun." His breath is volcanic against my ear.

"No games. Please. I just want *you*."

Now, the slip is undone to my belly button.

He runs his hands up and down my bare torso, massaging my breasts every time he passes them, pinching my nipples with a rising fury that matches the fire in his blood.

"Miles!" I fumble behind me until I've cupped his length again.

I start stroking him fast and furious, squeezing harder with every pump.

This guttural "fuck" drops from his throat like a hammer, and the slickness running out of his tip tells me he's losing control.

You'd better believe the unfastening happens faster now.

My husband knows I don't play fair, and I've never asked him to with me.

With a ragged breath, he picks me up and drops me on the bed, then climbs up beside me.

I move my hand up and down his hard cock, languidly pumping, before I take him in my mouth.

His head snaps back as I engulf him, fully in rapture.

"Fuck, kitten. You and your little tongue—you *kill* me," he snarls.

I'm smiling as I suck him harder, deeper, faster, swirling my tongue just under his crown, worshipping the familiar spot that always leaves him undone.

"Fuck!" He thrusts harder in my mouth, grinding his hips, pushing until I can't take more and I'm less than halfway down.

His hands fuse to both sides of my head, thrusting so hard and still not hard enough because he knows what I can take, and just when I think he's about to come so sweetly for me—

"Goddamn. Enough," he rasps, jerking back reluctantly.

I smile as he catches his breath.

When his eyes lock on mine, they're fully molten.

Then he places two fingers on my collarbone, slides down between my breasts, past my stomach, between my legs.

"You're ready as hell for me and I haven't even touched you yet. I'm not wasting a pussy this tight and wet." And he emphasizes it by pushing between my legs until I gasp.

"Miles, oh!"

I want to fight, but I want to surrender so much more.

And I do.

I give my body over to his touch, to everything he wants.

It isn't long before he shoves me down, spreads my legs, and pushes his face to my core.

I thought I already knew what it was like to be devoured by Miles Cromwell.

But I didn't know how he'd consume me now that I'm his wife.

Every fierce stroke of his tongue, his breath, his teeth come just a little sharper, a little more intense, a little more blinding.

When his tongue lashes my clit, my vision whites out.

I come so hard I'm ruined.

I soak the sheets, and if I didn't see him proudly wiping his lips when he comes up while my senses reset, I think I'd be shamed for life.

"Always be my little firecracker. Love the way you come so hard for me, kitten," he whispers, fusing his mouth to mine before I can respond.

We kiss until we can't stand it.

Until his teeth catch my bottom lip and pull insistently.

Until his thick, rough hand sweeps my legs apart, and his full weight eclipses me like a second shadow.

His arms go behind my back and his hands find my hair.

I'm pressed to him without an inch of space.

In one thrust, he's in me, rendering us both breathless.

It's amazing, and still not enough.

"Miles, fuck me," I whisper harshly. "Be as rough as you want."

I tilt my head forward, frantically searching his eyes, offering him an invitation that will always be open.

And the silver-blue animal glint in his eyes says he gladly accepts. Then his mouth covers mine again and his tongue thrusts in, claiming me.

I'm mounted by a man who's more wolf than mild-mannered husband.

I'm invaded with pleasure, overwhelmed in every way.

I'm marked with his teeth against my throat, and I bite his shoulder.

His hips work like pistons.

I arch up to meet his thrusts with soft pleas each time, shocking myself with how fast I come on his cock.

When I'm close for the third time, his strokes quicken, throwing him into me so hard each stroke shoves me deep into the mattress. He uses me so good, his cock grinding my depths, his pubic bone raking my clit until my head snaps back and everything convulses.

I feel him swell and groan and shudder with release.

Coming!

Our first orgasm together as man and wife shreds me, leaves my body jelly, but deliciously tingly in all the right places.

I'm catapulted to the stars and brought down on a cotton candy cloud that smells, tastes, and feels like Miles Cromwell.

And my husband's tongue is urgent and intense as he rakes mine. As he holds himself in me like he wants to push his seed deeper—*so deep*—conquering me from the inside out.

"Fucking damn, Jenn. *Damn.*" His voice is so rough it's barely human.

He pulses inside me and my body clenches around him as he thrusts again, driving to the very limits.

"Miles, yes!"

Together, we go down shaking.

Together, we collapse as he drops his head to my shoulder and slowly, almost angrily pulls out of me.

Together, we hold each other, stroking each other's hair, staring into each other's eyes like we can see eternity ahead.

"Jennifer Cromwell, I love you more than life itself." His lips meet mine again.

"And I love you because you *are* my life," I whisper, remembering Gram's letter.

Call it sickeningly sweet. Cheesy.

I don't care.

It's branded in my heart.

Most importantly, it's *ours*.

* * *

ON THE PLANE the next day, I decide to let him in on my secret and hand him Gram's letter.

"What's this?"

"Gram's attorney delivered it before the wedding. The letter is for me, but I think you should read it too. What she did was as much for you as it was for me."

"What did she do?"

"Played cupid, bless her heart. She made sure we'd butt heads and fall madly in love." I'm almost giddy when I imagine the pointed smile on Gram's face as she schemed this up.

He leans over, smiling, and kisses me. "Thank God she did. Don't know what the hell I'd be without you."

I'm quiet for a minute, trying to figure out how to say this.

It's our honeymoon. I don't want things to get too heavy. But I've thought about it ever since I read the letter.

"I have to tell you something." I look at him intently.

He laces his fingers through mine. "As long as it's good news. Nothing else allowed on our honeymoon, kitten. I'm sure it's a law in the Turks and Caicos, too."

My smile goes lopsided as he brings our intertwined hands to his lips and kisses my fingers.

"It's been on my mind a lot lately. You've lost so much in your life. I know that, and I know you think everyone leaves you behind, but they don't. You were friends with my grandma. When she left, she gave us this."

His grip on my hand tightens.

"Your dad taught you to paint. He can't be here anymore, but you'll always have your art. I never knew your mom, so I can't guess what she left you. But I'm sure she's always with you, whether you know it or not."

"She showed me what love should be," he answers slowly. "They both did. I never forgot that, even when everything went to hell..." He pulls me into his lap. "Now, if you're done with the sappy shit, Mrs. Cromwell."

His mouth covers mine with a kiss that's warming and dirty and too enticing.

"Be nice. The flight attendant will get upset."

"It's a private plane. The flight attendant makes twice the usual commercial salary to put up with me breaking the rules."

I giggle and he kisses me.

* * *

A COUPLE DAYS LATER, I wake up in our suite and see the balcony doors are open.

Miles sits in the sunlight outside with a canvas on an easel in front of him and a standing palette beside him.

His bare torso is beautiful in the sunlight. He's working shirtless with a cup of coffee beside him.

I laugh as I pad over.

"Good morning, Mrs. Cromwell."

"I'll never get tired of hearing that."

"I'll never get tired of saying it."

"You're painting here? Really? Talk about dedicated."

"I'm working on my wife's wedding gift. Want to come help?"

"Sure!" Too curious, I lean over the bed, find my discarded nightgown, and pull it over my head.

Then I go to the balcony to help Miles with his painting.

I should know better by now, but I'm still not prepared.

It's me.

Me, shimmering like this fairy-tale goddess walking out of a sapphire ocean onto the beach of Turks and Caicos that looks so much like the pristine white sands below us.

"I can't believe you like to paint me," I whisper, wringing my hands.

"Believe it, kitten. You're beautiful, you're mine, and you're useful. Not every artist has his own model. I'd be a fool not to take advantage of it constantly."

I smile. He leans forward and kisses me.

"Do you like it?" he asks.

"Yes, it's more PG-rated than the last one." But honestly, I'll always adore everything he paints.

"There's a reason it's tame. This one is going in our bedroom. I'm almost done. You want to do the last stroke?" He holds out the paintbrush.

I look from the brush to the painting, then to the palette standing beside him.

Oof.

I have no idea how to finish it or what this last stroke even is. "Not sure... I'm a little afraid I'll mess it up."

"You won't. Let me show you." He hands me the brush.

I take it gingerly.

His fingers fold over mine, gently guiding the brush to goddess me's ring finger. The last stroke starts as a squiggle. I'm sure it's going to ruin everything.

But when we remove the brush, goddess me has a bee-shaped wedding ring on her finger.

"There. She's taken now," he says.

I smile like I'm one with the dreamy warmth streaming into our room. The same warmth that's shining inside me.

I drop the brush on the palette, lean over, and kiss him.

He deepens the kiss which takes on a life of its own until he picks me up and carries me to bed. He lies down beside me, and after the scorching kiss I expect he's looking for more—and I'm ready and willing.

"What do you think about expanding our family?"

"More dogs?" I hold my breath.

"Eventually. I had something a little more delicate in mind before that, though."

His hand slides down my side and curls up until his palm settles over my belly.

This man.

I kiss him long and slow, showing him how much I love that idea.

"Soon, Miles. I'd like that a lot." I laugh.

"What's so funny?"

"I didn't realize we never had this conversation until I was about to walk down the aisle and I started freaking out a little. Then I read Gram's letter..."

"So, you're saying I should thank Lottie for you not jilting me at the altar?"

Grinning, I smack him playfully. "Thank her for bringing me to my senses, sure. But I always knew we'd get through it."

"We will, kitten. We've already proven we can make it through anything."

The next time he kisses me, I'm smiling with the same loving happiness in that painting.

Unlike his painted women, I'm grateful that I get to be the only one who ever touches this god, this man who picked up a brush and offered me a destiny I couldn't refuse.

FLASH FORWARD: NO LAUGHING MATTER (MILES)

Years Later

*J*enn wobbles out from behind the front desk at the inn, careful to step over Cream snoozing at her feet.

"This is insane, kitten. You have employees," I say.

"I don't have another manager and we're in the thick of travel season. Every set of hands counts, especially with the odd drama bomb walking in."

"It's your inn," I say with a shrug and a grin.

"Yep. Which is why I need to put in overtime."

"At thirty-nine weeks pregnant? Like hell," I grumble.

Her hands ball into fists and she levels a look. Even when she's mad at me, she's the portrait of summer with her red hair spilling around her shoulders.

I've painted this look over a dozen times. I'm still waiting for the day I'll get sick of it.

Though maybe I should find a way to walk that back.

"You're really going to give me crap and just stare at me?" she asks.

"Yeah. You're more radiant than ever today, woman."

Her face softens.

"Easy for you to say. You're not the one growing a bowling ball with arms and legs." She flicks her hair back restlessly.

My gaze drops to her stomach.

Just when I'm about to march over and take her in my arms, no matter how much she fights, the front door swings open.

A college kid drags a nervous looking girl in behind him. They're total opposites. He's wearing jeans with a clean-cut polo shirt typical of our comfortable middle class Seattle summer crowd, and she's wearing a bright green modern dress with pops of southeast Asian designs.

"Wow, this place even smells good." The young woman smiles, drawing a deep breath.

She has an accent, but I can't quite place it. Almost British, maybe.

"I know. I've been coming here since I was fourteen. Perfect place to get married," the kid whispers in her ear, rubbing her shoulders.

I only need a quick glance at Jenn to see the panic on her face.

They both look at me and decide to cool it on the public affection.

"Oh, gosh. This town is the wedding capital of the Pacific coast and it's still so small. If I were home, there would be seven hundred people at my wedding," she says.

"If you were home, you'd be marrying some prick you've never met who isn't on track to be a doctor." The boy beams a smarmy grin, so sure of himself.

I fold my arms and try not to laugh.

She throws up her hands. "Jim! I'm risking a fortune to marry you, and this is the thanks I get?"

His smile widens. "Hey, it's not like my mom's breaking out

the confetti either. But I'll always choose you, Meera."

Nice save. That wins him a smile.

They walk to the front desk with smiles too wide for their faces.

"Hi, we'd like to get married here please? We'll pay whatever you want."

"You've come to the right place." Jenn smiles but I can see the worry with the way her mouth pulls tight. "Do you have a date picked out?"

"Today or tomorrow," Meera answers, batting her eyes at her beau.

Shit.

A deer caught in the headlights wouldn't look as spooked as my wife.

Jenn clears her throat softly. "I'm afraid that's not possible. We typically need six weeks notice for full wedding accommodations. Plus, this week there's a wedding cruise tomorrow, one in the garden, and even one in the lighthouse on Friday. We don't have another venue."

The girl bites her lip and looks at her boyfriend like she's about to cry.

"What if we just got married in a room?" Jim says, taking her hand. "We just want this done. It doesn't have to be big and fancy."

"Hmm. Well, the inn is fully booked." Jenn's eyes flick desperately over her screen, searching for anything.

"No, please. There must be an opening somewhere. We have to get married this weekend," the girl says, her face falling. "My father will kill me when he finds out we eloped."

"I'm sorry, but I'm afraid we're fully booked. Is there anywhere else you can think of? I'd send you to the boat club in town, but I know they're having a massive retirement this week, too, so..."

Despite the empathy blowing up my heart, I try not to laugh.

No wonder my wife never gets a dull moment. This place is a

damn soap opera set.

The couple lingers, staring at Jenn like they're expecting her to produce a unicorn from thin air. Holding in a sigh, I walk over, offering a firm but diplomatic smile.

"You heard the lady, guys. We're booked."

Jenn gives me a pained look. "She has to get married, Miles."

I blink. "We're booked. What can we do?"

"They're getting married in the garden," I say.

"My garden?" She tilts her chin and stares up at me, not understanding.

"The fountain we put in last summer. It's a perfect spot for two kids on the fasttrack to holy matrimony."

Her eyes light up as she realizes I mean *our* garden at what used to be my place. Now, it's ours.

It's not quite as homey as Lottie's, but since Jenn moved in, I've let her green thumb advise our gardener. In no time, she's added bursts of color and even a few vegetable plants that blend in seamlessly. It's rustic, yet perfectly elegant.

"Oh. Oh, right," she whispers, her face lighting up as she looks at the couple. "You guys are in luck. My lovely partner just reminded me of a recent expansion. We don't normally use it for weddings, but since there are only two of you..."

I listen as they prattle on about the details, and the kids are much happier. The relief shines in their faces.

"One thing, though," the almost-groom says. "We don't have an officiant."

"You can apply online in Washington," Jenn says cheerfully.

Her eyes flick to me every few seconds, the gratitude shining in her face even as the kids pepper her with questions.

"I guess we'll need a cake too, is there a bakery in town? Oh, and flowers!" Meera bites her lip.

Jenn looks at the girl with a no-nonsense smile. "Give us a couple hours. We'll clip a bouquet from the garden just for you."

The girl spins into her fiancé's arms. "You hear that? It's so on! We're really getting married."

"There's a nice bakery in town that might be able to whip up a cake for a rush fee," I say.

The girl throws up her hands, still doting on her fiancé. "Oh, we don't need a cake. I just want to marry him."

Later, Jenn winces as she fishes around in the back room for a spare set of shears. She bends at the waist, and puts her hand on her back. "Ohhh."

Coffee rears up and lets out a low woof. Cream's ears go back next to him.

"Kitten, you okay?" I rush over.

"I think I'm... I don't know. My back hurts."

I go around the counter, pull her against me, and place my hand on her stomach. "Let's get you to the hospital. The flowers can wait."

"But they need the arrangements tomorrow!"

"And you need a doctor, woman," I say. "I'm not losing my firstborn or my wife to a damn bouquet."

She opens her mouth to sass back, but I shut it with a kiss.

"Miles..."

I help lead her out of the room and we pass the couple again.

"Aww, look at them," the Indian girl coos.

Her boyfriend slides an arm around her and they watch us race outside. I'm glad as hell I got a head start because my wife is panicked now, her face tense with pain.

"M-Miles!" I-I think the baby is already coming! Oh, God."

Shit, shit.

This is what I was worried about.

I rip my jacket off and lay it on the ground for her, taking her hand. "Let me help. You just lay down, wait for the EMTs."

I've already got my phone pressed against my ear, barking information.

When the soon-to-be-newlyweds poke their heads outside, I point at the boy. "You. I need towels and hot water. You can grab them from the back room behind the office. Go."

They both go running.

"Miles, I'm worried," Jenn whispers.

Kneeling beside her, I kiss her forehead. "I'm here. Squeeze my hand when it hurts, as hard as you need. Break the fucking thing if you have to." I have no clue how much that really helps, but it's what people say and I'm no doctor, so it sounds as good as anything.

Jenn screams louder, twisting my hand.

By the time the almost-newlyweds show up with our stuff and a small white ambulance jerks to a stop on the curb, time no longer has any meaning.

The entire universe condenses down to me, my woman, and the beautiful little girl who's about to come into the world.

Everything is hazy from the ride to the hospital, bursting through the doors, the flurry of personnel in scrubs damn near everywhere.

When I can breathe again, I'm staring at the newborn baby wrapped in a towel.

"She's beautiful. Have a look, Mama," I help Jenn sit up and hand her the baby. "We still set on Charlotte?" I ask. It's the name we knocked around for a girl.

Smiling, Jennifer shakes her head. "I think we have to go with Rose."

"Rose," I echo, remembering it's the name of our kid she always mentioned from the dream. "Fair enough. She'll have siblings soon enough, and I think Lottie won't be too mad waiting for her namesake."

* * *

Five Years Later

COFFEE LAYS AT MY FEET, thumping his curly thin tail against the ground.

We're both watching my wife and kids.

It's a goddamned idyllic scene.

Jenn, down on her knees pruning weeds from our garden. Rose is beside her with fake toy shears, helping her mother 'cut.' Cream lays between my wife and daughter, drooling as she naps in the sun.

The Dobermans are lazy in their old age, two big lumps who only wake up these days to play with the kids or go for their walks on the beach.

Little Royal wobbles around in front of me, his arms thrown out like wings.

I mix the red and brown until I create that beautiful red-brown rust color. I take my time spiraling my wife's hair into the scene. It's always such a brilliant contrast with the soft pinks, purples, and yellows surrounding her.

My old man would appreciate this. He never met Royal and only held Rose once before he checked out in his sleep. His nurse said he was smiling and whispering my mother's name the night before he died.

Still, there are times when I feel him here. On a sunny spring day like this with a perfect scene to lay down on the canvas, my father is everywhere.

Royal waddles over and grabs my leg.

"What's up, buddy?" I look down.

He jerks his arms toward me. "Up, up!"

I stare at my son, pretending to consider it before I huff out an exaggerated sigh and plop him into my lap. He goes down laughing like the spoiled little munchkin he is.

Before I can say anything, he starts reaching for my paintbrush.

"You want to paint? Really now?"

His huge lopsided grin says *yes.*

"What do you want to paint?"

"Mommy!" he squeals.

I let him hold the brush, trying to guide his hand before he thrashes it around and spatters paint everywhere.

"Daddy, no! I paint!"

"You're painting, little man. I'm just helping."

"No, no! Lemme do!" Royal takes the brush, dotting that beautiful rust color all over the canvas.

In under a minute, my stark realism turns into a postmodern mess. "Well, I always wanted to get more abstract..."

Royal raises both hands above his head in babbling triumph.

The noise makes Jenn look at me over her shoulder. "Do you have your hands full?"

"Yeah, but the view is beautiful."

She grins. "It's Pinnacle Pointe. It's spring. When is the view not gorgeous, Miles?"

"Didn't mean the gardens or the ocean," I tell her, leveling a look.

Her mouth pulls into a smile that shows her teeth.

Meanwhile, Rose fake cuts a few more weeds and chucks her plastic shears down like she's a little farmer who's been at it since the crack of dawn. "Is it time for my birthday party yet?"

Jenn throws her clippings into a brush pile. "Yes it is, little girl! By the time we're all cleaned up, it'll almost be time."

Later that afternoon, we sit on our back patio with Jenn's parents, Benson, the Winthropes, and a random assortment of kids from preschool and play dates.

"What are the odds they'd be born three years and one day apart?" Jenn asks.

Pippa laughs. "I still don't know how you managed that."

I slide my arm around my wife. "It has its benefits. We can have one big party until they're older." Although the single party is technically two in one.

Rose has a Disney princess themed bouncy house beside Royal's PAW Patrol bouncy house. They didn't necessarily need different themes, but Jenn didn't want bigger kids pouncing on little ones, and I understand.

Rose bounces out of the air castle and bounds toward me.

She doesn't stop until she cannonballs into my lap. "Daddy! Come jump with me!"

"I'm too big, baby girl. I'll break your little castle."

"Oh. That's sad."

I shake my head. "I know. Never grow up. When you're older, we'll get you guys a trampoline big enough for me."

Jenn looks at me and bursts out laughing in surprise.

Yay!" Rose kisses my cheek.

Not to be outdone, Coffee stands up and stretches from his nap, lets out a single low bark, and then lays his head in my lap like the drama king he is.

"Puppy!" Rose pats his nose and then darts off as quickly as she came.

The dogs go flying after her, both of them suddenly wide awake.

Once she's gone, Jenn leans over and kisses me on the cheek. "That looked like fun."

I pull her into my lap. "It was. I love you," I whisper.

"Don't sweat the kids, Miles. You have an easier time with my daughter than I do," my father-in-law says.

I chuckle because I don't know what to say.

"I should go grab the cake," Jenn says.

"Need some help?" I ask.

"I've got it."

While I make small talk with her parents, she comes back a minute later with her grandmother's famous honeycake.

"Does that have the local honey?" her mom asks.

Jenn nods. "Straight from Bee Harbor's very own honeycombs." She takes her time, carefully lining up the candles for each kid on both sides of the cake.

When it's ready, we summon the crowd of kids over and watch as they fumble with their wishes, then blow out the candles together.

It's a long day with presents, cake, multiple rounds of snacks, and good company.

Once everyone leaves near sunset, Jenn grabs Royal and I take Rose. We each corral one kid at a time for bath time and bed. I spend over an hour reading them both their favorite stories.

When the kids are asleep, I head for my office and grab the flowers I clipped from the garden earlier while Jenn was busy chasing the kids around. I stole a ribbon from Rose's craft bucket and tied them into a bouquet.

I find my wife coming out of our bathroom and hand her my homemade gift. "Fresh picked just for you, kitten."

She beams like the sun. "Thank you! Um, what are they for?"

I shrug. "My wife. Do I need another reason?"

"You're too sweet."

For once, I don't try to deny it. I just turn to my nightstand.

"Calista, play *All of Me*," I tell the virtual assistant.

Jenn places the flowers on her nightstand as the music starts playing, doubling the warmth in the room.

"Mrs. Cromwell, may I have this dance?"

She stares at me with a messy grin. "Are you serious right now?"

"Hell yeah. It's been too long since I danced with my wife. Now get your sweet ass over here, woman."

"I think you're just doing this because it's the night we said we'd... you know."

I do, and the way she blushes thrills me to the bone.

It must be my day because she listens.

And I place my hands on her hips and pull her as close as I can. "Remember when I promised you on our wedding night that I'd always love you like crazy?"

"Miles, I love you."

We kiss and I spin my wife slowly around the room.

Family business is no laughing matter, but it's the only business I'll never trade for anything in the known universe.

And after tonight, if I have my way, we'll be making our family a little bigger.

ABOUT NICOLE SNOW

Nicole Snow is a *Wall Street Journal* and *USA Today* bestselling author. She found her love of writing by hashing out love scenes on lunch breaks and plotting her great escape from boardrooms. Her work roared onto the indie romance scene in 2014 with her Grizzlies MC series.

Since then Snow aims for the very best in growly, heart-of-gold alpha heroes, unbelievable suspense, and swoon storms aplenty.

Already hooked on her stuff? Visit nicolesnowbooks.com to sign up for her newsletter and connect on social media.

Got a question or comment on her work? Reach her anytime at nicole@nicolesnowbooks.com

Thanks for reading. And please remember to leave an honest review! Nothing helps an author more.

MORE BOOKS BY NICOLE

Bossy Seattle Suits

One Bossy Proposal

One Bossy Dare

One Bossy Date

One Bossy Offer

Bad Chicago Bosses

Office Grump

Bossy Grump

Perfect Grump

Damaged Grump

Knights of Dallas Books

The Romeo Arrangement

The Best Friend Zone

The Hero I Need

The Worst Best Friend

Accidental Knight (Companion book)*

Heroes of Heart's Edge Books

No Perfect Hero

No Good Doctor

No Broken Beast

No Damaged Goods

No Fair Lady

No White Knight

No Gentle Giant

Marriage Mistake Standalone Books

Accidental Hero

Accidental Protector

Accidental Romeo

Accidental Knight

Accidental Rebel

Accidental Shield

Stand Alone Novels

The Perfect Wrong

Cinderella Undone

Man Enough

Surprise Daddy

Prince With Benefits

Marry Me Again

Love Scars

Recklessly His

Enguard Protectors Books

Still Not Over You

Still Not Into You

Still Not Yours

Still Not Love

Baby Fever Books

Baby Fever Bride

Baby Fever Promise

Baby Fever Secrets

Only Pretend Books

Fiance on Paper

One Night Bride

Grizzlies MC Books

Outlaw's Kiss

Outlaw's Obsession

Outlaw's Bride

Outlaw's Vow

Deadly Pistols MC Books

Never Love an Outlaw

Never Kiss an Outlaw

Never Have an Outlaw's Baby

Never Wed an Outlaw

Prairie Devils MC Books

Outlaw Kind of Love

Nomad Kind of Love

Savage Kind of Love

Wicked Kind of Love

Bitter Kind of Love

Printed in Great Britain
by Amazon

25020779R00264